ANOTHER TIME,
ANOTHER PLACE

ANOTHER TIME, ANOTHER PLACE

NOVELLAS BY ZANE

RIQUE
JOHNSON

JANICE N.
ADAMS

SHAWAN
LEWIS

DYWANE D.
BIRCH

SBI

STREBOR BOOKS

NEW YORK LONDON TORONTO SYDNEY

Strebor Books
P.O. Box 6505
Largo, MD 20792
http://www.streborbooks.com

ISBN-13   978-1-59309-058-6
ISBN-10   1-59309-058-7
LCCN 2008925309

First Strebor Books trade paperback edition June 2008

Cover design: www.mariondesigns.com

10 9 8 7 6 5 4 3 2 1

Manufactured in the United States of America

For information regarding special discounts for bulk purchases,
please contact Simon & Schuster Special Sales at 1-800-456-6798
or business@simonandschuster.com

TABLE OF CONTENTS

INTRODUCTION

Love can be invigorating. Love can be full of surprises. Love can be frustrating. Love can be real. Join myself and four other writers as we take you on a journey of love, lust, and everything in between. *Another Time, Another Place* is a concept that first took flight many years ago. I am glad to finally see it come to fruition. While my time of doing anthologies is slowly coming to an end, I still feel it is important to showcase the works of others. Soon I will limit that to publishing the works of others as I miss being a full-time novelist—my first love.

Rique Johnson is a wonderful author. You all better stop sleeping on him. The man can work magic with a pen. Make sure that you check out his novels: *Love & Justice, Whispers from a Troubled Heart, Every Woman's Man*, and *A Dangerous Return*. Dywane D. Birch is the man who makes words flow like poetry and keeps the drama flowing from page to page as readers get drawn into his characters. Please check out his novels: *Shattered Souls, From My Soul to Yours*, and *Beneath the Bruises*. I publish both of these outstanding men and I look forward to seeing their careers flourish in the near future.

Shawan Lewis and Janice N. Adams are newer writers who are both gifted in their own right. Their novellas contained within are powerful and engaging. I would like to sincerely thank all four contributors for allowing me to share their talent with the world and for seeing my vision for this project: *Another Time, Another Place*.

Have you ever come across someone who seemed like the perfect person for you, yet they were already with another? Have circumstances ever prevented you from pursuing the possible love of your life? If you could go back in time, would you do things differently? Make other choices? Fight for what you believe in?

My story, the title story in the collection, has a lot of meaning to me. Throughout my life there have been men that I allowed to get away, only to wonder years—sometimes decades—later what could have happened if things had been different. Most of the time when one person is free to love, the other is not. Sure, a lot of people leave the one they are with to see if the grass is greener on the other side but then karma kicks in and leaves them in total despair. Sometimes we have to wait and see what happens. Always we need to pray. Love comes to us when it is supposed to, not when we want it to. We cannot force it. We cannot invent it. We must try to recognize it and cherish it when it crosses our paths, though.

I hope that you enjoy this book as much as we have enjoyed compiling it. Please feel free to email me your thoughts to zane@eroticanoir.com. Make sure you join my email list by sending a blank email to eroticanoir-subscribe@topica.com and you can visit me on the Internet at www.eroticanoir.com.

Blessings,

Zane

MIRRORED
LIVES

RIQUE JOHNSON

ONE

April Jonston sat in the seating area of her bedroom's bow window and watched the heavy rain pour down the windowpanes. She was lost, entranced by the varying water formations traveling down the glass. Flashes of light dancing at a distance indicated that a lightning storm was nearing.

She was in her mid-forties, or thirty-nine and holding, as she often stated when asked her age. She had shoulder-length black hair, dark sultry eyes and a smile as bright as the heavens. April remained high school skinny, a perfect size six, thanks to the personal trainer that worked her hard three times a week. Even though she was a college graduate, in a word she was a kept woman. She had never worked a single day; despite a degree in advertising. As fate dictated her future, she met her husband, Virgil Jonston, during her one and only job interview. He was the owner and CEO of the interviewing firm, Innovative Solutions. Virgil was captivated by her beauty and charm. He risked his entire fortune when he stopped the interview to tell her that he couldn't go any further because he'd be hiring her for the wrong reason.

"Sue me, but I've been looking for someone like you my entire life," were the bold words Virgil said to her that day. They still resonate in her mind today.

Shortly after that, April Miller became April Jonston and has lived a fairytale-like life since the first after-work drink on the interview day.

She looked down at the massive yard and saw an Olympic-sized pool, tennis courts and a putting green all being reflected by the flashing lights. She had everything she'd imagined; a large house, a huge yard, the picketed fence as well as a good man in Virgil. Virgil lifted his head from the pillow, wiped the crust from his eyes, and watched his woman gaze out of the bow window.

"Are you okay, honey?" he asked.

"I'm fine. I just couldn't sleep," April lied.

"You've had a lot of that lately. Is there anything you'd like to discuss?"

"Truly, I'm fine. I'm drawn to storms. I've always been this way. I think they're sexy."

Virgil was two years younger than his wife. This fact didn't bother him, nor did their height difference of two inches. Virgil was the shorter of the two. The one shortcoming that always weighed heavily on his mind was the size of his manhood. He carried plenty of mental anxiety because he possessed neither size, length, nor girth.

Throughout the years, upon meeting a potential mate, he used his wealth to buy gifts; all in an attempt to let his kindness outweigh his inadequacy. If the relationship turned physical, he used various creams, toys and things to please the woman. His size made intimacy a job instead of a pleasurable act.

Even though storm-gazing was pleasing to April, she was troubled and found it increasingly difficult to hide her sexual frustration.

"I've always known you to enjoy storms," Virgil said. "The more violent the better, but hearing that they are sexy is something new. Still, two nights in a row makes me wonder. Come on, can I entice you with some thunder from down under?"

April's head turned toward him; she boasted a bright smile. Virgil was pleased with her apparent acceptance of the invitation, but concealed behind her wondrous smile was an underlying agony of performing the act. She felt obligated to fulfill the duties as his spouse; even though neither her heart nor mind was into it. Eight years into the marriage, her husband hadn't changed. He remained affectionate, caring, loving and attentive. However, his penis-size compensation efforts had lessened. The tongue and the toys were few and far between. Lately, the use of these items lacked the passion and precision they once had.

TWO

Ariel Johnson turned away from watching the rain dance on the window panes to respond to her husband's sexual suggestion. The bright smile she returned to him accepted his invitation. She greeted the devilish smile from Steven with enthusiasm. Ariel was a woman two years younger than her forty-seven-year-old mate. Her hair was pulled back into a long ponytail. Her skin was flawless except for a scar just above her left eyebrow. Ariel took one step toward her husband and paused as a sense of déjà vu overcame her.

The flickering light coming through the window from behind, her husband's gaze, everything right down to the waterfall-like pattern on the comforter that flowed from the bed to the floor felt as though she had lived through it before. She shook off the feeling and skipped toward the bed. After all, Steven Johnson was a master at pleasing a woman. He was the artist; she was his canvas. This was what she believed. This was how he made her feel. The thunder roared, Ariel screamed, and jumped into the arms of her man. Ariel and Steven's sex life worked like a fine-tuned machine; much like other aspects of their lives together. They both were working middle-class that pooled the household's resources together. This being the case, they could well afford the four-bedroom, four-and-a-half-bath and three-car garage home that had a yard large enough for the planned in-ground pool and tennis court. So, when Ariel lowered the silk robe off of her shoulders, Steven's mouth closed around her nipple like a dance rehearsed a thousand times. Her body responded as if she had said, "You had me at hello."

Ariel was on her knees, head tilted toward the bow window that mimicked a strobe light. Steven was on his knees facing her; one arm held her closely around the waist. With the other hand, he pinched the opposing nipple from his mouth. Even with her eyes closed, Ariel could sense the lightning flashes. She was hot with a passion that burned deep inside of her. There was a plethora of ways that lighted her fire, but her nipples carried the most fuel for her eroticism. Steven held a nipple between his thumb and pointer finger with ample pressure. The oversized electrode flattened like a marshmallow and the part that escaped the pressure formed an umbrella. He used the tip of his tongue to stroke back and forth along the exposed area beyond his fingertips.

Ariel's womanhood had already moistened from the initial teasing with his mouth, but when he nibbled on the pressurized area, all bets were off.

"Fuck me now," Ariel panted out of desire.

The instruction was not a demand. It was a need. Steven gazed intently into her eyes. He slowly removed the robe from her shoulders and pushed her backward, with the palm of his hand placed between her breasts. Ariel willingly lowered to her back and positioned her knees up with the legs spread apart, waiting for whatever her mate had in store for her. Steven attacked her with his hungry, eager tongue. It dove deep inside her haven with determination and purpose. He shaped his tongue like a scoop, glided it through the natural juices and swallowed the tasty treat after each time. He placed a hand behind each knee, raised her legs upward and licked her rectum as if he was trying to determine how many strokes were needed to get to the center of a lollipop. Ariel moaned when his tongue penetrated the entrance. His stroke was slow, deliberate and precise. Ariel's passionate moans filled the air and seemed to drown out the periodic clap of thunder. His tongue moved up between her lower lips and danced artistically around her clitoris. Ariel screamed, uncontrolled and uninhibited, loud with vibrations that accompanied trembling legs.

His index finger slowly entered the lower passionate wormhole in conjunction with a thumb sliding through the womanhood's wetness. Steven heard, "Oh shit" when he closed his lips around her clit. He repeatedly pressed both fingers together while he sucked her man-in-a-boat as if he was trying to detach it from her body. For most women, his actions on such a delicate part of the body would be too hard and rough, but for Ariel, the rougher the better. Ariel screamed uncontrollably, electrified by all senses. Her hips jerked to a sporadic rhythm only she and the universe understood.

THREE

April screamed when Virgil pressed his lips together; her clitoris was between them. The pressure was too great. It would have been one thing if he'd let his naturally soft lips tantalize her jewel, but he sucked his lips back like he had no teeth and gummed down reminiscent of crushing a cherry. She pushed his head backward; the sexual mood vanished completely like a magician's sleight-of-hand trick. April slowly pulled an electric cord and freed the electronic device from her ass. A vibrant hum filed the air.

"Enough of this for tonight," April said.

"I'm sorry, honey. Don't be upset. I won't be so rough," Virgil pleaded.

"I've no idea of what's gotten into you lately. All you seem to be interested in is causing me pain. If it isn't squeezing me too hard, an overzealous roughness or the improper use of the toys, it must be a lack of interest. Maybe you no longer care about my needs," April guessed. "You got yours," April said emotionally.

She took a moment to reflect on how she sucked him off prior to him getting started on her. She recalled how she worked up an erection with her soft hands. It was Virgil's favorite thing to have done to him, her hand fondling his penis and her mouth sucking on his nipple. His reaction was always the same. He rose to a stronger, younger-feeling erection. April sat on him for no other reason than to let him feel her wetness. That was her thing; any type of foreplay got her jewel as wet as an ocean stream. The downside was, she felt no friction, little penetration because of his size and her extreme wetness. Virgil, on the other hand, had a different story; all aspects of April's womanhood felt like a warm cushiony gelatin.

As she rode his tool in the reverse cowboy position, different degrees of eroticism filled him. He was just that sensitive and neared a climactic state quickly. He never had real stamina, fully hardened or semi-hard. He could easily wear the three-minute man badge and could be the poster child for the organization, but not today. April recalled falling to the side and licked her juices from his joystick. Her tongue moved up his shaft and made slow circles around Virgil's head. She had always enjoyed her taste. Years of fingering herself to pick up where her husband lacked had turned her into a pussy juice addict. She would always have two fingers basking in her juices while masturbating and thought of them as sponges. She would let them soak in her haven before she placed them into her mouth.

The toys replaced the real thing for only a few short years. After that, she faked orgasms to prevent damage to Virgil's fragile ego. What allowed April to satisfy her needs without her husband's knowledge was the fact that a climax for Virgil produced an identical result as an electrical switch being turned off. Soon after he exploded and rolled over, he would sleep hard, out like a light. Snoring was his cigarette and often April would masturbate to the rhythm of his sound.

"It isn't like that," Virgil responded. "I do care about your feelings and your needs. You haven't been into it these days; I thought roughing it up a bit would bring you back to where you used to be."

"I'd be more into it if you were the same," April responded. "Something about you has changed."

"I am the same," Virgil responded defensively.

"No, you used to be caring and sensitive to what my body needs were, but now your caress feels like a chore. I sense pleasing me has become a job that you hate to do, but you toil your way through it."

Virgil watched the tears begin to fall from April's eyes.

"I'm sorry," he said. "I'll do better, I promise."

He hugged his wife and gave serious thought to getting a penis extension. April jumped from the bed as a thunder rumble sounded. She looked back at her man who had already started descending to Neverland even as he watched her back away to the bow window. She sat in the bow window for a short moment with her head resting on tucked knees. Her head turned toward Virgil's snore sound, a sound that tonight disgusted her.

Heavy raindrops danced and sounded on the windowpanes as they splashed into a million molecules. April watched the hypnotic act for a brief moment before entering the bathroom. She threw a face cloth into the sink, turned on the hot water, and then ran a finger through her wetness.

I taste good, she thought, after removing the finger from her mouth.

She grabbed the hot face cloth and wrung it out bravely. The steamy water that fell from her fingers was too hot for an average bath, yet she endured the burning sensation. She then folded the cloth in half, took a long wiping stroke through her haven's juices. She sucked the nectar from the cloth as if she was extracting micro-fibers from the item. April dropped the cloth into the sink, closed her eyes as one hand caressed her breast while the other massaged her womanhood until she created more tasty treats to taste. She repeated the heated-cloth, pussy-juice maneuver until the taste of her secretion had dissipated. She looked at herself in the mirror, and ran a thumb across the flesh mole under her right eye.

"Damn, the storm is getting closer," she said aloud upon hearing perfume bottles rattle because of the thunder.

Virgil continued to call hogs. He was unaffected by the noise that could wake the dead. It was a good thing. April wasn't satisfied. Her needs had to be satisfied and she knew exactly what had to be done. She straddled the pedestal sink and felt blessed that it could hold her weight. The reflection back was sensual, aided by the dark grayish moonlight rays shining through the window that flickered with each flash of lightning. She danced two fingers in a circular waltz inside her haven until sounds of wetness invaded her ears. She put the fingers into her mouth as if the fingers were the spoon that stirred the stew. The same two fingers then separated her lower lips, spread them as far as her fingers allowed. She pulled her fingers upward and her clitoris moved forward as if it was attached to a pendulum. She shoved the other hand's middle finger into her wetness, and then caressed the exposed cherry with the lubricated finger. April's sensations rose in little time. Her hips moved to the self-induced stroke as she touched the clitoris softly at first, then plucked it like a musician on a bass guitar string. She gazed at the intense look in the mirror. With each strum of the solo instrument her expressions intensified. The varying sensuous looks became hypnotic. She watched herself watch back. The area between her eyebrows wrinkled with the increasing circular motions her two fingers made on her jewel. April's breathing became thick and heavy. She leaned forward, her head less than a foot from the mirrored glass. The reflection in the mirror slowly vanished as if she performed a magic act because of the condensation from the heavy breathing in her excited state.

Her expression prior to the climax seemed to intensify, electrified her own arousal. Oddly, the reflection vanishing in the mist told of an explosion just seconds away...ticking like a time bomb. One would think as much as she adored storms that the lightning strike just outside of the house would have been the lever that opened her orgasmic flood gates. Instead, the loud bang, the slight house tremor, and the sound of bottles and things tumbling in the medicine cabinet startled her. She released a tiny scream. Somehow, she ended on her butt sitting on the bathroom floor.

That was very close, she thought.

She stood up and peeked into the bedroom. Virgil remained out like a light. The only difference in him was, he'd moved from his left side to the right side. April looked at herself once more in the mirror. The reflection seemed to speak, "Make me sing!" Therefore, she intended to capture the identical intense erotic expression of moments ago. Her womanhood remained moist and hot. She knew in a manner of seconds, she'd be back to the near climactic state.

She straddled the sink a second time and immediately started the process of picking up where she had left off. She paid full attention to her jewel. Instantly a tingly sensation rose from the toes, up the legs to the pulsating walls of her womanhood. Again, the sight of her turned-on expression ignited even more passion within. Her blood boiled. April's open mouth, flared nostril, passionate eyes and the scar above her left eyebrow had great sex appeal. She exploded hard and uncontrolled; her legs trembled so violently that the soap dispenser vibrated and fell into the sink. She continued the motion on her clitoris until she couldn't withstand her own action.

April leaned forward, rested and supported herself with her forehead against the medicine cabinet's mirror. She panted heavily and took long, slow deliberate breaths in an attempt to regain normal breathing. After a short while, she lifted her head, wiped the lingering condensation from the mirror with the face cloth and directed her attention to the mirror's image. She ran fingers through her hair from front to back and was very satisfied with the pleasure she gave herself. April looked intently at her reflection.

"I don't have a scar above my left eye," she spoke aloud.

April jumped from the sink, turned on the bathroom light and returned to the mirror to investigate under better lighting.

FOUR

Ariel was startled when Steven turned on the bathroom light. "What the fuck are you doing?" he asked.

"Nothing," she lied. "I'm just looking at myself in the mirror."

"Yeah, you look confused by that or you're embarrassed because I've watched you finger-fuck yourself while admiring your work in the mirror. Riding my dick isn't good enough anymore? You have to straddle a sink like it's a fucking horse."

Ariel turned toward her husband. With his tone and posture, embarrassment wasn't the emotion that swept over her. It leaned more toward fear. She had gone through a ritual. She had more than pleased herself and was pretty much wiped out from her act because her self-induced orgasm closely followed one from the lovemaking session between her and Steven. Her erotic state started to dissipate when she became confused by her reflection in the mirror. As she walked toward the bedroom, she ran a thumb across the scar just above her left eyebrow and felt things were normal. She'd swear her childhood injury scar was replaced by a beauty mark mole under her right eye.

"I saw a mole when I climaxed," she spoke aloud.

The eeriness that consumed her when she fell to the floor, spooked by the close lightning strike, seemed like a reflection of another place and time. She kept the strange thoughts to herself because truthfully, it sounded crazy to her.

Steven's mood can't handle my notions right now, she said mentally to herself.

"No violence," Ariel spoke as she passed Steven.

Steven gazed upon her as if she'd lost her mind.

How dare you, he thought. He was appalled by the insinuation. "Don't tell me," he scolded her. Each word was accompanied by what he considered a mild tap on the back of her head. "…what to do," he continued with three more corresponding smacks. The last one was a shove that quickened her descent to the bed.

"Stop it!" Ariel snapped. "I'm not in the mood for this. Alright!" She climbed under the covers, laid on her left side and gazed at the flashes of light through the bow window. Steven grabbed the corners of his pillow, and repeatedly struck her on the head in a one-man pillow fight. He called his spouse everything under the sun except a child of God.

"Why are you doing this?" Ariel asked. "I've done nothing to deserve your hostility."

Steven's assault stopped for a moment. "You've made me feel as though I don't know how to take care of your needs. Maybe I'm not good enough or maybe you were fantasizing about your secret lover as you stared into the mirror."

"What the hell are you talking about? I have no such person."

"Devin Alexander," Steven spoke confidently.

"Now you're being totally ridiculous. Devin recently got married. He has never looked twice at me since we split up," Ariel said. She sensed her husband was about to rebut her statement. "Before you say it, that night at The Drink, Devin was winking at his date. Not me."

"Yeah right!"

"This conversation is too damn old. I have to tell you the same thing every time you get a hair up your ass."

"I don't have a hair up my ass. You shouldn't step on my manhood by finger-fucking yourself immediately after we have sex."

"Your manhood, this is what's angered you? Haven't you ever jacked off before?" Ariel raged.

"Plenty of times," Steven quickly answered. "But, never directly after being with a woman."

"It doesn't matter. You having to stroke yourself when women are available should threaten your manhood."

"It doesn't."

"Nor should me masturbating."

Steven swung his pillow at Ariel's head again. She protected her head with her pillow and simultaneously drowned out most of the second round of verbal abuse. She cried under the concealment of the pillow, very much confused by what she'd done wrong.

FIVE

April carefully slid under the covers; she hoped not to disturb Virgil. The foolish notion made her chuckle because her husband was in full snore mode. She laid on her side, watched flashes of light dance outside through the bow window and wished that each flash would damper the sound of Virgil's snore. She hugged the pillow tightly around her head; used it as a gigantic earplug. Oddly, the same eeriness consumed her. April opened her eyes to the darkness, as if that would aid her understanding of why the moment felt familiar to her.

I've been here before, she thought.

The premonition bothered her because the notion came with the belief that the experience was something unpleasant. The weary thoughts kept her awake for hours. Ultimately, the body grew tired and she fell asleep just before sunrise. The next morning when Virgil removed the pillow from her head, she woke tired, her face was clammy from sweating, and her damp hair was matted in place like a wet curl.

"I'm sorry, honey," Virgil apologized. "Was my snoring unbearable last night?"

Realistically, Virgil was a good man. He provided a daydream life for her. April's needs were met and her wants were never questioned. She was a pampered, placed-on-a-pedestal, stay-at-home wife, so dealing with a snoring issue uncontrollable by her spouse was easy. Years ago, she decided it was pointless to make him feel bad about it.

"No…it was nothing more than usual," April said, responding to his question. "The constant thundering had more to do with it," she lied. "You and the storm combined aren't the best lullaby to fall asleep to."

Virgil smiled.

"That was a pretty nasty storm," he said.

"You slept through the worst part. It got crazy out there for a good while. I'd swear that lightning struck somewhere in our yard."

"Maybe you shouldn't play human lightning rod and watch the storm from the bed."

Virgil glanced out of the window. The rain continued to fall, but with far less intensity than the downpour of the previous night.

"I believe the forecast calls for more thunderstorms tonight," Virgil spoke. "Maybe you should try earplugs tonight?"

"That may not be a bad idea."

Moments later, the aroma of bacon filled the air. April was in automatic mode when she prepared their morning breakfast. The meals varied, yet she remained efficient. The only difference between weekday and weekend meals was that she awakened naturally without an alarm clock. She placed Virgil's plate on the table, sat across the table and they began eating breakfast.

"The pepper jack cheese in the eggs this time really sets them off," Virgil complimented his wife. "Honey, did you hear me?"

April was in deep thought. She stared at the dark substance in her coffee cup as if the black liquid could sway her mind from the surfacing thought.

"Honey?" Virgil said a bit louder.

This time his word registered and the coffee cup slowly came into focus.

"Yes," April responded.

"What's wrong? Are you still troubled by my behavior last night?"

"I haven't given it much thought. That's water under the bridge; we'll get past this."

"Please explain the distance in the air today. What's wrong?"

"Really nothing," she lied again.

April felt bad with a second lie in such a short time. But, she wasn't about to tell her true feelings. The tainted mood began while she cooked. Mentally, she took inventory of her fairytale life. Even with his undying love, worldly possessions and money, a major part of her felt unfulfilled. She did a quick scan of her home.

How can a person with so much feel so empty? she asked herself.

Deep down, April wanted to contribute to her life's existence. Many women would say being a homemaker was a full-time job, but years of constant repetition had taken a toll on her spirit. She cooked, she cleaned, shopped for groceries, clothes and everything in between online. She and Virgil attended very little social functions, therefore, for years she felt like a prisoner confined to their home. Absent the visits from the personal trainer and an occasional call from her mother, her outside life would be nonexistent.

The one time April did voice her desire to contribute to the household, Virgil became irate, his old school chauvinistic views flared and they engaged in a major argument over the subject for days.

No wife of mine is going to work when I have the means to provide a good life without help, were Virgil's words. They were still prominent in her mind.

Virgil was the man of the house and throughout the years he reminded her of it countless times. It led April to believe that reviving a non-winnable stressful conversation wasn't worth the effort. Part of her believed her predicament was her own doing because she accepted the role from the very beginning. After all, it was his money, his house and his rules. It was a thought that tormented her silently for years.

"I'm a bit preoccupied with being spooked last night," April continued.

"Spooked? What happened?"

"I looked different in the mirror, but I'd guess the lightning may have played tricks with my eyes."

"Well, what did you see?"

"A reflection of me looked the same, yet uncommonly different."

"Explain."

"That's just it. I can't. I just felt as though I was seeing a near identical twin."

Virgil smiled. He slept through the worst part of the storm, yet April's explanation forced him to agree with his spouse.

"Sweetheart," Virgil said. "You're right. It was just the storm playing tricks on you. Don't waste energy worrying about a super-natural phenomenon," Virgil suggested.

"Maybe you're right," agreed April.

She was happy to have swayed the conversation without revealing her true feelings. Even though having Virgil believe she'd lost her mind forced a question about her motive.

SIX

Lying in bed the next morning Ariel had her back toward Steven's. She again focused her attention to the dancing rain on the bow window. It was a constant fall, but not the downpour of the previous night. Steven rolled over, placed an arm around her and then began running his fingers through her hair.

"I'm sorry I acted so ugly last night," Steven apologized. "I truly don't know what got into me."

Ariel remained silent.

"Come on," he begged, "don't be like that. After all, it was only a pillow."

Ariel rolled to her back, ignored his words once more and stared at the light fixture on the ceiling.

"You sound ridiculous," Ariel responded after a long moment of silence. "It didn't matter to you that it was only my finger. You reacted as though you caught me fucking another man. How fair is that?"

"I know," he spoke with a softer tone. "I overreacted and I'm very sorry."

"Truthfully," Ariel replied as she turned to look at him for the first time. "That was the second time in seven months you've apologized for striking me. Well, the first time, shame on you. The second time, shame on me. A third time isn't going to happen. I'm not sticking around for that."

"What exactly are you saying?"

"It's Saturday morning. Monday, I'm speaking with a divorce attorney."

"You can't be serious," Steven said a little animated. "You weren't hit hard at all with a pillow."

"So typical of a man, you attempt to justify a wrong by placing it on a grading scale. Striking me is wrong whether or not it's with your fist or with a pillow. I'd be a fool to sit here and wait for the next time bomb to explode."

Steven sat up, rested his back on the headboard, turned and gazed at his wife.

"I promise you on my life that I'll never abuse you mentally or physically again," Steven said slowly and concisely.

"If I recall correctly, wasn't it your mother's life you swore on the last time?"

Touché, Steven thought.

He was about to continue rationalizing why Ariel should reconsider her view when the "You've got mail" announcement floated through the air. Ariel jumped up, her naked frame seemed to glide on air. Their disturbing conversation didn't prevent Steven from admiring and thinking what a wonderful ass she had. Ariel left the bedroom; she had concealed what Steven deemed her greatest asset with a robe.

Moments later, she discovered the email notification was a communiqué from her office. The odd part was that she had never received a business email over the weekend before. She became alarmed with the subject matter of the email entitled "Presentation." She read the one-paragraph note that told her to rethink her approach.

"Rethink my approach," she said aloud.

Her mind drifted back to the presentation that she gave to a new client and fearful realizations surfaced like a submarine on a fast ascent. Ariel crossed her arms on the desk, leaned forward and rested her head on her arms. She took a deep breath to combat the mild case of depression that was suddenly consuming her. According to the email, she had Saturday and Sunday to put together a presentation that would rock the client's world. The exact approach eluded her, yet she sat for hours at the computer researching various products. Her result was a desk full of various white papers, but the best approach for her client still eluded her. Her eyes ached and at this point she experienced information overload and couldn't read another line of text on the flat-screen monitor. She left the home office and walked by the family room where Steven was watching TV. Ariel tussled through the pots and pans to begin dinner. Steven told her that he'd already ordered Chinese food and that it should be delivered shortly.

"Besides," Steven spoke softly into her ear after leaving the lazy boy recliner, "the rain has picked up again and the roar of thunder is getting louder by the minute. Another major storm is heading our way. It's too messy to go out, and just in case the lights fail, I thought it would be nice to have food delivered. See," he said, proud of a small accomplishment, "I have placed candles on the table already."

"That's very thoughtful of you," Ariel replied.

But, Steven's thoughtfulness hadn't lessened her anger. She understood the time away from the kitchen was a diversion to allow time to formulate a strategic presentation.

SEVEN

A s far back as April could remember she had enjoyed watching the brilliance of violent storms. She recalled her mother forcing her to get away from the window as a child. She sat at the kitchen table nursing a glass of burgundy wine. Virgil was placing the leftover Chinese food into containers. He'd had food delivered as an attempt to calm her because while they ate breakfast, he sensed that his wife was troubled even though she neglected to share her true thoughts. He was happy with himself because April really seemed to enjoy the General Tso's chicken and hot and sour soup that he presented her.

April listened to the rain increase its dance on the window-panes. It soothed and relaxed her more than her husband could understand. The sound of the rain coupled with the visual splatter of each raindrop on the panes was downright hypnotic. As she'd done many times before, she sat in the bow window with her knees pulled to her breasts. Her arms were wrapped around her legs holding them in place. She stared at the storm intently. Each flash of lightning was followed by a clap of thunder that increased in volume. April became lost inside a place only a lucky few can find. The flashes of light were like exploding bombs that streaked across the sky. Each burst of light gave her a multi-paneled view of her reflection. Oddly, she thought about the thunder from down under, but she knew it wasn't the answer to her being satisfied.

"Are you going to storm gaze all night again?" she vaguely heard but didn't respond.

April jumped; she was startled when Virgil placed his arms around her from the rear. She was mildly disappointed that he disturbed her solitude.

"Your butt is going to fall asleep if you sit here too long," Virgil joked. "You should come to bed early," he said with a devilish tone.

"Not tonight, honey," April responded without removing her gaze from the bow window. "The storm will help me relax and have a comfortable sleep. It worked last night. I slept soundly once I did fall asleep. I just want to watch it until my eyes get heavy."

"Okay, don't come running to bed scared when the storm gets closer to us. I'm not going to be used as your pillar of strength," Virgil joked.

"I'll be fine, dear."

Virgil kissed her behind the ear, and then whispered something nasty that prompted a swat on his leg from April. She watched him crawl into the bed with the reflection from the surrounding windowpanes. In a short time, Virgil was snoring. The louder Virgil snored, the closer the violent storm came. Brilliant flashes danced across the sky and brightened the darkness like fluorescent eels deep under the sea. Virgil was in full snore mode. His thunderous sounds competed with nature's voice, but ultimately became nothing more than a whisper compared to the howling winds that stirred outside. With each flash of light, April could see the trees take their bows as they conceded to the will of the wind. Paper and other debris floated in all directions, reminiscent of an unsteady, unworldly storm.

The lightning was plentiful. It complemented the roar of thunder waving through the air, seemingly making the Earth move.

April was fascinated and frightened at the same time. She had never seen such chaos in a thunderstorm. Her eyes widened, and her heart raced when two streaks of lightning thrown from the heavens approached each other from different directions and then seemed to collide and sprint toward her like a three-dimensional object. She let out a slight scream, stepped out of the bow window, and Virgil's words popped in her mind. She shot a glance at Virgil. He was dead to the world, oblivious to all noises around him.

April watched a foray of lightning engage in what could be considered a sword fight. It was magical, it lured her back to the bow-window seat, but she stopped short of planting her butt on the platform because of the surprise she felt between her legs. She sensed moistness while she stepped toward the window. As the flashes of light continued to flicker, she backed away with a hand already down her pants. She rubbed three fingers across her jewel and stopped at the juices. She curled her middle finger inside the wetness, tilted her head back because of the instant pleasure. She became excited about what she would do, thus seconds later, the bathroom door closed behind her.

April created an identical effect from the previous night by leaving the bathroom light off. It was eerie how different the nights were. The howling wind seemed to echo throughout the bathroom. The bass cymbal-like, thunder sound appeared as if a giant stood over their home and banged the two metal objects over the house. The flashes of electricity peering through the window made the bathroom appear like a disco.

She had no real reason why she approached the mirror so slowly and tentatively. She was in search of something, but she couldn't quite put a finger on it. Nevertheless, a middle finger worked her clitoris like a compass needle caught in a continuous circle. She elected not to straddle the sink; instead April placed a support palm on the medicine cabinet's mirror for the inevitable weakness in the knees. The muscles in the stretched arm grew tired. She bent her elbow and rested her forehead on the arm. She could almost kiss herself because of the proximity to the mirror.

April's climax was near, she was hot, and her body radiated steam that fogged the mirror like teenagers making out in a car. She was one step away from exploding juices all over her hand, yet she accomplished a difficult task; she prolonged the moment and wiped the condensation from the mirror with a series of "S" strokes to view her intense facial expressions. The continued flashes of light sparkling through the bathroom window made each sensual expression seem like varying degrees of eroticism. Each erotic view brought on a tingly sensation that radiated from her toes, up her legs and made her quiver as if she was cold. April began to pinch her jewel between her thumb and index finger. First gently, then gradually harder until it seemed to swell. She wiped the mirror once more and supported herself with the right hand. Her fingers clawed into the mirrored surface. She studied the extremely passionate reflection and knew in a matter of seconds no matter how hard she'd try to sustain the magic moment, she'd explode with vigor. She was so entranced, seduced by the ultimate orgasm, she cared little about the mole under her right eye.

"Oh," softly left her lips.

She repeated the phrase several times in succession. Each time, the word increased in volume.

EIGHT

Ariel had been watching a storm that was three times as bad as the previous night. She now sat in the bow window and got more turned on by the minute with the belief that lightning storms were sexy. She confirmed her thoughts when a hand slid into her panties discovered juices grander than on the chicken she had eaten. When her finger curled up into her wetness a sense of having already completed the task swept over her. She tasted her marinated finger and grabbed a toy before hiding in the bathroom. Behind closed doors, she inserted a pocket rocket deep that vibrated at the highest setting deep up her womanhood. Every pore on her body was electrified.

Tonight, she closed and locked the bathroom door to prevent the angry-husband syndrome. Steven was snoring, aided by a half-bottle of wine and four scotch on the rocks that he had consumed with dinner. Ariel drank the other half bottle of wine. Together with a slight buzz and the raging storm outside, her body yearned to be fulfilled.

The vibrations from the miniature vibrator hummed in her ears. It was a tune that gave her the rhythm for the circular waltz around her clitoris. She actually hummed the count one, two, and three in her head. The thunderous sounds outside orchestrated a different tune. The graceful glide of the waltz transformed itself into the electric energy of a rumba, illustrated by pinching that began on her girl toy. Her knees weakened nearly instantly.

Ariel braced herself with the left hand on the mirror, inserted her middle finger deep inside the wetness and rotated it around the vibrating object. She cleared a windshield wiper blade-like area on the mirror to view the climactic moment and then re-supported her weakened body. The reflection was everything she'd hoped for: sensual, erotic and intensely sexciting. The image of her was the same, yet it differed. She observed a mole under her right eye that she didn't recall having. It didn't matter; she was far too gone to be concerned with something so trivial when the flashing light illuminating through the bathroom's window might have tricked her eyes. Yet, she stared intently at the image.

April glazed back. For a brief moment both women thought they had lost their minds. Their moaned words were on a time delay. Ariel's passion cry was "Shit," but even under the heavy seduction of a near orgasm, the image in the mirror seemed to recite, "Oh." Nevertheless, both Ariel and April were lost to a beast-like passion. They ignored reality and continued to completion their "Oh" and "Shit" bellows. Suddenly, for each woman it became a race to the climactic finish. Both women exploded violently, roared and held a synchronized note.

The sound of thunder lasted longer than each woman's lungs sustained the note. The rumble seemed as though it was vibrating the room. They hadn't finished squirting juices onto their fingers when lightning struck both houses simultaneously. A one-half-inch crack on both bathroom walls traveled from the window, turned the corner and headed horizontally across the wall toward them. When the jagged crack reached their respective medicine cabinets, the mirrored glass shattered underneath their hands.

Both women jumped back and screamed for the first time out of fear. Both women suffered a cut on their palms—April's right hand and Ariel's left hand, respectively. They managed to pull up their panties with a lone hand and they stepped toward the sink holding their damaged hand at the wrist. They placed a face cloth in the hand containing the cut and clutched a fist around it. They looked into the mirror timidly, fearful of what they might see. To their surprise, they saw themselves as they were. Identical in every way except, Ariel saw a mole under her right eye and April now viewed a scar over the left eyebrow. April and Ariel were each in utter shock. Their minds raced a thousand miles a minute as they tried to rationalize what happened. The two women knew for the first time that they were seeing someone different. They simply stared at each other in silence, awed by the phenomenon. They both touched the broken glass with the fingertips of the uncut hand.

Virgil turned on the bathroom light just as glass from the shattered mirror fell into the sink.

"Honey," Virgil said. "What's going on in here?"

April was too startled by the glass and Virgil's sudden intrusion to respond. She slowly turned toward the voice and saw a man that she was vaguely familiar with.

Something's out of sync, April thought.

"April, are you okay?" Virgil asked based on the puzzled expression on his wife's face.

"I'm fine, other than my hand," April said as she extended the cut hand to him.

"How did that happen?"

"I was looking at myself in the mirror, and then all of a sudden, it shattered beneath my hand."

Virgil's eyes followed the crack in the wall from the medicine cabinet to the window.

"The house must have been struck by lightning to cause this much damage," Virgil said in awe.

April saw Virgil's head still locked on the window and for the first time she looked at the bathroom's destruction. Her eyes followed the crack back around the wall to the mirror. The odd thing was the bathroom wasn't exactly how she remembered it.

NINE

"Honey, are you okay?" Steven asked Ariel.

Ariel shook her head as if she was disillusioned.

"Open the door, Ariel," Steven spoke. "Why is the bathroom door locked?" she heard.

"Just one second," Ariel responded.

The vibrations within her reminded her of something. She used two fingers to dig into her haven and pull out the miniature vibrator that had all but run out of steam.

What the fuck? she thought.

Ariel panicked. She wrapped the device in toilet paper and threw it into the wastebasket. The louder bang on the door grabbed her attention. Tentatively, she headed for the door. She was slightly fearful without a total understanding of why. Steven immediately turned on the light.

"The house was hit by lightning," Steven stated excitedly. "Are you okay?"

"I was looking at myself in the mirror, and then all of a sudden, it shattered beneath my hand."

Ariel was dumbfounded. It appeared as though the words magically appeared into her thoughts for the first time and at the same time the words felt familiar to her.

"What in the hell happened to the wall?" Steven asked before he realized that he was asking the obvious. "The lightning strike did that?"

"I believe so."

Steven lifted the bloody face cloth from her hand, gazed at the quarter-inch deep cut and then closed his fingers around hers.

"It's a good thing only your palm was cut. Hell, glass from the mirror could have exploded and cut you in all sorts of places... something wrong?" Steven asked.

"Uh, nothing," Ariel lied.

She was stunned. The man before her she'd never seen before, yet he was so familiar to her. His look, the walk and the sound of his voice was as comfortable as a broken-in pair of shoes. Yet, she seemed to be living through a déjà vu moment. She looked around the bathroom, then the bedroom; all of the surroundings were different. Yet, certain details down to the pattern on the bed's comforter were part of her conscious memory. She didn't understand why and the fact scared her. Everything had a familiar feel and everything was new. She felt displaced, in a new reality, seemingly in another place and another time.

"Can I have a moment?" Ariel asked Steven.

She didn't wait for an answer. She walked out of the bedroom down the hall to the guest bathroom, closed the door behind her and sat on the toilet with her head between her hands.

"This doesn't make sense," Ariel whispered as if Steven was standing outside of the door. "None of it. My name is..."

Ariel could visualize a name, feel that she'd been called some-thing different, but the name could not be spoken. She stood, examining herself in the mirror. What Ariel saw was a carbon copy of herself. She had longer hair than she remembered, yet the length was familiar to her. But, for the life of her, she couldn't recall growing it that length. She leaned closer to the mirror, and then her heart pounded deep within her. It vibrated like a bass drum.

Since the lightning strike many things were memorable, yet most felt like a distant memory. The one thing she was certain of was that she never had a mole under her right eye. With an unconscious move she touched the area above her right eye, positive that a scar from a childhood injury had been there.

I've seen you before, she thought.

"I've seen you in the mirror just before the lightning strike," she stated aloud with nervous tension. "Am I you now? My name is..."

Ariel thought long and hard about it. She searched for an answer that eluded her.

"Ariel Jonston," she spoke to the reflection in the mirror. She somehow believed that personalities of two people were within her.

TEN

April watched her lips closely in the powder room's mirror. Her lips formed words that confused her. She spoke the name April Jonston. It stirred confusion within her that combined certainty with uncertainty. Deep down she felt the essence of another. She snapped her fingers as in "eureka."

"The woman in the mirror," she spoke aloud.

She instinctively went to rub a thumb over the mole under her right eye, but this time the familiar beauty mark was absent. Her thumb actually landed on the scar above the left eye.

"I didn't have this before the lightning strike," she spoke to her reflection. "Who am I now?"

"April?" Virgil said. "Are you okay in there?"

The question bothered her to some degree, but since the surroundings, the man, and the name she was called felt like a warm snuggly comforter, she answered him with less concern than before she entered the half-bath.

"Yes, honey," April said. "I'm fine. My nerves are much better now. I'll be out in a sec."

April intently looked at her reflection in the mirror for no reason other than to see if she could view her alternate self. Moments into the hypnotic gaze, a sense of peace overcame her. She didn't understand why, nor did she question it. She simply felt that a buried desire was about to be answered. As April exited the powder room, Virgil grabbed her cut hand by the wrist, swabbed the cut with peroxide and bandaged the hand.

"Your cut doesn't look deep," Virgil said. "It looks to be about a quarter-inch deep. However, it will take a few days before it heals, but you'll be fine. And, if I were you, I wouldn't plan on doing your aerobics class tomorrow," Virgil suggested.

April regarded her husband's caring in the same way that his words made her feel. It was a warm sensation already known, yet it felt new as it swept through her. She smiled.

"What?" he said. "The way you're looking at me, I'd swear you were seeing me for the first time."

"No. I'm looking at you like I have a husband that adores me," April responded.

"That I do. You are the core of my universe," Virgil replied. "And to prove it," he continued, knowing what he was about to say would please her, "if you really want to work, then by all means make yourself happy."

April regarded him strangely without an understanding why the statement baffled her. It just did. She stood, walked toward the bedroom and stopped when she saw the bow window. The deadliest part of the storm had subsided and passed over their area just after lightning struck their house. She walked toward the bow window hopeful that the remaining rain dancing on the panes like individual splashes of memory would add clarity to the confusion. She sat in the seating area of the bow window, pulled her knees toward her breasts and watched the rain. After a short moment all of their possessions came into view—the in-ground pool, tennis court and an exercise track. Suddenly, a good part of her felt blessed. Everything that she'd always wanted was before

her. She sensed that all the hard work of her life had paid off...
and couldn't understand why Virgil's comment about working
made her feel as though she'd missed something. Virgil approached
her from behind, started rubbing her tense shoulders.

"Honey," April said. "I work?" she asked with a state of confusion displayed on her face. "I mean, I don't want to work," she
continued tenderly. "I want to continue to be a homemaker. I
only ask that you share what's going on at work. This way I'll feel
connected with it. Who knows, maybe I'll be able to add an
insight you could take into consideration."

Virgil kissed the back of her head. April's usual comment was,
"How was your day?" He always felt that it was the proper thing
to ask, but this time he believed she possessed a genuine interest
in the company affairs. Something had changed within her. He
couldn't grasp the exact extent of the change, but her persona
and sentiment had evolved. Something about her was uniquely
different.

"You never cease to amaze me," Virgil said as he walked away.

He crawled onto the bed and spoke his favorite phrase. The
words "thunder from down under" made her giggle as if she'd
heard them for the very first time.

"I'll be in bed shortly," April said. "The storm has lessened and
missing the last part of the rainfall is like skipping the end of a
good movie."

"You get stranger by the day," Virgil joked.

"You may be on to something," April responded.

ELEVEN

Ariel watched the gigantic rectangular hole in the back-yard's ground through the bow window. She closed her eyes; she envisioned a pool filled with water. She vaguely recalled already floating in the pool, but the one before her now had yet to be completed. Both visions were real to her; both real-izations helped her understand exactly what had happened. She glanced at the bandaged hand and her memory flashed back to the sight of the crack traveling across the bathroom wall. Oddly, she remembered her attempt to move out of harm's way, but the hand wouldn't release from the mirror. It was as though her hand was glued to the glass with the strongest epoxy. The sting of the glass cutting her palm replaced the lightning's electrical energy. A quick pinch of the skin on the wave of natural phe-nomenon was all it took to allow the essence of another to enter a new soul. Memories, thoughts and feelings transcended be-tween April and Ariel, displaced between another time and another place.

Even stranger was her inability to stop the self-pleasing act. Realistically, she didn't want to. During the frightful moment she was far too close to the grand finale to be deterred by a light-ning strike. To top it off, the sight of the almost identical likeness of herself reflected in the mirror in an identical erotic state demanded a competition between the two before the crack reached them. Neither knew who came first. All they knew was they saw each other at the mystical moment.

"Sweetheart," Steven said. "Are you sad that the storm has pretty much passed over us?"

"I could watch them for days so I'm satisfied with the two-and-a-half nights of bliss."

"Understanding that my competition is weaker, I bet I can turn you on tonight."

Ariel smiled and turned toward her husband.

"You have always stimulated me. Lightning storms excite me in a different manner."

"How about this?" Steven suggested.

He stood on the bed and the lower pointer finger was erect like a spear with deadly aim. Ariel's curled legs swung around, straightened and her feet hit the floor with a rapid pace. She was summoned by the magic wand.

"You're lucky the storm has passed. Otherwise, one might think you're trying to attract lightning with that thing." When she touched his member with her hand, the strangest thing happened. A vision of holding a penis with two fingers flashed through her mind. She gazed at the hand holding him in awe. She became amazed at the new reality and allowed the memory of a smaller pleasure tool fade into the distant past. She closed her mouth around a bigger and better treat. It was new; it was different so much that being electrocuted would've been considered an understatement. She marveled at the grander size and attacked it with reckless abandonment. April was so pleased to have something to work with; her aggression was well beyond an animal in heat. She became so overbearing with excitement, Steven became apprehensive about the forcefulness.

"Chill for a minute," Steven said. "This isn't your last meal before execution. What's gotten into you?"

"I'm sorry," she said while holding the hardened member just out of the sanctuary of her mouth. Her warm excited breath blew heavily from her nostrils. "I'm just captivated by your size tonight."

Steven regarded his spouse strangely.

"I'm the same size as I was last night and the many nights before."

For Ariel, his statement held truth, but intertwined with the truthfulness was a recollection of never being pleased by this amount of manly meat. Needless to say, Ariel continued the aggressive assault on his manhood where she left off, still enthralled by the seemingly new length and thickness. It was new, different and felt wonderful in her mouth. In no time Steven became pleased with his wife's sexual onslaught. Her actions were like a breath of fresh air. Ariel's sexuality had finally crossed over into another dimension. Although, at times she didn't execute well, but this very moment her actions seemed veteran-like. That was until her hastiness caused her teeth to scrape painfully across his flesh.

"I want to feel me inside of you," Steven spoke tactfully.

He stepped backward, sat and then lowered to his back holding his greatest hard-on captive. Ariel crawled on the bed between his legs.

"Say that again," Ariel said as she replaced his hand with hers.

"I want to feel me inside of you," he said again.

"No," Ariel responded, entranced by a new sexual energy. "Tell me you want to fuck me," she spoke in a sultry voice unknown to Steven.

Steven's mouth fell open, but no words left it. He hardly believed his ears.

"What did you say?" he asked astonished.

"There is too much chit-chat at a time like this, but if you must know, I said fuck me hard. Do it now before I jerk you off with my hand."

Steven was speechless. For years the slightest mention of those words was a huge turnoff for her.

What a difference a day makes, he thought more turned on than ever.

Ariel sat on his pole and it slid through her wetness like a submarine diving to unknown depths. When the vessel stabilized, his tool was touching the inside back wall of her womanhood.

"Mercy," Ariel panted.

Parts of her realized it had been years since a non-manmade object satisfied her so. She gazed at Steven, eyes wide; she was almost afraid to move her body. The fear faded faster than it materialized. She began a slow and steady pelvic movement on what she deemed a new dick, yet she recalled being in the position with him before.

A recollection, a familiarity, whatever it was, it felt damn good to her. Ariel's entire body warmed as if it was being heated from the inside. The small of her back was the first to become clammy, followed by the glistening of her forehead. By the time sweat flowed down between her breasts, she was in full bronco buck mode. Ariel was literally slamming herself down onto his hardness. She then began a deep abrasive grind as if her haven was a mortar and his tool was a pestle.

Ariel was being fulfilled beyond her wildest dreams, yet she bathed in the notion that it was nothing new. It didn't matter; the old and new memories only added more fuel to her erotic state. The "fuck me" verbiage and other uncommon words spawned by Ariel became a real turn-on to Steven. Everything about her tonight was a side of his wife never seen before. He would no longer consider her slightly reserved. Her extra passion coupled with the verbal expressions gave him a whole new outlook on their sex life. He believed it was enhanced and his enthusiasm about the belief manifested itself into a grander, twenty-years-ago stamina.

Ariel exploded violently and loudly as she worked her way through an intense release. Her climactic state was so different, Steven thought for a quick second that she had been possessed. Never had he heard such an erotic bellow from his wife. She continued to ride his manhood until she could no longer stand the slightest brush against her clitoris.

"My juices," she panted as she leaned forward and rested on his chest.

"You are incredible tonight," Steven interrupted. "What about your juices?"

"My juices are all over you," she responded, still winded from the bronco ride.

Steven gave her a caring snuggly hug and then Ariel's own thought caught up with her.

"My juices," she stated clearer, "are all over your dick."

Her statement was sensual with a hint of excitement. Before Steven knew what was happening, Ariel dismounted the joyous toy and began licking the sweet nectar off his tool as if it was a Popsicle. She made long strokes with her tongue that began at his testicles and ended at the mushroom shape of his manhood. She repeated the maneuver until she had made a complete circle around the hard cylinder. When she was satisfied that none of her secretions remained on him, her mouth engulfed his hardness. She took it deep into her mouth. She choked.

"Don't kill yourself trying to tame that beast," Steven joked.

"I won't," she responded after regaining her breath. "I moved just a little too fast. Now it's your turn."

TWELVE

April watched the raindrops stop as if she'd never see them again. Parts of her believed the thought was a delicate truth. She had gazed storms in the past, but to survive a life-altering incident was something she truly believed would never happen again. As she stepped away from the bow window, she was a bit saddened that Virgil had fallen asleep. She stood beside the bed and admired his chiseled frame. The one benefit of being the head of his own company, that he continually boasted about, was it allowed him to become an amateur bodybuilder. His short stocky frame was well-defined. The arms, legs, chest and back showed years of dedication to the craft. Virgil's only sorrow was in his attempt to make himself more attractive. He, at the same time, made this already small manhood appear even tinier.

April was aroused by her husband's body, but for the life on her, she couldn't recall being so before. Nevertheless, she thought about the one thing men desire more than a two-woman orgy. That is to be wakened by their mate for a surprise fuck. She spread his legs, ran her fingertips upward on the inside of his thigh and positioned herself between his muscular legs. She replaced the fingertips with a wet tongue and licked the remaining way up his legs to his testicles. Virgil lifted his head and looked down at his ambitious wife. He closed his eyes and lowered his head again to assure himself that he was actually awake. His eyes opened wide when her soft lips kissed his sacs. It prompted him to raise and rest on his elbows.

"Something wrong?" April asked devilishly.

"No, nothing," Virgil responded with a tone indicative of being surprised. "I had to make sure I wasn't dreaming."

"Dreaming," April stated. "Let's call it a fantasy coming true."

Her tongue swiped up his testicles, along the shaft on his manhood and ran through thick pubic hair. April smiled to hide the frustration that she had reached his hair too quickly. She grabbed his penis with a hand and was happy that Virgil had closed his eyes because there was no hiding the utter shock on her face. Flashes of a larger tool popped into her mind like an implanted memory. With a little concentration, what she had before her became familiar. Both visions comforted her; she knew simply by holding it that its size would fall short in the pleasing department without direction.

"Shall we get a toy?" Virgil asked.

"Ah, no," April replied confidently. "You are fine just as you are."

Virgil was surprised by April's passing on a toy. "No thunder from down under? How about my thunder-tongue?"

"I'm yours for whatever you want."

Virgil and April switched positions. In a matter of seconds Virgil was caressing her inner thigh with his fingertips. April eagerly anticipated a gentle tongue from her husband. She liked being on her back, legs held up in the air by her mate. She recalled his name. The thought brought April to her elbows. She gazed at her husband and spoke his name.

"Virgil," she said as natural as she'd done for years. Yet, the other name thought of before the spoken word felt as real as the warm air coming from his mouth. "I want you," she continued, despite knowing Virgil's size would present a challenge.

Virgil stopped his tongue just short of tasting her peach. The comment pleased him; it frightened him and caused a certain type of anxiety. Like a high wind that swoops down and changes the complexity of a golf round, Virgil's mood digressed to something short of fear. He moved and sat on the side of the bed, his head hung low as he contemplated how to best serve his wife without his tongue and without the toys.

"Sweetheart, I'd do anything to please you. We both know that I lack in the size department. After years of frustrating you, I wouldn't mind if you found someone to satisfy your sexual needs. Just as long as I have you, I'd be fine."

"I don't need that," April said defensively. "All I've ever desired was your love."

"All I've ever wanted to do since the day I laid eyes on you was to love you and take care of you. A huge part of taking care of you includes the physical arena, too. I'd give up all of my wealth to be able to make you climax with what God gave me."

Virgil's words moved and captivated her heart. The emotional tremor in his voice revealed just how troubled he really was. As if it was the first time she truly listened, she heard the words in a whole new way. It was because she was different. As she thought of her near-perfect life, for the first time, none of the wealth and material possessions mattered. That's what April would think; it's what April thought.

"Sweetheart, I'd like to help you with this. Care to give it a try?" April asked.

"I know what you're trying to do, honey, but we both know I don't penetrate deeply enough for intercourse to be effective."

"It's just a matter of tactics. What's our objective?" April asked.

Virgil's smile delayed his response. For the first time in his recent memory, the issue was identified in the plural form instead of singular. Somehow he felt revived and it was apparent in his reply.

"To make your ass cum," Virgil responded.

"That's the spirit. Have you ever heard the expression, 'Dance with the girl you brung'?"

"Yes, a time or two."

"Then that's what we're going to do."

Virgil remained unsure how her new enthusiasm would accomplish the task, but he was more than eager to find out, even at the risk of disappointment.

"First, let's get him ready," April said. "All of this chatter can't be good for your thunder."

Virgil gave her a warm smile.

"Straddle my face," April instructed as she lowered to her back.

Virgil crawled on his hands and knees until both were respectively on the left and right side of her body. His grandness hung over her head.

"Lower," April said.

Virgil spread his legs wider, thus, automatically lowering his goods toward her hungry mouth. April teased him with the tip of her tongue. The wetness and warmth of the caressing instrument sent pleasure ripples throughout his body. A wider stroke from her hot tongue had every imaginable form of eroticism moving through him like the constant repetition of ocean waves crashing on the shore. The erection that Virgil had was one from years gone by. It was strong and felt unbreakable. He looked down at the steel-like manhood; despite the size, he believed it would be a powerful tool tonight.

April licked his testicles for a few minutes until they loosened and hung like two heavy sacks. Virgil heard the words "teabag" announced in the form of a question. He was motionless for a brief moment while he deciphered the meaning of her inquiry. After a quick glance at April's open mouth, he understood what she wanted him to do. He spread his legs further apart very slowly. The process lowered both sacs into her wide opened mouth, reminiscent of dunking two teabags into a cup of hot water. April closed her mouth carefully around his crown jewels. They felt like soft marbles and she swirled her tongue around them. With a delicate touch, she pulled on the sacs and was surprised when her ears intercepted the repeated word, "harder." Her mouth's grip tightened, she pulled down, added the swirl of her tongue and felt his flesh stretch. When he felt her mouth go through the motion of a swallow, Virgil thought his wife had been possessed by a sex goddess. Nevertheless, it had been years since there was this much excitement with their intimacy.

Hell, a great part of him felt like he was being fucked; especially when April started massaging the outer rim of his rectum. His first reaction was to tense his muscles, one that included clamped butt cheeks that a hydraulic drill couldn't open. But, after a few moments of a guitar strum tenderly across the forbidden zone, Virgil relaxed and enjoyed the extra special touch April performed. With Virgil's jewels still in her mouth, April somehow articulated to him that it was time.

Virgil's take on the sexual encounter thus far was something far more than thrilling. April could have hung him upside down on a rope by his big toes and he would have complied. He backed his body away, positioned himself on his knees between her spread legs, and held his iron rod in his hand, waiting for the next command. April raised her legs, bent each knee and held them in place opposite each of her ears.

"Give it to me now," April spoke.

In the vulnerable position, Virgil had easy access to April's wet jewel. He was excited with anticipation. A new freak in his wife, a high school-like hard-on coupled with the excitement of the unknown made him manly and confident. He slid his tool into her wet haven as if he had ten thick inches and began grinding his hips onto her with a decisive objective. Realistically, he wasn't deep enough in her to be anything more than an object out of place. Virgil was in the girls' pushup position. He gazed at her with a childlike innocence.

"Don't move," April spoke seductively.

She lowered her legs; the maneuver automatically rotated the pelvic area downward on an arch. Virgil managed to keep himself from being disturbed when he felt his manliness begin to escape from within her womanhood. April's "right there" comment restored his confidence. April's pelvic swing positioned his penis from just penetrating through the haven's opening to where Virgil's hardness rested diagonally across her clitoris. The mushroom part of his tool was a mere movement away from her part that needed to be stimulated. A sensual nod from April was her way of instructing him to proceed. All Virgil had to do was start a continuous friction movement on her clitoris. At first he tried the in-and-out, up-and-down thing. He received great pleasure in feeling his head travel back and forth between her silky wet lips, but the session wasn't about him. It was about her and finally pleasing the one he loved with what he was born with.

He moved back to April's original position. She smiled. This time he performed a friction creating a sawing move instead of pumping her. The sensation of her wet lips remained present, but he also sensed April getting into what he did. He watched her face deliberately, captured each expression in his mind like Tivo would a movie.

As April's facial expression began to intensify, passionate moans accompanied them. Each time the rim of his head rubbed against and over her jewel, he felt a tremor in her legs. For April, the repetitive movement of his shaft sliding against the sensitized cherry, and then abruptly changing to the softer mushroom cloud, had her in the midst of a slow-climbing climax. She enjoyed what was best described as the "snap on, snap off" sensation. This sensual feeling occurred for a quick second when the rim of his head pulled against her clitoris, then released to the softer outer mushroom. When the direction was reversed, the outer mushroom gave her an increased sensation as her clitoris rode the edge of the umbrella and then fastened itself back in place to ultimately gain a different eroticism from sliding on the harder sawing shaft. Virgil's mind recorded everything from the intensity of her eyes to the speechless way she sometimes held her mouth open.

He was pleasing her with his manhood. It made him proud, and it elevated his ego and made him feel like a real man. Somewhere between the passionate cries and moans, Virgil heard the words, "almost there." Two simple words electrified him greatly. His lifelong dream was being answered. She was about to explode absent the aid of hard plastic, gelled toys and vibrating objects.

"Cum on my dick," Virgil demanded.

He spoke the words as if he'd recited them a thousand times. They bordered on the chauvinistic line. April might have chuckled inside if she wasn't too far gone under the eroticism spell. She had reached the plateau.

"I'm…," April screamed.

Virgil heard the last word to the familiar phrase held and sung like a long note in a song. It stretched, increased in volume and pitch, and ultimately ended with a loud squeal. Virgil continued to move until his wife begged him to stop because her jewel had become overly sensitive. He kissed her all over each breast, up her neck and passionately in the mouth. It wasn't their first kiss, yet it was. The kiss carried a new sentiment and deeper love for each other.

April breathed heavily. She lowered her legs, straightened them out and slid them together. This move forced Virgil's tool outside of her entrance. April then felt Virgil's manhood throb. She held her legs as straight as possible, caressed his tool with all of her steamy wetness and despite the state of her clitoris, April began to move her hips up and down.

"You feel damn good," Virgil told her.

"No," April countered. "Words can't describe the orgasm I had. Now it's your turn," she expressed while she moved faster.

She felt his steel shaft throb harder like a heavy heartbeat. Virgil would have been satisfied simply because he'd crossed new boundaries, but her sloppy-wet-feeling pussy lips that moved frantically on his thunder had him wanting more. He didn't have to move, he couldn't move; everything April was doing made his toes curl. April moved so fast, she wasn't sure if he was still within the containment of her haven, but it mattered little. Somewhere within her act to please, she found pleasure. In a matter of seconds, her sensitive jewel would climax again.

"The thunder," Virgil panted. April understood this to be his telltale sign of the imminent explosion. "The thunder," he moaned louder. "Feel my roar!" Virgil said as he released his juices between her lips.

All April was able to muster was "fuck" when she felt his hot climactic spray ooze between her lips. She exploded a second time, right after Virgil.

"Damn you!" April screamed.

She held him tightly with both arms. An uncontrolled heavy breath warmed Virgil's ears.

"Did you…again?" Virgil asked.

"My scream didn't tell you?" she responded.

"I love you so much," Virgil spoke endearingly.

"And I you," April replied as she caressed his face tenderly.

"You'll never understand the depth of what you did for me. One day I hope to explain my emotions in a manner that's clear to you."

"Sweetheart, I'm your wife and I love you with all of my heart. That's all of the explanation I need."

Virgil kissed her on the forehead, laid his head next to hers and held her tenderly in a silent communicative embrace.

THIRTEEN

"My turn for what?", Steven joked.

"Just enjoy," Ariel said.

This time she took his manhood slower. She made sure her soft supple lips tenderly caressed the hardness all the way down the shaft. The good-cop, bad-cop, rough, smooth maneuver excited him. He had no idea what to expect next. Ariel's two point zero seemed capable of anything. Steven freaked completely out when her head tilted back, thus opening a path down her throat. Ariel took the beast entirely in her mouth and rapidly vibrated her head from side to side just to prove it. He was beyond impressed; he was damn awed.

When Ariel pulled her head back a strand of saliva was attached from his head to her bottom lip. The further she moved from his tool, the more the natural juice stretched until it ultimately broke in half. The part attached to her lip retracted and fell between her breasts. Steven watched more saliva travel down her chin, fall like a lone teardrop and join the other wetness at her breasts. Ariel massaged the juices onto her breasts before she positioned his hardness between her twins. She held his manliness captive with soft stokes of her breasts that she moved up and down in alternating directions. She held them in place with her hands. On queue Steven started pumping himself in a slow rhythm between her soft skin as if he was stroking her womanhood.

"I never knew breast fucking could feel so good," Steven said.

"I'm so uninhibited tonight. Liberation at its best," Ariel responded. She was barely able to control her excitement.

Without another word, Ariel was back to work on his joystick with her mouth. The hand-mouth combination was in full effect. She sucked his tool up and down with her mouth, lifted her head and then stroked him rapidly with a twisted hand motion while swirling her tongue around the mushroom part of his manliness. The continuous tongue swirling around his head combined with a masterful hand stroke was too much for Steven to bear. He feared he'd explode any second and he believed Ariel could sense it, too. He moaned heavily and loudly. The pleasured cries carried a state of excitement that was sweet music to her ears.

"Uh-huh," Ariel said after each of his moans.

Steven wasn't sure what her verbiage meant. He was near-orgasm drunk, too tipsy to comprehend anything but his ultimate release. He was certain since he throbbed like a swollen big toe that she would mount and ride him to the joyous state. He was wrong. His eyes opened wide, seemingly protruding out of their sockets as the massive explosion ejaculated like hot lava from a volcano into her mouth. Still, her hand pumped the shooting cannon until the last round was fired. Ariel swallowed the nectar with ease. Steven breathed heavily. He was entranced and literally amazed he'd been taken all of the way for the first time.

Ariel crawled up his body like a sexy lion about to devour its prey. Their lips met, Steven parted his, and Ariel pressed back firmly against his soft lips and sealed their lips. Her mouth opened slightly. She then transferred a portion of her treat into his mouth. The slimy substance felt foreign in his mouth, appalled his taste buds and made him realize exactly what had happened. Steven pushed her upward by both shoulders; Ariel wore a warm frisky smile. The opened hand smack on the side of her face was delivered with so much force that it knocked her off of him. She bounced off the edge of the bed and fell onto the floor.

"What the fuck are you doing?" Steven yelled angrily.

Ariel stood, looked at him with cold eyes, but her hateful expression was nothing compared to the verbal onslaught Steven gave her. Instantly, the sting of his strike announced itself like a jackhammer on a tiny nail. Instinctively, a hand moved to the warm pained area. All of a sudden Steven's abuse didn't feel new. The entire yelling and hitting thing had been jolted to the forefront of her mind.

"You're an asshole!" Ariel screamed back.

"At least I'm not the one spitting cum into another person's mouth," Steven raged.

"We were being adventurous and liberated, remember?"

"You should ask me before you do some nasty shit like that."

"So what you're saying is, I can taste and swallow your nasty shit, but you can't. What, you're afraid of becoming gay?"

Steven jumped from the bed. His hand was back ready to wreak havoc again, but, Ariel took a step toward his aggression; seemingly daring him to strike her. She stood her ground, her eyes were concentrating on his as fear ran rampart throughout her body.

You'd better back down before you get smacked down, Steven thought.

But, Ariel's stance made him second-guess himself so he simply pushed her backward between the breasts. Ariel sensed an anger she'd never experienced. Her piercing eyes were like two laser beams that burned perfectly round holes through his body. She stormed off and ended up at her computer with tears rolling from her eyes like mercury from a broken thermometer.

"Crazy bitch!" Steven yelled as she ran away.

Ariel sat with her feet in the computer chair holding her face in her palms. She cried for countless minutes and realized that something had to be done.

I will no longer be a punching bag, she thought and then realized the notion wasn't new.

Even though anger flowed through, she was able to regain her composure a short while later. A new reality seemed to hit her. Ariel gazed at all of the whitepapers before her, and then picked up the email from her supervisor. Initially, her reaction was one of concern.

I work? she questioned herself oddly.

The question puzzled her. A rush of knowledge bombarded her as if to answer her own inquiry. It changed the complexity of the question and made it a statement.

"I work," she spoke aloud.

The thought had remnants of something she'd always desired to do. Oddly, she was completely satisfied with the notion, yet it felt as new as a sunrise on a different day. The notion gave her a wholeness, as if the last piece of a puzzle had just been connected. Ariel read the white papers with a renewed determination and discovered that each white paper detailed software capable of capturing data from a device or database. Her task, as she understood it, was how to best collect, sort and display different sources of data in one webpage where it could be clearly understood. She leaned back in the chair, hands clasped behind her head and thought about the predicament.

What I need is a manager of managers, Ariel thought.

Another detailed search over the internet began.

FOURTEEN

Monday morning after April picked up Virgil's breakfast plates, she looked around her home and was pleased with her life. Happy that for once she was fulfilled both emotionally and sexually. As she put the plates in the dishwasher, Virgil's words of not being able to do aerobics came to mind. Her head turned toward the basement steps, she stared at the door's opening as if it led to someplace evil and headed toward the basement almost afraid to enter it. When she descended the stairs and entered the room, a wave of emotions swarmed her. The right half of the basement contained various pieces of exercise equipment, and on the other end, a jump rope, dumbbells and two huge exercise balls.

"I've had sex in this room," she spoke aloud.

The odd thing was she knew it wasn't with her husband. She walked over to the giant exercise ball, sat, balanced herself and then rocked back and forth. The simple motion triggered a memory that made her stand and step backward away from the ball. She stared at the huge light-blue circular object and a reflection of her personal trainer's muscular frame flashed across her eyelids. April's lover was five feet ten inches, with a huge chest and a small waist with large developed legs. Once, sometimes twice a week, the aerobic session would be replaced by a sexual escapade, and the last time April recalled it happening on the ball. The memory swarmed her like a hive of bees on a honey stealer. She pictured her naked frame sitting on the ball, legs spread apart. She saw herself rocking back and forth with the trainer's mouth positioned so that his tongue would swipe her jewel on a downward motion. She recalled not being tall enough to bend backward to have her hands and feet touch the floor simultaneously. But, a vivid memory of her balancing her butt on the exercise ball as it was wedged in a corner consumed her. She visualized her legs again spread wide with him deep inside of her warmed her.

April tried to shake the reminiscing session. She kicked the exercise ball away, but what she accomplished was a reminder of the first time she attempted to roll backward on the ball until her shoulder blades rested on the floor. At that time, the exercise ball shot from between her legs, bounced once and hit the trainer in the groin. She remembered once having succeeded. Strawberry jam popped into her mind. Visions of his two fingers spreading the treat onto her lower lips supported the odd thought. She sensed how the chill of the jam had given her goose bumps. She remembered how his warm mouth's delicate pull on her lips had made her juices flow. She recalled the long amount of time he had spent licking and sucking on every part of her moistened box. He brought on orgasm after orgasm with his well-trained tongue.

April's recollection of the incident felt almost real. She'd swear her clitoris was throbbing by simply visualizing their sexual moments. She remembered him balancing on the ball and how she carefully sat on his hardened manhood. She faced him with her hands locked behind his neck. She saw herself with her head back screaming with pleasure from the up-and-down bounce on the exercise ball. The bouncing started as a gentle motion in order to perfect the rhythm, but it ended with him literally dropping their weight on the ball to have the spring-back effect plunge his manliness deeper inside her pleasure box. April nearly cried tears of joy the first time he moved her legs from around his waist, placed her ankles respectively on each shoulder and stood. The recollection made her remember she liked occasional roughness because as he stood, he held her hips and pounded his rod hard into her excited moisture. The sound of their bodies violently colliding became a huge turn-on. She remembered always having multiple orgasms while suspended into the air.

April unknowingly started rubbing herself by simply rehashing the sexual encounters she'd had with her trainer. Her fingers touched the wetness of a lake.

Damn, she thought in the midst of the vision.

When a finger began circling her clitoris, her mind jumped back in to the memory like it never left. The one thing she remembered most was that the trainer always went for overkill. As if eating and pounding her hotbox wasn't enough, many times he would end with her positioned ass up on the ball. The exercise ball provided perfect feedback because it allowed him to grind all of his manhood deep inside her hotbox. She recalled his penis throbbing and how it illuminated her to wits' end.

"I thought...," April said aloud. She panted because of her masturbation act. "I'd be able to end our sexcapades, but the things you did to me let me know I was alive."

Visions of their last time together was as vivid as the moans she made now. She recalled saliva being dropped between her buttocks. The warm natural juices seemed to sizzle between the two mounds of her fiery hot body. He rubbed the wetness around and into her rear door, pulled his moistened hardness from her haven and carefully entered the black hole. The exercise room still carried the echo of her intense passionate cries. She remembered how delicate and slow the trainer's in-and-out motions were. They consisted of a rhythmic push forward, a pull backward to relieve pressure and then another push forward that was a fraction of an inch further than the last push. She bellowed louder the deeper his tool got into her. She recalled holding her mouth open when she felt his genitals rest against her butt as if the slippery snake had slithered its way out of her mouth.

The long, slow stroke deep into her black hole made her knees tremble. They shook today because of the vivid memory and the two fingers that worked a rapid motion around her private jewel. The best, most intensive climax April recalled was when his hardness reached her clitoris from the rear, through the backdoor. Visions of them making the exercise ball move in small circles as he ground himself as deep as possible to touch the magic pea. A lone hand reached backward, pushed against his hips in an attempt to relieve pressure from her hardening jewel. But the pain of the pleasure principle was too great to ignore and was too pleasing to be denied.

She remembered lowering her hand and taking a series of deep breaths to relax. April's legs trembled so badly when she came, it was as if she had no control over them at all. The trembling legs helped her body release an orgasm so grand, the creamy substance ran down the ball. But when she felt his manhood throb, expand, and become steel-like before it sprayed hot juices into her rear, she brought God into the equation. She disregarded the rear door and moved against his manliness as if he was entrenched inside her womanhood. She bounced her hips against his exploding tool until he collapsed. She pictured them slowly tumbling sideways to the floor gasping for air when all of his weight fell onto her. The self-induced orgasm she gave herself while she relived a past memory took her to her knees. She supported herself with one hand and made her body jerk recklessly as she continued to tantalize her overly sensitized clitoris. April lay on the floor with her body curled and waited for the sensation to dissipate.

FIFTEEN

Monday morning Ariel stood in front of the bathroom mirror with a great sense of accomplishment. She felt as though something grand had happened, but she didn't understand why. She shrugged her shoulders, and gave credit to the work she completed last night. She was positive the new approach would please both the client and her superiors. One hour and five minutes later, she stood next to the projector screen in the conference room detailing a new plan.

"The icons in the left column," Ariel said as she pointed and circled them with an infrared pen. "Represent various types of data you have in your infrastructure. The next column is a listing of devices or databases in your infrastructure that collects data from the varying types of sources on the left. These are managers... managers of data if you will."

One of the clients' nods didn't go unnoticed by Ariel.

"What you don't have is a mechanism that can pull all of the various sources of information together and paint a sensible picture of your infrastructure. Am I right?" Ariel asked, already knowing the obvious.

"There lies our dilemma," the lead client commented.

She showed them an example of a failed print queue and the effects it would have on their network. The second example was a collection of trouble tickets and how easily they could be shown in a report. The last example was sales figures extracted from a financial database.

"What you see before you are three separate pieces of information displayed on three different computers. How can a top-level official make an intelligent business decision like this?"

Ariel paused. She wasn't searching for an answer. The time was to allow the clients to ponder the question.

"You can't," she continued. "Not with one quick view. What you need is a manager of managers."

The solution to the client's problem was presented in the next slide. The slide showed the three data managers from the previous slide pointing their collected data to a business engine model of the solution software. The business engine was capable of collecting data from all industry standards.

"And this data could then be sorted, filtered, reported and/or displayed in a digital dashboard on one computer screen. All of this information can be accessed through a web portal," Ariel said confidently.

Ariel detailed to the client the security features of the software. She showed, based on company security policies, users would be able to drill down to more detailed levels of the infrastructure. She performed a brief walkthrough of the Executive, Manager and Operations logons. She smiled when the clients nodded when they were shown the "Executive" level that provided an overall picture of a company's infrastructure.

"With that," the client asked, "I can take one quick glance and determine hot issues?"

"Yes, sir," Ariel responded.

"Can it be tailored to other types of data?"

"That's the beauty of this solution. It doesn't matter what the data is, if it's being collected and stored in any type of database format, the information can be presented in a format that suits your needs. We can initially concentrate on your major heartburns, and then expand to other aspects of your business."

The two clients nodded as if accepting the notion. Ariel concluded the presentation by giving the clients the opportunity to manipulate the software through a workflow engine. What a difference a day makes. This time when Ariel left the conference room, her boss and clients were discussing the infinite possibilities the proposed solution offered. Her boss gave her two thumbs up as she closed the door.

A moment later, Ariel stood at her office window looking into the clear blue sky. She had nailed the presentation and the wonderful feeling gave her a new commitment to her craft. She was refreshed.

"I work," she spoke aloud. "And I'm damn good at it," she said proudly.

Later that evening during the drive home, Ariel reflected on the magnitude of her day. She was elated. An on-the-spot promotion moved her into a larger office. All of these things mattered little when she walked into the thick air of her home. The air remained thick without Steven being home from work. She somehow managed to push their domestic problems aside to have a productive day, but as she stood in the foyer, a rush of anxiety bombarded her. Part of her felt Steven's physical abuse was a first-time occurrence, part of her believed the opposite, but all of her stood firmly with the belief that the abuse would never happen again. Everything they'd accomplished as a couple meant nothing while her mental and physical stability was in question.

I ought to cut his dick off, she thought.

She quickly abandoned the notion because it would ruin not only what she accomplished this glorious day, but her entire life. The renewed commitment to her job came with a greater sense of independence. She would start anew, everything fresh and clean.

"Begin with an ending," she announced as she poured herself a glass of wine and began preparing dinner.

She sat at the table, crossed her legs and to her surprise, she realized she was wet. A vision of the woman in the mirror flashed in her mind and made her wonder what the other woman was doing.

She had just started eating the low-carb stir-fry when Steven entered the kitchen.

"Something smells good," he said before he kissed her on the neck. "How was your day?"

"There is more on the stove," Ariel responded. "Shall I fix you a plate?"

"I got it, enjoy your food." Seconds later, Steven sat across from her at the table. "Your day was?" he inquired again.

"Fantastic! No, my day was way, way better than that. It was more like super-duper fantastic," Ariel spoke with glee and began to eat again.

"I take it your presentation went well?"

Ariel only nodded.

"You're still upset about last night?" Steven asked.

Ariel's piercing glance told all.

"Honey, don't be. You dropping cum in my mouth took me by surprise. Yet, I know that I should have handled the situation better."

Ariel raised her head and displayed a "no shit!" expression.

"How long are you going to hold this against me?"

Ariel dropped the fork heavily on her plate. The loud sound indicated to Steven that the redundant question bothered her.

"Just until I walk out the door?" she responded.

"What does that mean?"

"It means…I'm leaving you tonight," she spoke evenly. "I have one suitcase packed."

"You can't be serious," Steven spoke in disbelief.

"Heart attack serious," Ariel spoke evenly.

"Why? Because I slapped you?"

"You just don't get it. No where in our vows did it say I had to be fed mental and physical abuse. The better or worse comment, in my book, means to stay by your side if you got sick, lose your job or something. Not!" Ariel yelled to drive the point home, "to put me through what you've done too many times to count."

Steven sat speechless. His mouth was open, shocked by his wife's words.

"Can we talk about this?" Steven asked.

"We just did. I suggest you enjoy the last meal my hands will ever prepare for you." Ariel stood abruptly, and the chair's legs scraped and sounded against the marble flooring. "I'll be back at a later date to gather the rest of my things."

"You can't give up on us like this. We have a good life together," Steven pleaded.

"Stevie," Ariel replied in a nasty tone. "I haven't given up on us; I gave up on you."

Steven swallowed a couple more forkfuls of food, then forcefully pushed his plate across the table toward her. The plates collided and split into several triangular pieces. Steven stood, clasped his hands together as if he was praying and began to beg Ariel to reconsider her decision. Ariel never allowed her eyes to leave his.

She was frightened, but she blanketed her fear with the notion of a new life, one minus the abuse she sometimes took. In one short movement, Steven stood in her space, nearly face to face with her. His compassionate words moved from a soft-toned, sorry-filled sentiment to a scornful, harder, threatening one. His eyes transformed to hateful ones, the red veins prominent as if he hadn't slept for days. The level of his voice rose with each passing second. Like cannonballs shot at a battleship, the verbal assault exploded against her vessel, rattled her spirit, but didn't break it.

"See what I mean," she spoke evenly with a hint of defiance.

Steven turned around, his blood boiled inside. Never did he consider her argument for wanting to end their sometimes strained marriage. He believed marriage was ordained by God and that meant forever. He couldn't let it end, no matter what the cost, no matter how he acted at times.

"Damn it!" Steven yelled. He knocked over a chair with a frustrated swing. "Think about what you're doing. We have a good life."

"Is this and the hostility you're showing now a part of the"— Ariel raised her hand and made the quotation mark move with two fingers—"good life? If it is, then I'm in search of a better life. There is no shame in that."

"You'd shame me with a failed marriage."

"I shamed you when I spoke to Devin when he was with another woman. I shamed you when I played with myself, and now, I've shamed you simply by talking about a divorce. It's always all about you. Know what," she spoke with conviction while Steven walked back into her personal space. "I'm putting me first, putting what I want ahead of me trying not to shame your sensitive feelings."

Steven felt belittled. Never in his life had a woman talked to him in such a degrading manner. A familiar thought of putting her in her place spoke volumes to him. The thought lit the blood in his veins like a match to a fuse of a dynamite stick. His flying fist originated from Georgia, possibly south of the equator, intended to prove who was boss. His right arm swung in front of her face with so much force, Ariel felt the breeze from the blow. However, Ariel's sight never left his revealing eyes and they prepared her for the onslaught. She had one hand resting on her hip and the other supporting her weight on the table. Steven's blow was fast, but Ariel was quicker. She grabbed a piece of broken plate, held it in front of her as she leaned backward out of harm's way. The plate cut a gash five inches long and an inch and a half deep into his forearm. Steven grabbed his arm, grimaced in pain as blood seeped through his fingers.

"I can't believe you'd do this to me," Steven yelled.

"You tried to hit me with your fucking fist," Ariel screamed back. "I can't believe that. I've done nothing to you except ask for a new life. You," she spoke with a shaky voice, "tried to beat me into submission. I have every right to defend myself."

Steven kicked at her. Again, Ariel dodged his aggression.

"Maybe instead of causing me harm, you should direct your attention to your bleeding arm. It looks fairly severe."

Steven wanted to dispute her suggestion, but the pain accompanying the blood had announced itself; it couldn't be ignored. He cursed her, called her everything except a child of God as he walked toward the bathroom. Ariel stood at the bathroom's entrance and watched him tend to his arm. The compassionate side of her wanted to reach out and help, but the deadly intention of his swing killed all chances of her taking action.

"Do you feel a slight pain in your stomach?" she asked.

"I'll never forgive you for what you just did to me," Steven responded.

"Good. Let the resulting permanent scar be a constant reminder that a real man would never strike a woman. More importantly, remember, a woman scorned is a deadly thing."

"You're just lucky that I missed."

"Truly, darling, you're the lucky one," she said and smiled devilishly afterward. "If you had struck me with that much deadly force, I wouldn't be inclined to tell you how to dilute the poison," she said nonchalantly.

Suddenly, the question about stomach pain resurfaced in his mind. He was unsure if paranoia had set in, but if he allowed himself to feel something other than the anguish of the arm, there was a discomfort residing in his belly. His unharmed arm instinctively held his stomach as if he was holding back severe cramps.

"What in fuck's name did you do to me?"

"The poison I put in your food was intended to be my safety net. The factor that would allow me to get out of the house without you kicking my ass. As it turned out, the arm accomplishes the same thing."

"You poisoned me, you bitch! I'll kill you," Steven roared.

"Not today. I wouldn't spend too much energy. It will make the poison spread quicker throughout your system."

"How could you stoop so low and do this to me?"

"As it turns out, seems I did the right thing. You'll be fine as long as you follow my instructions."

Steven hated to admit it, but he was scared. However, the "man" in him wouldn't allow it to show.

"What do I have to do to get this shit out of me?" Steven asked.

"Finish wrapping your arm, then check your Verizon personal email account. Detailed instructions are there."

Ariel watched him watch her back away. She went into the guest bedroom, grabbed the packed suitcase, car keys and left the home she'd known for years without saying another word. Steven's attention moved from the care of his arm toward the sound of the front door being closed. He stared from the bathroom into the empty bedroom. Suddenly, the house no longer felt like home. Suddenly, he had surpassed lonely, fell hard on alone. Suddenly, he remembered the need to check his email.

SIXTEEN

The doorbell woke April from her slumber. She had fallen asleep after her self-induced orgasm and had a dream about being liberated. She ran toward the stairs and yelled, "just a minute," as she dashed by the front door. She sprinted upstairs to the bedroom, and returned in seconds to answer the call. Somehow, as she opened the front door, she sensed that she had already left. She paused, shook off the notion that she would always be connected to the vision of herself.

The door opened to the sight of her personal trainer. As usual, he flashed a bright perfect smile, except this time, the gold-outlined front tooth was a distraction. He wore a muscle shirt too small for his well-defined physique, and biker shorts too tight that made his pelvic area scream "Look at me." He entered the house, greeted her with a customary kiss on the cheek and squeeze of her pinky finger.

"Sunshine, how are you feeling today?" the trainer asked.

"Liberated," April spoke and smiled bright as the sun.

The trainer wrinkled his forehead in confusion. April acknowledged his stunned look as she equated her comment as having the same effect when someone responds, "I'm blessed." Experience had taught her that it stunned most people. "I'm great. Really great," April spoke.

For the first time in months, there was an awkward silence between them.

"So," the trainer blurted to end the strange moment, "have you worked on the latest things I've shown you?"

"No, because the pushups exercise would be difficult with this thing on my hand," she responded and held her hand up.

"What happened to your hand?" he asked as he grabbed her wrist and kissed the bandage.

"The truth is too unbelievable, so I'll just say glass shattered in my hand."

"Poor thing. How can I make you feel better?" he asked as he pulled her near and pressed his body against hers.

Before the lightning strike, April might have draped her arms around him and responded with, "Ravish me." Today, however, was different. Her arms remained at her side, dictated by the notion that she rather not be touched.

"Okay, I give," the trainer stated. "What's up with you today? I feel the cold-shoulder treatment."

"My dear friend, please don't consider my action as mistreatment. I'm a changed person; the old me is in another time, in another place," she responded. April captured his full attention with her eyes. "Therefore, in essence, I'm a different person who's focused on doing the right thing."

"I'd guess by your 'doing the right thing,' the hot, steamy sex," he spoke sultrily, "has to end."

April inhaled deeply, exhaled as slowly as the intake had been. "You are intuitive," she responded. "Things are different now."

"Different?" the trainer said a little put back. "Mr. Virgin...I mean, Virgil, has his dick grown five inches longer?"

April gazed at him with hard, cold eyes. She was appalled by the belittling question.

"Whatever the case," she responded, "big or small, our extra-curricular activities have ended."

"You know you're going to miss...how does he say it, the thunder from down under."

"That may be true, but I no longer require sexual services from you. Besides, I told you his pet phrase in confidence. It was not meant to be used against me. As a matter of fact, the personal training services can end also. I've learned enough from you to maintain my fitness absent your assistance."

"Seriously?" he responded puzzled.

"Heart attack serious," she replied as if the words were spoken for her. "I'll maintain my fitness from this point. More importantly, I'm rededicated to my marriage and for the first time in years, I get it. I get how to cherish these things and have a great sex life despite inadequate challenges. I get that the time I've been fooling around with you, I could have devoted to discovering ways to make intimacy with my husband more pleasurable for me. How would you feel if you could no longer make a woman climax with your dick?"

The trainer pulled down the biker shorts to mid-thigh and let his "Johnson" hang freely for her to see.

Damn, April said to herself. *Even soft, he is larger than Virgil's erection.*

The trainer caught the mild excitement in her eyes and felt that she was trying to be strong. He held his manhood at the base, slapped it against his leg until it started to rise.

"When I can't get it up like this, I'll take Viagra," he boasted. "By the time I need help, it will probably be available in an aerosol can. You see," he said, directing her eyes down to the thicker, longer erection, "size does matter."

"You're right. I totally agree. The size of your big-ass attitude and inflated ego sickens my stomach. You can kindly leave. I'll send you a check for the week. I'm through with you."

April had the front door opened and an arm pointing to his exit. Her serious, distant expression silenced his words. He put his tool away, picked up the workout bag, hung the strap on his shoulder and walked out the door shaking his head. April closed and locked the door behind him. Her sense of being liberated was now far grander than moments ago when she responded to the trainer's question. She was proud that the feeling was her own and not a sensed notion.

SEVENTEEN

I n three days' time, Ariel had secured a ninth-floor, moderately priced condo a few blocks from her job. She was sitting on the living room's hardwood floor waiting for all new furniture and a window decorator to arrive.

"Hello," she said after she answered her cell phone.

"That was a funny trick you played on me," the caller spoke.

"Steven, you're alive. How is the ole stomach?" Ariel asked.

"You're still the comedienne. You have no idea of the anxiety I had thinking you'd actually poisoned me. To top it off, when I went to check my email, the DSL line was down. I almost dialed nine-one-one. All I thought about until the line came up was to drink plenty of water...which, by the way, had me pissing all night long. When I read your email that said, 'Fool, I'm not crazy, nothing is wrong with you,' I could have killed you from the scare alone."

"As I recall it, killing me was pretty much your plan the last time I saw you."

"I wouldn't harm you like that," Steven responded.

Ariel removed the cell phone from her ear, gazed at it strangely and closed the device to end the call. She had counted to seven when the cell phone rang again.

"Steven," Ariel said. "What do you want?"

"You're right," Steven confessed. "My anger had gotten the best of me. However, since that time, I've taken a moment to reflect on what you must feel. I have been abusive mentally and physically to you. I truly apologize," Steven relayed somberly. "It hadn't been an everyday thing, but I'd imagine enough to turn your heart away from me."

"That's a wonderful summation," Ariel replied.

"Let me make it up to you. Come home," Steven pleaded.

The loud laughter Ariel bellowed carried on for a long moment, long enough for Steven to interrupt the solo laugh.

"Okay, I understand. Not a chance in hell, right," Steven spoke.

"Precisely."

"I do want to make it up to you," Steven repeated again.

During the small moment of silence, Ariel bit down on her lip to prevent herself from laughing again. Steven sensed Ariel's need to quantify his statement.

"I'm selling the house, and half of the profit will be sent to you. I can't see myself living in this big-ass house alone."

Note to self, Ariel thought. *Cancel divorce attorney meeting tomorrow.*

"And another positive note," Steven continued. "I've scheduled a counseling session to talk about my anger issues."

"That's a big step. I'm proud you're addressing them."

"Well, if I'm to have a new life, I'd better fix what's wrong with me. So, how have you been?" Steven asked.

Ariel heard the sadness in his voice. She hoped he was sincere with his apology, hoped he would seek help, and hoped he wouldn't try to track her down with what she was about to say.

"Steven," Ariel spoke slowly, "you should know that I took half of our joint savings to have money for my new home."

"I saw that."

"I wasn't trying to piss you off. I'm entitled."

"Calm down," Steven replied. He sensed a bit of tension in her words. "I'm not upset and yes, you are entitled. We both have been adding money to that account for years."

"Don't worry, when I was in the credit union, I removed myself from the account," Ariel explained.

"Hmm…very noble of you, even though I've never known you to be vindictive."

"Just being fair." Ariel paused unknowing what more to say.

She appreciated Steven's gesture and somehow believed a different, more civilized person was speaking to her.

"Well," Steven said. "I just wanted you to know what I was planning. I won't hold you." Steven paused. The realization that he wouldn't hold her in his arms saddened him. "Good luck with your new place," he said and fought the notion to ask the location.

"Thank you."

"Sounds good."

It appeared they played a game of who would end the call first. All it accomplished was another moment of uncomfortable silence.

"That must be the furniture people," Ariel said upon hearing a knock on the door.

The distraction was great timing. They needed something to break the awkward moment.

"Got to run," Ariel said. "Let's talk soon."

"Sure thing."

They ended the conversation with an understanding of separate lives. The living room furniture Ariel purchased was ultra-modern leather pieces, angular in design. She chose a bright-red color to offset the varying shades of pastel wall paint. She sat on the footstool and mentally chose a new color for each room. The living room where she sat, the dining room, kitchen, bedroom and bath were all slated for a makeover.

Ariel stood, cautiously walked toward the bathroom for no other reason than a need to be there. It summoned her like a ghost's whisper. She walked into the plush bath that had yet to be decorated and gazed into the mirror trying to find a sensation familiar to her. After moments of examining herself, the sense of belonging and the presence of another were absent. She turned around, rested her butt against the pedestal sink and a notion called upon her once more. She closed her eyes, held them shut for a moment, then her head turned to the left as if she was sniffing down a scent. When she opened her eyes, the oversized tub was in sight.

Ariel dug through a box on the counter. It contained bathroom necessities and other things to pamper herself. She pulled out a twenty-four pack of votive candles, placed them strategically around the tub and placed another item on the floor before she started a steamy bath draw. She had no rational reason why she only lit every other candle; she just did. She then turned the bathroom lights off. The multiple flickering flames created an array of different feelings within her. She tossed the head of a single rose into the water and waited for the petals to separate before entering the alluring bath. She then carefully stepped over the burning candles and stood in the tub.

Ariel anticipated lowering her body into the deep, hot bath laced with baby oil. She lowered to her knees, splashed water on her thighs to help adjust the water's temperature. Ariel supported her weight with both hands, respectively on each side of the tub, straightened one leg in front of her, then the other. At a snail's pace, she bent her elbows to descend her body into the water. The baby oil-laced water felt like liquid silk as her legs slowly submerged under the water. The sting of the hot silky water on her womanhood forced an arched back; she composed herself and ever so slowly lowered her body into the water. The water level was just below her breasts in the full sitting position. She placed both hands into the water, immediately felt her fingers energize with warmth and cupped her breasts with her hot hands. Her sensitive nipples were pressed centered under her palms.

Ariel wasn't prepared for the erotic sensation the fire-like hand gave her. It was damn near an aphrodisiac. Needless to say, the hand-to-breast maneuver became repetitive. It eventually led to nipple pinching with fiery fingertips. She had difficulties determining whether the self-pleasing or the water's temperature made her forehead sweat, but streams of water began to roll down her face. The one sure thing was that her womanhood demanded attention. One hand swam toward the yearning.

Damn, all of my toys are boxed, she thought.

She touched herself, it felt different. Maybe it was the new sense of freedom, or possibly the aura of her new home, but something had changed. Then it hit her—she was now able to please herself without the repercussion and the thought excited her more than any tongue lashing or hard-on Steven ever gave her.

Ariel carefully reached between two burning candles, picked up the plastic item, submerged it under water and waited for all air bubbles to stop. Seconds later, Ariel moved the flesh from around her jewel and then shot her clitoris with liquid bullets. The water gun's stream was strong enough to penetrate through the bathwater and tantalize her cherry in a pulsating manner. Each pull of the trigger felt like a makeshift shower massage. The good part was, she had an endless supply of ammunition as long as her trigger finger still had strength to pull the trigger hard. Within minutes, the water gun's jet stream had her in full moan mode. Not only was her forehead sweating, all non-submerged body parts had rivers of water feeding back into the giant lake-like bath. Oddly, she wished she could hear the sound of rain.

Ariel had reached the boiling point. Her flesh was not to touch, her blood pressure rose to where her erotic state couldn't combat the sense of dizziness. Her trigger finger halted, the gun remained underwater, but normal breathing was a difficult task.

"Shit, I'm too hot," she panted.

She stood and steam rose from her skin as if she was emerging from the deep fryer. She waved a hand at her head attempting to cool herself. Yet, her jewel spat on the neglect. It throbbed and reminded her that it hated to be teased. She crossed her legs, held them tight attempting to control the beast, but the move was the prelude for what she did next. Her fingers exposed the clitoris naked to the universe. Then, as if she needed to slay a beast that just wouldn't die, the trigger finger moved in a rapid session. The liquid bullets without the bathwater's resistance felt more like the pressure from a fireman's hose. The intermittent sprays instantly caused her body to jerk. She accepted a challenge within herself to climax before the pistol ran out of water. The machinegun-like spray ignited a roar within her. She took a deep breath and held it captive for a moment.

"Aahhh!" she bellowed in a loud-pitch rising tone.

She dropped the water gun and finished the orgasm with a finger. She was exhausted. Her weakened knees collapsed into the tub. It sent water over the sides of the tub like a tidal wave caused by an underground earthquake. Her heart pounded violently, its vibrations echoed in her ears and her sensitive cherry stung like it had been whipped.

Ariel remained on her knees until normal breathing had returned, until her jewel felt less fiery, until she could lay back in the tub with her head resting against the top rim. With her eyes closed, she used the remaining heat from the bath to send her down a road of tranquility. She didn't remember falling asleep, but when she awoke, the chilled water was overshadowed by her pruned skin.

EIGHTEEN

I t had been a few days since April ended the sexual affair with the personal trainer. She believed she had succeeded in concealing the separation anxiety from Virgil. However, her spouse's overabundance of pampering made her wonder if he suspected he'd done something wrong. His latest treat included the couples shower they were in. He was washing her back with soapy hands that felt more like caressing to April. His fingertips pressed the muscles in her back with just the right amount of force. This had April eagerly awaiting what he had in store. He had strategically placed aromatic freshly cut lilies throughout the bathroom. A faint whisper of Jazz played on the bedroom stereo, but Virgil's attentiveness was what made the evening enchanting. He undressed her, pinned her hair up and had administered a perfect manicure and pedicure. His pampering relaxed her; she was very much in need of the attention.

In a short time, Virgil had washed every inch of her body. Her head fell backward when he dropped to his knees in front of her. The overly hot water massaging her face felt slightly less than how acid might on her face. But the discomfort was easily dampened by Virgil's mouth collapsing around her jewel. She arched her back for a greater effect and pulled her lower lips apart and then upward. This allowed her jewel to become a lonely stone on a desolate beach. At first, Virgil tantalized her with his soft tongue. He made wide deliberate strokes followed by a narrow, piercing tip that caressed her ever so gently.

After a couple of minutes of Virgil's precision-like tongue movements, April felt as though she was losing her mind. He continued until her legs wobbled like jelly.

"I can't let you have that big 'O' just yet," Virgil said. "Let's see just how long we can prolong it."

April didn't know what to think. The erotic state clouded her judgment.

"Whatever…you…want," she spoke barely legible to Virgil.

He caught the excess water falling from her womanhood in his mouth until the natural chamber overflowed. He replaced her fingers with his, spread her lower lips with a "V" formation of his fingers, pressed against her and pushed upward. Her man-in-the-boat stood at attention ready for commands. Virgil sprayed a pinpointed stream of water between his teeth onto her exposed clit.

At first she was startled, but the next time was twice as pleasing. April's head slowly fell forward; she watched the timed liquid bullets strike her jewel like a lawn sprinkler, intermittent, yet constant. When his mouth emptied, he refilled the chamber and repeated the process until his tongue became too sensitive from pressing against his two front teeth.

April's legs began to shake. She believed if a faint breeze traveled through the bathroom, she'd climax. Instead the telephone rang. Virgil wasn't bothered by the distraction and April was skilled at staying tuned through tremendous thunderstorms. Therefore, when the machine's greeting filled the air, she was far from fazed. Virgil began darting his tongue in and out of her wetness at a supersonic pace. Her control had all but vanished.

She merely held the release to make the climax more explosive. Virgil knew that she was an instant away from erupting when her fingernails scratched his shoulder with a rhythm that increased after each movement.

"Steven, your wife ended our affair," the personal trainer spoke. His voice floated through the answering machine's speaker like a sour note played on a violin. "I just thought you should know." There was a small moment of silence, followed by a panicked, louder tone. "Oh fuck," the trainer said, "I thought I'd dialed your cell."

The personal trainer hung up the phone without another word. April's sensual mood vanished quicker than the Titanic sinking into the black depths of the sea. She hastily backed away from his hungry mouth, under the shower's stream until her back hit the shower control knob. She managed to ignore the pain traveling down her leg caused by the octagon-shaped object. She gazed at her spouse disillusioned. Virgil's sad-eyed expression was identical to hers. Even the shower's stream that caused his eyes to bat a mile a minute couldn't conceal his new turbulent emotions.

April carefully stepped out of the tub. She neglected the drying towel and laid her wet body onto the bed. Moments later, Virgil entered the bedroom with a towel around his waist. He sat on the side of the bed unsure of what to say. April was dealing with an internal struggle. Part of her raged while another part of her had guilt for her actions. She turned to her stomach, eyes open in a dead stare, and attempted to make sense of what she was feeling. She got up, returned from the bathroom wearing a robe, and then paced in front of him for a moment. The time Virgil spent watching his wife walk battling her confusion felt like eternity to him.

"You're going to wear a hole in the carpet," Virgil said with his head hung low.

"You paid him?" April responded. She easily ignored his comment. Virgil's head lifted, his eyes met her anger. "You paid him to fucking have sex with me!" she yelled.

All sense of sensibility had left April. The guilt of her participation was squashed like a bug under a shoe. Knowing that her husband set her up to fail was bewildering.

"I did," Virgil responded shamefully. His spirits ran low. "But still you…" Virgil stopped his sentence. The old saying about leading a horse to water flashed through his mind. *Drank the water*, he thought. "I did it because of my…" Virgil paused again. This time he simply stared at her.

"You paid someone to fuck me. Sure, it took care of a need," she said as she paced back and forth again. "But, at the same time, the guilt I've had to live with outweighed most of the pleasure I gained."

"I just wanted you to feel like a real woman," Virgil responded.

"Virgil, I felt like a real woman just having a man like you. I'll admit, often I grew tired of not being fulfilled, but I knew what I was getting into before I married you. It's not like after we said, 'I do,' your dick suddenly shrank. So you see, I was willing to deal with our love life."

April's hands approached her head; she grabbed two fistfuls of hair and felt a need to snatch out chunks of it.

"I understand now," she spoke as her eyes filled with water, "why your efforts ceased. As I look back on things, your attentiveness to please me changed about the same time the personal trainer came along. You hired him to give me what you couldn't, yet, you couldn't handle the reality of your action. Am I right?"

Virgil acknowledged his wife's assessment with a nod. Indeed, it was a shameful bounce of his head.

"I also understand," April continued, "why you once stated you wouldn't mind if I slept with another man. You already knew I had because the trainer had told you. Didn't he?"

Virgil's head lowered again. He was embarrassed. He suppressed speaking the horse–and-water thought again, but at the same time understood the leading part of the phrase.

"I was wrong in surrendering to the flesh," April confessed. "You were wrong for putting me in a position to surrender."

Virgil gazed at his wife with a passion she'd never seen before. She felt a certain sympathy for him. She tried desperately to understand his motive, to find an appreciation in his action, but nothing surfaced. Both personalities within her tried to rationalize the angry feeling inside.

"You don't give a diabetic sugar," April said. "Just like you don't give a sex-starved person a chance at sex. Virgil, I wronged you. You wronged me, we wronged each other." A thought of liberation developed within her. "I want a divorce," she stated unexpectedly.

Virgil understood her anger, yet hearing her talk about divorce was the last thing he wanted to hear.

"You can't be serious," Virgil stated out of shock.

"Why can't I be?"

"Because you've never worked a day in your life," Virgil stated a little too sarcastically for his own taste.

"I work," she responded. The words felt true, but after she considered Virgil's statement, she continued, "I mean, I have an education. I have a skill and I'll find a way to take care of myself."

"April, think about it," Virgil pleaded. "Starting a first job at your age…"

"What!" April snapped. "You think I'm too old to find a job?"

"I didn't mean it that way. Times are hard out there. Most companies, mine included, seek the college grads because we can get them cheap. We both know you're accustomed to a grander lifestyle than what the salary of a person starting out in the workforce will bring." Suddenly, Virgil's head lowered, as did the tone of his voice. "I suspect I'm headed for a nasty court battle."

"It doesn't have to be that way. Besides, I don't want your money. Being liberated means me taking care of me. However..." She paused. "I'll initially need your help. So, let the love you claim to have for me guide you to do the right thing by me."

"My love for you wants you to stay. We can work out our troubles."

"I can't be with you right now. There is so much I need to sort out."

"Sort it out," Virgil pleaded. "Find yourself; just don't divorce me...not after you've shown me how to be a real man."

April's anger lessened to the point where she could think logically. She wasn't convinced to stay, but she'd take his words into consideration.

"I'd like to explore all of my options," April responded. "So, why don't you come up with an amicable solution? I promise you, I'll contemplate both options. Let's talk later, okay?" she suggested.

Virgil was troubled by thoughts of his precious April's departure. The loss of her love was enough to tear his heart into pieces.

Eddie, I want half, popped into his mind.

The comedic thought relieved some emotional tension for a quick second, but the bitter reality of the thought became something greater to be concerned about. His company was successful, a Fortune 500 top one hundred. He had worked too hard, for far too many years, to simply give up half of everything, thus, he sat for hours contemplating the predicament. After much debate, he rumbled through a file box in his home office for a specific piece of paper. He joined April in her favorite spot in the bow window. She made room for him and they sat silently.

"Virgil, I'm not feeling good about myself at all," April spoke. "I've broken my vows, tainted your trust in me...I know I'll never be the same if I stay with you."

"We can learn to trust one another again," Virgil responded.

"I'm just not in a good place right now. I'm me, but not me," she said. Her eyes never left the window.

Virgil watched his wife struggle with some sort of inner turmoil and realized pressuring her to rekindle their marriage would be like two positive ends of a magnet forcing each other away.

"I have a suggestion," he stated. "Why don't we start from the beginning?"

April's head turned toward his. She gave him her full attention with her eyes and waited for him to continue.

"Hello, April," Virgil said as he stood, faced her and extended his hand for a formal greeting. He concealed the other hand behind his back. "I'm Virgil Jonston, president and CEO of Innovative Solutions."

April's mind went back to their interview many years past.

"You studied at Penn," Virgil continued. "You seem to be over-qualified for the position you're applying for. Are you sure you'd like to work for I-S?"

Is he playing with me, April asked herself.

Her baffled expression wasn't missed by Virgil. He gave her the piece of paper from behind his back. To her surprise, it was her first and only résumé.

"Seriously, honey," Virgil said. "I have a solution that may be mutually beneficial to us. Why don't you work for me? Like you should have years ago."

"Wouldn't that be a conflict of interest?"

"I own the damn company. It seems I should be entitled to bend the rules. Here's what I propose…you get paid a handsome salary while you gain experience. When you feel the time is right to move on, do so."

"That's a generous offer, but I can't work and live with you. Nothing would have changed."

"I've got that covered, too. I'll provide the down payment for a place of your own. The job and down payment will be separate from the terms in our di…" Virgil paused. He looked at her with a more saddened expression. "Divorce," Virgil continued.

April took her turn at being a mute. Her head lowered, and she twisted two of her fingers in thought.

"Virgil," she spoke. "Understand that I don't want your money. Our divorce papers need not reflect anything more than what you just stated. I'd argue that I've sponged off you for years. You provided me a life beyond my wildest dreams. Helping me get into a place I can call mine and the job is enough. I want to be my own woman as I started out trying to do years ago. Liberated, remember me saying that?" April asked, not requiring an answer. "I'll change it to having my own independence."

"I understand a desire such as that can drive you on to greatness. Take your time, though; don't decide this very moment. I just want to be fair."

"You'd be more than fair just by honoring what we've discussed. That's all I need."

"Then it's settled. Despite everything and what you may think of me, you know I'm a man of my word."

NINETEEN

T hings moved fast for April. In three days' time, she started her lower-six-figure salary job. Two days later, she stood inside her sixth-floor condo within walking distance away from her job.

April started her new life with no bills other than the mortgage, utilities and food expenses. She decided to take her time to decorate. She had no kitchen table to speak of, an air mattress to sleep on, and one pan to cook with. Virgil insisted on taking care of these minor necessities, but she decided to experience independence at its fullest.

She walked to the living room window, glanced at the people walking the busy street below and then looked upward to praise the heavens. She saw in a short time the blue sky transform into a threatening gray one. April grabbed her purse, umbrella and headed toward the elevator. Moments later, she stepped into the revolving door of the condo lobby just as the skies let loose. The sound of thunder roared as lightning ripped across the sky. The storm seemed to drop buckets of rain along its rolling path. People ran for cover.

Ariel turned around just as the torrential rain fell and stepped back into the revolving door of her building. She pushed the bar to circle through, but it remained still. She looked left and saw someone familiar to her.

"It's you," both April and Ariel spoke simultaneously.

April let the door turn, her eyes never left Ariel. After a complete amusement park-ride-like circle, April and Ariel stood face to face, awed in silence. Both women touched each other's face in a place familiar to them. One woman's finger rubbed a face mole and the other stroked a scar above the eye.

THE END

ဆာပ

Rique Johnson was born and raised in Portsmouth, Virginia to proud parents Herman and Dorothy Johnson. He finished high school and then joined the U.S. Army six months later because he believed the world had much more to offer than his not-so-fabulous surroundings. After a three-year stint as a soldier, he moved to the Washington, D.C. metropolitan area in 1981 and has made his home in Northern Virginia since 1992.

Rique has always had a passion for the arts. From his desire to be an actor; demonstrated by his role in a homemade "Kung Fu" movie to him writing a monologue to be performed on the original Star Search. *He trained as a commercial artist and became a proficient photographer in high school. He was a fashion/print model during the first half of the 1980s and has been featured in magazine and newspaper ads for the Hecht Company. He was a local favorite for the fashion designers in the D.C. metro area and has done runway modeling for the Congressional Black Caucus. He was Mr. October in the* Black Men of Washington *calendar in 1985.*

Yet, he has always penciled something. As far as he can remember, his passion for writing started well before his teenage years with love notes to girls that he liked. One of his earliest memories was a love letter he wrote to his fourth-grade teacher. Since that time, he has penciled many songs and various pieces of poetry. He writes things that he simply calls thoughts. Sometimes these thoughts expressed the particular mood he was in and other times they were derived from things that were happening in the world at the time.

His imagination comes across in his novels as creative, bold and sometimes edgy. Rique is often called a storyteller. He writes so that readers can place themselves into the pages of the story and make the pages play like a movie in their own imaginations. He is a passionate writer who is unafraid to reveal the sensitivity of a male or himself, thus, evoking an emotional response from the readers.

He lives in Springfield, Virginia.

Rique Johnson is the author of the Detective Jason Jerrard novels, Love & Justice, Whispers from a Troubled Heart, *and* A Dangerous Return; *and of a novel,* Every Woman's Man. *His story "Life Happens" appears in* Sistergirls.com, *edited by Zane.*

You may visit the author at www.riquejohnson.com or email him at rique@ riquejohnson.com.

FOR THE GOOD TIMES

SHAWAN LEWIS

SIMPLY BEAUTIFUL
SAPELO, GEORGIA, 1965

I n Sapelo, Georgia, we call the promise of a new day *dayclean*. When the clouds dissipate from a velvet sky, and the sun penetrates its rays through sand imprints of lovers from the thick of night. This is *dayclean*.

Sapelo is beautiful to me. The freshness of a morning sky; the mystic Sea Islands bordering South Carolina, Georgia, and the northern part of Florida; tropical breezes over white sand beaches; and live oak trees with Spanish moss—all these things I admired about my paradise home.

Sand dunes, scattered along the edges of saltwater, were the perfect refuge for romance. Naked bodies entangled in love, lust, or whatever felt good inbetween. My boyfriend Adam and I spent most of our free time melting together in the dunes. We met in his hometown of Washington, D.C., on the campus of Howard University. I was a third-year law student. He was in his last year of medical school, courtesy of the United States Army. A few months after we started dating, I took him to Sapelo. He immediately fell in love with the island. Carefree living. Dusty dirt roads without traffic lights, and the friendly nature of my people. Geechee folk, we were called. A name inherited from our African ancestors of Sierre Leone. The beach was our retreat. No worries about school, or the challenges we faced in the future. Offering our hearts to each other was all that mattered.

***

I lived for lovemaking on the beach. I'd lost my virginity years before I'd met him, but every time I took his sweet temptation inside of me, it felt like the first time. His manhood was smooth mahogany and thick, well matched to his toned torso and muscular thighs. A scrumptious chocolate package that could make my melodic cries pitch past the stars. I loved the way he rocked his pelvis, pumping passion into my core. Each sweltering inch of his penis carved a kinetic notch of ecstasy against my throbbing walls. His girth, incomparable. The pleasure it gave me, insatiable. He savored the sensation of parting the warm layers of my flesh with his density, plunging deeper and deeper as crystal waves of the sea anchored us.

Moans of excitement roared from our mouths as the tide kept pace with our climactic journey. We rode each other fiercely for what seemed like an eternity. Then slowly, our erotic calls to the heavens cascaded down. Lower and lower, until the moans turned into comforting whispers. When all the tension of what our bodies had conquered was released, the whispers transformed into soft sighs.

Under the shelter of a magenta sky, we collapsed on the sand, spent from our exchange of surreal sex. "Jasmine, you know no man is an island," Adam whispered in my ear.

I smiled at him as my fingertips swept the curve of his muscular arm. "I believe I've heard those words somewhere before."

Adam gently took my hand in his, running my palm over the hair stubble that accentuated his jawbone. He closed his eyes for a moment, then focused on me. "Well, my father used to say that a man whose *words* are true, will win the hearts of many. But a man whose *actions* are true, will move mountains. The Army has afforded me the opportunity to see the world, and to pursue my dream of being a doctor. A poor, knucklehead boy from Anacostia, finding success. But Jasmine, achievements mean nothing without you. The solace of being in Sapelo...the peace you bring to my life. My place is with you. If you'll be my wife, I'll make sure you never regret it."

The bass of his voice, each word husky and strong, sent chills down my spine. Overwhelmed by his proposal, my body trembled as tears ran down my cheeks. Adam quickly moved closer, caressing me as I cried on his chest. My body language gave him the answer he wanted to hear, but I managed to collect myself, shouting to the world that I'd be his wife.

LIVIN' FOR YOU

1966

When Adam and I finished our studies, we returned to Sapelo to live. There were only two hundred residents on the island. There were no doctors or lawyers; we were the first. Sapelo, historically known for its rice and cotton crops, was a breeding ground for greedy developers. Land that was once harvested by the sweat of our slave ancestors' backs was now looked upon as a gold mine. Investors saw opportunities for hotels, shopping plazas, and even tourist theme parks. Our community saw the need to construct a medical facility and a library, but we wanted no part of a development frenzy. We circulated petitions, and worked with the Sapelo Island Restoration Society to inform Georgia lawmakers about the threat to our land. Thankfully, the Sea Island Foundation, endowed by the Rayman family, heard our pleas and extended funding. The only major employer on the island was the tobacco company, owned by RJ Rayman.

Support from the foundation was a blessing, but I knew in my heart we'd have to keep our guard up. Most people didn't know Sapelo existed, much less populated by a black majority. During slavery, white folk took our dynasty in Africa away by force. Sapelo was the twinkle in their eyes now, and they flaunted the almighty dollar in our faces, which was just as brutal. Natives wanted to build what was needed, not what some rich mogul had in mind.

***

Geechee culture in the Sea Islands originated during the slave trade in 1810. My people managed to outsmart the slave master, buy the land, and cultivate it. We grew our own vegetables and herbs. Some of the natives were basket weavers, missionaries, net casters, storytellers, and tour guides. We entertained visitors long enough for them to get a taste of our culture, but not to stay. You wanted lodging, Hammock Lodge was it. If you wanted a fancy hotel, you were better off vacationing some place else, which suited us just fine. There were no hospitals, schools or big stores. Sapelo was reachable only by boat. Five communities encompassed the area: Belle Marsh, Raccoon Bluff, Lumber Landing, Hog Hammock, and Shell Hammock. Traveling beyond them meant you had to go to the Marsh Landing Dock, and take a state-owned ferry across Doboy Sound to the mainland, known as St. Simons Island.

The people of Sapelo were family, and family took care of one another. I could've made more money practicing in a major city, but financial security wasn't a priority. My husband and I strived harder than ever. Adam had successfully built a medical mission, run by him and the aunt that raised me, Frances. My law practice was growing. I had implemented two land trusts to protect parts of the island, and even defended the Rayman family in a liability case. Building practices in a big city would have been too stressful for us, and our marriage. Modest living kept us humble, and we loved it.

YOU OUGHT TO BE WITH ME

1967

Life on Sapelo was good, but even isolation didn't provide immunity from the troubles of the world. The country was at war—Vietnam. The phone call I used to will out of my dreams, rang loudly this morning, waking the both of us. Adam literally jumped out of bed. He answered after the first ring.

"Hello. Yes, this is he. Yes, sir."

His posture straightened as he clenched the phone. The seriousness of his stare sent flutters to my stomach. He acknowledged his commanding officer, exchanging formalities I didn't want to hear. I slowly closed my eyes and exhaled as I touched my abdomen. The sensation of nerves I experienced was supposed to be from the baby growing inside my womb. Deep in my heart, I knew it was too soon to feel the awakenings of the seed Adam surged in me four months ago, on a warm July evening at the beach. The night I gripped his ass tight, wanting every drop of his warm climax. The night the candles around our sandy abyss highlighted the tears in his eyes—when he asked me to have his son. No, there were no signs of life rousing the pit of my stomach, only nerves. For the first time nausea set in, because I feared losing the life that gave me reason to wake each day...Adam. Flesh of my flesh, connected by a rib, in a story once told. Given to me by God's grace. Fear of him leaving had me scurrying out of bed, straight to the bathroom.

My chest heaved as I hunched over the commode, releasing tears and contents of an unsettled stomach. Adam's fingers made soothing circles over the center of my back, as I slowly rose from the plank floor. The morning chill radiated the soles of my feet, and I shuddered under the strong arms of his embrace. I tried to get myself together, but Adam holding me made it difficult. His touch was comforting, and like breathing, it was something I'd taken for granted. I leaned my head further back on his chest and whimpered.

Adam kissed the nape of my neck, resting his chin on the crown of my head. "Shh…Jasmine, honey. Everything's gonna be fine." His voice was a little groggy and hoarse, but sexy nonetheless. The warm air from his breath to my scalp sent tingles to a place below, right where my body wanted. My mind battled the urge to face his direction, hike my cotton nightie up, and mount him. Just the thought of his hands squeezing my bottom, with my legs wrapped around him tight, made me moist. Moans coming from my lips. A husky, *Good morning*, coming from his, as his dick greeted the leverage of my narrow tunnel. A snug fit every time. This morning's phone call, now jeopardized the groove with my husband. The intimacy we shared each morning, and the bond of friendship that sustained us long after the tools of love were unlinked. Damn this war.

I pulled away from him and turned the faucet on. I brought the cold water briskly to my mouth, rinsing away remnants of morning sickness. Adam was in back of me again, gently massaging the small bulge protruding from the middle of my petite frame. I slowly looked up in the mirror to see his beautiful image, focused on me. The lone vertical crinkle in his brow, the one that I thought was so sexy when he'd cum, was now a concerned scowl.

"You want some lemon tea?" he asked.

I slowly shook my head, *no*.

"Warm milk with nutmeg?"

My eyelashes were sticky from blinking away more tears. "I want you to stay," I said, despite the emotional knot burning my throat.

He turned me towards him, caressing my face with his hands. "The triage unit. They need doctors."

I swallowed hard as I looked up at him. His six-foot-five frame towered over my five-foot body. He got a kick out of teasing me, saying I had a complex about being short. *Feisty Geechee girl, trying to be Cleopatra*, he'd say. Memories of the good times we had came rushing in. I winced for a moment, holding my head. "When?"

Adam sighed. "I gotta take the first ferry out tomorrow, to make a flight from Savannah to Atlanta, then…"

"I'm cold," I interrupted, unlocking his arms from my waist.

I brushed away his attempt to keep me in his embrace and walked back to bed. A huff of air escaped my lips as I plopped down on the mattress. I wrestled the sheet over me. The cotton cocoon formed was my wall of anger against the world, and now to Adam, who was leaving. His travel details were too much for me to take. Suddenly, I felt weak, uncharacteristic of my usual nature. I was a feisty Geechee girl, who usually didn't hold her tongue. Bold in nature, I was told. When it came to Adam, though, I was a lamb. He knew my insecurities. Whenever there was fear inside of me, he would get to the heart of the matter.

I waited for him to come over, as I set my eyes to the sunrise peeking through the curtains of our bedroom window. Dawn was steadily pushing through the night, another *dayclean* crowning its way over the island.

Adam slowly came to my bedside, kneeling beside me. He slowly peeled away the bed sheet with one hand, while he pulled down his pajama pants with the other. His engorged member was ready to take action. It was time to forget about life, laboring in our minds. I took him in my hand, adept at stroking his entire shaft to ultimate stiffness, while he unbuttoned my gown.

"Damn, baby, keep workin' me like that," he moaned as he moved on top of me.

We had foreplay down to a science. He knew what I needed, and I knew how to serve him, unselfishly. For the first time, since that phone call from Vietnam, smiles covered our faces. Fear would not win over our love.

Adam was the security blanket that covered me. His dark chocolate skin blended with the butter-cream color of mine. He tenderly kissed my forehead. The sincerity of his eyes stayed with me as his hot tongue licked the middle of my cleavage line. He then focused on my breasts, drawing one slowly into his mouth. The sensation of his tongue circling my areola made me call out his name. I brought my legs up, spreading them wide to allow Adam to do as he pleased. I was captive to his touch. Whatever he wanted, I gladly gave him access to get it.

Adam teased my private place. I loved the feel of his tongue on my sensitive petal of pleasure, which was swelling underneath soft curls. He licked up and down my dark triangle, with intense strokes that made me squirm beneath him. My legs clamped the sides of his head, locking his face on me.

"Adam, baby, you gonna make me cum too soon; you keep doin' what you're doin'," I moaned.

"Let it flow, sweetheart," he said. "You know I love when you make it rain. Make it rain, Jasmine."

His tongue entered my hole, probing the spot that would send me off the edge.

"Ooh," I cried, my legs shaking from my orgasm.

"I pray I'll be home to see my baby come out of this beautiful pussy," he moaned. "Open up for me, Jasmine. I want every ounce of this sweet stuff covering me. Give me something to dream about while I'm away."

My hands held the top of his head firm, as my fingers feathered through the silky black curls of his cropped afro. I wanted him to enter me. I put my hands under his arms, and gestured for him to come up. He gave me a seductive glance as he followed the commands of touch.

"Give it to me now," I said, my voice quivering. Adam cradled my thighs as he penetrated me.

"Jasmine, you're making me weak," he moaned in my ear as his thrusts became more intense. "I love you so much."

He pumped me steadily to the brink of gratification. Each crash of our pelvises, louder than before. My juices were plentiful from the pregnancy, and the induction of passion.

"Baby, I'm about to flood you." Sweat scattered down Adam's forehead as he looked at me.

I battled my own rhythmic release. "Adam, not yet. No...!" I cried out to him, clenching my eyes shut. I pulled my legs down from the edge of his shoulders, resting them on the bed.

"Jasmine, you all right? Look at me." He changed his pace to a slow grind, mindful of the tears streaming down my face. "Tell me you're okay, baby."

I couldn't tell him that. "Don't stop."

"Was I going too deep?"

"No, Adam. I just don't want it to end."

"Me neither, baby," he said, gripping the fullness of my ass. "Fuck, this feels good," he moaned, pumping me harder.

His shallow breaths were warm against my earlobe, heightening my satisfaction. Adam enjoyed the way my muscles contracted around his dick. The same muscles making me feel good now, would inevitably cause me pain five months from now, when I'd push our child into the world. A day, I painfully felt in my heart, Adam would miss.

He plunged into my softness, calling out my name when he came. His upper body collapsed onto me. I exhaled as I held him close. *Why would this war separate us now?* I thought. Things were going so well. We were happy together, which was something most couples couldn't say, honestly.

My soul was stubborn, but I believed through faith, my uncertainty about Adam's safety would settle. He'd go to Vietnam, and do great things, as always. He'd come back home and love me, like he never left...and we'd be fine. I prayed that was the right conclusion, because I wasn't accepting anything else.

PERFECT TO ME

When I awakened, Adam was staring at me, just as I remembered before I drifted to sleep. Folks of Sapelo had given Adam a shrimp boil the night before. Our neighbor Winston let us use his store for the festivities. We ate shrimp and roast beef, then danced to Marvin Gaye until midnight. By the time we got home, I was exhausted. All I wanted to do was make love to my man, and rest in the shelter of his arms. Now, I had to face the fact that tomorrow was today. The *day-clean* I usually welcomed was suddenly intruding on me, like a thief stealing precious gems.

Adam's fingertips feathered my cheek. "Morning, sweetheart."

"Mornin'," I said, trying to sound cheerful. Adam saw right through my lukewarm smile, and edged closer to me. The trace of mint I smelled from his breath stirred my senses, and I wanted to freshen up for him. I tried to sit up, but he eased me back down. He aligned his body to mine, bearing his weight on his arms, as if he were about to do push ups.

"Jasmine, I want you to remember this: *I'm never beneath you, or above you, always one with you.* You have my heart. That will never change." He moved to the side, cradling my body with his arms. I nuzzled against his chest. "I'm gonna be fine, and you're gonna be fine. When I come back, I'll be holding you, while you nurse our baby to sleep. Life will be better than before, I promise."

I bit my lip as I looked down at my gold wedding band. "Life is good now."

Adam lifted my chin, his jaw slightly clenched. "Sometimes, love clouds the reality of life. We got obligations, Jasmine. Your career, my work here at the mission, and now my call to treat the injured in Vietnam. Going away wasn't in the forefront of my mind, but definitely not an afterthought. Just reality. Hopefully, my efforts will help prevent casualties. Being a good doctor is about saving lives, no matter what the cost, or where I have to do it." His expression brightened. "Your job is to stay happy and healthy, making sure this bug-a-boo is fine. All right?"

I nodded. "You'll write me?"

"Every day."

"You'll continue loving me?"

"You don't have to ask."

***

The waves from the Doboy Sound were calm. Adam leaned against a pier post, and I was wrapped in his arms. The ferry approached the dock, dividing the still waters with its hull. The ferry horn sounded from a distance. I looked up at my husband with weary eyes. For a second, I saw us back in time. A slave ship, parting still waters. A husband being taken from his wife, against his will. Civil Rights and Black Power ideology were integral to blacks in the sixties. In the whole scheme of things, though, I felt like a black man still didn't belong to his family. Adam called the war an obligation. I saw it as neo-slavery.

The ferry docked just as my tear landed on Adam's hand. I wouldn't be joining him on the ride to St. Simons Island. We both felt it was best to savor the moment in Sapelo, where we married. Clinging to him across the waters would only deepen the pain.

Anxious tourists, and a few school-age children, were bustling around us, preparing for the ride. Adam turned me around. "Remember what I told you," he said as he caressed my face. "*I'm never beneath you, or above you, always one with you.*"

"I love you."

He smiled and kissed my forehead. "I love you, my Geechee girl."

I sighed and shook my head. "I know there's nothing you can do, but I still don't want you to go."

"Don't worry, Jasmine. I'll be back soon," he said, his voice confident and strong.

"I know," I said softly. Anxiety churned my insides. While the weather had been mild for late November, a breezy current formed off the water. "Hold me." I shuddered into Adam's chest.

"Always, right here." He took my hand and placed it on his heart. "For life." We stared into each other's eyes and danced slowly, immersed into our silent love song. Sunrays from another *dayclean* descended down upon us, and together we remained... until the ferry operator made the final call for Adam to board.

STRONG AS DEATH, SWEET AS LOVE
1968

My head was on fire as if I'd been bludgeoned. The bedroom seemed to be spinning, sorta like the Turbo Spin ride at the Georgia State Fair that made me sick, when I was ten. I massaged my temple as I sat on the edge of the bed, trying to block the images of Adam drowning in his own blood.

Oh God, this can't be real, I prayed. "Wake me up," I said, slowly opening my eyes. Adam wasn't dead. No, not my Adam. Adam was a common name...it was someone else's Adam. Not my Adam. *Some bastard made a crank call,* I concluded. A hoax, I could accept. April first was a couple of hours away. News of a bomb destroying the medical tent where Adam was located, I refused to accept.

I'd gone to sleep early last night, due to constant back pain and pinches to my side. I was nine months' pregnant, and the baby had been kicking a lot. Like he had no room to get comfortable. The phone rang loudly, startling me out of a peaceful slumber.

"Good evening, this is Lieutenant Kramer. May I speak to Mrs. Jasmine Kelly?"

"This is she. Now why are you calling me at ten-thirty at night?" I asked, holding my swollen belly. I rose to my feet. "Is my husband, okay?"

A pause, then the words I never imagined: "I'm sorry."

His tone of voice, neutral. No persuasion of emotion, more like routine. Perhaps I was one of many on his casualty advisory list. I didn't need his sterile sympathy. I needed Adam.

The remainder of his dialogue was incoherent. I stood there, holding the phone down by my side. The phone cord swayed as I gripped the receiver with my sweaty palm.

Anger set in.

"Liar!" I yelled, slamming the phone into the cradle. I wailed so hard, the heavens must have heard me. All God had to do was give me a sign. Prove I was right, and make a liar out of that lieutenant. "Please, Lord, let Adam call!" I cried to the ceiling, as my body slumped to the wooden floor.

Aunt Frances arrived. I'd managed to call her between bouts of hysteria, and pangs in my belly. She rushed over and fell to her knees, pulling me close to her bosom. "Lawd, Jesus. I'm so sorry, baby," she cried.

My eyes were glazed from wetness. I was in shock, and the water gushing out of me let her know I was in labor. "Jasmine, you gettin' ready to be a mama." She gently grasped my shoulders, trying to raise me off the floor. "Baby, I know you hurtin' in all this madness, but your miracle 'bout to come." Aunt Frances was plump and solid, over 200 pounds easily, but I managed to jerk away from her. She sighed in frustration. "You ain't makin' this easy for me, gal." She grunted as she leaned her body over to retrieve the phone. "I ain't gonna fight wit ya, 'cause you need to save your energy. Auntie gonna get you some help, and we gonna get through this."

I leaned my head against the oak nightstand, clenching my stomach. Bearing the brunt of bad news. Aunt Frances called Dr. Tate and Sarah, the elder midwife/spiritual advisor of Sapelo.

The cramps to my stomach were getting worse. I curled into a fetal position, feeling defeated.

"Baby, you can't stay like this," she said, wiping my damp brow with her palm. "I gotta get you to the bed and check you." I didn't resist this time. She scooped me up into her arms and put me in the bed. When she rolled up my drenched, cotton nightgown, she gasped. "Lawd, this baby got plans of his own. Jasmine, I see the head. You gon' have to push! Pull your legs back and push!"

"God, no!" I screamed in agony. I couldn't believe what was happening to me. The pain raging through my body was nothing compared to what I thought Adam had endured. All I could see was his beautiful body, mangled by missiles. A dog tag to them, but he was everything to me. Our love, destroyed over senseless shit. There was nothing patriotic about a father, a brother, a son... Adam sacrificing their lives to protect political interests in foreign lands.

"Dammit, push!" she screamed, bracing my legs.

"I can't! I can't!"

"We gotta get this baby out! I know you can, do it. Do it now, Jasmine!"

I pushed with all my might, desperate to give birth to the only joy I had left.

"Owwl...!" I yelled, sweat beading on my nose. I couldn't hold my trembling legs anymore. It felt like my vagina was being ripped apart. I grimaced from the burning between my thighs, but tried to push again.

"That's it. Push!"

"Adam!"

"Bear down!"

I was weak from grief. I tried to bear down, but it was too

painful. Just as I mustered the strength to push again, everything went dark.

✳✳✳

When I blacked out, my baby got stuck in the birth canal. Through prayers mixed with tears, Aunt Frances reached inside of me, and pulled him out...but it was too late. His heart had stopped beating. I often wondered how I survived that horrifying night. I'd lost a lot of blood. Dr. Tate wanted to cut me open, and take out my uterus to stop the bleeding. Aunt Frances and Sarah told him, hell no. Sapelo women believed in the healing power of spirits. Sarah called upon the souls of my husband and son to save me. A miracle, some cabbage compresses, and old-wives roots prevented another life from being washed away.

KEEP ME CRYIN'
1972

Do four-and-a-half years change anything? Not when you live like you have nothing to lose. Ain't no closure in watching caskets close. I'd had the best in Adam, so finding love again was not an option. I consumed my days with practicing law, and ended my nights masturbating into an erotic lull. Warm bubble baths by candlelight, legs looped over my ceramic claw tub, with my hands squeezing my nipples to hardened satisfaction. My life had come to this...pleasing me, and me only. I couldn't risk someone, or something else, shattering the last piece to my fragile heart. Callousness was the pill I swallowed every day, to prevent sadness from driving me insane.

✳✳✳

I'd gotten used to the feeling of my fingertips teasing the fleshy ignition switch cushioned between my vaginal walls. I needed more. I deserved more, which was why I agreed to Aunt Frances setting me up with Eugene, the son of one of her childhood friends in Atlanta. We had some stuff in common: he was a lawyer; a Gemini, born on the same day, June seventh. He'd gone to law school at Howard, graduating five years ahead of me. He contemplated relocating to a coastal area, like St. Simons, which was just across the water from Sapelo. After exchanging a few letters, and receiving his picture, I decided to invite him to my home for dinner. I certainly never imagined I'd be accepting blind dates, but based on his description: six feet tall; medium-brown skin; athletic build; and the likeness of Arthur Ashe, I figured, *what the hell?*

Needless to say, when I heard someone knock at six in the evening, and I opened the front door, I was not charmed. My Arthur Ashe was all of five foot feet eight; splotchy medium-brown skin, the likeness of sandpaper; and a hairline that may have once been a thick afro. Time had made a bee-line straight through the middle of his damn head.

Once again I figured, *what the hell?* But this time I answered the question. Tonight was strictly need-based. Dinner, sex, and his ass on the next ferry back to Atlanta.

"Good evening, Jasmine," he said, almost sung. I knew his glance of me was more breathtaking than the air I almost choked on, after seeing him.

I was never much on makeup, but tonight was my rite of passage into the lion's den of dating. I wanted to spruce up pale cheeks that were accustomed to tear streaks. I had applied a light dusting of amber rouge, a touch of cranberry lipstick, and brown mascara to accentuate my teal-colored eyes. The baby oil I'd brushed through my hair, gave my bun a satin finish. I was one of the lighter sistas of Sapelo, thanks to my no-name white father, who obviously didn't want more than a fuck from my runaway black mother. Curly locks, wrapped in a tattered blanket. That's how my Aunt Frances first met me, when she opened the door to her porch thirty-one years ago. She had sacrificed her aspirations of becoming a registered nurse to care for me, like I was her own. She wanted me to be happy, and feared I was too young to be alone. I didn't think I was too young to be alone, but I was getting too old to let a traumatic past blindside the nuances of life. Aunt Frances said a woman had yearnings that couldn't be denied. I agreed, which was why I accepted my date's bouquet of roses, and stepped aside as he walked in. Tonight would not be the makings of rocket science, but whatever happened, I hoped I wouldn't regret it.

"Eugene, the roses are simply gorgeous," I blurted out with glee, my attempt at enthusiasm.

He grinned. "Beauty is truly in the eyes of the beholder of those roses."

I kept a strained smile after his corny comment, keeping my disappointment about his appearance at bay. I cleared my throat. "Please make yourself at home," I said, pointing to the sofa.

When he removed his trench coat and sat down, I bit my lip to prevent from cracking up. His copper-colored polyester suit clashed with the floral slipcovers of my living room sofa, creating a piece of work louder than the Matisse print hanging above. I couldn't hold back the low chuckle that escaped my mouth. The wine I had been sipping on while cooking dinner had me giddy, and I wondered if his body was just as tasteless as the suit.

Relax, Jasmine, I thought as I sat beside him. It wasn't that serious, I rationalized, but I still felt foreign to this whole dating scene. I mean, Eugene seemed nice enough. He wrote beautiful poetry, and I dug the Billie Holiday record he sent me. I just wondered if he had something under that polyester that would make me appreciate more than his personality. Like I said, it had been a long time.

He took the luxury of placing his hand on my thigh, slowly letting his fingertips take cover under the hem of my black rayon miniskirt. I enjoyed the warmth of his palm running up and down the smoothness of my sheer nylon stocking. I could feel an itch coming from a place that had been estranged from the excitement of a man's touch. I quickly crossed my legs, knocking his hand down. I knew he saw me blush as I bent over to straighten the *Ebony* magazines on the coffee table that were already neatly arranged.

"Sorry if I seem a little nervous, Eugene," I said softly. "It's been a while since I've kept a man's company."

He chuckled. "My love life was barely in existence until Frances and Berta introduced us. First dates can be a little awkward, but I'm sure we'll make out fine," he said with a wink.

I took notice of his nice smile as I leaned back against the sofa pillow. Pearly straight teeth were his first brownie point for the night. Two things I didn't like on a man: stained teeth and dirty fingernails. Eugene licked his lips as he eyed the hint of cleavage showing under my red sleeveless, V-neck angora sweater. The eagerness in his eyes, and the tingling of my sweet spot, indicated that dinner would be cut short.

He kissed my hand. "Thanks for inviting me over. You have a lovely home."

"Thanks," I said, admiring the fresh coat of French vanilla paint I'd put on the walls a few days ago. The bright color made the space in my cape Cape Cod seem a lot larger. "My house is simple, but tasteful, I think."

"Ah...tasteful. Leaves something to the imagination."

I squeezed his hand. "Speaking of taste, dinner's ready. Would you like to try some of my seafood casserole?"

"I'd love to try everything," he said, giving me a sly grin.

I slowly got up, smoothing the edges of my sweater over my hips as I sashayed to the kitchen. "Follow me," I said, a seductive smirk lingering on my face.

"Umm…my pleasure," he said as he followed close behind. He was a gentleman, helping me bring food from the kitchen to the formal dining area that I'd created out of unused porch space. He pulled out my chair, allowing me to get comfortable, then sat across from me.

"You're stunning," he said, reaching for his wine glass.

I nodded. "You're…so kind." I prayed the Merlot waiting in my glass would make him look fine by the end of the night.

✳✳✳

My mind wandered during dinner. I snapped back to reality when Eugene called my name.

"Jasmine, what's wrong?" he asked, wiping his mouth.

I looked down as I folded the napkin in my lap. "I guess I don't have much of an appetite for the casserole."

He reached for my hand. "Is there anything I can do?"

I put my cloth napkin down next to the plate of half-eaten food. I smirked as I got up and went to his side of the table. "Yes. Make me dessert," I whispered as I sat in his lap.

"Right away," he said, molding the contours of my ass in his hands. His lips sucked the side of my neck. I pressed my hips against his pelvis. "I've been waiting for this night." He lifted me out of the chair as I wrapped my legs and arms around him.

We were kissing and petting so much, we didn't make it to the bedroom. He laid me down on the paisley area rug of my living room floor. I swiftly pulled my sweater over my head and unfastened my red lace bra. He breathed heavily as he splattered sloppy kisses all over my chest, like a ravenous beast. I clamped my eyes shut, blocking out emotions. He groped my breasts, roughly squeezing them together.

"Eeeh...!" I screamed in pain. I firmly pushed his mouth away, frowning up at him as he loomed over me. Carnal pleasure was one thing, but his awkwardness would make for a long night.

"Are you okay?"

"I will be, hopefully. Do you have protection?"

"Yes," he said, anxiously pulling the condom from his pocket. He wiggled out of those ugly pants. "Right here."

He put the Trojan down on the coffee table as he watched me slip out of my skirt and nylons. When he removed his starched boxers, I realized something was missing in action. I had turned off the living room lamp, which left only light from the candles on the dining room table. Perhaps my vision was compromised from the dim lighting, but I could have sworn I saw a Tootsie Roll instead of a bratwurst peeping at me.

Get it together, Jasmine, I thought. *Your eyesight is probably blurred from drinking too much wine at dinner.*

"Are you ready, baby?" he asked as he moved beside me.

"Yeah, but let me make sure you are." I got up and massaged his shoulders. I planted soft kisses on a hairy back, which could have used a dab or two of Brut to camouflage his musty scent. I moved my right hand over his not-so-athletic chest, causing him to grunt like a boar in heat. My fingernail got snagged on his beady hairs.

The snag didn't hurt him, and nothing about him aroused me. This called for desperate measures.

I straddled my body at his legs, and bent my head to give his penis pleasure. My mouth received more oxygen than meat from him.

"That's right, baby," he said. "Get me ready."

Get what ready? There's nothing there, I thought, frowning at his shriveled prune.

I decided to remain optimistic. I took his penis in my palm, and stroked him. Talk about getting your rocks off. My massage to his marbles pleased him only. I kept rubbing, wishing a genie would come and be a miracle worker on Eugene, or grant me another man. I took the condom off of the table and put it on him. I watched it parachute off his sorry dick. Convinced that somebody had it out for me, I made a mental note to see Sarah about getting some "good luck" roots. Damn, the irony of it all. Another year, another April Fools' Day gone badly. Leaving me on my knees—staring at a toothpick, poking out of a sponge cake.

He got up from under me and wrapped his arms around my body, guiding me down.

"It's been a while since I made love to someone as beautiful as you." He crawled on top of me and somehow managed to get the condom to cling. His penis enlarged somewhat as he dabbed near my moist reservoir. Nothing impressive, but at least I felt something as he entered me. He slowly grinded, but the rhythm was off. Billie's "This Bitter Earth" had just finished playing. When the record player needle hit the last vinyl ridge, blasting static through the speakers, I realized tonight had been a big mistake. I'd had enough sexual incompetence for one night.

"Ah, Eugene," I said, prodding his doughy rib cage. "I'm sorry to disturb you, but I am not enjoying this."

"Just wait a minute, baby," he said as he continued to hump, out of breath. "I've been under a lot of pressure lately, so my body is a little tense. Give us a few minutes to get adjusted to each other."

I rolled my eyes and sighed as he continued the pointless stirring in my body. *No, negro, that's the problem. Your ass ain't tense enough.* Finally, the bitch in me climaxed.

"Stop, Eugene!" I yelled. He lifted his weight off and pulled out of me. I moved from under him.

"Jasmine, I'm sorry," he said. "I guess I'm just tired tonight. Let me find another way to please you." He ventured down to my pubic area. I scooted away.

"No, that's not necessary," I said.

"We just need more time. I can...."

I raked through my hair in frustration as I looked at him. "I don't mean to sound crass, but there's not that much time in the world, Eugene. My pussy is not that patient."

He frowned, throwing his hands up in exasperation. "What's with the attitude?"

I snatched my panties off of the floor. "Attitude!" I shouted, putting on my clothes.

"Yeah, what's the problem?"

I stood directly above him, pointing in his face. "My problem is you. Put your clothes on, and stop asking questions." I marched to the lamp and turned it to the highest brightness.

Eugene looked like he had just lost his puppy. He remained idle on the floor, knees prone, dick deflated. "Can we talk about this?"

I gave a sarcastic cackle as I flung my arms in the air. "Why not? We damn sure can't have a productive fuck!"

He raised his palms defensively. "Calm down."

I put my hands on my hips. "I will not calm down. I'm still horny, and you expect me to calm down!"

"Why are you so angry?"

I went over to the end table and snatched his photo out of my journal. "How old is this picture, Eugene? Where's the full afro? Hell, is this really you?"

He finally rose to his feet, and stared off in space as he got dressed. His silence to my inquisition told me he had been deceptive all along.

I sighed and shook my head in disgust. "I can't believe you. All the personal things I shared with you in my letters. The poetry and gifts exchanged. You had me worked up, thinking just maybe it was time to open my heart again. But as it stands now, you had me...and I had a fraud."

He touched my shoulder, but I pushed his hand away. "Wait! You act like I violated you or something," he said.

I paced the floor. "I willingly had sex with you, which makes me an ass, but you misrepresented yourself, which makes you cruel." My bottom lip trembled as I tried to hold back tears. "This fiasco makes me miss my husband even more."

He sighed as he stuffed his hands into his pants pockets. "So, what are you saying?"

I stopped pacing and stood directly in his face. "I'm saying, I want you to leave, and please lose my phone number on your way back to Atlanta."

He straightened his tie as I handed him his overcoat. The door tapped his back as I slammed it, and supported me as I slid down. I cursed my desperation. I don't know how long I cried, but sadness eventually led me to sleep. When I awakened, I didn't feel any better, but I got up and put the record player needle back on Billie Holiday. At least I knew her blues would spell the truth... this earth was indeed *bitter*.

TIRED OF BEING ALONE

A fifth of Scotch, and two bubble baths still couldn't erase the image of Eugene pumping hot air inside of me. His stature was rotund in all the wrong places...a damn shame. I sucked my teeth as I stormed into the tiny office at the medical mission. Aunt Frances was reclined in her wooden swivel chair. Her eyes closed, she hummed a tune all her own.

"Frances, Frances!"

"Huh?" Her pudgy cheeks jiggled as she opened her eyes and sat up straight. She grinned deeply, exposing dimples that made her mocha-colored face radiant. "Hey, baby gal," she said in a bass drawl. "You done snuck on in here, and surprised your old auntie." She moved the Bible that had been resting on her round belly to her cluttered desk.

I folded my arms as I leaned my butt on the edge of her desk. "I called your ass three times. You all right? I thought maybe you were praying, but I ain't hear that *humna hadasa* stuff you be puttin' down, when you in spiritual mode."

"Jasmine, hush up. It's called, 'speaking in tongues,' but you wouldn't know nothin' 'bout that, you heathen!"

"Look who's talkin'. You spend more time sleeping than tending to the sick in this mission." I had to hold in a laugh, because she was senselessly fanning herself. Overheated from her too-tight, white uniform.

"Lawd, I need another fan up in here. Turn dat thing up, would ya?" She motioned toward the buzzing steel fan.

I glanced at the fan and didn't move. "Humph. I wish I would. You need to boil in your sins, Miss Part-time Nurse, Full-time Practical Joker."

She squeezed her wide hips out of the seat and bumped me as she bent over to turn up the fan. "Whatcha talkin'?" she asked.

I shook my head as I watched her butt settle back into the chair, each spring underneath creaking from her load. "I'm talking about that munchkin you set me up with last night." I pouted and folded my arms, waiting for her response.

She held her belly as she chuckled. "Well, he didn't look that short, last time I saw 'em, 'bout ten years ago when he was in college."

"Ten years and twenty pounds lighter would make anyone look taller, you old fool!"

"Why you gotta be angry all the time? That's the problem. You frustrated below. And since you ain't fit to get into nobody's convent, you might as well put that thang to use, 'fore it dry up."

"You talkin' from experience, Old Settler?"

"There you go with that smart mouth. When you was a baby, crying those blue eyes out, I shoulda taken you to the beach and fed you to the porpoises!"

I sprung to attention, hands on my hips. "They wouldn't have eaten me, 'cause they know you their family! Now hush, and listen to what I gotta say."

She pouted a little as she took a handkerchief from her pocket to wipe her brow. I could tell I'd hurt her feelings, but she'd get over it. She always did. We were so much alike. Mouthy and in charge. We fussed all the time, our way of loving each other.

Aunt Frances didn't mean any harm. I gave her a kiss on the cheek.

"Shoo now, go on," she huffed, trying not to smile.

"I know you constantly worryin' about me, since Adam been gone, but I'll be all right. You've seen me through the best and the worst, and I know you gonna always be there. Just give me a little more time to figure out my love life, okay?"

She nodded in agreement as she looked me over. "You mighty casual."

"I don't have any appointments today," I said, running my hand down the side of my form-fitting, strapless sundress. "I'm thinkin' about taking a walk along the beach."

She picked up a wicker basket filled with boxes from off of her desk. "Well, we short one orderly. Can you help your auntie out for a few minutes before you go?"

I took the basket from her. "I reckon. What you need?"

She swirled in her chair with her back facing me. "Unpack those boxes, and stock the medicine drawers in the triage area with bandages," she said, picking up the telephone receiver. "I gotta make a quick phone call to the Red Cross, then I'll come out and relieve you."

I poked her in the shoulder as she started dialing on the rotary phone. "A *thank you* would be a nice touch."

Aunt Frances turned to face me with the receiver nuzzled against her ear. She reached for my hand. "*I'm sorry* would be even better."

I raised my brow, confused.

"You know? For Eugene and all."

I squeezed her hand. "Eugene wasn't the problem, just the wrong answer."

"Jasmine, I want you to get out and meet new people. Start enjoyin' life again."

I hugged her. Gripping the basket with both hands, I walked to the doorway. "Maybe I should leave the island. Seem like each day I stay in Sapelo…in my house, it gets harder to forget the past." A frown crept on her face, but I walked out.

***

The humidity in the mission was overbearing. I wiped the sweat off the nape of my neck, and pulled the slightly frizzled locks of my mane into a make-shift bun. My mind was on a much needed nap on the sand, soothed by a misty breeze. I placed the last bandage in one of the drawers, and headed back to the office when I glanced at a patient, unraveling the blood-stained bandage on his head. He noticed me watching, and motioned with his finger to come over.

"No, no," I mouthed. "I'm not a nurse."

He put his hands in a prayer gesture, and mouthed, "Please."

I licked my lips that were dry from the humidity. I smiled at the young man as I walked closer. He looked like a mummy, with his head wrapped in gauze. The closer I got to him, the more attractive he became. Tight pecs shadowed his sweat-laden tank undershirt. His muscular arms glistened from the sun shining through a nearby window. A bright smile, with the prettiest white teeth I'd ever seen, complemented his flawless cocoa skin. When we were only inches apart, he gently took my hand and kissed it. The warm and wet tingling on my flesh from his smooth lips sent butterflies to my stomach. I jerked my hand away, feeling flushed in the face, and ignited below by his continuous stare.

"What's your name?" I asked as I opened the medicine drawer.

"Name's Harrison. Harrison Holmes."

I looked back at him, fixated on the smile that was suddenly familiar. "You Charlotte's boy, aren't you?"

He smirked. "I'm Charlotte's son. Thank you for obligin' me, Miss Jasmine."

I fiddled with the heart pendant resting on my chest. "You know me?"

"I've seen you in passing plenty of times." He grabbed my hips and pulled me closer. "But with those sexy eyes, and this soft ass, I sure as hell wanna know you."

I was stunned by his forwardness, but I didn't move away this time. His hands felt good on my curvaceous bottom. I could only imagine what would happen next if we were alone on the beach, instead of sweating in the confines of this stucco mission building. I cleared my throat, and slowly removed his hands from my waist.

"We're not alone, you know," I said, peeking behind us at a few of the occupied gurneys. A couple of patients were sleeping; another one had a girlie magazine, but was getting more enjoyment watching me and this young man.

Harrison pulled a cigarette pack from the pocket of his khakis, and tapped it against his palm until one came out. "You want to be alone? I can arrange that."

I ignored his proposition, and took some more gauze and bandage tape out of the drawer. "Looks like that bandage needs changing." I slowly unraveled the soiled gauze from around his bald head, gasping when I got to the gaping wound at his ear. A part of his earlobe was gone, the remaining skin jagged and bloody. The dog tag around his neck let me know he was a soldier. I thought of Adam. "Maybe I should get Dr. Tate or Frances," I said, abruptly placing the gauze on the side of the bed. "I don't know what I'm doing, anyway."

He touched my arm. "Just keepin' me company is enough; please stay." His deep brown eyes were persuasive. I gave him a slight smile as I picked the gauze up.

I resumed wrapping the bandage around his head. He winced when the fresh gauze grazed his ear.

"Sorry," I said as I rolled the remainder of the dressing around his wound.

"If you don't mind me asking, how'd this happen?"

He lit the cigarette. "Air strike. My unit's helicopter was shot down. Only two of us survived. I lost enough hearing to get me out of that damn war. I'm all right, though. Coulda been worse." He took a slow drag from his cigarette, blowing smoke out the side of his mouth as he surveyed my dress. "Those shells coulda blinded me, and I wouldn't see all this beauty standin' before me."

I smacked my lips as I opened the medicine drawer and dropped the tape in. "Did you practice that line on your wife before you got here?"

His jaw clenched for a second as he leaned over to put out his cigarette against the cement wall. He let his finger glide down the smoothness of my bare arm. "Now why you wanna ask a question that you don't wanna hear the answer to?"

I braced my hands on the gurney as I leaned in closer to him. "I'm a lawyer. I like to know the truth."

He shrugged with a blank expression. "I got a wife. Ain't much of a marriage, though. I get done fightin,' come home, and now it feel like I'm battlin' secrets. My gut tells me something went down with her while I was away. I'm back in Sapelo, searching for the truth. Lately, it seems like the truth and lies are the same thing. Sorta like rum and Coke. Sometimes one is stronger than the other. Sometimes you can't tell the difference, but you drink the watered-down stuff, until you come across something more potent." He smiled. "Something strong enough to warm your soul." He placed his hands on my shoulders and gently began a massage that almost melted me to the floor. I steadied myself and closed my eyes as he rested his cheek against my face. "Miss Jasmine, I guess what I'm tryin' to say is that I want more than what I got right now."

"Ahh...I see."

"Ahiem...," a motherly tone bellowed from behind me. I abruptly pulled away from Harrison when I heard Frances' interruption. "I see you and Mr. Holmes got acquainted," she said, tapping her big foot.

I nervously played with my damp bang, smoothing invisible wrinkles from my dress. "Uh...I was just leaving."

She puckered her lips. "Some beach water would do your hot tail some good, right about now."

Harrison chuckled. I rolled my eyes at the both of them. "Hush, Frances," I whispered, brushing past her.

"Miss Jasmine?"

I glanced back. "Yes, what is it?" I asked, crossing my arms.

"You got a nice touch. Thanks for taking care of me."

I grinned. "You're welcome." I turned and walked towards the door.

"Uh...Florence Nightingale?"

I stopped, shifting one hip to the side. "Yes, Frances?"

"Thanks for taking care of Mr. Holmes," she said with a gap-toothed grin.

I turned my nose up to her, and headed out when I heard her cackle, "Eugene who?"

I had to laugh.

✳✳✳

I sat on a rock near the sand dunes, admiring how the sunlight made the tips of the water waves sparkle like fine crystal.

"Thinkin' of me." The sound of someone's voice startled me. When I turned to see Harrison directly behind me, I got goose bumps. His tenor-toned words, and an infectious smile, seemed to stir desire in me that had been dormant for too long.

I smiled. "Don't flatter yourself," I said turning back towards the water. He straddled the rock as he sat down, pulling my body back towards his chest. I rested my head against his taut chest muscles. I didn't know this man, but for some reason I enjoyed his flirtatious nature—the feel of his arms around mine.

"I apologize if I was being fresh earlier."

"I don't have a problem telling a man when he's out of line. I'm just wondering why you got a fondness for my company."

"Seem like you'd be good company. Damn, you smell good," he said as his chin whisked over the crown of my head.

I moved a loose strand of hair away from my eye. "You smell Apple Blossom, the scented shampoo I use. How old are you?"

"More lawyer questions."

"And?"

"Now, I'd be rude if I asked a lady, such as you, her age."

"No, you'd be informed. I'm thirty-one."

"Well, bless you. I'll get there next decade, God willing."

"Shit, twenty-one? You just a baby."

He smirked, putting my hand on his crotch. "These feel like baby balls to you?"

I blushed, but I continued to feel. When his erection became too tempting, I removed my hand.

"Why'd you move your hand?"

"I'm not an adulterer."

"I don't think I called you one." He pulled me up to my feet. "Come with me."

"Why?" I asked, hesitant to walk toward the water with him.

He smiled. "Just come. I bite, but it don't hurt."

"You're crazy," I said, laughing at him.

"I guess Vietnam will do that to a brotha. Uhmm...the water is nice today," he said, holding my hand as we treaded into the calm waves.

"Yeah, it is pretty warm, I reckon," I said, looking around to see if anyone was watching.

"Nervous?"

"I just feel silly, is all."

He pulled me close to his body. "Guess I'ma have to do more, 'cause that ain't what you supposed to be feelin.'"

I shook my head. "Harrison, this whole seduction thing is tempting, but I like privacy, like at night? There's an old man fishin' over there," I said, pointing in the distance.

He shrugged. "He ain't botherin' us, and he look too old to know what's goin' on. Come on and enjoy yourself. He won't see nothin.'"

He trailed wet kisses down the middle of my neck, circling all the way to my collarbone. The pressure from his lips caused a shiver to escape my mouth. I closed my eyes, leaning my body into the confines of his broad shoulders. He moved us further into the water. When the water line reached my shoulders, I felt him unzip my dress.

Harrison's strong hands cupped my breasts. He merged them close together, massaging each nipple with his thumbs until they hardened like raisins. I opened my mouth, but only moans came out. He smiled as he went under water. He sucked hard on my breast, increasing my breathlessness. I wanted more, but when I felt his hands underneath my dress, I knew he wanted something else.

Within seconds, I felt my silk panties against my thigh. He slowly came up for air, looking sly. "I think I see a pearl down there." Before I could respond, he was under water, parting my legs. He got straight to the point, licking my pussy furiously, back and forth. The way he devoured me with his mouth was incredible. He was under the water so long, I feared he'd drown. I pulled Harrison's shoulders upward, but he resisted. His firm grip on my ass assured me that he was doing just fine. My hands held his smooth head, drawing him closer to the folds of my sweetness. The staying power of his tongue flicking my clit, then plunging inside me, sent a fever through my body. My lip quivered as I felt my release come over me. I bit down to prevent screaming out in ecstasy. Harrison slowly surfaced, his wet body shining under the sun. I felt something hot and strong poking me. I panicked, pushing my body away from him.

"Let's get out," I gasped. "Jellyfish."

He reared his head back as he laughed. Then he pulled me back to him. "I'd like to think I'm more like a stingray." He winked, poking me again below.

I curled my lips seductively as I wrapped my arms around his neck. "What you thinkin' about doin' with that?" I asked, looking down at his torso.

"I ain't much for words, but I think you'll feel what I'm sayin'," he said, raising my thighs effortlessly. The bottom half of my sundress was now a lavender tarp, covering the waves as Harrison raised me higher on his pelvis. I felt like a flower, whose petals were being opened by blazing sunlight, as I slid down his dick. "Ohh...," I sighed as I took him in. "Please, be gentle with me. It's been a while."

He kissed my neck. "Oh...you can't take it deep from Charlotte's *boy*, huh?" He tightened his embrace around me, kissing my cheek. "I got you, big girl. Don't worry, it's gonna hurt so good in a second." He lowered my body on the water, securing my back as he smoothly grinded into my tight canal.

"We shouldn't be this careless," I said, breathless. "I mean, we just met and all."

Harrison licked his lips, staring into my eyes. "Careless is dunkin' a stitched-up ear into some damn salt water." I giggled as he playfully nibbled on my earlobe. "Don't worry. Doc Tate said my health is fine." He nuzzled his head against my neck. The warmth of his rapid breaths to my skin made my heart race. "Ease your mind, and let me take you where you wanna go," he said in a soft whisper.

It took my body a minute to get used to him. The friction from his pelvis clamping my clit gradually lessened the discomfort. "Sweet Jasmine, you feel soo...good," he moaned as he kneaded my ass, spreading my cushion into a comfort zone that had me crying out for mercy. He looked dazed as he peered into my eyes. This gratifying infusion, and the oneness I felt, made my eyes mist.

"You all right, Miss Jasmine," he asked, his powerful hands gliding up and down my thighs.

The sensation of his thrusts was so intense. "Don't stop!" I cried. "Please, don't stop." I threw my head back as he pumped harder and longer. The water around us splashed from our bodies being together. His shoulders stiffened, and the velocity of his shaft pummeling through my ribbed tunnel, sent a tickle inside of me. Harrison grunted as he dove closer to the point of climax.

"Damn, I'm about to cum," he muffled into my shoulder. He made contact with the tip of that erotic spot, giving me so much pleasure.

"Harrison!" I screamed, feeling my walls contract around him, like a butterfly trying its wings.

"Jasmine, I feel you grippin' me, baby," he said out of breath. "Ahhh…!" he screamed, banging me beautifully until he came. We held onto each other, gasping for air. The waves were tranquil again.

There was golden silence surrounding us, until we heard, "Hey, young fella. I see you done caught yo-self some good fish out dere, huh?"

It was the old fisherman's raspy voice, giving Harrison a toothless grin, and a "thumbs up" from afar. Harrison returned the gesture as we kissed and laughed at the same time.

RIGHT NOW, RIGHT NOW

A cabaret-style celebration, and live drummers banging sultry African beats, had folks celebrating at the Heritage Parade. I'd just finished my rum punch near the bandstand when I saw Harrison. It had only been a couple of days since our rendezvous at the beach, but I missed being close to him, safe in his arms. He rocked to the rhythms of the conga drums, holding an adorable baby in his arms. The baby boy wore denim overalls, and appeared to be around a year old. He giggled as Harrison proudly raised him up to the sky, and then glided him back down like an airplane into his arms. The little one had a smooth bald head, like Harrison, whose ear bandage was covered with a nice red-and-black crocheted tam. His festive gait lessened when a lanky, ebony-brown woman, dressed in a tube top and capris, approached.

By the small crease to his brow, I could tell he was unsettled. I assumed the baby was his son. I knew the woman in red was the community whore, whom I gathered was his wife. Her name, Naomi; the smart-mouthed gal who back-talked me years ago, when I caught her making out in my shed with the neighbor's son, Marcus. She had a reputation for dividing her private goods between the young men of Sapelo and St. Simons Island. I heard that she'd married a soldier, but I didn't know it was Harrison.

Harrison was an amazing stud, who knew how to talk to a woman, and didn't back down until he got what he wanted. His joking nature, coupled by his earnest gaze at my delight from the pleasure he gave...those images were hard to resist. Though he was here with his family, I felt a connection to him. Naomi talked to Emma, one of the island elders standing beside her, while my focus stayed on Harrison. Finally, he felt the desire of my soul searching for relief. His almond-shaped eyes shifted from the young child, straight through the partygoers, to me. He smiled as I let my hair down, swaying my hips to the beat of the drums. I raised my arms, waving them in time with the dip of my hips. The split to my sarong widened. The fluid moves of my body had him in a seductive trance. We both enjoyed this playful hunt, and my thighs became increasingly moist, hoping he'd find a way to join my dance.

I put my finger to my lips, slowing parting the fullness of them, smiling as he watched intently. I sucked up and down my fingertip. I could tell the gesture excited him, based on the slow lick of his lips. I pretended that he was my fingertip, and I was locked on his dick. Sucking him as he slurped the sensuous juices of my pussy. The thought of us making love this way had me aroused.

The beats got harder. My hips shook faster, my body sweltering from the mixture of island humidity and bridled passion. The dancing bodies around me were engrossed in their own world of excitement. Some fueled by the liquid spirits they had consumed; others aroused by the hypnotic drum force. I swept the newness of sweat drops from my chest into my mouth, moaning his name. Harrison read my lips and stepped closer. He studied the roundness of my breasts as I opened the top button to my yellow knit midriff. I sauntered closer, licking my lips, enticing him. He took more steps, at a calculated pace, opening his mouth slightly. We were still a few feet apart, but bonded by sensual chemistry. I gyrated harder. The dance of his eyes followed my lead. We created a private code. A passionate body language, longing to be unleashed.

Naomi moved into my line of sight, pulling Harrison away. The drums stopped. Her eyes threw darts at me as she took the baby out of his arms. They walked near the food tent. He broke free from her grasp and faced my direction. Naomi's calls to him were unanswered. His hearing had been impaired from the war, but he knew she was speaking. He wasn't paying attention to her. The hunger in his eyes spoke to me. We remained still as the music began again. Slowly, I turned my back, ignoring his silent pleas. The fantasy was over. Frustrated, I swiftly removed my sandals, and wormed through the crowd. I ran toward home, where I would endure another sleepless night.

HERE I AM

The tears streamed down my face as I sat in a tub of water so hot, it had reddened my skin. I wasn't ashamed of how I'd performed for Harrison at the parade; I was mad at the world, for being lonely. Confused as to why his mere presence weakened my defenses, replacing them with primal vulnerability. The Merlot that had settled in fine crystal now flowed across the wooden floor. Deep red wine with a quality so pure, it could've been mistaken for blood. The glass I had flung was wedding crystal. My fury caused it to shatter against the bathroom wall. Beauty defiled to broken fragments. I stared at a jagged edge from one of the pieces alongside the tub. The enchantment I felt from Harrison between my legs had turned to numbness.

Solemnly, I picked the piece of glass up from the floor. I trailed it steadily against my wrist, then my hand began to shake. The glass fell from my wet fingers into the water.

"Damn you!" I screamed, splashing water to the ceiling. I exhaled and slowly reclined back against the tub. I let the water cover me to the neck, as I tried to calm my emotions. The tightness and tension in my upper body began to lessen, but a faint knock at the door suddenly roused fear.

"Who's there!" I screamed as I straightened my posture. I had one leg out of the tub, trying to step cautiously.

"Miss Jasmine, it's Harrison. I didn't mean to scare ya."

Relieved that I recognized the voice, I found a safe place to plant my feet, and exited the tub. Water dripping from my body, I tried to figure out how to step around the glass to get to the towel draped against the vanity. "How'd you get in here?" I asked, shivering.

"The door was unlocked."

"Well, that's news to me, but you wouldn't have known it was unlocked, unless you tried it. What do you want?"

"Can I come in?"

"I'm not decent."

I heard a soft chuckle. "Let me decide that for myself. Can I come in, Miss Jasmine?"

I didn't protest, which obviously was his cue to open the creaking door slightly. He peered in, observing me with my hands strategically placed over my private areas.

"Whatcha tryin' to hide, huh?" I looked down to the floor as he approached, glass crumbling under his dusty work boots. "I've seen and tasted your sweetness, lady." He pulled my hands down. "There ain't no shame in that." He lifted my chin up.

"What's all this glass doin' on the floor?"

I shrugged. "I had an accident, is all."

His hand gently smoothed over a wave of my damp hair. "You all right?"

My lip quivered as I recalled what he'd said to me, our first meeting at the mission.

"Don't ask a question you don't wanna hear the answer to."

He grabbed the towel and took care in drying me off. "You grown, and you don't owe me no explanation." He smiled as he eased the towel between my thighs, then secured it with a tuck under my arms. He kissed my neck, applying suction with his lips. I moaned and squeezed my thighs tight to suppress the erotic itch he'd just sent through me. Harrison smiled as he pushed a curl from my bang to the side. "I just want you to know, I been thinkin' of you, nonstop. I do carpentry, and I drive supply trucks for Mr. Rayman. When I got off work, my walking led to you."

I flung my damp hair as I sized him up. "You don't know me. You might know how to make me feel good, but you don't know anything about me."

He circled his arms around my waist. "I know more than you think. You Frances' niece, and Dr. Kelly was your husband. He's gone, and you left here, missing him."

I looked down at the amber polish on my toes. "I don't wanna talk about it."

"Miss Jasmine, you ain't got to be scared no more," he said, his tone mellow. He lifted my face to meet his. "You damn sure ain't gotta be afraid of me. This crystal on the floor will hurt you more than I ever will."

I shook my head as I placed my hands on his chest, trying to pull away. "You're talkin' foolish. You're a married man."

He kept me locked in his embrace. "Being married has nothin' to do with this wine on the floor, and those tears in your eyes. Unless lightning lucky enough to strike me dead, I'ma be married tomorrow, so talk of that mess can rest for another time. This mess here looks like a damn emergency, and I believe I'm the one to save you." He caressed my shoulders. "Lay those burdens down on me; I'm strong enough to carry 'em."

Harrison scooped me into his arms and carefully guided me out of the bathroom into the bedroom. After laying me down on the bed, he took off his work boots and his denim shirt, exposing a chiseled chest. I raised my head as I watched him remove the belt from his dungarees.

"Let me get my robe."

"You lay back and relax," he said, guiding me back down. He gave me a tender kiss. "Where is it?"

"In the bureau," I said softly as he lifted from my body.

As he got the blue robe, he noticed the record player on the dresser. "You like Al Green?" he asked, looking at the singer's record mounted to the turntable.

I looked up to the ceiling, as I fingered my gold heart pendant. "Adam did. There was a song on there I really liked, though."

He raised a brow. "Was it this one?" He turned the player on. When I heard the introduction, I got to my feet.

"Could you turn it off, please," I said, shutting my eyes for a moment.

"I wanna dance with you," he whispered into my ear as he tied the robe around me.

I put my palms up in desperation, shaking my head. "Please."

He thread his fingers through mine, pulling me close to him. "Shh...this the one you like? Does it remind you of Adam?" I nodded slowly, sighing as I rested my head against his chest. His arms became a warm blanket, covering the satin fabric that graced my shoulders. "Well, I ain't selfish. You need him here, use me. I'll do whatever you want. Whatever he did, just as long as I know you gonna be all right. Don't let sadness take your life, Miss Jasmine. Hold onto me. That's all you gotta do. Just hold on."

Harrison locked his hands around my waist. I looked up at him as he kissed my forehead. A tender melody serenaded us.

Don't look so sad

I know it's over...

Harrison caressed my face, wiping wetness away with his fingertips.

But life goes on, and this world keeps on turning....

We swayed to the music. Harrison comforted me, rubbing my back as I rested my weight on him.

Let's just be glad, we had have this time to spend together
There is no need to watch the bridges that were burning...

The lyrics made me reminisce. Fond memories of loving Adam more than myself; thoughts of losing our son; and my battle to mend scars of being orphaned and widowed came crashing down. Harrison bore my cries. It felt good to let go, with him holding me tight.

Lay your head upon my pillow
Sweet baby, hold your warm and tender body close to mine...

"Look at me," he said. "I'm yours."

I sniffled. "For tonight."

"Let that be enough for now. God himself couldn't make the world in a day. Be patient. Time gonna bring good things. Like rain falling on flower seeds, helping them grow into somethin' sweet, like *Jasmine*."

I smiled for the first time, enjoying the warmth of his arms.

Hear the whisper of the raindrops blow softly against my window
pane late at night
Make believe you love me...one more time
For the good times...

When I woke up, I thought Harrison would be gone, but he was still here. Sleeping peacefully beside me.

LOVE WHAT YOU DO FOR ME

Harrison gave me innocence last night. As a new *dayclean* shined across the bed, I slipped my hand into his boxers, taking what I needed now into my hand.

He smiled and moved onto his back. I removed his shorts.

"Mornin,' beautiful," he moaned.

"Umm...Good morning," I said, kissing the bridge of his nose as he opened his eyes.

He licked his lips. "I see you feelin' better."

"I am, but this Rock of Gibraltar gonna tear my insides out," I moaned, easing down on his rod.

"That's because you like to take control of everything," he said with a wink. "Sometimes you gotta let a man handle his business before you start running things."

"Is that right?"

"That's right, now take it easy," he said. He guided my hips, sliding me up and down the vascular desire that became more delicious with each stroke. "That's it," he moaned as he closed his eyes. Harrison gave in to the feel of my triangle swallowing his dick. I rode him until my body collapsed onto his, weakened from my orgasm. "My turn," he said, as he placed me on my back. I welcomed him into my warm shelter, wrapping my knees over his shoulders. We both succumbed to the depth of our lovemaking. Harrison being with me made life beautiful again. His skillful touch to all the right places helped me experience uninhibited intimacy.

As we rested, I rubbed his taut back, gliding my hand up and down his spine.

"You gotta get home?" I asked, giving him a peck on the lips.

He exhaled as he touched my necklace. "I gotta shower, kiss my son, and get to work, 'fore Mr. Rayman fire my ass."

I smiled. "He won't fire you, if I put in a good word."

"What?"

"I work for him, too. I'm his lawyer."

He playfully pinched me. "Damn, you somethin' else. Why you still in Sapelo? Seem like you'd be makin' mean green in a big city, like New York or Chicago."

I wrapped my arms around him. "I like being around familiar faces. People who make me feel good, like you." I looked away, towards the oak tree hovering outside my window.

Harrison touched my chin, easing my face his way. "What's the matter?"

"Naomi. She gonna be wondering about you."

He shook his head. "I doubt that. She stopped asking me questions about my whereabouts when I started asking about her late nights."

"Well, I just wanna say thank you for last night...for everything."

He frowned slightly, rising up on his elbow. "You thankin' me like you ain't gonna see me again."

I shrugged as I touched his thick eyebrow. "There's no guarantee."

Harrison shook his head. "That's where you're wrong, Counselor. I done traveled the world, and come across many fine ladies in my day, but..."

I burst out laughing, pulling myself up against the headboard. "Yeah, you're such a wise, old soul." He wasn't amused. I stopped smiling when I realized I may have been too sarcastic. "Harrison, I…"

His eyes narrowed as he placed his index finger over my lips. "Like I was saying…I've seen many a fine woman, but I'm old enough to recognize when I'm in good company. You got my attention, lovely lady, and if you don't mind, I think I wanna stick around."

I glanced at the small piece of gauze taped to his ear. "Your ear is gettin' better."

Harrison grinned. "I guess there's hope for me yet." He took a deep breath and clasped his hands behind his head, lying back down on the pillow. His expression was reflective, directed towards the fan circulating from the ceiling.

I nudged him. "Deep in thought?" He smiled as he pulled himself up beside me, placing his forehead against mine.

"Yep. I was thinkin' about a beautiful woman I once met. How her eyes changed colors with the movement of the sun. How the switch of her hips when she walked made me stand at attention. The sexiness of her bottom lip, pouting at me, waiting far too long for my kiss. Sorry to keep you waitin'," he whispered as his lips covered the fullness of mine.

TO SIR WITH LOVE

I had a meeting with Mr. Rayman at his mansion. He'd recently taken quite ill, and needed to review some of his legal affairs concerning the estate, and delegation of a successor for his cigarette company. As I walked toward the long stretch of willow trees and restored plantation houses, I noticed Harrison hollering through the open door of his cedar bungalow. Next thing I saw was him storming inside. A minute later, he was back outside, throwing a pile of women's clothes, and an old suitcase to the dusty ground. Naomi stood crying on the porch as he threw her business outside for all of Sapelo to see.

I didn't want to see Harrison upset, but whatever business he had with his wife was between them. I knew we'd be able to talk about it when he was ready. I shook my head as I continued walking down the plantation path toward the Rayman Mansion.

***

Regal ivory pillars towered over the intricate entrance to the mansion. The solid oak doors opened as I made the last stride up the slate steps. Gladys, Mr. Rayman's housekeeper, stood smiling at the doorway.

"Mornin,' Miss Gladys," I said, kissing her on the cheek.

"Mornin,' chile," she said, rocking me as we hugged. I'd known Miss Gladys ever since I was a little girl. She was petite, and always wore her thick hair in a neat bun. Her rosewater scent, and neat posture always made me wonder if she'd ever wanted to be a model or actress, instead of working for the Raymans all these years. I'd never seen a frown on her flawless bronze skin, and I never heard her complain.

"How's Mr. Rayman doin' today?"

"Still himself," she said, shaking her head. "Fussin' and sneakin' cigarettes every chance he gets."

I laughed. "Where is he?"

She pointed to the west wing. "In the study. Go on, he's expectin' you."

As I strolled over the emerald marble tile corridor, I saw Mr. Rayman, settled comfortably in his leather reading chair. He had a paisley cigar robe belted around navy cotton pajamas. He appeared to be dozing off when I entered. I approached him in the vast library corridor, and his head lifted slowly.

"Jasmine," he said, extending his arms for a hug. He'd seen me grow up, so I was used to the light peck he'd placed on my hair when I hugged him. He shook his head, almost with a melancholy glance. "You get more beautiful by the day, you know that?"

I waved my hand. "Don't make me blush, now," I said, sitting on the sofa near him. "How you feelin' today?"

He huffed. "Like I got one foot in the grave."

"Stop that talk. You just had a setback, is all."

He pointed at me. "A smart woman like you should know better. Emphysema isn't some nightmare that will go away." He swallowed hard, wringing his hands.

I got up and poured him a glass of water from the pitcher.

He nodded in appreciation. "Thank you kindly," he whispered, taking a sip.

"Did you bring all the paperwork with you?"

"Yes, sir," I said as I sat back down. I pulled a file from my briefcase. "Here are the documents you requested. I believe I amended everything, per your instructions over the phone. We just need to go over some minor details, and make any final changes you see fit."

He drank the rest of the water, then handed me the glass. "Tobacco business is still good in Sapelo. I employ many people, trying to help folks take care of their families."

"Yes, sir," I said, folding my hands. "I believe your company is what has kept the people here. It's the only viable industry on the island, and you've always treated people fairly."

He looked over at the grandfather clock, chiming in the background. "I don't know about all of that, Jasmine. I've tried to do my best, but I'm not perfect. I've made plenty of mistakes. Even hurt some people." He looked back at me, sadness creeping across his face. "There are things I wish I could take back, but I can't. So, I'm gonna make sure mistakes are minimal from this point on. I want future generations to keep the plant going, and hopefully give something back to Sapelo, as I plan on doing."

I reached for his hand. "You talk like you're on your death bed."

"It's necessary talk. You didn't become a lawyer, thinking just about today. I didn't build a company, thinking about what someone built yesterday. We're visionaries, you and I. You gotta always plan ahead, because life is sure to catch you sleeping, if you don't."

I smiled. "Words of wisdom, sir. I thank you."

He sighed as he squeezed my hand. "Don't thank me anymore.

You're my attorney. You've done an excellent job, handling my business matters. I thank *you*." He let my hand go, and began to rub his chest.

I stood up, concerned. "Mr. Rayman, do you want me to call for Gladys?"

He coughed violently, motioning for more water. I hurried to the end table and poured him another glass. He took a sip, shaking his head. I touched his shoulder as he exhaled. "No, no. I'm fine. I just get choked up, sometimes." He picked up the papers. "Let me look over things, and we'll talk again, at the Board of Directors meeting. I'm appointing two new members, effective first quarter of the New Year. My son, Victor, who will replace me, and my first female appointee."

I smiled. "Really? Let me guess, Mrs. Rayman?"

"Good guess, but no cigar," he said cheerfully.

"Who?"

"Mrs. Jasmine Kelly, Esquire."

I was speechless. He slowly rose to his feet, as I offered my assistance. "Mr. Rayman, you're appointing me to the board? Why? I mean, you already have separate counsel managing the operations of the corporation." He patted my hand.

"I'm tired. I need to rest now. We'll discuss it further after the meeting next week."

HOW CAN YOU MEND A BROKEN HEART?

When I walked back through the Hog Hammock community where Harrison lived, I saw him chopping wood. He had a cigarette dangling from his mouth, but managed to belt a loud roar after each hit to the stump. Sweat poured from his face, more so from anger than the hot sun beaming down. Even a scowl didn't diminish his handsome features. Since he was situated right outside Otis' furniture shop, I thought it'd be all right for us to talk. Otis, a disabled veteran and constant nuisance, sat on the shop porch with an oriental female companion. She massaged his shoulders, while he enjoyed watching Harrison's rage.

I walked by them gawking, and stepped cautiously towards Harrison. "You ready to talk?" I asked, watching his bare back flex from manual labor.

He didn't respond and continued to chop away at the wood.

I spoke louder. "Harrison, you hear me? Can we talk?"

He stood chopping, wiping his brow with the back of his hand. Nothing more than a grunt came from his mouth as he stood straight, staring at the trees before him. Harrison's face turned casually to me for a second. He threw his cigarette down, and didn't say a word as he continued to vent with the wood. I sighed as I removed my pumps. I unraveled the beige suit coat I'd wrapped around my hips, placing them on another stump where his sweet tea rested. I picked up the Mason jar, taking a sip as I tucked a bra strap that had fallen to my shoulder back under my rayon camisole.

"Man, you shoulda listened to me when I told you 'fore, Naomi was nothin' but trouble." He smirked, pointing at me. "And this one here, she'll send ya to an early grave." I gulped down my sip, drawing my cheeks in as I flipped Otis the bird. His simple ass cackled, stomping his foot on the porch.

Harrison gritted his teeth and hit the wood again, keeping the ax in the stump as he stared at Otis. "Otis, I ain't for your two cents. All I want is some wood. Keep your opinions to yourself."

Otis held his hands up. "All I'm sayin' is, some of these Sapelo women too high maintenance. That's why I brought me back a real Geechee girl, ain't that right, rice puddin'?" he said, tickling his woman.

I tightened my lips, placing my free hand on my hip as I walked to the porch.

"Well, if things so Peachy and Geechee in Vietnam, why don't you take your ass back there? Be fewer headaches for all of us. Ain't that right, rice puddin'?" I asked, acknowledging the woman.

She stood up and bowed at me. "Yah, yah," she replied through a million teeth.

"You speak English?" She nodded and smiled, not knowing what I'd just asked. I was gonna have fun with this. I shook her hand. "Welcome to Sapelo. Lemme help ya learn a couple of words... Hot grits." I mouthed the words slowly, "H-O-T G-R-I-T-S."

She smiled. "Yah...yah."

"Yah, good for attitude problems," I mimicked, tilting my head toward Otis. He played with the toothpick in his mouth, eyeing me from head to toe. I sucked my teeth. "Otis, you need a damn tutor yourself. Who gonna teach her English?"

He gave me a sinister stare. "Whatcha doin' here, homewrecka?" He howled again, as if he was truly funny. I threw sweet tea in his face. He jumped up, looking at his wet tank shirt, then back at me with a deep frown. Harrison dropped the ax and flew over, getting in between us.

"Woman, you lost yo damn mind!" Otis screamed, wiping his face. His woman did the two-step, all in a tizzy that her man's shirt was soaked.

Harrison tightened his fists. "You better not even look like you gonna hit her. You make a wrong move, and I'll be sure to give you another bum knee."

I threw the jar to the ground. "He ain't gonna do nothin.' He just pissed off, 'cause I told him to eat dust off my shoes, after he said he wanted to fill Adam's shoes—asking me for sex."

"What!" Harrison yelled, positioned like he was ready to punch Otis.

I pulled him back. "Let's go. He ain't worth your time."

We gathered our things and started to walk away when Otis yelled. "That's right. Get off my property! Damn vanilla house negra, keepin' a henpecked joker."

Harrison ran back to the porch, knocking Otis flat on his back. "Whatcha talkin' now, fool!" he hollered, throwing punch after punch on Otis.

I tried to intervene, grabbing him by his belt. "Harrison, that's enough!" Neighbors were starting to come out on their porches to see the show.

All Miss Saigon did was fling her arms, screaming, "Ha gris! Ha gris!" Like she thought that meant, *stop*.

Harrison heard her and suddenly stopped, shaking his head at her efforts to settle things down. I pulled him off the porch as Otis stammered to his feet. He had a swollen eye, and was rubbing his jaw. I smiled at the woman. "You keep practicing, rice puddin,'" I said. "You'll need those hot grits sooner than later." Harrison tried to hide a smile. I pinched his side, letting him know I'd caught him holding a laugh as we walked away.

***

Harrison and I sat quietly on a rock near the dunes, watching seagulls hunt for fish in the water. I touched his shoulder. "How long you gonna be mad?"

He looked down, rubbing a piece of seaweed between his fingers fingers. "As long as I gotta see her."

"Seem like a long time. Sapelo ain't that big."

He flicked the seaweed down to the sand, shaking his head. "Big enough to make a fool out of me. I can't believe she was with my best friend, Floyd. The whole time, screwin' him on the side. Carryin' his seed while I was in combat, fighting for my life. Nobody tell me nothin'." He put his head in his hands and broke down in tears. "Keenan mean the world to me. I bust my ass, working long hours to make sure that little boy got what he need. And he ain't even mine?"

I bit my lip, not knowing what to say. I reached for his hand, but he resisted, opting to crack his knuckles instead. "Floyd was smart to run off to Atlanta. Can't figure out why Naomi's ass ain't follow him?"

I smiled and kissed his cheek, trying to make light of the situation. "She doesn't wanna have him for a husband. She got you. She just needed somethin' extra."

His jaw tightened as he looked at me. "That's always what I am, somethin' extra. Ain't that right, Miss Jasmine?"

I looked at my hands for a second, then touched his thigh. "I didn't mean it that way."

"No other way 'round it," he said, looking off to the water.

I happened to glance behind us, and thought I'd pee on myself from the sight.

I swallowed hard as I slowly turned back. "Harrison," I whispered. "Don't look now, but there is a big-ass gator, sun bathing three feet behind us."

He did exactly the opposite of what I told him. He slowly peered back to find the gator, grinning under fangs, like we were Labor Day ribs. He turned slightly towards me while he kept his peripheral vision on the gator. "We got three seconds to put his ass on a diet," he whispered. "We jump on...shit!" The gator made the first move, jaws wide open.

Harrison pushed me down to the sand, miraculously throwing the blanket we'd sat on over the gator's head with his free hand. By the time the gator gripped the blanket, unveiling his elongated head, we'd haul-tailed it up shore. When we reached the dirt road, we slowed down. "That was close," I said, laughing as I massaged a cramp out of my side.

"You ain't never lie," Harrison said, bending over to catch his breath. He rose back up and pulled me into his arms. "You all right?"

I nodded as I looked up at him. "You?" I asked, concerned as I caressed his face.

He pulled my hands down, holding them against his chest. "I don't know, Miss Jasmine. Seem like life shouldn't be this stressful."

I kissed his fingers. "Harrison, you're a good man. Don't let Naomi's lies make you bitter."

He shrugged. "A good man that got played for a fool. Naomi and I wasn't right, even before I left for the war. We got married too young. She got childish ways, and I ain't been the best husband. The minute I got home, the fussin' started back up. My relief was spending time with Keenan...and then you." I smiled as he took my hand, and we began walking to my house. "This mornin,' when you saw us fightin,' I'd just told her to leave. That's how I found out. She knew she could hurt me by using Keenan. She said I wasn't the real daddy, but if I stayed with her, she'd let me adopt him. She told me to pick between you and Keenan. I told her if I couldn't bargain with God, I sure as hell wasn't gonna bargain with her."

"What about Keenan?"

He sighed. "He's over at her folks' place with her. 'Less Naomi plan on gettin' a job, she ain't goin' nowhere. I'll try to see him when I can. If she act ugly, and keep Keenan from me...I'll just have to wait until he gets older, where he can decide for himself."

When we reached my door, I hugged him. "Harrison, I know the pain you're going through, losing something precious."

He nodded. "I know you do. That's why I don't want you worryin' about me. It's been a helluva day. Go on inside, and get some rest."

I held onto his arms. "Won't you come in? I can make supper."

He kissed my forehead. "Ain't got much of an appetite right now, Miss Jasmine."

"What can I do for you, Harrison? I love..." I swallowed hard. "I'd love to help."

He touched my cheek. "I may need some legal help, separating from her and all, but right now, I just need time to clear my head." He gave me a soft kiss on the lips. "Night, Miss Jasmine."

I leaned against the porch banister, crossing my arms. "Night," I mumbled as I watched him leave me.

OH ME, OH MY

Harrison had been avoiding me. I'd call, he wouldn't answer. The house never had lights on. Even in the daytime, he didn't open the door when I knocked. I knew he needed time to sort through some things. One morning, I left a note taped to the back door. I knew he'd see it, when he went out to the yard to lift weights. It simply read, *I miss you*. The next morning, I found a bouquet of fresh cut flowers on my doorstep. Harrison had been missing me, too.

The demands of maintaining a law office kept me from day-dreaming about romance too much, especially since Mr. Rayman had been referring new clients my way. I was reading a brief, on the verge of calling Mr. Rayman to discuss his will, when Naomi stormed through the door. I peered at her from under my wire-rimmed glasses, unfazed. "Need help with that divorce?"

"No, I need you to leave my man alone!" she yelled in front of my desk. Her chest heaved under a hot pink blouse that clashed with the black polka-dot micro mini she sported, two sizes too small.

I put my glasses on my desk calendar and got up, walking right up in her face. "You got some nerve barging into my law office, makin' accusations, when the flies on the wall can't even keep up with all the men you been fuckin'!" She backed up a little, when she realized I had a sharp letter opener in my right hand.

"Harrison and I got some problems we tryin' to work through, and you ain't helpin,' with your Geritol ass!"

I looked her up and down. "Humph. Last I heard, you're the one that needed the K-Y Jelly."

She pointed in my face. "Looka here, Harrison ain't perfect. Neither am I, but I wanna work things out." She smoothed her hand over her belly. "For our new baby's sake." She curled her lips, looking indignant. "I'm pregnant."

I gave her a blank expression. "So? What's that mean to me? You like to multiply, similar to creeping rats."

Naomi slapped me, sending the letter opener to the floor. I had her falling back in the visitor's chair, once I knocked the wind out of her.

"Pregnant my ass!" I hollered down at her. "You would not have tried me like that if you were with child. I bet you won't try me again, now will you?" To add insult to injury, I yanked her freshly pressed ponytail before I picked up the letter opener and went back to my desk. I had semi-renovated an abandoned church house for my law practice, but this drama made me realize I needed a bigger place, with a receptionist to screen assholes.

She crossed her arms over her body, whimpering like a baby. "I love Harrison!"

I patted my French roll and put back on my glasses. "The next time you wanna fool yourself into thinkin' you love Harrison, think about how you hurt him. He was in Vietnam, praying he'd make it through, just to come home and find out his son isn't his. Despite your deception, he still wants to make a life for that boy, because he's a good man. He can teach Keenan something decent."

She stood up, adjusting her clothes. "Like sleeping with a slut?"

I raised a brow. "No, like divorcing a Looney Tune."

She put her hands on her hips. "People make mistakes!"

I twirled a pen in my hand. "And people pay for mistakes."

She banged her fist on my desk. "I agree, heifer. This ain't over!"

I waved my finger at her. "You know, you're right, Naomi. Please forgive me for forgetting one last thing." I pulled a card from my stationery box, scribbled a message, and tucked the card in an envelope.

"What's this?" she snapped as I handed it to her.

"A *thank you* note, for not treating Harrison right. Your ignorance, my bliss."

She stormed out. I ran to the door, watching her switch up the road. "Naomi? Be sure to check your mail, 'cause you gonna get a bill for wastin' my damn time!"

***

Harrison fed me grapes, drenched with Sangria. A midnight moon illuminated the white sand where we sat.

"Thanks for meeting me," he said.

I leaned against his shoulder. "Thanks for rescuing me from work."

He kissed my forehead. "Everything all right?"

"Yeah, just a lot of late nights reviewing paperwork for Mr. Rayman."

"He ain't doing too well, is he?"

"No. He's not doing too well. I gotta meet with him tomorrow. Help him get his affairs in order." I smirked as I looked at my fingernails. "You know your old lady paid me a visit earlier this evening."

Harrison frowned. "Say what? That woman is stuck on stupid. She ain't hurt you, did she?"

"No, but I kinda feel bad about givin' her an Ali blow to the belly. She said she was pregnant." I tried to read Harrison's eyes.

He waved his hands. "Don't put that one on me. If she ain't lying, she definitely knocked up by somebody else. We ain't been like that since I've been back." He held my face as he nestled his nose against mine. "I been with you, and you only. That's the God's honest truth."

I felt his cheek. "I believe you, Harrison."

"What you and I got together ain't conventional, but it feel more sacred than anything I've felt before." He wrapped his arms around me. "I love you, Jasmine, body and soul."

I blushed like a school girl, as I reached behind me and pulled a present from my beach bag. I handed it to him. His eyes brightened. "What's this?" he asked, opening it.

I laughed. "A peace offering from the gator. He said he's sorry for biting the blanket, 'cause he was really goin' for your ass!"

Harrison laughed as he held the crocheted black-and-red quilt up in admiration.

"Well, we ain't in alligator territory tonight, but I got my pistol, just in case one of 'em gets lost." He shook his head as he pulled me close to him. "What am I gonna do with you?"

I gave him a sly grin. "I'm sure you'll figure out something."

He smiled as he pulled a banana from the wicker fruit basket beside us. "Ever had a banana split before?"

I nodded. "I love 'em."

He licked his lips. "Alright, I want you to try mine." He handed me the blanket. "Spread this out, take your bathing suit off, and lay down on your belly."

"My belly?" I asked, removing my peach-colored bikini.

"Yep," he said as he removed his Bermuda shorts, exposing a pleasingly erect penis.

"Can I have this instead of the banana?" I asked as I pulled his body onto the blanket. I swirled my tongue around the head of his shaft, then took it all in my mouth. I tugged him at just the right pressure.

"Baby, you suckin' me so good," he moaned as he held my head steady. I made popping noises as I released, then wrapped him in my mouth again, exciting him further.

"Turn this way," he said, rotating my bottom to his face. He waved his tongue down the valley of my juicy pussy, then he traveled back up through the middle of my plush rear.

"Ohhh...Harrison," I whined. "Right there." His tongue rolled rhythmically over my folds. I continued to suck appetizer juices from the tip of his goodness, when I felt him massage his finger in the crevice of my ass. I tensed for a second.

"Relax," he said, moving from under me. He peeled the banana, placing it near my mouth. "Take a bite." I went down on the banana, like it was his dick. I closed my eyes and moaned as I slowly pulled back, clipping a chunk off into my mouth. Harrison looked mesmerized. "Damn, baby. Lay down." I got on my stomach and felt him part my legs with his strong hands.

I watched him mash a piece of the banana between his finger-tips. As he rubbed the sticky, sweet consistency, he lowered his body on top of me. I shut my eyes tight as he lubed my crack with the banana paste. He was gentle, tracing his finger lightly over the hole. "Jasmine, just relax. Let your body trust mine, and give into the feelin,' okay?"

"Okay," I said under a muffled moan. I hoped my thirty-two-year-old ass could hang with the virile, young-ass dick that was about to go up my anus. When he slowly penetrated me, I thought I was gonna lose my mind.

"Ahh...!" I cried, clenching the blanket.

"Easy," he whispered as he massaged the small of my back.

"Harrison, your cock is so thick," I moaned as I rubbed my clit, trying to get used to him stretching me.

His strokes were steady and smooth. He placed wet kisses all over my back. "Breathe. Breathe, baby," he moaned in my ear. He gripped my hips, raising them further up his pelvis. "Lawd, Jasmine, this gonna take me there, I swear. Is it hurtin'?"

"Stop talkin'!" I mumbled, clawing sand with my fingers.

He chuckled. "That delicious, huh?"

"Ummm...give me a little more. That's it. That's it! Oh shit!"

"You sure you wanna do that?"

"Shee...it!"

"Gettin' backed up, ain't ya?" he grunted, pumping me.

"Yes!"

"You like my banana split?"

"Uh...huuhhunh..."

"I didn't hear you good. Say it's the best."

"It's the best. You feel so fuckin' good!" My whole body was shaking.

"All right, let's get full. You ready?"

I was delusional at this point, eyes rolled back in my head like a possessed woman. He was pleasing the hell out of me.

"We gonna top this shit off with some whipped cream," he said, his breath shallow. I felt the tension increase in his body as he wrapped his arms around my neck. He rocked me hard, but I didn't want him to stop.

"Ooooh...Aaaaw...!" Love sounds from our climax together. We molded our bodies into a warm cocoon.

"You believe I'm ripe enough for you now?" Harrison asked, sucking moisture from my neck.

I glided my hand over his bald head. "Yes, Harrison. That was so good."

He stared deeply into my eyes. "I'm always gonna be good for you, Miss Jasmine."

GOOD MORNING HEARTACHE

"I'm glad you could make it a few hours earlier, Jasmine," Mr. Rayman said softly from his sick bed. He gently reached for my hand.

I blinked back tears as I sat in the chair, holding his frail fingers inside mine. Mr. Rayman had been too weak to attend the Board of Directors meeting, so I brought the minutes and documents to him. He was losing his battle with emphysema. I tried to be a composed professional, but it was difficult. I'd known this kind-hearted man all of my life. He nurtured my love of books over the years, giving me Shakespeare, Mark Twain, and even Zora Neale Hurston, a graduation gift he'd selected with the help of Gladys. I worked in his office as a clerk, from high school to college. While I'd received academic scholarships to Howard, he still offered funds to Aunt Frances, for expenses that weren't covered.

His blue eyes were glassy, and each breath he took was more labored than the previous one. "How'd the meeting go?" he asked in a hushed tone.

I nodded with a smile. "Everyone seemed fine with the appointments." I bit my lip. "Except for Victor. Your son never has liked me too much. He didn't say a single word to me the whole time."

Mr. Rayman looked solemn as he bent his head. "He'll come around. The world is changing, and we all need to embrace new things. I appointed you both, because you bring so much talent to our board. Victor is a physician in Burlington. You're an attorney, here in Sapelo." He smiled proudly. "I believe your collective ideas and energy will be good for the company."

"I brought the file for your Will and Testament, Mr. Rayman," I said, carefully placing it on his lap.

He put his hand over the file. "Jasmine, I've thought long and hard about these changes, but I still need your opinion on how to proceed."

I folded my hands. "Yes, Mr. Rayman, I'm listening."

He took a deep sigh as he rested his head against the headboard. "In the event of my death, I will need someone to manage the reading of my wishes efficiently. My family does not know about some of the revisions, and will not know until the reading is rendered. Emotions may run high, and I want to make sure order can be restored." He coughed. "Do you...do you understand?"

"Yes, Mr. Rayman," I said as I poured him a glass of water from the crystal pitcher.

I handed him the glass. "Do you have reservations about me handling the reading?"

He took a long sip, then handed the glass back to me. "Normally, I wouldn't. You're competent counsel. I know you'd do a fine job." He shook his head slowly. I frowned, confused by his hesitation. He gripped the folder in his hand. "The contents of the will affect many people, including you."

I placed my hand on my chest. "Me?"

He nodded. "Jasmine, I've asked Jake Rogers, who you know as company counsel, to read the will, with you present."

I moved closer to the bed, placing both hands on his. "Mr. Rayman, Jake has a fine reputation, and we get along well." I raised my shoulders. "I just don't understand why you've asked him to conduct the reading."

He looked at me, apprehension evident from the creases to his brow. "There is one section in the will that might present a challenge, if you were reading it. The section that lists the heirs of my estate."

I narrowed my eyes. "Sir?"

"Your name will be included on that list. Jasmine, you are my daughter."

My lips trembled. This great fortress of a bedroom suddenly felt like a coffin, cutting off my airway. I stood up fast, gasping for air.

"Jasmine, please sit down." He raised his weak arm in the air, attempting to reach for me. I shook my head violently, backing far away from the bed, over to the large windowsill. Hard rain tapped against the pane as I stared at this man in disbelief.

Finally, my emotions poured out. "Why!" I wailed. "Why did you keep this from me?" I paced the floor, holding my head in my hands.

"Jasmine, please hear me out," he said, his voice faltering. He motioned for me to come closer. I stood still, fuming as tears trailed my cheeks. "Please sit down."

Every step closer to the chair felt like lead, weighing down my feet. I stood paralyzed in front of him. His tears ran as fast as mine. "I know I should've told you years ago, but I wasn't ready for you and my family to feel shame. There was so much racial tension in the world, back when you were born. I didn't want trouble brewing on the island, causing scandal and embarrassment for everyone."

I laughed, rearing my head back. "You wanted to save your precious reputation, Mr. Rayman." I waved my hands. "No one could know about the generous tobacco farmer turned fortune king, fathering a child out of wedlock. All hell would break loose, if anyone knew you'd been unfaithful to your precious Marilyn."

"Jasmine, I made a mistake, and..."

"Yes," I interrupted. "And that mistake was me...your competent counsel, bastard child!"

His face reddened, distraught by my hurt. "Jasmine, I would say I'm sorry a million times, if I thought it would ease your pain...but I know it would not. You have always mattered to me. I believe the bond we have as business associates is just as strong as a father/daughter bond."

"How would you know? You never gave me a chance to be your daughter. I respected you, and I loved you as client. I believe that love could have blossomed even more, had I known the truth. You banished that opportunity, so your family wouldn't be dishonored. Did you think hiring me as counsel would make amends for your betrayal?"

He took a breath and clasped his hands. "Please, Jasmine, don't hate me."

"I don't hate you. I'm disappointed. You are facing your last days, trying to clear your conscience, while I'm sitting here, wondering how my heart still beats from all the turmoil I've endured."

"Jasmine, I did what was best at the time."

"Mr. Rayman, you did what was best for you. You swept an affair under the rug, denied a child, and decided to go about business as usual. Maybe if I was simply your attorney, I would have said, good decision. But as a woman who cried her eyes out, longing to know who her parents were, you made a horrendous error."

He was silent as I walked back over to the windowsill, staring at the falling rain.

"Did you love my mother?" I asked, peering back at him.

He looked at his hands, then smiled up at me. "Yes. I loved her very much...I still do."

I walked back over to him with my arms crossed. "As your lawyer, I wanna make sure I understand you correctly. Let me re-phrase the question. Were you *in love* with her, or were you just lusting for something exotic. Like a slave master with an affinity for dark meat."

"No!" he cried. "Jasmine, it wasn't that way." He closed his eyes, holding his chest for a moment. I was angry, but a part of me felt like I needed to make peace with him.

"Do you want me to get Dr. Tate?"

He shook his head *no* as he stared at me. I sniffled and sat down, accepting the fresh handkerchief he'd offered to dab my eyes. "Mr. Rayman, I'm upset, not just from this news, but from wounds of the past. It's too late for us to start over, but I will always remember the good things you brought to my life, as my mentor and friend." I slowly took his hand. "I agree that Jake should oversee the proceedings, whenever the need arises. Don't fret over this anymore. I'll be fine."

He smiled after I kissed him on the forehead, seemingly comforted by our truce. I got up and walked towards the door. "Mr. Rayman, I have one more question," I said, looking back at him. "My mother? Where is she?"

Mr. Rayman looked through tear-filled eyes, but before he could say anything, Gladys appeared at the door. "I'm right here," she said softly. "I'm your mother, Jasmine."

"You?" I whispered through trembling lips. A tear rolled down her face as she cautiously wrapped her arms around me. I stood numb, resting my chin on her shoulder as she held me tight.

"I'm not proud of what I did, but I gave you to Frances, so you'd have more from this world than I could offer. Every time you set foot in this house, I wished I could tell you that you was my own."

I moved away from her. "You could have!" I shouted, crossing my arms over my body.

Gladys wrung her hands. "Tellin' you then could've changed the good future you had ahead, and tellin' you later, wouldn't have eased the pain I see on your face right now."

She reached out to me. "I'm so sorry, Jasmine. Please try to understand."

Blinded by my tears, I backed out the door in silence, running down the hallway and then down the marble steps.

***

"Start talking!" I shouted after I stormed through Aunt Frances' front door.

I plopped down in her recliner as she stood in the middle of the living room floor, staring down at the tea steaming in her mug.

"I'm sorry you had to find out this way, chile," she said, shaking her head.

I snatched the throw pillow from behind me and smashed it between my hands. "I didn't need to find out this way!"

Frances sighed as she sat on the sofa across from me. She rested her mug on the coffee table, scratching her head. "Gladys say anything to you?"

I swallowed hard. "She tried, but I couldn't take it anymore. I had to get out of there."

"You know Gladys and I been friends for years, don't you?"

I slowly nodded.

"Well, when we got outta school, I decided I was gonna be a nurse, and she wanted to go off to design school, in New York. When they told her she didn't get accepted, I reckon because of her color, she was crushed. Eventually, she started working for the Raymans. She said it would be temporary, until she saved up enough to have her own little boutique on the island. Rayman took a liking to her. At first, she thought he just wanted to get under her skirt. After a year of her working there, though, they got close. Mrs. Rayman was into being a socialite more than a wife. Gladys was Mr. Rayman's confidante. They shared their dreams and decided to be lovers. She had been seeing a young man from Belle Marsh, named Leonard when she got pregnant. Rayman was the only man she'd been with, and when she told him, he didn't question it. Mrs. Rayman didn't think nothin' of it, either. She was expectin,' preparing a nursery for their boy, Victor. When Leonard stopped courtin' Gladys, everybody just assumed he was a deadbeat, leaving Gladys in a family way. Rayman offered to send her to Paris. That was her dream. To travel the world and study fashion."

I raised my hands. "What happened? Did she go?"

"Naw, 'cause she didn't wanna be no brushed-off mistress, pregnant and alone in another country. Her folks moved to Decatur, and told her to make a life for herself. So, she stayed with me, and I delivered you. When she went back to the Raymans, she asked me to raise you."

I sucked my teeth. "So, the secret was safe."

"Jasmine, Gladys has always loved you."

"Humph, not enough to keep me," I said under my breath.

She slapped her knee. "Stop being so spiteful!"

"Why did *she* abandon me!"

"Why are *you* sleeping with a married man?"

I looked down, slightly embarrassed by her inquiry.

She pushed herself up. "Yeah, shut ya up for a second, didn't

I?" she huffed, putting her hand on her hip. "No need to pout, 'cause your actions say you grown. Life ain't a bed of roses. We human, and things happen. You just gotta pick yourself up, and keep goin' the best way you know how." She pulled me up into a bear hug. "Sometimes when you keep lookin' back, you miss the rainbow God tryin' to show you ahead."

"Aunt Frances, you're the only person I've loved that's never left me," I muffled as I rested my head on her bosom.

She stroked my hair. "There's two things I'm most proud of... being a nurse, and raising you to be the fine woman that you are. You've helped people. You've mentored our young girls on the island, giving them a slice of your spirit to succeed. Don't let that beacon of light go out, baby. Your survival through all the madness thrown your way—let that strength inside you be your redemption." She patted my back. "Why don't you go back to that mansion, and talk to Gladys?"

I shook my head slowly as I pulled away. "I'm sorry, Aunt Frances, but I'm not ready to do that. I'm not ready," I cried, walking out.

YOUR HEART'S IN GOOD HANDS

I purposely missed my father's funeral, opting to spend the day grappling with myself in solitude. The next morning, I attended Jake's meeting with the Raymans. I claimed my generous inheritance in silence, among the curses and cries of a family who would never claim me as their own. When the reading concluded, I bustled out, ignoring the calls of Gladys. Our newfound fortune combined...well over a million dollars. Time invested together, as mother and daughter—still bordering on bankrupt.

***

I felt warm hands caress my shoulders as I stared at my husband's headstone. "Seem like you got more time to spend in the cemetery than with me," Harrison said, wrapping his arms around my waist.

"Harrison, I wanna be alone right now. I got some things on my mind."

"I don't have a say in this? Been a month since Rayman's funeral, and I ain't seen ya. Talk to me."

I sighed. "My whole life has been one big question mark."

"Ain't that how everybody's life seem?"

"You don't understand."

Harrison held me tighter. "I know you gotta stop staring at these bones, if you ever wanna get out of livin' in the past."

I pushed him away, cutting my eyes at him. "Don't be disrespectful, Harrison. This was my husband."

He grimaced, pointing to the ground. "This here is dirt and bones, and over yonder is dirt and bones for your daddy, too!"

I hauled a hard slap to his face. Harrison grabbed my arms, shaking me against his body.

"Let me go!" I screamed.

"I'ma let you get away with hittin' me, 'cause you hurtin' and tryin' to deny it!" He released my arms, but still held me close to him. "I got your number. You ain't as big and bad as you think, and I ain't Otis. You not gonna treat me like some chump. I may be younger, but I'm not a fool with his dick hangin' between his legs, foamin' at the mouth." He toyed with a strand of my hair, softly kissing my temple. "You can stop this tough-girl routine. I wanna help you through hard times," he said in a softer tone. "Mourn if you gotta, but don't let sadness take over who you are. Dirt and bones? That's how you want to remember love? Or do you want to feel alive with me?"

I sucked my teeth, turning my back to him. "What am I supposed to do? Fuck you until you forgive Naomi?"

He wrapped his arms around me, rocking me amidst the chill of an autumn breeze. "I don't love her no more, and you know it. I love you, and you love me, so quit looking at this grave. You mighta been Adam's baby doll, but you my Eve, now. You gonna sin and make mistakes, just like everybody else. A degree don't save you from being lost in this cold-ass world. We the same, Jasmine. Brokenhearted and trying to find our way back to somethin' safe."

I placed my hands over his, giving in to his touch. He turned me to look into his eyes.

"I coulda died in Vietnam, and you coulda died the night you lost your baby. But we didn't. We made it...and I believe we're made for each other." Harrison held my chin. "I don't want nothin' from you, but your heart. What we got is real, and I know you feel it. Stop actin' like you don't need nobody. That's all I ask."

"I love you, Harrison," I said, holding him tight.

He picked me up into his arms. "I love you, Miss Jasmine, and as long as we got each other, we gonna be all right."

I WANNA HOLD YOU

Under a cloud-covered sky, Harrison removed the black silk scarf that covered my hair. Unbuttoning my black satin blouse next, he planted a kiss on my neck as I loosened his trousers, sending them to the floor.

We stood naked behind the shield of oak shutters that adorned his bedroom window. The slats were open just enough to allow the moon room to cast a hue against our silhouette.

"I've missed you so much," Harrison said as he held my face.

"I don't wanna be without you again," I whispered.

His smile met mine, brewing a passionate kiss. The dance of our tongues screamed fire and desire.

"I need to feel you now," he moaned.

"Take it, Harrison. I belong to you," I said, lying on the bed.

He sucked my pussy as I stroked his manhood, loving the feel of him pulsating against my palm. I spread my legs further, in anticipation of his thickness breaking through my flesh. When he entered me, I gasped. "Harrison, you inside of me feels like Heaven."

He smiled. "That's how love should feel."

His deep thrusts matched the rise of my hips in perfect time. Tongues intertwined, we smothered each other with kisses. Our breathing was labored, but not to the point of climactic heights. I moved on top of him, grinding my being into his. He closed his eyes as I leaned my body closer and flexed my muscles around his dick.

"Umm...Jasmine, I can't get enough of this tight-ass pussy," he moaned.

I arched my back and bounced up and down his glistening rod. "Ahh...Harrison. Ooh...I'm cumin'!"

"Shit, I'm lovin' all this sweet nectar coming from your pussy!"

I slowed my ride back to a grind, collapsing on his chest. He positioned me on my back, and widened my limbs against his shoulders. He plunged into me. "Harrison, don't hold back," I whimpered.

Harrison pressed my legs back further. "You okay?" he whispered in my ear. I nodded *yes* as I caressed his head, knowing that even in his most vulnerable moment, he still cared about me. My hands massaged the sweat on his back as I savored his dick thickening against my walls. Our pelvises beat like a drum. Harrison went deeper...I winced, he hollered as he climaxed. I held his shivering body firm, fully satisfied from the privilege to be one with him.

He kissed my lips softly as our bodies rested side by side. "You're so beautiful to me."

I smiled as I snuggled under the bed sheet with him. "Tell me why you think I'm beautiful."

"Your touch makes me feel like I can trust a woman again. You gotta way of erasin' the pain, like it wasn't even there. Jasmine, I need you so much. Please don't give up on me."

I held his hand. "I love being with you, and I want nothing more than to share my life with you. I just hope you don't grow tired of me."

He frowned as he touched my chin. "Whatcha talkin,' woman?"

I shrugged. "Harrison, there's ten years between us. Every day when I look in the mirror, I see changes. A woman's looks change."

He wrapped his arms around me. "Looks don't have nothin' to do with being beautiful, in my book. I married a good-lookin' gal; but I pray I'll get a chance to spend the rest of my days with a beautiful woman."

I blushed, looking down. "I found a gray hair down there."

He smiled. "I saw somethin,' but it wasn't gray." He eased his hand between my thighs, and fingered my pubic curls. "What I saw was precious silver, making my heart want you more and more." He cupped my full breasts. "You a mature woman. That's what I love about you," he said, removing the sheet from around me.

Harrison kissed the faint lines of stretch marks along my hips, resting his lips on the small bulge in my midsection that had not shrunk from pregnancy. "Any man that can't appreciate a woman's body changin' to bring forth life, ain't a man. I'm never gonna give you reason to doubt yourself, Miss Jasmine. Don't let ten years keep you wonderin'. Every new discovery gonna be good for us, and I can't wait for the good times to come."

GUILTY

A loud bang sent Harrison and I scrambling out of bed. I was groggy from sleep, but I clearly saw Naomi's pistol pointed at my naked body.

"Naomi, what the hell ya doin'!" Harrison screamed, running toward her.

"Get back!" she spat, aiming the gun at his chest. "I'll deal with you in a minute."

She walked over to me, pulling my hair so hard, it made me crouch down. "I told ya this wasn't over, bitch!"

"Please...lemme go!" I cried from her yanking my head.

"Naomi, don't do this..."

"Don't do what, Harrison? Don't make her beg for her life! Shut up, and stay back. You didn't wanna talk things out before, so don't talk to me now! This between me and this yella heifer, who think she gonna replace me."

"Jasmine..."

"Don't talk to her! Get on your knees," she ordered, pushing me down. "You ain't hot stuff now, are you?"

I shook my head as tears ran down my face. My body trembled in fear as she placed the gun to my head.

She looked at Harrison. "Go get the extra laundry rope from out back."

"Naomi, don't hurt…"

"You got two seconds to move the other way, 'fore I shoot this tramp!"

"Harrison, do what she says!" I yelled. He ran out as she pulled me up to my feet, keeping the gun snug on my temple. "Naomi, please just lemme leave…I'll go away, peacefully. I'll leave Harrison be, just please."

"Shut up!" Naomi hollered. "I ain't bargainin' wit ya!" She shot a glance at Harrison holding the rope. "What took ya so long?" He gripped the rope in his hands, his brow saturated from nervousness. Naomi smirked. "I know what you was doin.' You tried to find your other shotgun, but I got that one, too. Wives know they husbands' hidin' places. You too busy stickin' it to this one, you ain't move your guns, or change the locks. Guess you wanted me to come back, didn't you, baby?" He kept quiet. "Didn't you!"

"Yeah…yes, Naomi." He raised his hands in the air. "Now, please…."

She shoved me into him. "Use that chair over there in the corner, and tie her up!"

I gasped for air as I cowered against his chest. He slowly stepped to the side, with his hands in front of him. "Naomi, I wronged you, and I'm sorry. Don't hurt Jasmine. It's me you want."

"That's right, and no one else gonna have you, but me. Tie her ass up, now!" Sorrow covered his face as I held out my wrists, and he bound them. Naomi held the gun with both hands to keep steady. She sniffled through tears. "You made me do this, Harrison! Leave me for Vietnam, and then leave me again, for her! I cheated on you, because you always found some excuse to leave me! That's why I had Floyd's baby! He had time for me!"

Harrison frowned, shifting his body as if he wanted to charge at her.

"Don't...," I muffled softly to him.

"Don't try me," she said, getting closer to us with the gun. She shook her head at Harrison with contempt in her eyes. "You had no right to throw me out! We got vows, you and me. You run off to fix her problems, instead of fixin' the problems in your own damn house! Tie her to the chair!"

He did as she instructed, looking at me the whole time. My body shook as I stared at the sincerity in his eyes. I didn't blame him for this. It was me who entertained the indiscretion that jeopardized our lives.

Bound in the chair, I watched in horror as Naomi pointed the gun to Harrison's penis.

"I was never good enough for you, was I?"

"Naomi...," he said softly.

"Answer me!"

He clasped his hands in prayer fashion. "You were good, Naomi. You were good, and I'm sorry for all this. Please..."

"Show me." Naomi tugged at her flowered silk dress, busting all the buttons. "Show me how good," she said, curling her lips seductively as she exposed her nude body. "Lay down on the bed, with your hands above ya head."

Harrison slowly backed up to the bed with his hands in the air as she pointed the gun to his chest. She groped him until he was hard, then mounted him rough.

"Ummm...," she moaned, rocking back and forth. "I'ma make sure you remember whose dick this is, you hear?"

I closed my eyes, not by the scene taking place in front of me, but from the tears spewing from the corners of Harrison's eyes.

"Open your eyes, bitch!" she screamed at me.

"And you open your mouth!" she hollered at him, probing the gun between his lips.

"You willin' to die for this pussy, huh?" she moaned, as she jerked rapidly on top of him.

"Uhhhmm...," Harrison groaned, nodding his head.

She reared her head back in chilling laughter. "Well, darlin', cum...and die!"

I heard a snap from the gun at the same time Harrison tackled Naomi.

"You bastard!" she cried.

"Harrison, no!" I screamed.

Bang!

"Harrison!" Naomi and I both screamed in unison.

Bang!

"No!" I cringed, holding my head in my hands. Harrison's eyes bulged. He fell back hard to the floor, unconscious, as Naomi's lifeless body collided with his.

FULL OF FIRE

Crimson, the color of blood. Tears, clear in color—I'd tasted the saltiness of them both, too many times. Like waves from the deep blue sea, pain can wipe you out. In the midst of a storm, you drown, or you find strength you never knew you had, to fight for your life.

Three people, different in so many ways, soldered together by lies. Ignoring the truth, casting patience to the wind, wanting fulfillment for selfish needs. Harrison, Naomi, and I gambled with hearts, and we were forced to face tragic consequences.

The gun jammed the first time, giving Harrison opportunity to fight. The second shot overpowered him, and I knew I'd lost another soldier whom I'd loved. Naomi witnessed the agony on Harrison's face, blood streaming from his body as he hit the floor. It was at that moment, I believe she realized how much she loved him. Her cries of regret echoed the walls, and she put the gun to her head, taking her own life.

LET'S STAY TOGETHER

APRIL, 1973

Does a year change anything? I believe it does, when you allow time to remove pride, and order your steps in its own way. Each tragedy had drawn me closer to death. Fallen lives I'd cherished, etched forever in my brain to the brink of madness. Just when I was about to give in to the storm's tide, a miracle supplied a lifeline. Harrison survived the gunshot wound to the chest. I let go of the past, and embraced the opportunity to start over.

I released the bitterness that had dulled my senses. I lost a father, but I was grateful to still have Gladys. The day after the shooting, I visited her new home on St. Simons Island. We embraced, talked for hours, and began a legacy that I prayed would beautifully transcend time. Her gift to me, my identity. My gift to her, forgiveness. We planned a vacation to Paris, a place where we could dream together and explore the world, happy.

Aunt Frances had prepared a "Bon Voyage" breakfast. Everyone was gathered at the table, eating honey ham and biscuits. I felt blessed to have been given a second chance to love my family: Harrison—the best friend I married on New Year's Day; Keenan— a sweet bundle of joy, the son we adopted; Frances—the devoted aunt, whose tough love gave me the courage to stand; and Gladys— the beautiful woman I welcomed into my mended heart. Our time together, now cherished like a rare jewel.

***

Gladys and I said our good-byes and held hands as we walked along the dock. Aunt Frances held Keenan, while he waved and blew kisses. Harrison lugged our bags to the ferry. I laughed at him as he held his back, teasing me about the load of "must have" outfits that I probably wouldn't wear. He kissed Gladys on the cheek and pulled me into his arms.

"Good luck on your contractor's test tomorrow," I said, kissing him.

He winked. "I'll ace it."

"Holmes Construction, Incorporated. Sounds good to me."

"You sayin' it, sounds even better. Thanks for believin' in me." I smiled as I trailed my finger over the thin mustache he'd allowed to grow above his sexy lips. "Thanks for being everything I need."

As the ferry pulled off, I hugged my mother tight. We released tears of joy, while sunrays trailed brilliantly along the rippling water. *Dayclean* in Sapelo is still beautiful. When light erases the dark velvet of night, and the sun's warmth awakens us, hope begins.

ଚ୍ଚର

Shawan Lewis received her bachelor of science degree in sociology from James Madison University. After years of working in the insurance industry, Ms. Lewis stepped out on faith to pursue a career in writing. She is the author of the novels Help Wanted *(2007) and* Final Game *(2008), published by Urban Books. In her spare time, she enjoys reading, collecting Billie Holiday memorabilia, dancing, listening to jazz music, and traveling. She resides in Baltimore, Maryland with her daughter.*

Shawan would like to thank her family, Zane, Jonathan Luckett, Urban Soul, and agent Audra Barrett for the support of her literary endeavors.

Please visit the website at www.shawanlewis.com for author updates and book information. Shawan can also be reached at shawanlewis@aol.com.

THE GODDESS OF DESIRE

OF DESIRE

DYWANE D. BIRCH

RAGHABA
WHO BEHOLDS ME, BEHOLDS THE DESIRES OF THEIR HEART

Curvaceous, perfectly formed, I was masturbated into existence by my father who took his engorged phallus in his grasp and repetitiously stroked so that he might create an orgasm. And so I am that which men and the gods crave. I am the longing that slips into their dreams and settles into the basin of their loins, then erupts into delicious pleasures. Alluring, enticing, I am she who breaks their resolve, fulfills their wants, and leaves them longing for more. Though I will never be spoken of, or listed among the goddesses of ancient Kemet, which will one day be known as Egypt—the mother of civilization—I do exist. And my story—yesterday and today—along the edges of the Nile, during the rule of Ramses II, shall be written on the papyrus by the scribe of cunning fingers who will attempt to bury my treasured memory into the earth. Yet, he will fail. For it will be during the *Akhet*, season of the flood, when the Nile rises and swells across the land that I will be uncovered. And all that I am, all that I shall be, will be filled with tales of lasciviousness and reckless abandon that will extend across the continent, and throughout the universe, spreading into the hearts and minds of mortals for centuries to come.

And just like the gods and goddesses before me who guide and direct the natural forces of the mind and body, these mortals shall bear witness to the carnal aching that consumes them and causes them to act out deeds that may fulfill them, or become that which destroys them. They shall be driven by desperation and obsession which shall poison their will to deny themselves, and they shall seek out enjoyment anywhere, anyhow, anyplace—by any means necessary; for I am all things that will manifest themselves in good, bad and indifferent.

Until such time, I shall sit before you and bring forth the pleasures of all whosoever might yearn. Without fear, without regret, I share with you bountiful fruits of passion. Come... breathe in my intoxicating beauty, savor my scented womanhood, and relish in the joys that overwhelm and stretch the imagination. Behold, I am Raghaba...the Goddess of Desire.

⊷═◉═⊷

"Raghaba...Raghaba...Raghaba...come to me, my love. I am restless with a fire that flows through my being, causing flames to erupt from the eye of my loins. Only you can quench these embers that threaten to ignite and spread. I awake craving you..."

It is this voice, crisp and clear, that stirs me from a peaceful slumber. I open my eyes and stretch. It is the awakening of another day as the sky opens up to receive the sun on the eastern horizon, its brightness shining the promise of another glorious day.

I rise early, eager to greet Horus—son of Osiris, the god of the dead. He has summoned me in his dreams for two seasons, and I have ignored his prodding. In my mind's eye, I have seen him stroke himself and spill forth the milk of his loins in hopes that I shall greedily lap it up and become full with his seeds. But I have not been keen to satisfy his carnal urges...until now.

It is the dampness between my thighs, and the intense desire that spreads through my body and consumes me, enticing me to slip my fingers into the center of my being and lightly brush over the front of my vagina—awakening my clitoris, that brings me to the decision to have him. And today, as he has dreamt and fantasized, I shall bring him into my home, spread open my legs, and welcome him into paradise.

It has been almost six seasons since his return to the Upper Nile from the Nubian Desert in the land of Kush—which shall be called Nubia. And, though he has kept his distance from me, his roaming eyes have been filled with adoration each time he lays them upon me. But I am not amused with such lustful stares. He has not gone without the pleasures of other goddesses who have thrown themselves at his feet and have allowed him to suckle at their breasts and journey through their womanhoods, whetting his sexual appetite. His seeds have been planted deep into the womb of plenty. Yet, he still remains unsatisfied, thirsting for more—for none have been able to feed his insatiable hunger for sex. And because I have not given into his persistent imaginings, his urges have intensified.

But tonight, when the sun greets the moon and kisses the points of each star, Horus will be granted a taste of what he desires. And to ensure that he does not weaken when the time has come to roll down the bed coverings and take to the bed, I will prepare him a hearty meal of roasted hyena seasoned with sesame and fennel (along with antelope that has been lightly brushed with fenugreek) and he shall be served bread and hummus while I eat my dish of bolti and lentils with onions.

Nefer…nefer…you capture me with your eyes…

"Beautiful, beautiful," the voice in his dream is calling. And in the eyes of the gods, I *am* beautiful. I smile as I head to the flat, thatched roof to light the cylindrical clay oven before the sun's rays blaze down onto the earth, and it becomes too hot to bear the oven's heat.

I busy myself around my modest mud brick home with the double-thick walls. I sweep the clay tiles in the central room—the room in the center of the house where it is most protected from the heat—shake out the reed mats on the floor, wipe down the area for eating, fluff and shake the mattress made of woven cords, then sprinkle jasmine and rose petals over the linen sheets. I draw the net covering around the rectangular wooden bed to keep the gnats and mosquitoes from pestering the space that will become drenched with the sweat of passion upon the fall of the sun.

I glance out of the open window along the length of the north wall. It is still early enough for a breeze, which blows from the north, to air the house. The rest of my windows are close to the ceiling to maintain the cool temperature. But as the sun rises to its resting point, so shall the heat and its burning strength. I try hard to block the thought of the looming high temperature out of my head, but its presence is all around me.

I sigh as my eyes fix on the sand dunes slightly to the right of the house, erected as barriers from the Nile's floodwaters, and think about the water that flows from the heart of the tropics—which begin to rise at the summer solstice as a result of the rainy season of Ethiopia, and continue to do so for one hundred days, before it recedes. It is the rise and fall of the waters that holds the fate of our land. Too little, or too much, could mean sad devastation—the loss of crop and famine. I imagine myself naked splashing about in the waters, alongside the banks, and chuckle at the thought of wrestling crocodiles in the nude and riding the backs of muddy hippos.

Then, somehow, I imagine myself climbing, naked and free, traveling the distance of the framed rocky walls that form cliffs which dip down to the Nile's edge, then shoot up with covered tips of fine white limestone, to rich yellow sandstone, then higher up to red granite and black basalt—all these cliffs forming the horizon of all landscape views in beautiful Kemet. Then I imagine lying under the stars with my legs spread wide—the sand beneath my bare bottom gleaming like endless diamonds—exposing the golden brown lips of my smooth vagina as I pull open its slit with my fingers and wait for probing fingers, lips, and tongues to explore its sweetness. I can hear the low roar that escapes me as I lift my hips and grind and grind and grind against the sensations until I start to shake, then explode in ecstasy. From whence such thoughts originate I am unsure, but they amuse me, nonetheless—at least for the moment.

The sight of two lion cubs playing catches my attention, and pulls me from my daydream. I inhale a deep breath, close my eyes, and silently pray to Min, the god of fertility and sexuality, asking him to keep the blessings of my sexuality and high sex drive bestowed upon me in this life and in the afterlife, so that I might continue to engage in sex as part of the joys of paradise. Even as gods and goddesses we are earthy enough to copulate, and to enjoy the pleasures of sex. And I want to be able to satisfy and indulge my libido here and into the world beyond.

When everything is finally prepared, I place a clay jar of beer and of wine on the table. Though Horus will not need libation to be in the mood, it will loosen his tongue and allow him to speak out to the heavens so that the gods before him might hear his moans of unadulterated and uninhibited ecstasy. Tonight, there shall be no line drawn in the sand; there will be no boundaries. And I shall quench his thirst, and my own, for sexual pleasure.

I burn kyphi, an assortment of myrrh, henna, cinnamon and juniper, and allow its fragrance to soften the staleness that has lingered in the air while I bathe. I enter the washing area—a recessed room that has a square slab of limestone in the corner, for standing—and oil my pubic area. I will shave to ensure it is smooth as silk. Next are my eyebrows. Removing body hair is not only for beauty, but it rids the body of lice. Though I shall not ever shave my head, I have been fortunate to not be visited by such nuisances as fleas, bedbugs or lice.

I use ground beans from the ricinus communis plant and oil to rub into my hair. It is what maintains the lustrous growth of my flowing mane. I let it set upon my head while I shave. When I am finished, I use a cleansing paste of water and natron to cleanse my body, then shampoo my hair. I rinse myself, watch the water empty out into a bowl in the floor below, then dry off and wrap my body in a linen towel. Another towel is wrapped around my hair as I saunter into my bedroom and sit at my dressing table. The day is quickly beginning to take flight, the sun's rays already dancing against the brightness of the room. And I am struggling to not break a sweat. I can already feel beads of perspiration popping up against my skin like goose bumps.

I fan myself a bit so that I might cool, then pull out a solid gold hand mirror and stare into it, studying my features. I smile at what I see. Skin the color of honey, thin nose with full, inviting lips. Tall and sultry—with oval, mesmerizing green eyes that sparkle like precious stones—I am the fairest of them all. I thank Hathor— mother goddess and goddess of all that is best in women—for the blessings she has bestowed upon me. My exquisite beauty is striking, and oozes with sensuality. My presence alone announces my sexuality—free-spirited and open-minded, willing to indulge in all things pleasing to the body. And it is a reminder of why no man can deny me. It is no wonder that men are unable to resist me against their own temptations. And no wonder that I am every woman's nightmare.

I rub myself with almond oil to keep my soft skin moisturized and protected against the harshness of the sun. Though my flawless complexion does not warrant much, I reach under my table and retrieve a jar of khol and a pencil made of reed to line my eyes and eyebrows. When I have perfected the signature lines about my upper and lower eyelids, extending to the sides of my face, I dip my thin reed brush into a jar of henna and paint my lips. While most of the goddesses don wigs made of human hair or wool, I maintain natural tresses—thick, long, shiny black hair—that falls to my shoulders—with blunt-cut bangs. From the roots, I run my fingers through my silky hair, then brush and pin it up with jeweled pins. I dab Lotus oil behind my ears, under the crease of my breasts and along the inner part of my thighs. The use of unguents enhance my *khaibt*—special body odor. It causes the gods to draw to me like hungry flies swarming over a rotted carcass, and I will shoo them, swat at them, but allow them to dance with their fantasies afar.

I return to the central room and lay out a bronze bowl of cactus figs, grapes, plums and dates, then wash and rinse the tall, straight lettuce and press its leaves for its milky substance. It is an aphrodisiac. And tonight, I will drink its secretions and prepare myself for the feast of lovemaking. And to prevent the seeds Horus will plant deep inside of me from spreading and taking root, I grind together a measure of acacia nuts with honey, then moisten seed-wool and insert it into my vagina, covering the mouth of my uterus, to prevent pregnancy; for I am as fertile as the Nile.

And—in a land where a woman's femininity and desirability is contingent on her ability to bear sons and daughters—pregnancy is something to be proud of, and motherhood is venerated. However, bringing forth a child is not what I crave. The thought of nursing a child for three years, its teeth sinking into my breasts, nauseates me. Where the women strive to emulate Isis—mother goddess to Horus—because she represents all that a mother should be: loving, clever, loyal and brave, the purest example of the loving wife and mother, I am not motivated by such beliefs. My womanhood, my femininity, my sensuality, is not—nor will it ever be—defined by my ability to conceive or bear children. If it were, I would have taken a mate and be in a lifelong monogamous relationship, which by custom, should have occurred around age twelve or a bit older since it is common practice to wed young. Oh, joy! I would just as well slice my wrist, then toss myself into the Nile to be eaten by the crocodiles before becoming a *hemet*—wife, or be saddled down with three or four children, provided, that is, they survived the birthing.

So, no, I shall not be lured into such trappings, nor shall I ever live a life of unhappiness just for the sake of conforming to the whimsical thoughts of others. And I will continue to defy all things that apply to such beliefs that have to do with marriage and children. I am young—twenty and vivacious—and full of carnal passion. And I will live my life according to my own will.

I return to the roof to check on the meats, which are roasting well, brushing them with more seasons. When the meats are done, I store them in a clay pan, then return to my bedroom to finish beautifying myself. Once I am satisfied with all the preparations, I slip into my white diaphanous gown of fine linen, its transparency revealing the tips of dark, succulent nipples—erect and inviting. I adorn myself with a gold and diamond headband, hang a gold ankh and lotus necklace around my slender neck, then slip in earrings made of lapis lazuli—the deep blue stones catching the sun and sparkling about the room.

I walk out the door, greet the day with a smile, then stroll along the groves lined with sycamore and persea, one foot in front of the other. I am as graceful as all the goddesses before me were, my dress billowy, my stride giddy and light as I step on the earth.

Along the way, my mind begins to wander again, and I conjure up thoughts of how I will seduce Horus and shake the heavens. My clit begins to swell and peek out beneath its hood with the images that now swirl about in my head. Images of what might hang in the center of his crotch and the heaviness of the pouch of skin that holds his seeds, slapping against me as he slams and twists and grinds and snaps his hips into me flash through my head. Images of gyrating myself atop him, tempting him, taunting him, to reach for me as I roll my hips fast and deep, gripping the length of him send a heat coursing through my skin, through my breasts and that heat settles on the tip of my clitoris, waiting to be released. I dare myself from taking shade under a willow tree and pinching away at the prickly sensations that are nagging me. It has been three moons since I have pleasured myself. And now these images that have found space in my head have sprouted a dire need for release.

My thoughts are quickly disrupted by a deep, piercing voice calling out to me. "Raghaba, Raghaba..." I hear, cutting into my space. I glance over my shoulder, keeping pace. A sly smile forms across my face. Behind me is Hapi, god of the Nile, running to catch up to the scent that leads him to me. His full breasts, naked and free, bounce about as he closes the gap between us. "Wait for me…"

I slow my steps.

He sprints up to me like a gazelle, fast and graceful. "… *hotep*," he says, his breath catching in his throat, "You have trampled my thoughts, my awakened moments consumed with the beauty of Raghaba."

I am not amused. "And may the gods bring peace unto you. Now, why have you come?" I ask, keeping my eyes ahead, dismissing what has fallen from his tongue. I ask, but I know. He has smelled the honey that gathers between my thighs, and longs to drink from its cup.

"Are we not destined to feast on the passion that stirs between us?"

I stop, stare, then allow my eyes to linger. Hmm…his lips are beautiful; full, juicy, suck-able, mocha-colored lips that look as soft as lambs' wool. His strong face is that of a man, but his body, with breasts that nourish Kemet, is not to my liking. He shall never enter himself, nor empty himself, into me. A hermaphrodite god is not my fancy. But, I entertain vibrant thoughts of feeling his lips against my clit, and become tempted to indulge. "Foolish one," I say. "There is no passion that stirs itself within me for you. You can offer me nothing, but the warmth of your tongue."

His gaze wanders lecherously over my body, his eyes traveling the curves that form me. "Then I shall caress your sweetness with my tongue under a *nehet*, and quench my thirst for you."

"So be it," I say, walking off toward a willow tree to catch the shade. "Let's be quick so that I may race the sun before it reaches its highest point. I do not wish to sweat out my hair or have my body reek of messy deeds."

He keeps step behind me, removing his loincloth, then spreading it out onto the ground. I lift my gown up over my hips, and sit, facing him. I glance up at his manhood. It is long and skinny with a curve, its head as thick as a plum. *No*, I think, *he shall never slither his snake inside of me.*

"My *ba* shall be rested now," he states, kneeling down before me, licking his lips.

My eyes roll up in the back of my head. "Spare me. Your thirst for me has nothing to do with your soul," I snap, leaning back and spreading my legs. "Now, cease talk and allow your mouth and tongue to do what's in your thoughts."

A smile forms on his face as he parts the lips of my sweet basin with his fingers, then blows on my clitoris. The opening of my vulva, filled with the richness of brown and pink colliding together against the center of its seam, is waiting, soft, wet and ready.

I lean back on my forearms, and watch him bury his face between my thighs. He licks in the center, his tongue thick, long and warm, flapping up and down along the seam of soft flesh. He darts his tongue in, then out. In. Out. In. Out. Flicks it against my tender clit, nudging it ever so gently; then he mounts his mouth around it.

A moan escapes me. I am starting to hear the song of birds overhead. "Oh, yes...eat me...mmm...devour my goodness... leave nothing untouched," I say.

He is slurping me, exploring me, ravishing me. "Mmmm," he moans, kissing the space his tongue journeyed. "You are as sweet as a melon..."—he flicks his tongue against my clit, again and again—"...Oh, Raghaba, between your sweet thighs lie my greatest desires."

He dips his tongue back into me, massages my clitoris as I raise my hips off the ground and grind against his mouth.

"Mmmm…uh…uh," I moan.

Beneath the burning sky, beads of sweat threaten to roll down my face and back as I am nearing orgasm. I clutch the sand with my toes as he digs deeper into me. He is trying to unearth hidden treasures with his tongue, trying to unlock a jeweled chest full of liquid passion. I brush my hardened nipples with the tips of my fingers. My long lashes flutter, my eyes flit up, then roll up in my head as I let out a deep moan that causes everything around us to pause and take notice. The plover burying its egg in the sand, the lion grazing, the gazelles running to and fro, the scarab beetles rolling dung about, the vulture stalking over the carcass of a jackal, they all become paralyzed in the throes of my moans. I arch my back, lift my legs, wrap them around his neck, and let him lap his way to the key until its locks snap open and a warm fountain of joy gushes out, filling his mouth, and dripping down his chin. My body shudders as I soak the cloth beneath me with my juice and scent.

Hapi keeps his mouth mounted around my vulva, suckling and moaning—begging for the last droplets of my overflowing juices. When he is done, he kisses my vagina one last time, then pulls his face from between my legs, his lips glistening, his chin streaked, with pleasure, his face and chest shining with sweat. I close my eyes for a moment, toss my head back and attempt to recover from the powerful orgasm. My insides are still trembling. I pull in deep breaths. Inhale. Exhale. Inhale. I wait for my heart to stop racing about, then open my eyes. Hapi stands, his serpent-looking phallus swaying about, its head swollen and large. He strokes it, looking down lustfully at me.

"I have drunk from your lips and have been filled, and now my loins seek release."

I raise my brow, wiping myself with his loincloth, then standing up. "Then I suggest you suckle on your breast," I say, tossing him his garment, "and stroke your own organ so that it may find the release it seeks; for I will not be the one who pleasures you."

He brings the soiled cloth to his nose and inhales, deeply. "Then I shall breathe in your scent and unleash the fire that burns within."

I have no further use for him. The sight of his breasts and skinny phallus sicken me.

"Do what you will. Leave me so I might continue on my way."

"*Hotep*," he says as he begins to stroke himself.

"And peace unto you."

I too inhale the scent that still hovers in the air, and gather myself, leaving him under the *nehet* where he will spill his seeds into the earth with thoughts of me, Raghaba—the goddess of desire.

Looking forward I see the mud brick palace that once belonged to Khnum, the creator of all things, and wonder what will become of all things that shall be. There is a light breeze that is stifled by the searing heat. But, despite its intensity, I am thankful. I am blessed. I lift my head to the sky, and allow its fiery rays to fall upon my honey-golden face as I give praise to Nut, the sky goddess, and Ra, the sun god, for harmony. I smile to Sekhmet, the goddess of war, and thank her for peace and protection. And, then, I spread my arms wide and give glory to Ma'at, goddess of truth, balance and order, for keeping all things aligned.

Through the gardens, I hear the frolicking and chatter of female voices, and silence finds itself before me as I pass by, glaring eyes pierce me. Suddenly whispers move with the wind and I strain to hear. I wonder if it is the same wind that has carried my moans through the air.

"Ssh, Raghaba is coming. She will hear."

"Let her," Nephthys says snidely. "She is useless dung."

How dare she insult me! I fight the urge to summon the gods for her head so that it may be put on display. She is hateful and bitter because she is as dry as the desert, and as ugly as a camel. And because she is not fertile, she is not for the taking in marriage. Yet she hungers for the love and attention of Horus whose eyes do not flicker with desire for her. Ha! Foolish one! Yet, it is I whom she chooses to blame for her despair. Little does she know I do not want him or his affection, just what hangs underneath his garment between his strong, muscular thighs. And when I have tired of him, I shall discard him as I do all the others. A wicked smile forms on my lips as thoughts of what the night will bring dance in my head. I am everything she wishes to be, and all things she will never possess.

Her eyes follow me as she continues, "I will pray and give offering that Ra will scorch her womb and blister her skin."

"But she is adored by the gods."

"They are feeble fools," she snaps, "who know not what she is. She lures them in with her exquisiteness, contaminates their minds with fantasies, then thickens their hearts against love. Beneath her lies the goddess of deceit."

I stop and turn to face her. Her stare is locked on mine. I throw my head back and laugh at Nephthys and the pettiness of the rest of them, keeping my glare on her. She is taken aback. "Do not hate on my youth and beauty. Nor speak malice with your tongues because your gods turn their necks and massage images of me into their heads. I give your men and the gods what you shall not dare."

"And it is you," Nephthys spats, "who poisons them from our beds. Your lair is a scorpion's nest."

The ludicrousness of what she speaks tickles me. She is confused and clearly desperate. Sex and sexuality are important parts of life, here and in the afterlife. There is nothing taboo about experiencing the joys of pleasuring oneself or another. And I shall not be left to feel ashamed for indulging one's heart's desires, or for feeding my own pleasures. I do not wish to deprive or be deprived.

"And yours," I snap back, "is a maggot's delight. Your rancid womb reeks with the stench of death. Even the beetles refuse to touch your flesh. You are the worthless shell of a woman."

Despite the relentless sun beating down on us, and the sweat upon her face, her eyes turn cold, then become enflamed. "You, Raghaba, goddess of desire, are a man eater, a lecherous, conniving thief of the soul."

"And this," I sneer, "is coming from the same tongue of the woman who seduced her own sister's husband, and took him to her bed so that she might spring forth the fruits of his loins. You deliberately disguised yourself as your own sister and had drunken sex with her husband, and now you have eyes for your nephew. Yet, you part your lips to call me a conniving thief."

I grin, wickedly. "No, barren one," I say, taunting her. "You are the treacherous one. Unlike you, Nephthys—goddess of the desert, I entertain men for pleasure, not to steal them from their wives, or to manipulate them into planting seeds into my womb. I amuse their fantasies and allow them to experience the pleasures you and these others so willingly deny them. So, do not ever confuse me with your wickedness.

"And though I am capable of satisfying the appetite of a thousand gods, tonight I seek only one. The rest of your gods are safe— tonight. So sleep well with them. But come the awakening of dawn, when the sun rises and falls, I will make no such promise. And for you, Nephthys," I say, pointing in her direction, matching her slit-drawn glare, "you had better pray to the gods that I find favor in you and not allow vengeance to flow through my veins. For if I do not, your vagina—the wasteland that it is—shall be pulled out and tossed into the wilderness so that the vultures may peck it apart, and then I shall have your tongue removed."

The young goddesses cast their eyes downward, flush with embarrassment. Nephthys glowers, but holds her tongue in fear she will awaken and find it cut out and fed to the dogs that lie at her feet. I smile in victory, her eyes burning into my back, as I saunter my way toward the temple of Amun, where the gods offer food to the ancestors, and gather in recreation.

◄═══○═══►

There is a sprinkle of goddesses donned in stylish wigs and flowing gowns—perched up on stools—vying for the attention of Horus. He is acutely aware of this. He sheepishly flirts with them with his eyes, but there is no twinkle that holds any promise. I toss my head up and leisurely stroll past them, catching their glares from the corners of my eyes.

"Why has she come?" I overhear Uadjet, goddess of justice, time, heaven and hell, ask. Her tongue, sharp with indignation, hisses and cracks as she holds the neck of a cobra in her right hand, its body wrapped around her arm. "Has she not spoiled enough fruits of our gods with her clever and cunning ways?" She squeezes the asp's neck in my direction and its jaws pop open, displaying long, sharp fangs, dripping with venom.

I come to take that which you tremble to have in your bed tonight, I think, rolling my eyes and dismissing her meager attempt to intimidate me. I am admired by few, envied by most, but hated by many. I am a threat. Knowingly, I smile and take a seat across the room so that I might enjoy the view.

"Raghaba," Khonsu, the moon god, says, briskly walking over and greeting me with a wide smile. "Most desirous and gracious one, you are lovelier than ever. My heart has longed for your presence." He leans in to kiss me.

I catch the snarling glares of the other goddesses across the room. Jealousy and hate swim around in their pathetic eyes. Lucky for them, I am not in the mood to entertain them. Had I not already had my way with Khonsu, I would have given them an eyeful. But, Khonsu holds no purpose for me.

"Your lips"—I put the palm of my hand up in his face to stop him—"shall never rest upon mine again, nor shall you ever enjoy the pleasures that flow between my thighs."

"*Nefer*, my heart bleeds. Have I done something to offend you?"

"Don't *nefer* me," I say, feigning a pout. "My beauty has nothing to do with this. Why have you not called upon me?" I ask this, but it is of no real concern to me. I only inquire to see if his tongue will flap truth or lies.

"I have been to Elephantine and Hermopolis since the last season. But I have kept you close in my thoughts and, even now as I cast my eyes upon you, you have kept me deeply aroused."

I glance down at his short and very thick penis, pressing up and straining against his loincloth. And in a flash, I see his testicles—tiny bite-size radishes—clinging tightly up against his body, and instantly I remember being shocked at how such little things could produce a heavy load of cream that shot out of the tip of his dwarf-like phallus like rushing, curdled milk. I remember how he lay there on his back, after the illicit act, with the slippery thickness of his seeds on his stomach and thighs, breathing heavily, then falling into a deep, heavy snore as if he had slain the wombs of a hundred goddesses.

Traveling along these memories, remembering how the several nights with him had been such a waste, disgusts me. *What a waste*, I think, rolling my eyes. Being with him was like going to a feast of the gods with very little meat to fill you. He always left me hungry for something more. However, I shall admit that his only saving grace is his tongue. Other than that, it is no wonder I bored with him so quickly. But I dare not tell him these things. To bash his manhood would be most unbecoming. Yet, I will not lead him to believe he was a great lover, either. Or that he was a master of pleasure. To do so would be a calamity. Still in all, I accept the reality that fulfilling the sexual desires of one's heart will never guarantee the fulfillment of my own, all the time.

"And when did you return?"

"The beginning of *peret*," he replies.

I laugh to myself. *Hmm…and we are now in the shemu, the season of harvesting. How interesting*, I muse. While others were planting seeds into the fertile earth, he was out doing a little planting of his own seeds—seeds which will sprout and flourish during the growing season, then spring forth fully grown crop during the harvest. I do not know why this foolish man feels the need to be dishonest. We are not bound together by commitment or marriage, so there is no need for insincerity.

I let out a disgusted sigh. "Stop with your lies," I say, looking over his shoulder. Seth, the god of chaos and destruction, is eyeing me. Lust is smoldering in his eyes. He discreetly strokes himself over his loincloth, challenges me to cast my eyes downward onto his ever-growing bulge. He does not make my clitoris throb, so I refuse the bait. I frown, giving him a sickened stare. I dislike him almost as much as I do his miserable sister, Nephthys. He winks at me, and I roll my eyes—returning my attention to the Khonsu. "It has been revealed by the gods that you have taken up with Meshkenet down in the Delta. So, now, let that swamp creature soothe your yearnings."

"Raghaba, it is you I adore. Meshkenet does not hold my heart."

"And it is your heart that is the seat of the soul, and shall be weighed against your deeds. So, be careful of what your tongue speaks."

He is blocking my view of Horus and I am becoming annoyed. "I don't wish to continue this; please leave me."

"Then I shall visit with you when the moon lights the sky."

I clench my teeth. "And, if you dare," I say, narrowing my eyes, "I shall summon the gods to strike down upon you."

"Raghaba," he whines, clutching his chest, "why have you turned on me? It is you that has captured my heart."

"But it is she who has captured your semen, no?"

His eyes widen, surprised that I am aware that she is with child. He is as foolish as a mongoose. Does he not know that Raghaba knows the desires of all?

He opens his mouth to speak. Again, my hand stops him. "Khonsu," I say. "I've had enough. Go suckle the sagging breasts of Meshkenet. And let me be."

"You are as beautiful as you are evil," he says. "Your tongue, as soft and loving as it can be, has the hiss of a snake. But it captivates me."

"And your tongue," I say, narrowing my eyes to slits, "is rotted with lies. Good day."

I excuse him with the flick of my hand, but he still stands—waiting. For what is of no concern to me. I am done with engaging in idle conversation with him. *Humph. What a waste*, I think, rolling my eyes in my head. *He couldn't even stir the bottom of my honey well, right.* Oh, yes. This conversation is definitely over. I blink, blink again…make him invisible.

I see Toth—god of sacred writings and wisdom, coming toward us, his manhood swaying beneath his loincloth. He is lean and muscular with chiseled features and the goodness of the sun burned into his shiny, bronzed skin. His eyes are big, brown and bright. I smile, knowing he has also held me in his dreams. A vision of me on my knees with my face down, back arched and Toth inserting himself slowly into the back of my vagina, straddling me, clamping the inside of his bulky thighs around my hips, then pumping deeply in and out of me while pulling me by the hair flashes through my head, and I quickly decide that I will engage him in frolic. That I shall climb atop of him, lower my womanhood down onto the length of him, then close its opening around the width of his penis—snapping it shut, like a crocodile taking a bite. Yes, when opportunity presents itself, I shall melt myself all over him, fuse my vagina onto his manhood, and we shall become one.

Until such time, I strain to keep focus on Horus—who is still seated at the table playing senet with Khnum—instead of the meaty lump that bounces in the center of Toth's crotch. I shift in my seat, cross my legs and pinch off the swelling in my clitoris.

Toth greets me with eyes dancing and with a smile and lustful gaze. "Raghaba," he says, his voice deep and masculine, looking directly at Khonsu, "have we a problem here?" He lifts my hand and kisses it, keeping his eyes locked on Khonsu.

"Not at all," I reply, allowing him to hold my hand in his— much longer than he should. "Khonsu was just leaving."

Khonsu nods. "Indeed I am." He bows his head slightly, in my direction. "Raghaba, as always…it has been a blessing to lay my eyes upon you." He nods to Toth, who graciously returns the nod.

"Be safe in your travels," I offer snidely as he walks off.

When Khonsu is safely out of earshot, Toth leans in and whispers, "You, beautiful goddess of desire, have certainly caused quite a stir among the gods today."

I smile. "And so I should."

"And, as you can see," he says, nodding in the direction of Uadjet and the other goddesses, "none of the goddesses have found favor in your presence here."

"Nor should they," I offer, dismissing his comment with the flick of my wrist. I roll my eyes in their direction, then return my attention to the beautiful specimen that stands before me. Our eyes lock and we share a smile.

He moves in closer, inhaling me. "You smell sweet as the lotus."

"And I taste even sweeter," I tease.

His hand finds its way to the small of my back, tracing light circles. "Perhaps I shall taste for myself?"

"Perhaps…," I offer, pausing, my eyes traveling across the room. Toth beholds my face as I look forth from my seat at Horus. He is immersed in his game. Its ivory and ebony board sits on four legs carved like bulls' feet. I keep my eyes fixed on the hands, thick and long, that hold its pawn in an attempt to outwit the evil forces so that he may reach the kingdom of Osiris—and win. I silently cheer him on, hoping for his victory, and for what lies in wait. My mind lingers on…imagining his fingers kneading my nipples; the warmth of his hands enveloping my breasts, then gliding along the curves of my body. I clamp my smooth thighs tight, shutting off the dew that collects along the creases of my labia. The other gods who are present slyly find cause to gather around me. They smell my excitement, but dare not touch. My erotic scent floats around them, the faint aroma of sex and sweat that has been baked into my skin by the sun.

Horus looks up; his eyes find me. His hunger for the pleasures that only I can bring him ripen in his gaze, and without words, I am certain, as I have always been, that it is I he desires. I hold his gaze for an endless moment, then smile.

My smile, slight, yet seductive, is an invitation for what's to come. He knows I am aware of his salacious thoughts, just as I am of the wanderings of the gods who sit before and around me. They, too, yearn to be pleasured, their erections straining against their garments for release. Perhaps release shall come, but not today and not with me.

My attention returns to Toth. "...You shall," I continue. "But, not in this hour, nor on this day."

He follows my eyes, glances over his shoulder, sees Horus, and knows from whence my passion grows.

"Then perhaps," he responds, kissing me lightly on the cheek, "we shall walk under the moonlight, and share a moment, exploring each other. I look forward to such time."

"And the time shall come," I say, taking him by the hand, "where we shall meet beneath the stars, and I shall allow you to feel the sensation of my tongue, my mouth, my lips, against your flesh."

He kisses me again, softly on the cheek, and says, "Then I shall wait until such time." He excuses himself, gliding back to the other side of the room. I turn to find the burning eyes of Nephthys, and decide to give her something extra to toss into her fire.

I get up from my seat and saunter past her and the others, then make my way toward Horus and the other gods who are gathered around the board game. I maneuver my way in between them, then lean in, pressing my soft lips flush to his ear. "Do not speak," I whisper. He nods. "Dine with me tonight, and you shall act out what you have kept locked in your dreams. I have prepared you a feast that will take you through the night, and greet you when the sun awakens." Horus keeps his eyes locked on the board game, but he smiles. I blow lightly into his ear. "I shall await your arrival."

He nods.

I walk off, leaving him and the others admiring the flawless curve of my backside, and sultry sway of my hips, drooling.

"She is absolutely breathtaking," I overhear one of the gods say.

"Mesmerizing," another says.

On my way back across the desert, I visit the shemayet, the office of musician, the highest position to be held, to fetch Rahjidaha so that she may play the harp in the private garden while Horus and I dine. Then she can leave when it is time to begin an evening of splendor. I busy myself around the house until the hour arrives.

⊷≡◎═⊷

"So you've come," I say, as Horus steps through the door, greeting him with a smile. Although no man has ever refused me, there is always a first time. I am glad tonight was not it. My earlier encounter with Hapi has left my insides churning for something more.

"I am not one to turn down an offer to be in the company of a woman, especially one as lovely as you," he says.

"Come," I say, taking him by the hand. I lead him to the table.

"Sit with me by the fire so that we might eat and drink from the cup of passion."

"I do pray that the cup from which we shall drink is large enough to quench both my thirst and my hunger for you."

"And if it is not," I say, smiling, "then we shall keep filling it until it does."

He takes his seat as I begin serving him his meal that has been kept warm in clay pots. We give thanks to the gods, then eat. Very few words are said during the meal. Yet, he can barely keep his eyes off of me long enough to finish eating. I smile with this knowing, but say nothing. I sit across from him and watch him wrap his full lips around the neck of the clay bottle from which he drinks beer.

"You are a very mysterious woman, my dear Raghaba."

"Do you not like mystery?" I ask, sipping my cup of wine.

He leans in, places his elbows on the wooden table, interlocks his fingers, then rests his chin on his hands. "I do like the element of surprise; being kept on the edge of suspense can be quite intriguing."

"And quite uncomfortable," I say coyly.

"Nothing makes me uneasy," he states, licking his lips. "Nothing," he softly repeats, his voice dripping with innuendo.

I smile.

"Tell me about you," he says. "Share with me everything about Raghaba."

Hmm…to share or not to share? That was the question I mulled over in my head as I looked him in his piercing eyes, then locked my eyes on his lips, imagining what it would be like to feel them—full and wet—all over my body. I think for a moment. Contemplate whether or not I should invite him into my personal space.

About me? I think. Do I tell him that I am a woman who cannot be bothered with love, that there is no room in my heart for hurt and disappointments? That I shall not allow myself to be loved? Do I tell him that I am a woman who holds neither regrets nor guilt for loving, wanting, needing, sex? That I am comfortable in my sexuality; that I am liberated? Do I tell him that I will make sweet, sweet love to him, give him all there is to give of me—tonight, but come the beginning of dawn, there will be nothing else left to give? Do I tell him that there will be lots of sex, but will never be any intimacy? That the only thing that causes my heart to race with joy is thoughts of illicit affairs that bring forth roaring orgasms? Does he want truths? Do I bare all and tell him these things? *No,* I answer. There is no need to. This is not about me.

He takes a heaping gulp of beer.

"There is nothing to tell," I say.

"Ah, yes, beautiful one, there is always something to be told, something to be shared."

Perhaps, I think as he stares at me. "Not in this hour," I state, looking at him over the rim of my cup as I slowly sip, "nor in this life."

"Does that mean you will not indulge me, my love, so that I may grow close to you?"

"It means that there is nothing that I wish to uncover about Raghaba."

"Then I shall wait to unearth all there is to know on my own—in time, of course."

"Of course," I offer, filling my cup with more wine. I take a slow, deliberate sip. My patience is running thin. "Until such time," I say, "tell me what is in your thoughts?"

He smiles, seduction dripping from his lips. "You," he says.

"From the first moment my eyes came upon you, I have wanted to feel you beneath me. I have wanted to taste you, and explore you. And now, here I sit, before the woman in my dreams." He takes a slow, deliberate sip from his drink, pushing his empty bowl to the side. He wipes his mouth with the back of his hand. "Why have you not taken up with a man?"

"Because no one man satisfies me," I want to say, but decide against it. He will learn soon enough about the ways of Raghaba.

"And why should I be taken by a man?" I ask, scowling.

"To share the joys of love and companionship," he answers. "You are most desirous, Raghaba."

"And I am also most satisfied being unattached."

"But what of home and family?" he asks, taking another large swallow of beer. I watch him guzzle down the remainder of what's left in the jug, then belch. My face forms a frown. "Do you not wish to bask in the delight they bring?"

I control my breathing. This line of questioning is what will sour my mood and have me excuse him from my company. I realize he is only trying to be polite, but I am not interested in politeness. I am not interested in this type of chatter. The only things that I am engrossed in at this moment are images of him running his hands lightly over my body, his lips gathering around the lobes of my ears, sucking and nibbling; his fingers prying my flesh wide open to reveal my wetness as he slips himself inside of me and stirs my excitement. These are the things that I am concerned with. Not blurred visions of being chained to a man and a house full of children.

I stare at him. Decide not to answer.

There's a pregnant pause, one that gives birth to annoyance.

"Your eyes are hypnotic," he says, staring deep into them. I suspect he recognizes my disinterest in entertaining his questions about my views on life, love, and the pursuit of family. I am not looking for a happy-ever-after—just a never-ending orgasm, be it with him or someone else. I regain my focus, and shift my mood back to why I invited him.

I coyly bat my lashes. "Then I warn you to be very careful how you look into them."

He smiles. "It is your spell I crave to be under."

I have to admit, although he is moving as slowly as a turtle and I am growing restless, there is something I find quite charming about him which keeps me indulging him. But, my mind is made up—charming or not—if he does not gesture to explore my passion, sooner than later, I will send him out into the night air.

"Again," I warn. "Be very careful. You may get more than you're prepared to handle."

"Why and wherefore am I kept a prisoner from love?"

"Because," I reply, "it is your mouth that speaks full of love, but it is your heart that is filled with lust. Behind your eyes, there is a longing." I reach over and place my hand over his. "Tell me your desires so that I may fulfill them."

"Are you sure you can deliver?" he asks, grinning.

I am feeling relieved. Finally, we are moving toward a night of explicit action, instead of one cluttered with useless discussion.

"My dear, dear, Horus," I answer, slowly pulling in my bottom lip. "I am a woman who is most adept at delivering all things without delay. And there is nothing...and I do mean *nothing* that I won't do to ensure it."

He laughs. "We shall see," he says. "Raghaba, goddess of desire, we shall surely see."

"Then let us not continue this cat-and-mouse chase," I say,

eyeing him seductively. In that moment, there is a silence that comes between us; it briefly visits, then exits. "Don't tell me the cat has come and eaten at your tongue so quickly."

"No cat"—he sticks his tongue out and rapidly flaps it up and down—"shall ever take hold of my tongue."

"Then let's hope you know how to use it, and use it well," I challenge.

"Tonight," he states, "I want you to bring forth a mighty orgasm." I smile, standing up. I slowly begin to unfasten my gown. I decide I had better be swift in making my move before he opens his mouth and spoils the opportunity with another string of foolishness. "Then you have come to the right place." My garment drops around my ankles. Horus soaks in my flawless beauty as he gets up from his seat, drinking in the round firmness of my breasts, delighting in the curve of my hips. He walks around me as I stand on display for his taking.

"How ample and lovely your backside is," he says, eyeing me lustfully as I step out of my white linen dress. He basks in my nakedness as I slowly turn to face him and allow my breasts to bounce and dangle freely before him. He walks up on me, places his hands—strong and warm—upon my agile hips and pulls me into him. "I have longed for you. And tonight, I will have you."

"Yes, my love," I say as he tilts his head, then kisses me, filling my mouth with his tongue. He tastes, um…good. No, better than good—delicious! My loins become the heat of the earth as his hands trace along my back, then rest on my backside. He gently squeezes. I inhale his scent. Get lost in the smell of mint, warm and stimulating.

"Tonight," I continue, in between mint-flavored kisses, "I will give you all the things you have desired. And together we shall perform for the gods, and they shall smile down upon us as we become one."

"And together," he responds, brushing his full lips against mine, "we shall do what prompts us and revel in its pleasure."

"And so it shall be."

His lips devour mine, and I am getting lost in pleasure. Abruptly, he pulls away and steps back. He walks to the other side of the room, leaving me wondering, wanting, imagining, what's to come. He removes his loincloth and my eyes become glued to his manhood. It is as thick as a cucumber and as long as the branch of a willow. Instantly, I feel myself becoming hot and moist.

I peel my eyes from his center, and allow them to soak in his majestic presence. He is almost glowing from the flicker of the fire. He stands before me with shiny dark skin as rich as silt, the fertile soil that feeds all of Kemet, and he is tall and sturdy like a mountain. His broad shoulders and smooth muscular chest entice me to touch, to taste, but I deny myself…for now.

I gesture forward to close the space he has created between us, but he stops me. "Stay," he commands, his voice booming. "Come to me when I call, and worship all that I am."

I stretch out my arms, palms outward, and, with a slight tilt of my head, I nod.

"Tonight, I shall worship you like no other."

"And what of tomorrow?" he asks, slowly stroking himself. I struggle to keep my eyes on his; struggle to ignore the excitement that expands in his hand, full and dark with bulging veins.

"Tomorrow," I say, taking hold of my breasts, kneading them, squeezing them, pushing them upward so that I may twirl my tongue around each nipple, "is of no consequence for that which stands before us at this very moment."

"Then let us not waste time," he says. "Come to me on your knees. And allow me to slip myself in between the warmth of your succulent lips."

I run my tongue longingly around my lips as he wags his engorged phallus at me. Saliva gathers in my mouth as I crouch down and crawl to him like a hungry lioness keeping its eye on its prey. I stop. Arch my back, slowly wind my hips, then raise one arm, remove the pins from my hair and allow my hair to fall against my shoulders and face. Horus stands enthused, eager, watching me make my way to him. I swing my head and purr. He spreads his legs apart, strokes himself in anticipation as I continue to make slow, seductive moves toward him. My insides shake with mounting excitement as he strokes his penis. Long, thick, and leaking. And I hunger to touch it, taste it, feel it.

Finally, I am upon him, kneeling before him with his phallus hovering and waving over me like an arm. Just beyond reach. I reach for it and grab it by the base with both hands, then squeeze until the veins bulge and the head swells. My lips part. I wrap them lovingly around the width of his smooth, powerful penis, then welcome him into my mouth—invite him to use it as if it were a vagina. I swallow slowly, purposefully. Allow him to stretch the back of my throat until I lose him past my tonsils and down into my neck. He pushes his manhood in and out, quickening his pace against the suckling sounds that escape me. I am well-attuned to what he craves, and so I give it to him. This is what has consumed his dreams.

"Oh, Raghaba," he moans in a harmonious melody against the suction of my mouth. "Oh, Raghaba...suck me with your sweet lips...uh, oh, yes...Raghaba, wet it like the Nile."

My lips, my mouth, engulf him. I am sucking and licking and

nibbling the sensitive spot just below the head of his penis, causing him to dip at the knees. His right leg begins to shake. I look up at him—his face twisted and his eyes shut tight as he bucks his hips—and smile. I slowly remove my lips, then swirl my tongue around and over the eye of his organ to collect the clear, sweet and sticky nectar that begins to dribble.

"Mmmm," I moan greedily. I place a hand between my legs, then press two fingers against my clitoris and massage it in quick circular motions. "Mmmm…"

He grabs the back of my head, picks up his pace. I slowly run my hands along the back of his thighs, down across his calves, then back up again, grabbing his muscular behind. "Give me the milk of your loins," I say in between breaths. "Feed me, Horus, so that I might feed you." I swallow him whole again. Bury him deep in my throat; swallow, gulp. Swallow, gulp.

"Oh, yes…oh, yes…Rag…ha…ba…"

His body shudders as he expels warm, creamy seeds of pleasure. I slowly pull the length of him from out of my throat, then lick my lips and swallow all of his sweet love cream. My lips linger around the head of his still erect phallus so that I can lick it clean. He begins to stroke himself, milking and squeezing his erection, squirting out the last few drops of milk that I willingly suck.

I look up and see Horus is dazed. His chest heaves in and out. I stifle a laugh, knowing I have emptied his sac, and sucked him into a room-spinning delirium. He braces himself against the wall as his legs threaten to collapse under the weight of his body. He attempts to walk, but stumbles. He grabs hold of the wooden pillar that supports the roof in the middle of the floor, clinging to it. I rise from my knees, a satisfied smile spread across my face, and grab him by the head of his penis. I place my other hand between my legs, press on my clitoris, then slip two fingers into my throbbing wetness, my vulva swollen and aching with excitement.

"The night is still young," I say, pulling him by his manhood through the hall toward the bedroom. "Let us finish off in the comforts of the bed. Your loins have been chained for far too long. It is time we unlock the passion that dwells in the pit of your soul and allow it to flow. It's time to release, and be free."

"I must rest a spell," he states, eagerly following behind me, "so that I can give you my greatest performance. You have worked me over swiftly. I wish not to disappoint you."

"Nor shall I let you," I say, massaging the head of his penis. *But if you do*, I think, *I shall put you out*. "By the time I'm done with you, you will know the goodness of Raghaba and all that she brings. And you shall remember this very moment, always."

"The gods have truly bestowed their blessings upon me," he says, cupping my backside. "You are everything I hoped for, and more than I ever imagined."

"And there is still more to come," I say, pulling my fingers out of my sweet, sticky love chest, then offering them to him. He accepts, his mouth sliding down to my knuckles, his tongue in between each finger, sucking and licking my juices off. He licks his lips.

"Aaaah," he says, "I savor your sweetness."

"And you shall delight in more."

When we reach the bed, Horus sits and watches me take a strip of linen cloth and fold it, then wrap it around his eyes. The room is aglow with the flicker of the wall torches, orange and blue flames dancing about. "Lie down on your stomach," I command, "and let me have my way with you."

He does not question me; does what he is told and allows me to take him where he has been afraid to venture with others. I straddle him, then pour jasmine oil into my hands and massage his wide back, his steely shoulders, and thick neck. He relaxes under the soothing scent. His beautifully sculpted body, dark as the rich silt of the Nile, glistens under my touch. I lean the warmth of my smooth body against his, slowly easing my way down to his backside, rubbing and pulling at his cheeks, then down across the back of his thighs, then down to his calves, kneading his muscles, his legs long and strong. I inch my hands back up, pull open his backside, then lightly blow. He flinches, tenses, then relaxes.

"Is this not what you've desired?"

He nods his head and whispers in a voice straining against itself, a voice that should not belong to him. "Yes," he says.

I allow my drool to drip into the seam of his rear.

"Who am I?" I coo in a seductive voice.

"Raghaba," he moans.

I flick my tongue across the opening of his anus, then lick all around it.

"Who am I?" I repeat.

He gasps. "Raghaba."

I stick my wet tongue deep in. Tongue him longingly. Tongue him lovingly. He slowly twirls his hips and lets out a loud, rumbling moan that shudders the night and shakes all of Kemet. I reach up and gently tug his testicles which are the size of two ripe plums, and plant warm kisses on each one, then slip them into my mouth, rolling my tongue around each one, licking the back of them, then gliding my tongue back up along the crevice of his rear, resting it—wet and hungry, back in the center of his hole.

He moans again, grinding himself into the mattress.

"Turn over," I demand. The erotic odor of his manliness lingers against my lips, lays along my tongue and I am anxious to share its taste with him. As he turns over, a rush of excitement flows through me as I watch his overly enlarged organ bounce across the ripples of his muscled stomach, and drip a thin string of nectar.

I kiss him and share his scent with him. My tongue swirls deeply into his mouth, then pulls his tongue into my own mouth. I straddle him and suck on his tongue as if it were his thick phallus. His hand grabs at his penis, pulling and stroking it, slapping it up against my backside. I begin to massage my clitoris and allow my juices to drip against his thigh. I grind against him. I moan with him. I lock my eyes on his. And as he strokes himself, I stroke myself. Match the rise and fall of his breathing.

"Let me remove this cloth that binds my sight," he says, reaching for the cloth strip with his free hand. "I want to lay my eyes upon you. Want to see you worship me."

"No," I snap, grabbing his hand. "There is plenty of time to see me with your eyes. Tonight, use your other senses, and allow your imagination to savor me."

"You are teasing me," he says, his voice low and sensual.

"No," I coo in between soft, wet kisses. "I am preparing you"—more kisses—"and preparing me." My tongue slithers down his neck, over his shoulders, then to his chest. I gingerly lick around his dark nipples and trace wet circles around each one, causing him to moan in delight.

I reach behind me, grab the base of his phallus and squeeze. My loins become engulfed in flames, as I await his entry. The tip of his penis brushes against my wetness. I am teasing me, and teasing him until we both can no longer take it. He anticipates what I want…his erection massive and long. I am trembling as I mount him—half-sitting, half-squatting. I brace myself against his chest. Slowly, I ease down on him and the head of his penis kisses my hungry lips. They flare open and allow him inside of me, the mouth of my vagina stretching wide to fit around him, then snapping snugly around the girth of his manhood. A soft moan escapes me as I envelope him—bury him in my wetness, and squeeze him. "Mmmm…"

"Oh, Raghaba," he whispers. "You know not what you do to me."

"Is this not what you desired?" I question, sliding all the way down onto him, the base of his phallus tickling my clit as I lean forward and place my lips flush against his ear. "Did you not crave the wetness of my valley? Did you not dream sweet dreams of riding the wave of pleasure?"

"Yes," he says, panting, cupping my breasts, then pulling softly at my nipples.

"Who am I?"

"Raghaba…"

"Who am I?"

"Goddess of desire…uh, oh, yes."

We are both trying to find a rhythm that matches our needs as we travel uncharted territory. I slowly rise, then plunge deep down onto him, gyrating my pelvis. Rise. Plunge. Rise. Plunge. I am pulling him up and down with me. He is pushing up in me. I am pushing down on him. His hands steady on either side of my hips, bracing my ride. I lean in and devour his lips with my mouth, darting my tongue in and out until he catches it and pulls it deep into his mouth. Our tongues swirl around one another. Warm and moist, he sucks on mine. I suck on his.

And with each stroke, my body is flooded with joy. I have become a river, flowing along the sides of his shaft, a waterfall cascading down, around and across his balls. I am wet. And I am wetting him. The slippery, smacking, slurping sounds of my vagina play sweet music. I lift my hips and place my hands back upon his chest, then remain still. Instinctively, Horus raises his hips up into me. "Uh...mmm...oh, yesss," I purr. My vagina clenches and throbs as he moves himself inside of me with slow, measured strokes. "Take me, Horus," I whisper. "Let the gods see how well you feast in my womanhood."

Up.

Down.

Up.

Down.

I am pushing. He is pushing. I am chanting. He is chanting. We are calling out to the gods who have crossed over into the afterlife. We are seeking refuge and temporary solace in each other's arms, in each other's lips, in each other's movements— fluid, fast, rippling movements of pleasure.

"Oh, Raghaba," he moans again. "You are so wet. I could lose myself in your every move from now until eternity. My heart beats for you, Raghaba. And I shall lay down my life to live out the rest of my days with you here and in the afterlife."

I blink, blink again. His tongue announces the thoughts of his heart. And I feel myself slipping off this pleasure ride. But I say nothing. Just press my lips against his to silence him, and continue to ride. I do not share his sentiments. Does he not know that I will allow him to soil my sheets, but never my heart? Does he not recognize that what he speaks is not of love, but of lust? After tonight, though I may ride him through the sun and back again, I do not want his heart, or his undying love.

I give him more of my tongue; shove it into his mouth as deep as it will go to keep him from speaking words that may clog up the surge that rushes through me. Like the mighty Nile that extends four thousand miles from the mountains of Ethiopia, forming the Blue Nile and the White Nile that flows through Sudan, then converging and emptying into the Mediterranean Sea, a giant orgasm is swelling inside of me. I hear its roaring rapids crashing against my inner walls, splashing against Horus' pulsing organ as he thrusts deeper inside of me. I reach around and cup his balls and jingle and gently squeeze them. They too are full...and heavy, ready to erupt. Our silhouettes sway about the room like two sensual dancers looping around each other, dipping and bending.

I flip my wild and tossed-about hair out of my face. I feel the eyes of the gods looking down upon us, my womb calling out to them. I move down into him. He moves up against me. We are fighting to outmatch each other.

Up.

Down.

Up.

Down.

I am galloping him. He is bucking me. Our pelvises are crashing against each other, the clanking of bones, the smacking of skin, desperately seeking release. I hold my breasts in my hands, pull one up to my lips at a time and suck and lick them, alternately. I slow my pace, moaning. "Uh...uh...oh, yes!"

Horus runs his hands along the small of my back, his fingertips slowly gliding down my spine. "Raghaba," he whispers, "my sweet, sweet Raghaba. Your insides are like the center of the earth, deep and hot. My loins burn with desire for you."

He slides his hands and fingers all over my flesh, causing it to tingle and become hot. Finally, his hands rest on my two soft, round humps. He digs his fingers into the flesh of my backside, squeezes the fat of my cheeks together and rapidly thrusts himself up into me, his eyes rolling back into his head. His moan becomes a growl, deep and hungry. He is panting and howling and pulling at the bedcovering. I pull in my bottom lip. His begins to quiver. And, together, we explode against each other. The intensity forces me to shudder and collapse against his chest. Drenched in a mixture of pleasure and sweat, we drift off to sleep, limbs intertwined with his organ still lodged inside of me.

⊷⊨◉◉⊨⊶

We both awaken to the kiss of the sun, bright and gleaming. The heat is already creeping in, causing beads of sweat to line the bridge of my nose. I am on my side, back facing Horus, and he has me pulled into his chest with his arm locked around me, and one leg draped over both of mine. I can feel the rigidness of his manhood poking me. With his arm still wrapped around me, I maneuver myself so that I can turn my body around to him, face-to-face. Although, I am full from the pleasures of the night before, I cannot believe I have allowed him to stay. Cannot believe I am looking into his face, breathing in his breath scented with stale passion. Can not imagine why I did not wake him in the still of the night and send him on his way. *Probably because I will have him another round*, I think.

"Good morning," he says, placing a gentle kiss on my forehead. "The gods have poured down their blessings upon us this beautiful day." He pulls me into his arms, and buries his face against my neck. His breath is warm and tickly, but I do not become aroused. "Oh, Raghaba, what have you done to me?"

I slowly pull back from him; look into his eyes. There is another kind of wanting in them, a wanting I will not provide. "I have given you what you have so desired."

"And I yearn more."

"There is nothing more to offer you."

"Oh, my sweet Raghaba," he says, leaning up on his elbow, "how wrong you are. There is still so much more of you to give. You are so full of vigor, so full of adventure. I want to spend every wakening moment exploring the depths of your spirit."

I force a slight smile. I do not want to sound callous, do not want to breed cynicism, but he is asking for things he will never be given. Things I will not allow him to lay claim to. There is no one man I wish to share more than what I am willing to give him, a night or two of unadulterated, endless bliss. Anything more would be a lie chaining my spirit. I am not of this world to be tied down to matters of the heart. Not one to be hostage to emotions, or to expectations, or to vulnerabilities that come with opening up and giving of oneself—not in mind or heart, and definitely not to any one living, breathing being.

"This," I say, running my hands all over my nakedness, "is all I wish to give. And when I have fulfilled your desires, I shall move on to someone else's."

He presses his lips against me, hard. Silences me from speaking what he does not want to hear, slipping his hand between my legs and stroking the front of my vagina, nuzzling two fingers between the spaces between each lip, then massaging my clitoris with his thumb.

"Mmm," I moan. "Mmm…"

His fingers play a sweet melody against my clitoris, strumming along the opening of my vagina, causing drums to beat in and around and against my inner walls. I clamp my legs shut, and begin humping his hand, thrashing about the bed in a fit of unrequited ecstasy.

"Oh, yes…Oh, yes…Oh, yes…Mmmm…it feels…so…good…"

Horus plants his mouth over my nipple and sucks, then gently bites down. I scream. It is a sound not of pain, or agony, or discomfort, but of gut-wrenching explosions traveling from the bottom of my feet to the center of my being, transporting me from the here and now to another place, another time. I call on the gods, beg them, and plead with them, to keep me grounded, to keep me from slipping into another world. Horus's hand, his fingers, his mouth, his lips, his rhythm takes me to the edge, pushes me over, then lifts me back up.

I am coming, and coming, and coming—all over his hand, all over his fingers, wet and slippery, warm and sticky. I am drowning, drowning, drowning. A surge of orgasmic waves splash, pull me under, toss me around, awash me with pleasure. And I come a thousand times more. When I finally stop moving my hips and humping his hand, Horus pulls his fingers from out of me, then licks and sucks them. I catch my breath, watching him, then lean in and kiss him. I do not know why, but it seems logical in an illogical sense, tasting my sweet saltiness on his lips.

With his head resting against the crescent-shaped stone headrest, he holds me in his arms, and allows me to lay my head upon his chest. My eyes flutter and become heavy.

"Raghaba, do you not know my desires for you are endless…?" Horus asks. "…I want to love you, give you the same pleasures you have given me …" His voice begins to dry up the river that still flows through me. I hear him, but I am too weak to speak. Too exhausted to tell him to tie a knot on his tongue, or get out. I close my eyes, and pray to the gods that when I awaken, he's gone.

⋆⇌ ⊙⇋⋆

I awaken from a deep sleep to the smell of food, wafting about the room. I open my eyes, stretch and yawn, wondering who is cooking. I glance over to the other side of the bed. It is empty. The only remnant of Horus's burly presence is the big, round stain in the center of the bed that has since dried, and the scent of sex that still lingers between my thighs. I look up at the woven sticks and palm rafters of my roof, imagining it is the sky, and give thanks for the gods hearing my call. Horus has left. *That was thoughtful of him to not rouse me from my sleep*, I think, pulling myself out of bed and walking into the wash area. I am surprised to see the wooden bucket is filled with steaming water, and sweet-smelling lotus petals are floating atop. I scratch and shake my head and almost faint when I walk into the central room to find a feast of all feasts spread out on the table. There is fresh fruit, baked bread and honey, along with roasted mutton and sliced cucumbers, onions and carrots. My stomach becomes a roaring lion.

Horus enters the central room, naked, carrying a jar and smiling. "Good afternoon," he says, stepping into my space and planting a kiss on my forehead. "Were your dreams as sweet as you?"

"Sweeter," I say, eyeing him. He is really a handsome man with striking features.

"Here, sit," he says, pulling out a stool. "I have drawn your water from the well so that you may freshen yourself."

247

"Thanks," I say, taking a seat. "I thought you left."

"No, sweet Raghaba, I have not left you. I had hoped to spend another day with you. As you can see, I have prepared us a meal so that we may nourish our appetites and our urges."

I reach for the jar of *labna*—a soft cream cheese made from milk—and scoop out a dollop, then spread it over bread sweetened with honey. I sprinkle cassia over it, then bite into its center, savoring its sweetness. "This is delicious," I state, chewing.

"Not as delicious as you." I smile. "But it has been made by the hands of a man who wants nothing more than to please and spoil you, Raghaba."

I smile. It is the only thing I feel safe offering him; for anything I say will not be pleasing to him. I continue eating. I can tell there is something lingering on his mind by the way he looks at me. I try to finish up my meal before it is ruined by reckless chatter.

We eat in silence. He watches me as I eat.

"Travel to Elephantine with me," he finally says, cutting into the quietness of the room. I keep my face straight, continue chewing. I have no interest in visiting or taking that hot, long journey to the small island just north of the first cataract of the Nile, on the borders of Kemet and Nubia.

I suck my fingers clean, then dip them in water to rinse. "And why would I want to travel to Elephantine with you?" I ask, eyeing him cautiously.

"So that we may spend time together," he says, tilting his head as if I should have already known this, "while I hunt."

While you hunt, I repeat in my head. We are in a land rich and plentiful; a wet jungle of trees and thickets of reed and papyrus that thrive along the Nile; a land that is roamed by rhinos, hippos, elephants, wild boar, lions, and countless other wild animals.

Not to mention, the crocodiles, scorpions, ants, mosquitoes and pesky flies that bite. I fold my arms over my chest, and blink my eyes. I blink again. How dare he think to part his lips with such a request? Does he not know I am not destined to be a cheerleader of hunting or any other sport—except sex?

In my mind's eye, I can see the fluttering of ducks, startled from their nests in the dense reeds by the cats used to flush them out. Ugh! The gall of him to think that I would find fancy in being on a wild duck hunt along the banks of the Nile with him poised with his bow and arrow, and me sitting beside him petting a tame lion and handing him his next arrow. Or worse, watching him hunt crocodile or hippos as many of the men do for sport.

"Horus, you foolish man," I say. "Though I appreciate the invitation, do I look like a woman who would enjoy watching you or any other man hunt?"

"Would you not like to enjoy my company on the way? There will be other goddesses from all over the land there." He adds that as if it is supposed to entice me to consider.

I sigh. "I can find much more useful things to do with my time, than spend it in the jungle, cackling with a bunch of petty women who will fear my presence around their men."

"You'd be in my company," he says. "So there would be no need for them to fear you."

I sigh. Okay, this is the moment the gods above have been waiting for—the moment of truth. See. I exist because I am desire. I exist because I am cravings. I exist because I am forbidden fruits. I exist because greed is what will keep one wanting, taking, more than what they already have; more than what they need. However, if it weren't for the whimsical antics of the overindulgent and self-absorbed, I would probably not matter. But I do. And I will continue to live and flourish in hearts and minds because most can not deny themselves the pleasures of the flesh. So, I, the goddess of desire, will continue to cripple them, to weaken them, to entice them, to lure them into a moment of illicit passion. My lot in life would probably be most different if men and women could refuse temptation. But, because they cannot always deny themselves physical pleasures, they become impulsive, take risks, will do whatever it takes to satisfy the desires of the flesh, and will throw caution into the wind in order to fulfill real or imagined needs—without concern, without regard, for anyone. It is the love of pleasing the flesh which manifests itself in covetousness, whoredom, gluttony, wantonness, and drunkenness. So, I exist. Because, with all the heart and soul and might, we seek and delight in pleasure, no matter what is lost in the process. So, fear will always exist as long as I am present.

I lean in, resting my arms on the table. I tell him, "If her man's eyes wander upon me with lusty thoughts, then I shall quench his thirst if I so choose. If his thoughts are pure, and he can avoid temptation, then I shall leave him be."

He stares at me, hard. "And how many men shall you take to your bed, and allow to clutter your womb, before you set your sights on one man?"

"I shall bed as many as my womanhood allows," I state, matching his stare. "And don't you worry about the clutter in my womb. I shall keep it flushed so that nothing spreads and takes root inside of me."

"And have you no shame?" he asks, indignation coursing through his voice. I blink, blink again. How dare he question me, then become offensive? I do not want to bicker, or spew hurtful words about, but the slow spinning in my head indicates

I will say things that shall not be taken back if his tone escalates.

I pull in a deep breath to steady the thumping in my chest. It is obvious he wants to open up the conversation from last evening. But I shall tread lightly around the subject.

"Why should I? I am a woman who does not subscribe to the likings of others. I do what I please with whom I please, whenever I please."

He abruptly gets up from his seat, looks down on me, then pulls a deep breath in. "Then I guess my presence is no longer needed here."

I shrug as my eyes follow him. "I have enjoyed your company through the night, and will even allow you to share my bed and what lies between my thighs again. But, I have no other interest in you, Horus. Nephthys, with her rotted teeth and hollow womb, longs to spend every wakening moment with you, not I. She wants to bear your children and live happily-ever-after. Go chase dreams with her; come fulfill fantasies with me."

"Nephthys is not whom my heart desires," he says, lifting me up from my seat.

"Then Uadjet should suit your fancy," I offer. "Her eyes burn with passion for you."

He pulls me into him, pressing his body against mine. "I do not want Uadjet. My eyes burn only for you. I have longed for you from the very first moment I laid them upon you. It is you my heart craves."

"No, Horus," I snap. My lip begins to tremble, and I am unsure why. "You do not know what you speak. It is the warmth and wetness of my lips and vagina your heart craves. It is not love; it is lust."

"Why do you reject me?" he asks.

"I am not rejecting you," I answer. "I am rejecting that which you offer. There's a difference."

"Should we not endeavor to take a chance on love?"

I cannot believe him. He is relentless. And his frantic ramblings almost sound needy. Desperate. Clingy. I have no time or patience for either.

For some reason, hearing him say the word *love* makes me want to scream. Love, love, love…with all of its abstractions, with all of its uncertainty, there's concreteness about its meaning, about its intent, that frightens me. It is a feeling that is foreign to me, and one I do not wish to explore. I do not wish to feel exposed, or vulnerable to emotions that involve the giving of my heart to someone else. To lose any part of myself in the process of loving someone does not excite me. I am not lonely, nor do I starve for love and affection in my life. Beyond the barriers of sex, I do not consume myself with thoughts of being held, or caressed, or cared for. There is no yearning for warmth, tenderness or intimacy. Just sex, sex, sex and more sex; that is the only thing I desire to share. So, no, I shall not entertain love's possibilities. Nor shall I ever be plagued with lovesickness.

"To dance with love," I say, almost apologetically, "would be like walking barefoot across a thousand wild bees. I am not eager to embrace the sting of heartache should it come."

He looks at me with sorrow in his eyes. "Then you shall never know the joy it can bring."

"Nor shall I ever regret what I shall never miss."

He takes me into his arms. His touch begs me to reconsider his offering of love, but I am too detached and jaded for emotional connections. His hands, warm and gentle, embrace the sides of my face. "Who has cast a shadow upon your heart?" he asks, staring into my eyes. "Who has hardened your spirit against love? Tell me, dear Raghaba, who has trampled your heart? Will you not let me comfort you; help you mend?"

I do not answer. Do not breathe credence into anything he says. I stand, pressed against his chest. There is nothing to mend, nothing that has been trampled upon, and there is no need for comfort. I feel his heartbeat, his measured breathing. I feel him trying to melt himself into me, and me into him.

"Horus," I say, prying myself from his embrace. "I will revel in the pleasures we have shared. And I thank you for keeping company with me, but I shall not open the windows of my heart to invite love in. Not today, tomorrow, and not in the calendar years to come. So, please do not badger me with such notions. If you wish to share my bed again, you may. But nothing more than explicit passion shall ever come of it."

Solemnly, he keeps his gaze upon me as if he were attempting to burn me into his memory. Then he lightly presses his lips against mine one last time, before walking out the door, leaving me drawing in a long breath—wondering why things must become so complicated.

―――◦≡◦―――

Several days and nights have come and gone, and Horus has been silent. A part of me is relieved that there's been no word from him. However, there's another part—that part of me that has not grown tired of him, yet—that would keep company with him again through the night, and perhaps into the sunrise. I can not deny the truth: Horus felt so very good inside of me. And my vagina walls wish to wrap themselves around his manhood again.

However, I will not call upon him. And though he keeps his distance, I know I am still in his dreams. He still allows images of my nakedness to consume him. And I linger in his thoughts, against his morning erections, against the stroke of his hardness, against the flooding and release of his loins. I am fully aware that he will find comfort between the thighs of many others, but his thirst for me shall not be quenched. The well of his desires for me shall overflow and no matter how hard he tries to ignore these urgings, he shall give into them. He will seek to feel the heat of my skin against his. He shall find his way back to me to rest himself in between my bosom, and in the center of my thighs where I will allow him to taste the fruit of my clitoris, then release himself into the basin of my womb.

It is early evening and I have just finished washing my body and oiling it with jasmine oil. I have been as lazy as a cat, napping and nibbling today. And now I am sitting at the table in the central room, eating a bowl of boiled cabbage and a side plate of mullet roe—fish eggs—when my mind slowly begins to drift, along the edges of the desert.

I am running over and around the shifting sand-dunes of the Sahara; something is chasing me, but I am not exactly sure what it is. There are no faces. Just sweaty and musky bodies chasing behind me with long arms, big hands and long spidery fingers, stretching out to grab me. They are naked and salivating. And their grotesquely large penises have the heads of hissing asps. The scorching sand beneath the bottom of my feet makes running unbearable, but if I stop, these two-legged creatures will devour me. The heat and the want of water make it most difficult to keep my stride. My lips crack and my throat burns from gulping in the treacherous heat. I am screaming, but no one hears my cries for help. I am stumbling and falling. The sun is beating down on me, brutal and relentless, just like the creatures that are slowly closing in on me, determined to have their way with me. To do whatever they will. There is nothing but miles and miles of desert ahead of me and I do not understand what this means. But somehow, after all of my running, and all of my screaming, an oasis lies ahead of me. I crane my neck to look behind me, and there is nothing behind me. The creatures have gone. And I am now wallowing in the Nile, soaking in all of its wetness. This vision frightens and confuses me. I take a deep breath and wonder if the gods are trying to reveal my fate to me.

The sound of a man's voice saves me from finding out what becomes of me. A film of sweat lines my forehead.

"Is it I who fills your thoughts?" he asks, grinning. I stare up into his face. For the first time, I notice his straight, neatly spaced teeth. They have not been worn down over the years from the sand that gets into the food or the bits of stone that end up in the stone-ground flour. I don't know when he got here, or how long he had been standing here, but...

"Toth," I say, feigning surprise to see him standing in my doorway. But I knew he would come. The throbbing heat between his legs has led him to me. His dreams have become too much for him to bear. And now he stands before me, eager to fulfill all that has consumed him. Though I know what will fall from his lips, I still ask, "Why have you come unannounced?"

"I could no longer wait to be summoned by you," he says, his tone filled with a lust that matches his gaze as he steps into my space. "You seem to have time for everyone else, except me. You leave my loins neglected. You deny me your touch. Teasing me with promises you do not plan to keep. No, Raghaba, I have waited far too long. Tonight, I am here to take what I've been longing for."

For some reason, his jealousy entices me; the knowing that he is feeling slighted, that he has been wanting, longing for, this causes my nipples to harden. I smell his need. His pores leak with the scent of lust. I will not give in so easily.

"But I have not invited you," I say, backing up, "nor have I offered you any reason to make claims upon me." He is making his way closer to me, and I keep moving away until my back is up against the wall, and I have no more room to go anywhere else.

Though I am not frightened by his presence, I pretend that I am. I toy with him, giving him the illusion that he is in control; that he is taking what he wants. I allow him to think he is orchestrating this journey. He raises his arms on either side of me, then presses his palms flat against the wall, blocking any chance for escape. The element of danger, though imagined, ignites a flame inside of me which causes my juices to slowly simmer.

He leans in, presses his body against mine, and whispers, "Raghaba, sweet goddess of desire, give me what my loins so desperately need. Let me slip myself into your wet valley and lose all that I am in your pleasures. Allow me to melt against the scent of your womanhood."

He places his warm mouth around my left earlobe, sucks on it, then dips his tongue into my ear as he writhers his wide hand up my gown and reaches into the space between my thighs, searching for the center of my flesh. I let out a soft moan when his fingers find the slick softness of its opening. My hips move against my will, grind against his hand.

"You have not earned the right to such pleasures," I say coyly, catching the air that gathers in the back of my throat.

He presses his fingers against my clitoris and whispers ferociously into my ear, "And neither have the others whom you have taken to your bed. So, tonight shall be no different." He takes my hand and presses it against his hardness. "Feel the thickness and length of my desires for you. Squeeze it and feel its pulse." I squeeze. "See. It beats for your warmth. And tonight, I shall have it, Raghaba, goddess of desire. You will saturate me with your juices, and I will fill you with mine."

My juices are now coming to a rapid boil as he pins me up against the wall and grinds himself into me. I can feel the girth of his manhood pushing against my stomach. Strong hands encircle my waist. His lips devour mine.

I pull away. "I am not prepared for you." The wetness that drips all over his probing fingers defies what comes from my mouth.

He licks his fingers. "No, my sweet Raghaba, you are more than ready. And tonight," he says, scooping me up in his arms, then walking toward the back of the house to the stairs that lead to the roof, "we shall greet the gods who look down upon us under the stars and share with them our heated passion."

I do not protest. I allow him to carry me to the roof where he shall unleash his fantasies, and where I shall indulge them.

Once on the roof, he puts me down so that I can retrieve the rolled reed mat and coverings. Then he unrolls it, and covers it with the coarse linen sheet. Silence guides us as we both hastily remove our garments. We stand naked, my erect nipples, matching the sturdy erection of his manhood. I take in his muscular body, the broad chest and narrow waist with massive thighs and heart-shaped calves. Strong, smooth and assured, Toth closes the space between us, pulling me into him.

"Don't ever deny me," he murmurs, planting wet kisses along my neck and collar bone.

"Then don't give me reason," I respond, stroking his penis, "and you shall not be denied." *Well, at least not tonight,* I think as we tenderly hold hands, gazing deep into each other's eyes. For me, there is no genuine emotion attached to my words or the act. It is just a part in the script, an imaginary role I am more than comfortable playing—for now.

He rubs the edge of my vulva; wets his fingers in my juices. My clitoris is hard, sticking out, exposed and vulnerable. My vagina, hot and ready, contracts. As he moves his body, so I move mine. He fondles his testicles, and I manipulate my clitoris. Our eyes lock together.

Toth catches sight of a clay jar on a wooden stand in the far corner. He walks over to retrieve it. "What is in it?" he asks, making his way to the other side of the roof.

"Beer. Why?"

"Good," he says. He opens, and takes a long swig, walking back over to me. He kisses me, delivering beer into my mouth. He licks as it slides down my chin and down my chest. He tells me to hold my head back, and open my mouth. I obey, and he turns the jar up and pours, its contents spilling out of my mouth. He licks all over me, pouring beer all over my breasts, then sucking and slurping it up. "Mmm…you tastes so good."

I let out a soft moan.

"I want you to get on your knees," he says, "and spread your legs wide, then I want you to arch your back and stick your backside out. I want to taste and eat the forbidden hole."

My clitoris twitches as my juices run down my leg. I am excited, and more than willing to submit myself to him in any way he wants. I get on the mat and follow his instructions. He licks the seam of my backside, then flaps his warm, wet tongue against its opening. He buries his tongue in, then his finger. I moan again. Feel my breath catch in my throat.

"I will make sweet love to this tender jewel," he says in between moans. He buries his nose into my seam, then inhales—deep and hard. "Mmmm...you smell and taste as sweet as the nectar from the lotus."

He pushes two fingers in, gets them in down to his knuckles, then pulls out. Then sticks them back in. He is teasing me. I wind my hips. The tight ring of flesh, hugging his fingers, puckers and twitches with the flick of his tongue. He slips a finger inside and I moan—spreading my legs wider—and gyrate my hips as his finger burrows deeper inside of me. He removes his finger, replacing it with his tongue as he pulls open my cheeks, tracing along the outer edges of my hole. His mouth caresses me; his tongue makes love to me. I hump my backside against his mouth, twisting and rearing and moaning.

"Mmm...mmm...uh...uh...ooooh...that's right, Toth, eat me... tongue me deep and wet," I say, panting. Toth is slurping and licking and blowing my anus. Taking me places I never knew possible.

"Hold open your sweet cheeks for me," he says, slapping my backside. My buttocks bounce against the sting. I pull them open, wide and ready for what's to come. Toth is a master at eating my backside, and I feel myself slipping into a frenzied, mind-boggling orgasm as he slips one, then two fingers into my hole and reaches between my legs with his other hand and fondles my clitoris, then slides two fingers into my slickness. I lose myself in excitement and in pleasure as he slowly inches his manhood into my tight, burning hole. I grimace, clutching the mat cloth.

"Uh..."

"Relax...it will stop hurting," he says, leaning over and kissing my back. "Let me dig open your walls, and travel to where no man has been."

He inches more of himself inside of me.

"Uh…"

He reaches around and fondles my breasts as he pushes himself further, stretching the tight ring of flesh that now aches and burns and twitches to accommodate the length and width of him, the veined trunk of his hardness pulsing and pushing against resistance, against need, against want, against desire—piercing me, causing the intense sweetness of pain and warmth and pleasure to swirl in my lower back, then explode through my body.

"Oh, yes," I sigh, pumping my hips to meet his slow, thoughtful thrusts. "I'm so wet…mmmph….mmmph…"

"That's it, Raghaba…take it all," he whispers into my ear, the heat from his loins escaping through his mouth, causing my skin to tingle. "Oh, beautiful one, you are so tight," he moans. "You feel so good…"

I clench my teeth. "Uh…," I moan, craning my neck to see him. His eyes are closed and his bottom lip is pulled in. He plants his hands on my hips and moans as he maneuvers his hips in many different directions, hitting the center, the sides and the bottom of my rectum. "Uh…uh…it feels soooo good."

We are so caught up in rapture that we are unaware of the eyes that are taking in our every movement, savoring the rise and fall of our bodies. Inhaling our scents, and basking in the aroma of arousal.

Toth moans.

I moan.

Then we are both startled by a noise. It is of someone clearing his throat. We both stare with surprised looks on our faces. It is Horus standing in the doorway. His eyes are full and wide, dancing with lust from watching us. He smiles as Toth continues to thrust inside of me, makes no effort to stop. I am starting to feel uncomfortable knowing Horus is here, but Toth does not care. He presses his chest against my back, sucks on my earlobe, then whispers, "Let him join us." His thrusts become harder. His penis thickens.

"Nooo," I moan. "Ooooh...yes...uh...no."

"Let him join us," he says again, pushing harder, pulling my cheeks open wider as he stretches my rectum.

"Uh...mmm...oh, yes...mmm...noooo..."

I close my eyes, block out his request, and concentrate on the building sensation that stirs itself around my clitoris. I do not know how long my eyes have been closed, but when I open them, Horus is kneeling over us, hovering near my face. His penis inches from my reach. My lips quiver in anticipation; drool slides down the side of my mouth. Toth sees this and seems to be excited. He seems eager to see me suck Horus's organ while he inches my legs up over his shoulders and around his neck. My back bows as his hands lift my buttocks up off the mat. Then he slides his thickness into me, stretching the yawn of my vagina. I gasp. He fills me with the length and width of his phallus. He begins pumping deep inside of me, and my juices start to splash against the edges of his manhood.

"Do it harder," Horus eggs on, pinching my nipples. My vagina gets wetter and hotter with him tweaking my nipples between his fingers. "Make her beg for mercy from the gods above." I glance in his direction, eyes slick with pleasure, and see he is stroking himself in time with Toth's thrusts. "She likes it fast and hard," he says, licking his lips, encouraging Toth to deepen his stride. His shaft rapidly plunges in and out of me, like a hot spear.

I am on fire, blazing like the sun, my hips slamming up against Toth's, each thrust deeper than the one before. The sensitivity of my nipples is heightened by Horus's touch. It is feeling so good. Toth is feeling so delicious inside of me. Horus is looking so delicious over me. But I shall not give either one of them the satisfaction of bringing forth screams of pleasure. I bite down on my lower lip.

"Harder," I demand, stifling a moan that gets caught in the back of my throat. He slams himself into me. "Stop teasing me, Toth...feed me...lose yourself in me."

He is panting. He is grunting. His hips are thrashing. His body is slick with sweat, and glowing under the moonlight. His face is twisting. I am forcing him to deliver pain and ecstasy in deep, fast strokes; forcing him to bring forth an orgasm that bursts through my hot, sweaty flesh. And with each stroke, in all its intensity, he is determined to give me all that I am asking, with force and urgency.

"Uh...," he groans.

I catch the moon, full and bright, in the center of a cloudless sky, smiling down on me. I close my eyes, hold my breath, fight back the moans, and focus on the gold of dawn and the crimson of sunset that stretches across the back of my eyelids. I am coming. I bite down on my lip, pull Toth into me, dig my nails into his skin, and rake my nails along the small of his back.

"Deeper!" I yell.

"Faster!" I beg.

I open my eyes and turn my head to Horus. He is pumping his manhood in and out of his hand. The head of his penis is sliding in and out, peeking at me, taunting me. His heavy testicles hang loosely, swinging back and forth like a pendulum as he strokes himself. I reach up and touch them, feel the weight of them, then open my mouth to receive them as he lowers them down into my mouth. I suck and lick them as he strokes himself with one hand and strokes my clitoris with the other. I lap at them as Toth strokes the inside of me. I swallow and gulp them as I pinch my right nipple with my hand.

Overhead, I catch the glimpse of the rays of the sun as it begins to lower itself over the Nile, crawling against a burst of pinks, oranges, and blues that brush across the horizon. I am coming. A rush of heat is swirling through me. I am coming. The world around me is spinning. I am coming, coming, coming. Again and again and again, wave after wave after wave, my juices splash against Toth's thrusts. I will not scream. I want more. I need more.

"Harder," I urge.

"Harder!" I shout.

"Harder!" I demand.

I turn my attention back to Horus, taking hold of his penis, then slowly slipping its bulbous head into my mouth. I suck. I kiss and fondle his testicles, my finger tracing a slow, sensuous path over and behind each one. And he lets out a soft moan that seems to turn Toth on. The sight and sounds of me making love to Horus with my mouth excites him. I deliberately make loud sucking sounds. There's a twinkling in Toth's eyes as he locks his stare onto my mouth nursing Horus's manhood. He licks his lips, moistens them, as if he wants to pleasure the length of Horus, too. I may be in the throes of passion, but I am acutely aware of the attraction—or fascination—that stirs in Toth's eyes for Horus. It fuels my already burning fire, ignites prickly sensations that shoot through me, and expels into an explosion of throaty grunts and groans. Toth's excitement strengthens and lengthens inside of me. I wrap my legs around his waist as he lifts my hips up off the mat, and buries himself deep into my womb.

My hand finds the groove of Toth's neck and I draw him near, pull him to my lips and kiss him. My tongue darts back and forth between his mouth and Horus's phallus. I swirl it, fast and wet, caressing Horus's manhood and Toth's lips at the same time. I alternate between sucking and kissing, kissing and sucking, then both simultaneously.

"That's right, sweet Raghaba," Toth says, urging me on, "suck Horus like you have sucked no other. Take him down into your throat so that he may empty himself into your belly."

I moan and gag and gulp and swallow until I finally have Horus deep down in my throat. Tears rim my eyes, threaten to blur my vision. I fight them back. Stare into the center of the sky; see the moon slowly creeping out; feel the day's heat lifting; drag my long, red-painted nails along Toth's back, breaking skin.

Toth moans.

Horus moans.

I moan.

We are all moving to the same beat—Horus's hand rubbing my clit, my mouth and lips on his manhood, in sync with the thrashing hips of Toth who is trying so desperately to find a way to climb up into my vagina, crawl through my womb, then push himself out through my mouth. There is a hum, followed by a string of music playing in my ear. The sweet plucking of the harp, the jangling of the sistrum, the whistling of the flute, the ringing of bells, the thump-thumping of drums, the beat of rhythmic handclapping is all around me. I am coming, and coming, and coming.

Horus's left leg starts to shake. His head is thrown back; his eyes are closed; mouth wide open; face contorted with pleasure. It is a sign that he, too, is ready to release. I suck him harder as he grabs the back of my neck and thrusts deeper into my mouth. I am suffocating, gasping for air, but I am determined to bring him to ecstasy as I lose him past the hollow of my throat. Toth reaches up under me, and slides one finger, then two fingers into my anus, fingering me and pumping me at the same time. I am floating. I am losing myself in pleasure. I am craving more of Toth, craving more of Horus, gripping them both with orifices that are wet and dripping—the swish-swishing sound of fluids and air and friction rising in melody to the slapping of flesh against flesh.

I forget about the air I am fighting to breathe in; forget about the tears I am fighting to hold back, and greedily bob my head back and forth, slurping and sucking, hungrily throwing my hips up and down and around, meeting Toth's thrusts, greeting his slick penis, pulling his fingers deeper into my anus.

Horus's right leg now starts to shake. "Oh, yes…oh, yes…oh, yes…," he says, jolting his body forward as he releases himself down into my throat. I suck and gurgle and pant, trying to swallow all of his thick, warm cream. I remove his penis from out of my throat, keep my lips wrapped snugly around its tip and suck forth the remaining droplets of his semen.

He pulls his manhood out of my mouth and violently strokes himself, bringing forth another spasmodic orgasm that spills out onto the side of my face, my neck and chest. He rubs his penis on my face, then smears himself over my left nipple, causing a delicious current of heat and sporadic contractions to sweep through my uterus, pulling Toth further into the tightness and deepness of my valley.

Horus reaches down, scoops a bit of his thick, sticky milk onto his finger, then feeds it to me. I moan and swallow. Toth is watching me lick the cream off Horus's fingers. He whispers, "Yeah, eat the milk of his loins; swallow the bittersweet seeds of life." Then he leans in and kisses me, passionately, reaching into my mouth with his tongue for a taste of Horus. I smile, knowing what else he longs for. He looks into my eyes, and knows I will keep the secret of his desires. Nothing done tonight on this rooftop will be spoken of, or revealed to anyone else. It is what we shall take with us to our tombs and, perhaps, share in the memory again in the afterlife.

It is now Toth's turn to release the pleasure building in his loins. I continue to pump my hips up into his while Horus presses and rapidly massages my clit.

"Feed me your goodness...Oh, Toth," I moan. "...You are stretching me beyond the wonders of any pleasures known to mankind. Make the gods proud tonight, ram yourself deep into my valley." He thrusts himself harder, deeper. "Uh...mmm... don't stop. Yes, yes, yes..."

"Uh...uh...oh, yes...mmm...Raghaba...oh, yes..."

"Fill her womb with your seeds," Horus says in a seductive plea. "Make her womb beg for your release."

Toth grips my hips, then plunges ferociously in and out of me. "Uh...uh...oh, yes...mmm...uh." And when he finally comes, it is with a short, sharp cry and final thrust that propels me forward as he collapses on top of me.

⋅→═◦═←⋅

We are lying side by side. I am sandwiched in the middle—arms and legs enveloped. The temperature has dropped, and there is a soft breeze, fresh and cool against our damp, sticky bodies, glistening with sweat. The intermingling of juices, the sweet musky scent of sweat and unguents become reminders of our passion. There is nothing said between us, just the sounds of heavy breathing and hearts beating against the chorus of crickets.

Horus is slowly grinding himself up against my backside. I can feel the weight of his penis pressing against the seam of my buttocks. I moan, gently pushing back against it. I reach behind me and slowly jerk it in my hand. Toth is kissing me, and kneading my breasts, gently rolling my nipples between his fingers. Instinctively, without saying a word, Horus lifts up my right leg and Toth slowly slides his manhood into my wetness. The thought of having both of them inside of me, filling me up at both ends, causes my warm fluid to gush out of me. I smile, knowing the two of them have longed for this type of closeness.

Toth is now holding my leg up, and Horus spreads open my cheeks. He licks two of his thick fingers, then inserts them deep into my rectum. I moan and groan and grind. Toth flicks my clitoris and slides himself in and out of me. I offer him my breast and he sucks on my nipple.

"Uh," I moan.

When my hole is open and ready, Horus presses the tip of his penis against its center, then pushes in. I gasp. It is the cue Toth needs to quicken and deepen his strokes as Horus inches more of himself inside my aching anus. It is an ache that teeters between pain and pleasure. They are both deep inside of me now. I am grinding and pumping and squeezing my vagina to meet the wants of Toth. And grinding and pumping and squeezing my rectum to satisfy the needs of Horus. They are both riding in and around me. Their arms hang over me, clutching each other's. I have become a wet, willing vessel which they can enjoy, but they are so caught up in their own pleasures, that they become oblivious to me. They are pumping in me, but pulling at each other. I give them both what they want.

"Oh, yes...oh, yes...oh, yes...," I moan.

Horus grunts.

Toth grunts.

They both swell inside of me, ripe and ready to explode.

"Who am I?" I ask, moaning.

"Raghaba," they answer in unison.

"Who am I?" I whisper.

"The goddess of desire," they respond. The heat from our naked bodies pressed up against one another causes sweat to drip from our faces and down our backs. There is sweat rolling between my breasts and down my stomach, then gathering into the dip of my navel.

"Both of you," I moan, matching their grinds. They feel so good inside of me. "Come...come...come...oh, yes."

And, again, as if rehearsed, with their hands clasped and their fingers interlocked, they shake and shudder and fill me with warm, sticky seeds. We lay in one another's presence for a few moments longer before I lean in and kiss them both gently on the lips. It is a kiss full of secrecy and fulfillment. It is one that holds no promises. But it is what ties us, connects us, to our desires—and leaves us wanting more.

I stand, leaving them both with flaccid penises and empty sacs—drained and exhausted, wrapped in each other's embrace, knowing no other woman has pleasured them in the way that I have, nor allowed them to explore their hidden desires.

I am passion. I am longing. I am carnal pleasures. I am not to be tamed. Not to be confined. Behold...I am Raghaba—goddess of desire.

ಬಂಡ

Dywane D. Birch, a graduate of Norfolk State University and Hunter College, is the author of Shattered Souls, From My Soul to Yours, When Loving You is Wrong, *and* Beneath the Bruises. *He is also a contributing author to the compelling compilation,* Breaking The Cycle *(2005), edited by Zane—a collection of short stories on domestic violence, which won the 2006 NAACP Image Award for outstanding literary fiction; and a contributing author to the anthology* Fantasy *(2007), a collection of erotic short stories. He has a master's degree in psychology, and is a clinically certified forensic counselor. A former director of an adolescent crisis shelter, he continues to work with adolescents and adult offenders. He currently speaks at local colleges on the issue of domestic violence while working on his fifth novel and a collection of poetry. He divides his free time between New Jersey and Maryland. You may email the author at bshatteredsouls@cs.com or visit www.myspace.com/dywaneb*

A TWISTED STATE OF MIND

JANICE N. ADAMS

With downtown Atlanta in my rearview mirror and Sandy Springs north of me, I start my long commute. Thank the Lord, it's Friday. I'm completely exhausted and can't wait to get home. My crazy-ass manager, Ms. Collins, has worked my fingers to the bone. Every time that heifer plans to go out of town on business, she dumps so much work on me that I damn near lose my mind. She makes sure that I earn every penny Clark and Howard International, Inc. pays me.

Ahhhh yes, home sweet home. I enter through the garage, open the kitchen door and am hit with the aroma of sizzling steak, onions and peppers. The enticing smell leads me through the family room to the deck out back where I find my boyfriend, Keith Nelson, manning the grill. I stand at the sliding-glass door for a moment, taking in the sight before me: a well-groomed, buff, caramel brother wearing only a grill apron and a pair of knee-length jean shorts. Sweat beads on his forehead and glistens across his upper body from Hotlanta's ninety-eight-degree temperature and the heat of the grill. *Mmmm-mmmm, he's simply scrumptious.* He makes me want him every time I look at him. I open the door and his welcoming eyes greet me.

"Hey, baby. How was your day?" He presses his soft and sexy lips against mine and I can't help but to kiss and slurp them.

"Insane. Boss lady is at it again. She's out of town all next week and gave me a pile of crap to do between today and when she gets back."

"Well, that's what happens when you're the star. She trusts you. That's a good thing."

"Yeah, well, she doesn't have to work a sista like this to show her confidence. Some of the other assistant attorneys can share the load, too. Anyway, enough about work, what are you preparing?"

"One of your favorites, a big juicy steak, veggies on the barbie, and baked potatoes."

"Mmmm, you're making my mouth water."

"Yeah? Well, after dinner, I plan to put something else in your mouth."

"Oh really." I grab his sweaty shoulders, draw him closer, put my hand in his pants and take hold of his dick and scrotum. "Is this what you're gonna feed me?" I squeeze his groin harder.

"Oh, so, it's like that? Aight. We'll see who's holding what. Dinner should be ready in about twenty minutes."

"Fine." I release him with a smile and watch him regain his composure.

"Are you hanging outside with me?"

"Hell to the no. It's too damn hot out here for my cocoa behind. I'm going inside and get comfortable. Call me when dinner is ready."

"Cool."

After changing into a soft, cotton summer dress, I lay my head back and relax on the sofa with a glass of white Zinfandel. As I watch Keith's gleaming, athletic body put a hurtin' on my steak, I drift and reflect about him.

***

The rainy season is gone, been gone, and doesn't seem like it's ever coming back. I miss the days when I dated a freak as freaky as me. I wish Keith would let his cum rain down on me like I *really* like it, all over my face, tits, and belly. What better way to find out the taste of a man than to have him skeet on your face, right? I like to take my hands and rub the warm cream on my face like moisturizer. Every man's cum is different, some tart, some bland, and some downright sweet. Those are the ones I like the best. Keith thinks letting his creamy, hot fluid run down my pussy and thighs is exciting enough. Hell, I like that shit in my cookie, up my ass and all over my dark espresso skin. Quite frankly, his conservative attitude and behavior is getting on my last nerve. The drought sets in like the Sahara Desert and this shit is getting harder to endure.

I crave the dangling, long dong between a robust man's legs. Watching a huge cock bounce toward me with each step a man takes excites the hell out of me. How many more days and nights can I stand watching my boyfriend walk toward me with his six inches of dick that's only going to saturate my pussy and thighs? I'm dying for nine inches and my creamy, pearly shower.

I remember the first time I saw Keith's half-naked body. I knew I'd hit a homerun with his fine, athletic build, big hands and large feet. But when he dropped his boxers and I saw his thang, I snickered "pencil dick" in my mind but I didn't dare show my amusement. Hell, he spent two hundred dollars on dinner that night. Most ladies are happy with six inches of lead pipe but not my golden kitty. I need a dick that consumes the center of me. If I can close my thumb and middle finger around the dick, and the dick doesn't bottom me out, it's a small dick to me.

Damn, look at the time; it's four-forty-five p.m. on Monday already. Where did the weekend go? The last thing I remember is sitting down eating dinner with Keith. Anyway, let me stop sitting here thinking about his dick and leave this nine-to-five. Besides, I'm just trippin.' The brother treats me like a platinum princess. I get anything I desire. I'll just continue to deal with his thang and fantasize as usual.

I step onto the elevator, leaving the thirty-fifth floor, and as usual, it stops on almost every floor as we descend. I'm still getting accustomed to 191 Peachtree, a fifty-story skyscraper. Parked at the twenty-second floor, I hear a deep voice request, "Press fifteen, please."

I look up from searching my purse for my car keys to see who possesses the sexy baritone. *Oh, my damn!* It's the guy from the fitness center downstairs. What I wouldn't give to see what he's packin'! The brother goes to the gym as religiously as I do. I work out three times a week on my lunch hour, Mondays, Wednesdays, and Fridays. And each day, I wait until twelve-thirty when this six-foot-two, Hershey-dipped Adonis walks through the door. I play cool and pretend not to look at him, but any girl would be out of her mind not to. I study him intensely and know his routine by heart—thirty minutes on the treadmill or elliptical, thirty minutes of free weights, and two hundred crunches. One thing is for damn sure: The brother has strength and stamina, perfect for my sexual fantasies with him.

I freeze every time I see him do squats. I position myself in the room so I can watch his tight round ass go up and down while he balances the barbell. I lie on the leg machine to do my hamstring curls, rest my chin on the padded part and enjoy the sight, muscles flexing, sweat dripping, energy and strength exploding, man, what a turn-on. Usually, in his last ten squats, he makes an ugly face as he grunts to complete the set. I wonder if that's how he looks when he cums. Men can make some crazy faces when busting a nut. With all the weight he lifts, I know his legs and glutes burn like hell. If his legs can handle all that weight, I can only imagine what his strong legs can do when popping a coochie.

Personally, I just want to sink my teeth into his ass—better yet, grab him by the booty and navigate him deep into the center of me. He wears loose-fitting shorts over his spandex biker-like apparel, but I can still see the large bulge in the front. I know he's packin' but how much is the question. When he releases the barbell, I drool at his upper body that is exhilarating as well.

His arms are cut to a tee; every bicep, tricep, and pec flexes with each movement. I wonder what it's like being held in those muscular arms. I envision him standing, holding my five-foot-nine hourglass frame around his waist, while I ride his wild, black stallion. Keith is built, but not like this guy. To top everything off, this fine specimen of a man has those sexy, bedroom eyes like the well-known DJ, Donnie Simpson. His hazel eyes bring radiance to his chiseled face. And may I add, the faint shadow beard he sports isn't bad, either. Whew! The brother gives me chills and makes my pussy want him every time I see him. Six months of watching him, and I've yet to learn his name. Everyone at the gym is so into working out, I don't dare break the flow or expose my desire to know him by asking someone, who is he? That's how office rumors start.

After I lift weights, I wait for the boring step aerobic class to end. I go to the wooden dance floor to do my own aerobic routine. I open the closet door where the stereo equipment is stored and put in my own CD of hip-hop remixes. I turn that sucker up, face the mirrors, feel the rhythm in my bones, and let go of my own pent-up energy. I love to dance. I'm my own video vixen. I mostly combine moves from Janet Jackson, Ciara, and Beyoncé and generally end my routine with some Latino salsa. I gyrate my hips so fast I wanna holla, "You go, girl," when I see my reflection. By the time my workout is over, sweat beads down my face, and my cotton tank top displays puddles of absorbed sweat. Even my socks are damp with sweat. Some days, I hear clapping at the end of my routine from someone in the workout area, but I never see who it is because the equipment blocks my view.

When I walk to the closet to retrieve my CD, I admire my workout efforts in the mirror as I see my well-toned body. I love being in shape. I have strength and stamina, too. *Mmmm-mmmm, what wonderful things Adonis and I can do with these healthy bodies.* I chuckle at my nasty thoughts of having explosive sex with him.

The sound of the elevator closing jolts my mind from the gym back to our present close proximity.

Well, here's my chance. It's now or never. I break the ice. "Aren't you leaving work like the rest of us?" *Stupid question, but that's okay; he'll say something.* I just want to watch his sexy, delicious lips move.

"I need to get something from my office first, Miss?"

I ignore his curious voice inflection, signaling me to say my name. What fun would that be if I told him right away?

"Oh, I see," I respond, waiting for him to say more. If he's interested, he'll part his scrumptious lips and talk to me. He looks at me more intensely as if he's trying to figure out something. Then with a moment of realization, he inquires, "Hey, aren't you the young lady at the gym who dances after the aerobics class?"

"Perhaps." I'm not quick to say "yes" because I'm not sure what he thinks about my dancing.

The elevator dings at the twenty-first floor and more people enter. It's always a long journey to the lobby. The metal doors close and we continue to descend.

"That is you. You look good out there." His compliment makes me relax and enjoy our small talk.

"I didn't know anyone watches," I lie just to see what he says.

"I bet that you hear someone clap at the end of your routine. Who do you think that is?"

"I often wonder who's applauding. Is that you?" I ask, drooling over what I know is beneath his stylish attire—the big bulge and muscles for days. I try to maintain eye contact with him but I can't help but to look below his belt just this once. I don't feel too bad. Hell, he's looking at my 36DDs. Our eyes meet again.

"Perhaps it's me. How long have you been with Clark and Howard, Miss...? And what floor do you work on?"

Yes! He's diggin' me, too. "My name is Connie Winslow. I've been here for six months and I work on the thirty-fifth."

"The legal department, huh?"

"Yes." *Now watch him think I'm an administrative assistant or paralegal.*

"What position do you hold?" he asks carefully. The brother has tact. I like that.

"I'm an assistant attorney."

He clears his throat as if surprised at my answer. "Damn, that's impressive. You look so young."

"Trust me; I'm older than I look. People often think I'm younger than I really am."

The elevator stops again and more people get in.

"Forgive my manners, sir, I didn't catch your name." "Sir" is so formal but he looks at least eight years my senior.

"Bishop. Bishop Thomas. Pleased to meet you, Connie." He extends his hand and I feel strangely stimulated when we shake.

"Interesting name. Any particular reason you're named Bishop?"

"Yeah, there's a story behind it, but it'll take longer than this elevator ride to tell you." He smiles with each word and the people on the elevator pretend to look at the red numbers count down. I hear a man cough in the far-right corner, but I'm not fazed by Bishop's obviously bold response. I take it as a naughty, playful gesture. I see where this sly remark is headed, right where I want it. Silly man in the corner just doesn't know.

"Mmmm, let's see..." I cup my chin as if in deep thought. "Perhaps at some point in your life, you anointed someone," I say playfully.

"Yeah, something like that," he replies with a devilish grin. The man coughs again. The elevator bell dings at the nineteenth floor and more people step in, pushing Bishop and me farther to the back of the elevator near the man in the far-right corner. The door closes and Bishop and I continue to play our inquisitive game, but in a soft whisper.

"Really? Maybe one day you can show me how the anointing goes? I'm curious to know what type of blessing a man like you can give." I see the coughing man in my peripheral damn near choke at my response. I want to laugh because this is fun.

"Yeah?" Bishop asks surprised and as if interested in my request.

"Yeah," I solidify.

Damn. The sound of the fifteenth-floor elevator bell dings and ends my entertaining conversation with Bishop. *Mmmm-mmmmm, there goes Adonis, such a fine specimen of man.*

"See you around, Connie Winslow."

"Definitely."

He winks at me and exits the elevator. I watch his tight athletic ass walk away as my pussy starts to quiver with lustful desire. I look at the man in the corner shaking his head. "Whew, you young folks are something else. You're new here, right?"

"Yes." I can't believe he's admitting to listening to Bishop's and my conversation.

"Be careful, young lady. Everything ain't what it seems."

"Such as?" I ask, curious of the man's statement and irritated he blows my Bishop high.

"Know who you're dealing with."

"Thank you, but I already do. What are you, my conscience?" I act like I know what I'm talking about 'cause I don't want the man to know that his comment alarms me. He doesn't reply so I grin and return to watching the red numbers countdown to the lobby. I tell the man to have a good evening and exit the elevator with my head held high and shoulders squared.

I hope rush-hour traffic is light today 'cause I can use one of Keith's body massages right about now. He has great hands. If only he had the dick to match, what fun I could have.

Damn, my cell phone is always ringing when I got too much shit in my hands to answer it quickly. Uggh, how annoying, I've got to change this Bach ring tone to something funkier.

"Keith? Hold on. I'm putting my laptop and briefcase in the car." He patiently waits as I place my stuff in the backseat. "Sorry for the wait. What's up?"

"I want your naked, brown body next to me, that's what's up. How much longer will it take you to get home?"

"Looking at the traffic, at least an hour and a half."

"Damn, girl, my pipe is gonna burst by then."

"No, it's gonna burst right now. Listen to me. Take your pants off and walk to the kitchen."

"Word."

"Now get some olive oil out of the pantry."

"Got it."

"Sit on the sofa and put a few drops on the head of your dick."

"Done."

"Now lie back, close your eyes, stroke your meat, and imagine me straddling your cock."

"Ah, baby, you're so good to me. I needed this. But I'll still be waiting for you to get here."

I listen to Keith jerk-off. The sound of his ecstasy excites me; I can't wait to see him.

***

Shit! After driving through all that damn traffic, getting home in record time for a body massage and some sex, Keith didn't touch the bottom of me again, and no damn pearly shower! I roll onto my side with my back facing him, look out of the bedroom window and think, *Keith's small Johnson has got to go.* He peeps over and looks at my dead stare while I wonder how in the hell do I continue to deal with this situation.

"Baby, what are you thinking about?"

I want to say "Bishop," but I don't dare. "I'm thinking about Quincy's BBQ that we're going to on Saturday and I don't have a thing to wear."

"Is that all?"

I watch him reach into his wallet on the nightstand. "Here's seven hundred dollars. Treat yourself to something nice."

"Thanks, Keith. That's so sweet of you." I don't mean that shit. I'm frustrated and just want compensation for a year of this neglect. I sure hope I run into Bishop on the elevator again tomorrow.

***

I give myself a final check in the mirror on this fine, sunny Tuesday morning. This short black skirt, tight-ass slate-blue blouse, and black, ankle-strapped pumps will do.

"Kiss-kiss, Keith. Gotta get to work. See you tonight." I blow him a kiss from across the bedroom and try to rush out of the door.

"Hold up. Don't a brother get a hug or somethin'?" I hug him and entertain his everlasting tongue kiss, then release my embrace just enough to look at my watch behind his head. *Damn, now I'll probably miss Bishop in the lobby.*

I drive like a bat out of hell trying to get to work by eight a.m. Traffic is heavy and delays my commute by fifteen minutes. I rush into the building's lobby and wait for an elevator.

"Eight-fifteen. Kind of tardy, aren't you, Connie Winslow?"

The deep, tranquil voice penetrates my thoughts and the playful tone lets me know that the six-foot-two Adonis likes what he sees. Why else would he remember my name? My womanhood starts to throb as Bishop stands directly behind my short skirt. What is it about this man that strikes me so? I pretend not to hear him. He steps closer to my ass and breathes onto the nape of my neck, "Are you having a good morning, Miss Connie?" I refuse to turn around. I wait to see what he does next. He damn near presses his penis on my skirt. "Someone is definitely not having a good morning. Problems at home, Connie?" The elevator door opens. Interestingly, it's empty for a change.

"Ladies first." Bishop extends his hand with a gentlemanly gesture. My wet box is sending down uncontrollable juices. I feel the cotton patch in my panties saturate from my natural lubricants. The door closes. "Cat got your tongue this morning?"

"No. I have work on my mind. My manager is out this week and I have a lot of work to do," I finally reply.

"Really. Yesterday, you mentioned that you're an assistant attorney, but you didn't mention what you do." He takes two steps toward me and invades my personal space. I step back one.

"I review outsourcing contracts for the firm," I reply, trying not to look or sound too interested.

"Damnnn. No shit. Sexy and smart."

"I'll take that as a compliment and you should watch yourself. I could report that comment as sexual harassment."

"I know. But you won't," he says in an arrogant, matter-of-fact kind of way.

"Mighty cocky, aren't you, Bishop? Does your wife approve?" His wedding ring blings in the elevator light like rare African diamonds. He takes two steps toward me. I don't move, as I secretly desire him. His bulge comes to my mind. *Is his dick a six- or nine-caliber?* I wonder. He ignores my question—typical—and continues to walk toward me. I see right through his pants and can imagine his long dong bouncing in the air as it approaches me. He stops in front of me.

"Is there something over here that I can help you with?" I ask, trying to remain cool, but my wet pussy is a dead giveaway. I want his cock in me.

"No, there's something over here that I can help *you* with," he insists.

"And what might that be?" I look at the red numbers, only eight more floors before he has to get off.

"I can help you with this."

He reaches under my skirt and into my panties, getting a handful of my lubricants. I stand motionless against the back wall. As excited as I am, I forget that anyone might be waiting for the elevator doors to open to take them to the next floor. Just as I want to say something to him, I see the red number "15" above the door and the bell dings.

"I'll see you later, Connie," he announces.

"Uh, yeah. See you later," I reply still in a daze. The doors close. *No, he didn't just grab my snatch like that.* He did it so quick and smooth that my pussy wants a repeat of his middle finger in my wet, enlarged opening. He doesn't know that he's playing with fire. I'm a sexually frustrated, twenty-eight-year-old young lady who is dying to get bottomed out. And he just lit my fuse.

❋❋❋

The packed elevator stops on the fifteenth floor to let the lunch crowd in. I scoot to the side and stare up at the bright-red numbers and ignore Adonis' entrance to the increasingly packed elevator.

"Bishop Thomas? How's heading up the accounting department going? Haven't seen you or your staff since we closed the books on the Miller account. Love the work you did. Absolutely on point with our goals." The senior executive from upstairs obviously admires his abilities. I must admit that I want to know more about his abilities, too. Bishop moves closer to me. I stand catty corner to him and place the palm of my left hand behind my back and in position of his zipper. He covers my wandering hand with his briefcase so others don't see. I squeeze gently and get a huge handful of what he's packin.' He struggles to reply to the executive. "Ah, yes sir, Mr. Steinman. Thank you. Just let me know anytime I or my staff can be of service."

Mr. Steinman exits at the tenth floor. More people get on to journey out for lunch. The elevator is totally crowded now with lots of small talk. I slightly unzip Bishop's pants. His hazel eyes monitor the crowd as I search and find what feels like nine inches. I squeeze and rub harder. I hear him swallow dry spit. I grin at the lady across the elevator who starts to look suspicious at us. I ignore her, look up at the red numbers, and squeeze harder. At the fifth floor, I release Bishop's swollen dick and quickly zip his pants. I continue to look at the numbers, then at the lady. I'm certain she knows something is up, but I don't care. I have my thrills to fulfill.

The elevator bell dings for the first-floor lobby. Everyone exits except the nosey lady who tries to linger, but Bishops escorts her off in a gentlemanly fashion.

"Connie, wait," he insists.

He presses the "close door" button, then takes out a special badge, slides it across the sensor and presses "PH." *How the hell does he have a VIP badge to the penthouse?* I wonder. He's the director of accounting. Only senior executives have privilege to the penthouse floor. He must know someone important. His network connection turns up my fire another degree because someone of high status at the firm trusts him.

The ride to the penthouse is nonstop and for fifty floors we indulge ourselves with each other. He drops to his knees, raises my short skirt with his warrior hands, gnaws at my tissue-thin laced thong, then rips it away with one wild tug. My hotbox is so wet with anticipation. He lands his full, voluptuous tongue on my clit and teases my erectile organ like a madman, sucking it, pressing on it, and gently biting it. That drives me crazy. I grab the back of his perfect fade and hold his head right where I want it. He swirls his tongue all about my pussy, soaking my hair and inner meat. His tongue swoops inside my cavity.

"Keep it right there, Bishop," I moan.

Damn, this shit is off the chain. He tongues my kitty cat with his large, movable flesh and I cum on the substitute dick, long and hard. My creamy wetness covers his mouth. He stands and shares my pussy juice with me in a passionate kiss. I unzip his trousers and feel the heat of his desire to have me as I rub his overly warm penis and enlarged sacs. I continue to let him think he has the upper hand and allow him to slam his tongue into my throat while his middle finger goes into my vagina. I whisper, "more," into his ear to let him know I'm not a beginner. He includes his index finger and just begins to thrill me. "More." He gives me three. Now I'm starting to enjoy it. "More." Yes! The four fingers of this fine, dark-chocolate prince pumping in and out of me sends me into a spin. He watches me as I hump his foursome. He's more turned on. Damn, I want to let go of these two rails and do my thing, but he obviously likes this. I look up at the red numbers. We're halfway to the top. Only twenty-five floors remain. *Sorry, Bishop, but I got game, too.*

I release the rails and push his hand away while still locked in our passionate kiss. I unbutton his starched, blue-and-white-striped Sean John shirt, rip open his cotton tank undershirt, and rub his six-pack and chest with my free hand while the other drops his trousers. Now, what shall I do first to this panting, mostly naked specimen?

I quickly press him into the corner where the rails don't meet. I kneel and deep-throat his delicious meat. I watch his head toss back and feel his nine-inch dick grow another inch as I release it slowly from the back of my throat. I lick the tasty lollipop, up, down, and around with long intentional strokes. When I place Bishop's penis on my lips to enjoy his pre-ejaculation juices, I feel him motioning forward, wanting me to take it deep again.

"Not yet," I whisper.

I go to the base of his ass, spread his cheeks apart and run my tongue all around the outer rim of his asshole.

"Shit," he yells as he squirms with my tongue.

I spread his cheeks farther apart and poke his asshole with my tongue, making quick, wisp-like licks. Now, *he* grabs the rails. I stay there a moment, eating the athletic booty. I release his cheeks and hear him take a deep breath. I hope he doesn't think I'm done. I kiss his tight muscular thighs and venture to his scrotum. I engulf one ball, then the other. I hold Bishop's sac in my mouth and suck it like an ice cube on a hot summer's day. "Shit!" he announces, again. His satisfaction with my work makes me hotter. I release his nuts and look into his eyes; they speak with lust and desire. I place the circumference of his penis in my hand to lower him back into my throat. I can't touch my middle finger to my thumb. I'm more than pleased. I smile at him. He smiles back. I deep-throat him again. I feel his dick pulsate as the blood engorges the long-dong vessels. As I suck and lick, I feel the big dick swelling as Bishop begins to climax. He pants heavily and his body tenses. "Shit! Damn, Connie." His breathing is irregular and his dick is about to burst.

I hear the ding of the elevator bell indicating the arrival at the penthouse. "Fuck!" Bishop proclaims. I quickly released him from my mouth. He pulls up his trousers to find the badge in his pants pocket. He grabs it and hurriedly swipes the sensor just as the doors begin to open. I hear an executive say, "Hold the elevator, please." Bishop rapidly presses the "close door" button, then "L" for the lobby. I get another ride for fifty floors.

Bishop looks surprised when he turns around and sees my bare breasts standing at attention for him. I keep the excitement going, undisturbed by the ding of the elevator bell. Bishop approaches me, lets loose of his trousers. I watch them drop to his ankles, exposing what I long for—his ten inches. He lifts me with his strong, Hershey arms and situates my anxious pussy atop his perfectly round, thick-headed penis. He doesn't waste time. I'm glad because I want every moment to count. I grab the rails for more support and lock my long, espresso legs around his six-pack. The thick head penetrates me, in a little, in a little farther, in more, in deeper, in all the way. Bishop is huge inside my wet box. His girth reaches from one side of my pelvis to the other. His length touches my cervix and bottoms me out. There is no space left in me. He consumes the center of me, just how I like it.

"Damn, Connie. You got some good-ass pussy." He fucks me with repeated, fast motions, bucking my body like a wild rodeo bull. *Shit! This brother is laying it on me some kind of good!* I let go of the rails, crisscross my arms around his neck, and sink the tips of my fingers into his broad shoulders.

"Hold on," he orders. I hang onto Bishop as he grabs my ass and walks across the elevator. He smacks the "stop" button, causing the elevator to freeze at the thirtieth floor. He thrusts me into the far-right corner where that silly man stood and fucks me harder. We slide down the wall and onto the floor. There we lay, my blouse open, my short skirt hiked up around my belly, pumps in the air, Bishop's trousers around his ankles, his Sean John open, tank ripped, his bare chest against my excited nipples, and his ten inches at the bottom of me, pounding against my cervix while I drench him in my delectable juices.

He positions his arms under my knees and raises my legs backward over my head, pointing my moist box straight up to the ceiling. He descends upon my vertical pussy with such force that I moan his name, "Bishop."

"Yeah, baby? You like that big dick?"

"Yes!"

I feel his cock grow wider as more blood rushes to it. My body quivers and my vaginal muscles rapidly pulsate and send an uncontrollable amount of cum over his rod. I barely hear him say, "My turn." Bishop curls me into a ball under his Adonis body, squeezes me until I almost can't breathe, and then releases his white, gooey serum into my unprotected pussy with a long, satisfying grunt followed by *ahhhh*.

"You like that, huh?" I ask even though I know the answer. He looks at me, smiles, then answers, "Yeah. You got skills. I like that."

He rises off of me and presses the "stop" button again. We begin to descend the remaining thirty floors. His hazel eyes look at me ever so confidently, like he just conquered something. I gotta set him straight and let him know that I run this show, not him.

"You say that like this shit will happen again." I'm just fucking with his head now to hear what he says.

"Well, won't it? How can it not? And I wouldn't call this 'shit,' either."

See how easy a man's ego surfaces. He is so concerned about his Johnson and fucking capabilities. This makes it easy for me to control this conversation. I got his ass now.

"Well, I don't know," I remark.

He looks stunned, probably because he thinks that he laid something on me that I've never had before. He wants me to crawl back to him for more like I'm sure some girls have. Little does he know that he merely gave me what I've had in the past, and what I'm currently lacking from Keith. This makes me sexually dangerous, and him my play thang, if I want. He walks toward me, takes me within his grasp, and rubs his semi-flaccid penis against my saturated wet zone. He's determined to save face.

"So, what are you saying? This isn't what you expected?"

"Well—"

Before I can finish my sentence, he embeds his tongue into my mouth. During the midst of our kiss, he whispers, "You feel the heat like I do. I know it."

I don't need convincing, but it's fun to let him think that I do. I turn away from him and purposely look at the red numbers.

"Shit!" Bishop exclaims, realizing we're going to get caught if he doesn't let go and allow us to dress. We hastily fumble with our clothes as the elevator counts down from the fifth floor to the lobby. At the second floor, I ask Bishop how do I look as I fret over my skirt and blouse and fluff at my mid-length locs.

"Fine," he comments and rapidly continues to tuck his shirt into his pants and zip them. He reaches down and picks up his torn undershirt and stuffs it into his trouser pocket. I find my ripped lace thong in the corner and put it into my purse. The lobby bell dings. Bishop and I give each other one last smile as he stands overtop the wet spot we created on the carpet. The door opens and there stands the nosey lady. Bishop extends his hand in a gentlemanly fashion signaling me to exit first. I walk past the nosey woman and I hear Bishop say, "Ms. Claire, how are you today?" She doesn't answer him but informs him that his shirt buttons are crooked.

"Thank you, Ms. Claire. I hadn't noticed."

The lady steps onto the elevator and I briefly see her sniff the air and frown at the spot on the carpet. She raises her hand to catch Bishop's attention, but he ignores her and the door closes. He quickly catches up with me before I journey to the parking garage.

"Connie, wait. Where are you going?"

"To find the closest store to buy some new panties," I whisper with a smile.

"Word. Okay, well, um, I'll talk with you later."

"Okay."

I watch Bishop head in the direction of the café and I continue to exit the lobby.

The workday ends without me seeing Bishop again, but my kitty cat constantly reminds me of him. With his girth and that vertical position, he tore me a little. Every time I go to the bathroom, a slight stinging sensation occurs at the beginning of my perineum. My pussy hasn't been stretched out like this in a long time. It's only seen the action of Keith's undersized pecker for a year.

*** ***

At home, Keith is waiting as usual. He generally arrives first because his commute is shorter and he doesn't have to deal with the damn freeway traffic. I hate my commute. I could buy a new Prada bag every month with the amount of money I burn in gas. I'm glad Keith is good for something more than sex. After paying bills, investing ten percent of my paycheck, and setting aside my emergency funds, there's not much left for anything extra. I gotta admit I like how Keith allows me to save my money and spend his. That might be wrong, but hell, he can afford it.

"Hey, baby. How was your day?"

"Fine. I had an unexpected meeting that went very well. I'm worn out from it. I think I'll skip dinner and go to bed."

"Mind if I join you?"

Hell yeah, I scream in my mind. I don't want Keith messing up

Bishop's staying power. I want the essence of Bishop's sex to linger with me until I'm ready to wash him away. But I gotta do the right thing.

"I'll wait for you upstairs, sweetie," I reply to Keith in my platinum princess voice that he's accustomed to hearing. *Damn, so much for letting my encounter with Bishop marinate.*

***

I perfectly time my arrival at the office on Wednesday.

"Miss Connie, how are you today?" His delectable voice sends chills down my spine as we board the elevator with the others. I purposely stand across from Bishop to eye him face to face. He's so handsome, chiseled jaw line, soft-shadow beard, pearly whites, and cleft chin. My hot zone begins to throb as I think about what he's packin'.

"Other than dealing with my commute, I'm fine, Bishop. Thanks for asking."

"Heavy schedule today?" he wants to know.

"Not really. Just some contracts to review and have ready for my manager when she returns next week on Monday." I lie because I suspect he wants to do something today.

"Wonderful. I need your expertise to go over a bid that has some serious financials. Are you available at ten this morning?"

Check him out, trying to sound legit in front of everyone. I think it's cute.

"Sure. I'll meet you in the conference room on your floor."

"Ten o'clock, it is," he confirms.

Yes! I know his cock is crying out for my moist box. He likes my deep cavity and my hot box needs more exercise.

I watch his sexy body exit onto the fifteenth floor with a couple of other people. I grin at the other four people journeying with me and snicker to myself. *If only they knew what I'm thinking. That's right, in what position will I mount Bishop's pole at ten o'clock?* I exit at the thirty-fifth floor, rush to my desk, and utilize the first two hours of my morning to get as much done as possible. I know our ten o'clock meeting is going to take some time.

"Press fifteen, please," I say to the man next to the elevator numbers. Damn, we're stopping at almost every floor. It kills me when people take the elevator to go to the next floor. *Take the damn stairs, you lazy ass.* If only I could really say that shit. Finally, I exit the fifteenth floor. I approach the receptionist behind the glass doors that read "Clark and Howard International, Inc. Accounting Department."

"Bishop Thomas, please," I request. The receptionist presses the black button on her switchboard.

"Mr. Thomas? You have a visitor."

"Send her on back," I hear him say through the speakerphone.

"You may go back, Ms...." The receptionist stumbles to learn my last name.

"Winslow, Ms. Connie Winslow," I say proudly.

"Ms. Winslow," the receptionist repeats to Bishop.

"Yes, I know. Send her back, please."

"Turn right at the end of the hall, go halfway down. Mr. Thomas' office is on the left-hand side."

"Thank you," I reply and begin switching my derriere down the hall.

I check out the digs of the fifteenth floor as I walk down the long corridor, making the most out of my first visit.

"Nice office," I announce, standing in Bishop's doorway.

"Come in, Connie, and make yourself comfortable."

I walk in confident and sexy. Instead of sitting, I walk to the large glass window behind his desk and enjoy the skyline of downtown Atlanta.

"Your view is lovely," I comment.

"It's not as lovely as the view I see from here." *Damn, his baritone voice gets me every time.* I turn in his direction feeling horny as hell. He stands facing me in front of his closed office door with his ten inches exposed, saluting me. He steps out of his trousers, walks to his desk, and sits in his plush, black leather chair. "Come here," he suggests, extending his hand to me. I touch the palm of his hand and allow him to lead me to his awaiting penis. I hear the DJ on V-103 announce the song "Ordinary People." Then the voice of John Legend serenades us from Bishop's sleek stereo. I slowly crouch down on my knees between Bishop's muscular Hershey thighs, and begin my deep-throat action. He grabs onto the arm of the chair and watches me take him whole.

"Damn, Connie. Nobody handles me like this."

I suck harder and draw his big cock deeper into my throat. I go up and down on it, sending Bishop deeper into his chair with a tightening grip. He arches, he concaves, he arches again and concaves again. I don't want to engulf his sac or kiss his asshole today. All I want is the ten-inch pipe. I release his huge penis and stroke it up and down with one hand, spreading my saliva while I unfasten my blouse and bra with my other hand. I place his dick in between my excited 36DDs, squeeze my breasts tightly around his dick, and suck the very tip of his penis. His length comes in handy to do this. He loves it. I release his dick, grab it tightly with my hands, and slap my face all around with it. He gets my drift. I deep-throat him again and stroke around his asshole with my index finger. He's too excited and I know this moment of lustful indulgence is ending soon. I feel the blood rush to his penis and then out of nowhere, his damn phone rings. He slaps the intercom button.

"What is it, Barbara?" he yells at the receptionist terribly irritated. I don't stop. Through the speaker I hear, "I'm sorry, Mr. Thomas, but your wife is on line two."

He hangs up with the receptionist and looks at me stroking and gobbling his dick while his wife waits on hold.

"Don't stop, Connie," he insists.

"Not to worry," I reply with a devilish grin and continue my handiwork.

"Hello." All I hear him say is, "Hey, yeah, huh, uh, okay, see you then." He abruptly hangs up and I have his full attention again.

I swirl my tongue all over his groin, hair, dick, balls and all. I take him back into my throat, down to the base of his penis and suck intensely. He throws his head into the back of his seat, grabs me by my hair, and pumps my mouth forcefully, filling my jaws with his monstrous dick. After a number of hard thrusts, he pulls me off of his lead pipe and squirts my face with his gooey cum.

"Mmmmmm! Mmmmmm!" he moans and is speechless. I squint my eyes as his warm semen covers my mouth, nose, and forehead. Ahhhhh, yes, my pearly shower! The drought ends and the rainy season returns; I love it. I'm so hot and turned on. I rub his bodily moisturizer on my face, neck, and tits. When he catches his breath, he smiles at me and says, "So you like my anointment, huh?"

I say nothing as I lick the remaining cum off the palm of my hand. He has sweet cum which makes the rainy season even more delightful. I whisper in his ear with my large breasts resting on his chest. "Is this how you got our nickname?"

He chuckles and admits, "Actually, yes. One day after football practice back at Morehouse, some odd years ago, the fellas and I were sharing date stories in the locker room. After telling mine, they nicknamed me Bishop and it stuck."

"Does your wifey know you're a naughty boy who likes to anoint women in this manner? Did you anoint her?" I ask, licking him lightly on his earlobe.

"What do you think?"

"Don't know. That's why I'm asking."

"Why do you care?" asks Bishop while nibbling at my breasts and neck.

Why must he ask me that shit? I decide to tell him a lie. "I don't really."

"So, why ask?" he demands, still nibbling. *Damn, his lips feel so good against my exposed breasts.*

I ignore him because I don't want him to know that I do care. If only I can have something of him that she doesn't, he'll be more mine. I playfully laugh a little and then put his mind back to our business. "Bishop," I whisper, "we're not done with each other yet."

"True," he replies.

I turn around backward, descend on his long shaft, and give him a rump-shaking, lap dance with his joystick inside my hot box. He stands and humps me doggy style while I touch the floor with the palms of my hands still clapping his dick with my butt cheeks. Good thing I'm flexible. He then fucks me so hard we unintentionally travel toward the large pane-glass window. I spread eagle against the glass to brace myself from his force. If only the folks on the street could see us, what an eyeful they would get. Two naked jaybirds fucking sky high.

"Damn, Bishop, that's my spot!"

"Yeah? Well, come on with it then," he grunts. I moan as he

bottoms me out and my cum spills onto his engorged cock. "Oh, shit! Damn, your pussy is good!" I watch him throw his head back as he sinks his manly hands into the flesh of my ass. He holds on tightly and keeps his body close. I feel the bulging and pulsing of his penis as his cum meets mine. He squeezes my ass harder as if he wishes he could put all of himself in me. He slowly releases and backs away from me, staring in an unusual way. I can't tell if he's dazed or amazed. He grabs some Kleenex tissue out of the box on his desk and wipes his glistening, cummy penis.

"Damn! You know how to work a brother." He's definitely amazed.

"You may want to freshen up a bit in the bathroom down the hall to your right." He reaches for his boxers and every brown-skin, toned muscle flexes. *Shit, he's so fine.*

"I plan to. Don't worry."

He walks past me, slaps my ass while biting his bottom lip. He doesn't say anything but his slap insinuates he's a happy camper. I hope there are no finger marks on my ass from all of his grabbing. I couldn't explain them to Keith. He may have a small Johnson, but he notices everything about my body, everything except the fact that my pussy is being stretched to its limits these days. *Damn, I crave Bishop, but Keith is my source of stability. What is a girl to do? Have them both, right? Hell yeah!*

I scoot back into my size-eight skirt and affix my cleavage-making bra as Bishop stares me down from his desk chair. He sits charismatically, adjusting the knot in his silk, Armani tie. Even though our company allows us to dress business casual, apparently Bishop likes to top off his business shirt with an impressive tie. Lord knows, he stands out in my mind.

I purposely drop my tiny, black lace panties in Bishop's trashcan that sits adjacent to his light-maple wood desk—in plain view, of course. After dressing, he offers some small talk about the weather. I humor him and talk about the ninety-degree, hot, August day, then excuse myself to use the ladies room.

I wonder what he's thinking now, or better yet, if he's seen my panties. I push open the restroom door and discover that I have the place to myself. I moisten a handful of brown paper towels with soap and water, and grab some dry ones with my free hand. Just as I'm about to step into a stall, a soft, muffled knock is at the door. I place the paper towels in my intended stall and walk to the door, fluffing my locs in the mirror as I pass. I hear another muffled knock at the door. I open and peep around the door.

"Bishop? What are you doing here?"

"Anybody in there?"

"No, why?"

He slides through the small opening and quickly locks the door. Before I can utter a word, he puts his tongue deep into my mouth and grabs my naked ass beneath my skirt.

"You forgot something." With those words, he tosses my panties onto the marble vanity near the door. He lifts me off the floor and sits my exposed ass on the cold, hard marble countertop. I quickly get over the chilly discomfort and reach for the long dong.

"Connie, my dick is like a heat-seeking missile for your pussy." I feel Bishop inside me once more. He doesn't cum this time and that makes this encounter more challenging as only my vaginal juices moisten us.

Sweet mother of mercy, his penis girth is like the damn Grand Canyon. His dick is rocking against the breadth of my pelvis and at this point, it's hurting me so good. I want to let out a scream from the pressure, but I don't dare. A scream coming from the ladies room would not be good for either of us. Bishop sees my facial expression and knows; he is not only at the bottom of me, but he's giving me that bit of pain a pussy feels when a man has taken it all. I fake like I cum this time to make him stop. He can't have everything. I'm mindful Keith may want to hit something tonight. Bishop's last thrust interrupts my thoughts. Shit! He takes what little bit I could save for Keith. My pussy is a done deal.

Someone tries to open the door. Bishop and I look frantic as she pulls harder at the handle.

"Bishop, quick, hide in this stall. Close the door and stand on the toilet so she doesn't see your feet." I giggle at the sight of him pulling up his pants while scurrying to the stall. I pull my skirt down and straighten the rest of my clothes, walk to the door, and gracefully open it.

"Why is the door locked?" Ms. Claire, the nosey lady from the elevator, walks in like she's about to urinate on herself.

"Oh, I must have accidentally hit it when I came in." I play stupid until the fussbox enters a stall. I peep out of the restroom door, lightly tap on Bishop's stall, and hurriedly get him out of the restroom. At the door, he surprises me with a tender peck on the lips as he brushes past me. I'm not sure of its meaning. Does it matter? Maybe. I finally freshen up in the stall with the damp and dry paper towels, and then return to Bishop's office. I enter the room and wonder what can we say to each other. I don't know this man. I only know we have strong chemistry and great sex.

"I hear you are quite the assistant attorney at Clark and Howard."

"I do my best." I'm in shock. He's actually talking about business with me.

"Well, I would like for you to review this procurement contract with me. I can run the numbers, but some of the vendor's legalese is more challenging for us accountants. Do you mind helping me, like I asked on the elevator?"

"No, not at all." I'm still stunned but manage to switch gears like him. It feels good to know he appreciates my intellect as well as my lustful heat. How nice it is to be in the company of a smart, sexy, well-put-together brother. What a morning.

I call my friend Shelly Parker from my desk phone and excitedly tell her about my tantalizing encounters with Bishop. Between the whispering and fragmented code words, she gets the gist of my news.

"Connie, that's a trip. You gotta stop by after work and fill me in on all the details. Girl, you've only been at the job six months. Does he have a brother or a friend I can get *some* from 'cause you know a sista got *needs*?" We laugh at her playful desperation.

"I'll try to stop by if I have time. But I gotta go now. Chat with you later."

It's three p.m., the bewitching hour at work. I try not to hit the snack machine, but I'm always hungry around this time. Three hours after lunch and three hours before dinner. Almost daily, I walk to the snack machine and think I'll bring a piece of fruit for the next day. I never do. And to make matters worse, the company only has snack machines on every other floor. You gotta really want some sweets to go through the trouble, but a lot of people do, myself included. In goes another seventy-five cents. I'll get a bag of unsalted pretzels this time. They're better than chips. Normally, I take the stairs, but Bishop wore me out so much this morning, I think I'll take the elevator. Today, I'll be the lazy ass that I often complain about. Damn, I'm beat.

I stand waiting for the elevator on the thirty-seventh floor. The door opens. There stands Bishop and that damn nosey lady.

"Connie, what a pleasant surprise."

"Hi, Bishop. How are you?"

Ms. Claire pretends to watch the red numbers above the door, but I know she's hanging on to our every word.

"Fine. You know, I've been meaning to ask you, would you like to join my carpool? I'm driving this week. Friday is my last day. Then we rotate. We had three people, but the third just resigned from the company. You can take her place."

"Sounds like a good idea, but I—"

"You live in Sandy Springs, right?"

How the hell does he know that? I never told him. I hope his ass ain't no fatal attraction. If he knows the suburb I live in, I wonder if he knows my address. Oh hell, I wonder if he knows I live with Keith. Let me calm down and just answer the question.

"Yes."

"Well, so do I."

"Stop playin,'" I say surprised.

"Seriously. You can park at the Nort Springs Marta station. I'll pick you up there with the other rider."

"I'll think about it and let you know," I respond.

I already know my answer is "yes," but I'm not saying anything in front of Ms. Claire. Something about this woman unnerves me. The elevator bell dings and I exit to the thirty-fifth floor.

"Connie, let me know soon."

That baritone voice sends desiring chills through me. How can he have such an effect on me? I turn and say, "okay," with an appealing smile. The look that Ms. Claire gives me makes me wonder if she knows something.

I walk to my office thinking about Bishop's offer to carpool. The freeway traffic is horrible and the commute would be better with others. Maybe it will lessen my stress at the traffic congestion, not to mention the cost of gas. I tell Keith all the time that I don't need to drive the Acura MDX every day. But he insists because he says we can afford it. I know we can, but I still like to save whenever possible. That extra money could come in handy for something else. But as long as we're not feeling the pinch, I guess we're okay for now. *How in the hell can I explain carpooling to him? And suppose someone sees me at the station? Nope. No way, José. I can't carpool. It isn't worth the argument.* I sit at my desk and dial Bishop's extension. Butter-flies dance in my stomach to a Terrance Blanchard jazz tune on my radio as I wait for his sexy greeting.

"Clark and Howard. This is Bishop Thomas."

"Hi, Bishop. It's me, Connie."

"Hey. Hold on a second. Let me close my door." He quickly returns to the phone. "So did you think about my offer?"

"Yes, and regretfully, I have to say thanks but no thanks." I hear him sigh into the receiver.

"May I ask why? Does it have to do with this morning? 'Cause I—"

I interrupt him. "Bishop, this isn't about you. It's about me. I just don't think it's a good idea and it doesn't meet my needs."

"What do you mean, your needs?"

"It doesn't fit my lifestyle. I really don't need to carpool and I can afford the commute."

"Connie, everybody carpools or uses the Marta, even senior management. Most of us can afford the commute, but think about how much you can save in gas, time, and effort. If you carpool only once a month, the cost for gas is split three ways, and you don't have to deal with the stress of maneuvering through all the traffic. You know I'm right, so what's the real reason? Is it about us?"

"Us? Since when is there an 'us'? You're married, remember."

"Ohhhhh. So that's it. Well, you don't need to worry about that."

"Who said that I was worried?"

"May I ask you something, Connie?"

"Sure."

"Do you have someone in your life?

"What?" I nearly choke on my ice water. I fumble through my top desk drawer, searching for a napkin to wipe the drips of water from the front of my blouse.

"I assume that means, yes?"

Bishop wants to find out more about me, I think. Or he wants to find out if I'll answer honestly to whatever research he's been conducting on me. *Which way shall I play his game? Mmmmm. Well, he's not totally forthcoming, neither will I be.*

"Well, I'm kind of seeing someone."

He waits as if I'm going to say more but I don't. Let him squirm and show just how much interest he has in my world.

"Lucky man. He has an intelligent, beautiful queen like you but he's not treating you right. I know if you were mine, I'd spoil you with treats every day."

I say nothing to his comment. I'm not putting Keith out there like that. He does treat me good, I'm his platinum princess, and he's my stability. Unfortunately for me, he has a disappointing dick. A girl can't always have it all. I've gotta get control of my weakness for this good-looking, educated, well-paid, respectable man with an outstanding cock. For the first time in my relationship with Keith, I'm out of control because of my sexual frustrations with him. I could quit now and end this lustful venture with Bishop, but I can't. His spell is upon me and I'm captivated.

"Yeah? What treats might that be?"

"I think you know. The main two reasons why a woman messes

around on a man are for money or sex. We both know you're well compensated financially, so the sex deposits to your bank must be insufficient, aren't they? If you allow me, I want to give you a bigger deposit with a more favorable return on investment."

"Why should I?" I question to see where he takes this.

"Because you know our chemistry is sizzling, satisfying, and explosive. You like the heat we create and I like your fire."

Just hearing him speak these words to me sends surges of electricity straight down my spine, exciting my nipples and erogenous zones along the way. He knows that he's right and I can't tell him any differently.

"Yes, Bishop, you're right. But I still can't carpool. The North Springs station is too close to home."

"Well, what about if I pick you up at the Sandy Springs station? It's so busy there no one will notice. I can meet you early, if you like. I just want to spend more time with you. You do something to me no other woman has, and that includes my wife."

I pause to reflect on my answer. *I should stop this now*, I tell myself. I could stop it if I want. My pussy interrupts my thought as it pulsates with each of Bishop's pleads.

"Please, Connie, let's do this. I know you want to 'cause I sure as hell do. Nobody will know. I promise."

I know his offer means more than just a ride to and from work. *Oh, what the hell, I'll let him bottom me out one more time, then I'll stop.*

"Never thought I'd agree."

"So, that means yes?"

"Yeah, I'll carpool with you, Bishop."

"Terrific. I won't let you down."

"I'll park on the deck, then meet you curbside at Perimeter near the underground entrance. I'll be there at seven-thirty a.m. sharp. Don't be late," I order.

"Ah baby, don't worry. I'll come right on time. No pun intended."

I laugh at the innuendo, end our conversation, and finish my workday.

I'm so glad it's quittin' time. Wednesdays are always filled with meetings and conference calls. With my manager out of the office on business, the staff is more laid-back but the work never ceases.

Finally, it's five o'clock and my day is over. I drive home with the sunroof open, windows down, thinking about carpooling with Bishop tomorrow. *I wonder what naughty tricks he has up his sleeve? I know I plan to have a couple of my own.* I laugh at my mischievous thoughts while paying little attention to the road. Oh shit! I jerk the car to the right, cutting in front of an old Honda Civic barely making my exit. Whew, that was close.

Keith greets me at the front door with a hug and a delicious kiss when I enter the two-story, 5,000-square-foot home he bought shortly before we met a year ago. He says it's a real estate investment and when it's time to sell the house and invest in something larger, he wants me to be ready to join him. He often speaks of our future together and I wish with all my might that I could be totally happy with him. I just gotta find some kind of way to get past my stumbling block—his small rod.

Keith does well for himself as a record producer and distributor for underground rap artists. He's like an educated roughneck. He applies his 1997 bachelors degree in business administration from Towson State to his music business, making deal after deal, most to his advantage. I admire his sound business mind and how careful he is with his finances. He doesn't blow his money like a lot of young brothers who are getting paid. He's intelligent, handsome, built, and more generous than any other brother I've dated. Every time I offer to pay half the mortgage, he denies my attempt. He only asks that I pay the utilities and groceries. It's a sweet deal if I may say so. But there's one thing I know for sure about Keith—don't ever cross him. He's got a mean streak that is respected by many in his business. I guess he's gotta have that edge to be successful.

Occasionally, Keith asks me to review contracts, especially when he's questioning his own attorney's decisions. I don't mind, particularly because we work well together. Our situation is perfect, except he's not the best lover I've ever had—not because he doesn't know what to do, but because of his small pecker. But for now, until I figure out how to improve our situation, I'm gonna continue to bank every penny I can, so that if things don't work out with him, I can buy my own house.

"Hey, baby, how was work? Sit down and let me rub your feet."

We sit in the family room waiting for the Chinese takeout he ordered. I look into his dark-brown, cheerful eyes and for a split-second feel a moment of guilt as I remember Bishop's hard dick exploding in my aching pussy. The thought of Bishop's cock overtakes my guilt and I'm horny as hell again, desiring another bottom-out feeling. I want Keith to be able to reach my cervix, to pound it like Bishop does. I sit up, straddle his lap, and kiss him passionately to get his engine going; that doesn't take long. He is usually always ready for sex. He practically rips my blouse off, and throws me backward onto the sectional sofa. He kneels on the floor, yanks my skirt and new panties off, grabs my ass and pulls me closer to him. He throws my legs over his shoulders and eats my center meat so hard that I instantly cum.

"You like that, baby?"

I moan, "Yes, Keith."

"Who's your man?"

"You are, sweetie."

"Who takes care of you?"

"You do, Keith."

"That's right. Remember that shit."

He drops his pants, climbs on top of me, and straddles my face, letting his dick and balls hang into my mouth. He lowers himself onto my face and I take him whole. I suck his small dick like it's the best thing since sliced bread. He's moaning so hard I know he's getting ready to cum. I squeeze his cock with my hand and slap it on my face. I deep-throat him again. I want my pearly shower. *Please, Keith, just this once, let there be a rainy season*, I silently hope. I feel the blood rushing harder to his dick. I suck harder and wetter. I keep his cock close to my face. *Please, oh please, let this be our first*. Keith moans as he grabs the back of the sofa. I think he's gonna stay over my face. I'm so excited, I moan with anticipation. He humps my mouth with hard, deep strokes as if the moist palette is my wet box.

"Oh shit, Connie, I'm gonna cum!"

I don't stop; I can't wait to share this moment with him.

"Connie, don't stop, baby."

Doesn't he know I don't intend to stop?

"Damn, Connie, this shit feels so good!"

Almost there, I tell myself. He starts to quiver and I suck harder. He convulses and I beat his meat deliberately with one goal in mind—my man is gonna cum on my face. Yes, finally, I can't wait! A few more strokes should do the trick.

"Fuck!" Keith yells.

"Hell to the no," I scream. We're both pissed at the sound of the doorbell and the Asian guy hollering, "Chinese delivery." Keith tries to finish his last crucial strokes but it's useless. His concentration is further broken by the loud slam of the brass doorknocker. Being the protector that he is, Keith ceases our moment of truth to answer the door.

"Baby, I'm sorry. I gotta get that," he apologizes, then scrambles for his pants. I lie on the sofa disappointed as hell. I can't believe this. The one damn time I have him at the breaking point, fuckin' Ming Lee shows up at the door. Disgusted and unsatisfied, I get dressed and join Keith in the kitchen.

"Why did you put your clothes back on, baby? I ain't done with you yet," he informs as he places the delivery bags on the granite cook island. He walks me back to the sofa, stripping my clothes as we venture to pick up where we left off.

"Lay your sexy ass down," he says with a playful smile.

I oblige him knowing that the worst is about to happen. He enters my deep cavity and I can barely feel him, but I kiss and suck on his chest and neck to make him feel good. I can't let on that anything is wrong. He fucks me wildly and I go with the flow as usual. I moan and pretend like it's good to me. If I'm lucky, he'll cum quick. I'd much rather that he eat me. I always cum and get pleasure out of that. But this business about his dick in my pussy has got to get better, but how?

Keith grunts intensely, rapidly shakes his right foot like the little rabbit Thumper in the old Walt Disney movie, indicating that he's cumming. I hug and kiss him, making him feel loved and wanted. I know he can't help what he's blessed to work with.

"Did you cum?" he asks, always aiming to please me.

I don't want to lie to his face so I answer, "I came when you ate your snack."

"Word. I just want to make you happy, Connie."

"I know. I am," I lie. *Damn, this situation makes me feel awful.*

"Are you ready to eat?" I ask, hoping this fiasco is over.

"Yeah."

We dress and Keith holds my hand as we walk to the kitchen. Even for that short distance, he displays his affection for me. I'm lucky to have a caring man like him.

***

I look at the crystal dial of the watch Keith gave me on Christmas last year. Thursday, six-fifty-five a.m.—five more minutes. Suddenly, I feel a little uneasy about my carpool activity. I know this is wrong, but I yearn for the sex Bishop gives me. I think about my sexual encounter with Keith yesterday evening. *Lord, why didn't you bless him with the right equipment?* There's no way I can tell him how I really feel. It would kill him. What am I supposed to do? My decision comes quickly. I just want to feel Bishop one more time, then I'll cut him off. I promise.

At seven-thirty a.m., Bishop pulls up in a 2005, metallic silver Mercedes 500. I hope he doesn't think that I'm impressed. I often see cars like this and nicer. Some of Keith's clients have some serious James Bond-type rides, loaded with all kinds of gadgets. The doors unlock and I step off of the curb and into the plush vehicle. Bishop leans toward me for a good-morning peck. I oblige him with a warm, friendly greeting. I'm going to make this the best time ever, then leave his ass alone.

"Good morning, Ms. Winslow. How are you?"

"Fine."

"Good to see you."

"You too, Bishop. Did you miss me? 'Cause I sure as hell missed you."

"Damn, baby, your flame is combustible first thing in the morning, isn't it?"

I hope I can go through with my plan. Looking at him right now and smelling his fresh-out-of-the shower body is turning me on some kind of bad, making me want more than just *one* last time. *Can I do away with his fine ass? I hope so. Lord, give me strength.* He puts the car in drive, then rests his right hand atop my left thigh and rubs my slender, cocoa leg gently.

"So, Connie Winslow, tell me about yourself. Who are you? Where are you from? What's your favorite food? I want to know all there is to know about you." He inquires like he's genuinely interested. I place my hand atop his and lock my fingers with his. I can't help but to toy with him. Before divulging any of my personal business, I decide whether I want him to know anything else about me.

"Well, why do you ask?"

"I'm just curious. Just thought we could get to know each other better, that's all."

"Oh, I see. Well, does it matter? I mean, would it change anything?" I ask.

"You never know." He looks at me in that manly, matter-of-fact way. I know he's serious but I ignore him. His ass is married and I'm with Keith. None of this matters. I gaze out of the window as we exit onto the main road. He raises our hands to his mouth and kisses the back of my hand, catching my attention.

"It matters," he states, making direct eye contact with me. His sexy, hazel mirrors look at me sincerely. *Shit, why does he make me melt like this?*

"Well, Bishop, since it matters, originally I'm from Raleigh, North Carolina. I got a full academic scholarship to the University of Atlanta. I liked Hotlanta so much that I decided to stay after I graduated. I got a job as a pharmaceutical sales rep and hated it. Then, I decided to go to law school. So, I applied and got accepted to the University of Virginia. Earned my Juris Doctor. Moved back to Atlanta. Worked with the Circuit Court for about a year but didn't like that too much, either. The criminal justice system is a trip. Then my friend Shelly suggested that I apply for the job I have now at Clark and Howard. Someone told her about the opening. I followed her advice and here I am. I've been with the company for six months. What about you?" I'm curious as hell to find out more about him, too. With another kiss on my hand, he begins to share his life.

"Atlanta is my home. I grew up in Marietta. I left home and received my undergraduate degree from West Point. Then got my master's degree from Harvard's School of Business. At age twenty-five, I joined the Marines as an officer. Did two four-year tours overseas. Decided I didn't want to make a career out of the military. So, I moved back here. Got a job at King and Spalding for a few years, then joined Clark and Howard three years ago."

"Wow, you've been busy. So tell me, Bishop, where in all of that did you get married?"

"My marital status really bothers you, huh?"

What the hell does he think? Obviously, it doesn't bother him. *Plus, I'm just curious as to why he's steppin' out on his wife.*

"Well?" I look at him with raised eyebrows, waiting for his response.

"Connie, my marriage ain't all that. If it was, I wouldn't be here with you."

"I didn't ask you that. I asked when did you get married." Men always want to dance around a question when they don't want to answer.

"Well, let's see…" He starts counting the years backward like it's so damn hard. So, I help him out.

"Was it before or after you left the military?"

"It was before," he answers and doesn't say another word.

"That's it?" I ask, unsatisfied with his answer.

"Well, what else do you want me to say?"

"Where did you meet? Do you have children?"

I watch him squirm from this obviously uncomfortable subject. He fidgets with the control panel to adjust the air conditioner as he starts to sweat.

"Well, where did you meet?" I ask again.

"We met at Harvard. She was a professor at the law school."

Oh shit, no wonder he's choking. He's in an older-woman-younger-man situation.

"So what were you, her little boy toy?"

"Very funny, you got jokes. Go ahead, joke. I've heard all of them over the years."

"So, I gotta ask. How old are you, Bishop?"

"Thirty-eight," he announces modestly.

"I figured about right. So how old is she?"

He pauses, and then looks out of his side window like he doesn't want to answer. Naturally, I ask again.

"Well? How old?

"She's forty-eight," he replies reluctantly.

"Damn. No shit. For real?"

"Yeah."

"So what does she look like? Is she like Lena Horne still holding it all together or is she haggard looking?"

"She changed a lot after she found out we couldn't have children. She took it pretty hard. Next thing I knew, food was her best friend and our relationship went south. It's been a long thirteen years. The best years were the two we dated prior to when I left for overseas. I was away in the military, so there wasn't too much I could do to help her. When I came home during leave, she was always angry with me for being away. My visits never amounted to much."

"How has it been since you returned home? Things must have improved 'cause you're still married."

"To be honest, things got better—not great, but just better. She joined a weight loss program and I developed an exercise program to complement her diet. She did good and lost seventy-five pounds. Our friendship improved, but our relationship never really got back on track."

"So, if things improved and she got control of her depression, and your friendship improved, why not build upon that instead of cheating on her?"

"Connie, you don't understand. It's more complicated than that."

"Well, if you don't mind me saying, what's so complicated?"

He pulls into the Park and Ride at the Lenox Mall Marta station. A scrawny man approaches the car and Bishop unlocks the doors. I use every second to my advantage.

"Well, what's her name?" I know I'm pressing my luck. I got a fifty-fifty chance he'll tell me his wife's name. But surprisingly, he does.

"I call her Bernie. Now, can we drop this?"

He looks at me like he's hoping I'll end my inquisition before the man approaching the car opens the door.

"Fine," I reply.

"I'll tell you more soon." He quickly kisses the back of my hand and releases it, never to hold it again during our commute to work. The man standing externally to the car grabs the door handle and slides in.

"Mornin', B. Hey, who's this fine young lady?"

Bishop introduces me to the carpooler. He's a short, hyper, skinny man named George Lucas. He extends his hand and I shake the bony structure. I cringe at his corky attempt to hold my hand longer than I intend and curse him when he strokes my palm with his middle finger.

"What the hell is your problem?" I blurt. He immediately releases my hand. Bishop turns toward George and merely says almost in a joking fashion, "Man, George, behave yourself." Then he looks at me with an apologetic grin. "Connie, he didn't mean anything by it. He does it to every female that rides with us."

"Well, he shouldn't. Dirty bastard. Why doesn't he just catch the Marta since he's right here?"

"He doesn't like crowds," Bishop informs.

I turn around to face George to give him a piece of my mind. He greets my assertion with a snag-a-tooth smile that catches me off guard, and I lose my ability to cuss his ass out. All I manage to say is, "You need to get your grill fixed, you pervert." Folks say you can tell a lot by a person's handshake. George probably can't get any pussy and a nasty handshake is probably the highlight of his day and the best he can do. He talks a mile a minute as we travel south on I-695 toward downtown Atlanta. His motor mouth gabs mostly about the news and current events. He's like a damn walking broadcast station. And loud, oh my gosh, this man is loud. I can't wait to get to work to get away from him. His political conversation about President Bush and the Senate is boring me to tears. I try to change the conversation to the war on terrorism, like where the hell is Osama bin Laden and why the U.S. can't find his ass. But George is stuck on the latest Senate bill proposals. I stare out of the window while Bishop entertains the conversation all the way to work.

We finally arrive after more than an hour's commute. Bishop drives into the lower-deck parking garage and parks in a far rear corner. George, with his loud-ass mouth, has something to say about it.

"B, man, why are you parking down here? We usually park on the first level."

"Man, George, I'm tired of these fools putting dings in my car because they park too close. Every day, seems like there's a new one."

George exits the car, stands back, and looks along the side of the car. "B, I don't see any dings."

"That's because I have them fixed all the damn time. Do you know how expensive that shit is?"

"Yeah, I hear you, man. Well, look, I gotta run. Later. I'll see you at five o'clock."

"Later," Bishop agreed.

I watch George scurry off to catch the elevator to the lobby, laptop case in one hand and lunch cooler in the other. He looks rather comical trying to keep the laptop strap on his narrow shoulder while his little Oompa Loompa feet shuffle across the parking lot.

Bishop and I linger at the car. The lower level is sparsely occupied. He exits the car, comes to my door, and opens it. I gotta admit he does have nice, gentlemanly manners. I exit the Mercedes and stand close to him, allowing the sensational fragrance of his Sean John cologne and manly physique to fill my senses. Bishop presses me against the car door and softly says, "I can't restrain myself another minute." With those words, he parts my lips and slides his tongue into my mouth for a passionate French kiss. I can't help but to kiss him back. His warm breath wisps over my ear, "I want you, Connie. Can I have you?" We both know that shit means right here, right now.

"Yes," I answer as my pussy prepares for him.

He unlocks the doors, takes my purse and laptop out of my hands and places them in the front seat. He then opens the back car door and we slide in, me on my back and him on top of me. Thank the Lord for his dark-tinted windows. He reaches under my skirt to remove my panties, but I surprise him when he discovers there's nothing to remove.

"Oh shit! Damn, you're so sexy. You know just how to turn me on, Connie."

I grin but say nothing, and continue to kiss him wildly. I like being naughty. I unbuckle Bishop's belt while he unzips his pants. He presses down between my thighs and almost instantly his long, thick, brown dick finds my heated center. He puts his penis in me, one inch at a time. I gasp with each down stroke. I feel my walls fill up with him as he reaches the bottom of me. I'm so wet and he loves it. My vaginal juices drain out, soaking our pubic hair. My diva starts to sing with her sweet wet sounds. In and out, Bishop pumps my snatch and sends me into a daze. Shit! This man knows how to satisfy me. I grab his ass and navigate him a little to the right so he can hurt me so good. I want to scream but I can't. Damn, he's so big!

"You like that, Bishop?"

He breathes heavily in my ear. "Hell, yeah! You got the best pussy I've ever had."

"Fuck me, Bishop. Fuck my pussy the way you like it."

He braces himself firmly and thrusts me harder than before. I scream out, "Ouch, Bishop, you hurt me so good!"

"Yeah? Here's some more for you," he grunts.

He wraps his arms under my ass, pulls me more toward his swollen dick and takes everything I have. I feel myself blacking out as my vaginal walls pulsate, sending my cum all over Bishop's pole. I barely hear him say, "Oh shit! Connie, I'm cumming so hard." All I see are stars. His dick swells in my cavity so much that I can't move. He fucks me with quick, deep pulses as he ejaculates in me. He makes his grunt face like the one I see him do at the gym. I know that I please him, and for some strange reason, I feel proud.

Bishop opens his eyes and we smile at each other. My first thought is there's so much cum between the two of us, *how the hell am I going to wipe the gooey mess off of me?* I still have to go to work. It's not like I have on cotton panties to help absorb our cum.

"We've made quite the mess, haven't we?" I ask, looking down at our half-exposed bodies.

"Yes, we have. Hold on a sec." Bishop pulls up his pants, and then presses a button on his key ring. The trunk pops open. "Don't move. I'll be right back," he informs. I look out of the window to see what he's doing, but the windows are foggy. I can't see shit. I hear the trunk close and Bishop returns inside the car. He hands me a clean, white hand towel. "I keep a few extra towels in the car for when I work out at the gym."

"Thanks." I wipe my wet zone dry and watch him wipe down the long dong that turns me out each time we're together. I want to say something to him, but no words come to my mouth. As usual, he breaks the ice.

"What are you doing for lunch today?"

"Nothing. It's Thursday so I'm not going to the gym. I'll probably grab something from the cafeteria and eat at my desk." I hold up the towel by the corner. "Where should I put this?"

"Ahhh, let's see." He looks around as if searching for a bag, but his car is totally spotless. "Leave it on the floor. I'll get it. You should join me for lunch across the street at the Westin Peachtree Hotel. The restaurant has great food and we can finish our conversation."

"Sounds good to me. I've always wanted to eat at the revolving restaurant, but just haven't gotten around to it."

"Cool. I'll meet you there at noon," Bishop confirms as he completes tucking his shirt into his trousers. He points to my towel. "Hand me that." I raise it by the corner and hand it to him.

"Connie, you touch it like it's poison. It's just me and you," he jokes, exiting the car. I hear the trunk open and shut. He returns to my car door, reaches inside, and guides me out by the hand.

"Come on, we should get upstairs, but let me wipe this down first."

I look at my watch, eight-twenty-five a.m. *Shit! I'm late.* Even though my witch of a manager is out of town on business, she always leaves her secretary in charge of employees' time in and out of the office.

"Bishop, I gotta go. I'll see you at noon."

"Bet. Just give the hostess my name when you get to the restaurant."

I leave him wiping down his backseat and make a mad dash for the elevator to the lobby. I stand in front of the main elevators to go to my office, and goofy-ass George appears and has the nerve to approach me.

"Connie, right?"

"Yes."

"You're just getting inside? Where's Bishop?"

"I don't know. Excuse me, please." I gladly step onto the elevator to get away from him. I see him turn and yell, "Bishop, man, where have you been? I left you in the garage thirty-five minutes ago."

The elevator doors close, ending my tolerance of his annoying voice. I enter onto my floor and luckily, my boss' secretary is away from her desk. I rush to my office and partially close the door. Just as I log onto my computer, the secretary knocks on my door, asking a made-up question about the Harrison contract. I know she's taking a head count.

I watch the time elapse, counting down to twelve when I am to meet Bishop for lunch at the Westin Peachtree. There is so much work to do, but I need a break. My manager, Ms. Collins, should know better than to overwork her staff, whether she's here or not. She's not the nicest boss I've ever had, either, always demanding and controlling. She gives micromanagement a whole new meaning with her stringent ass. I wish the heifer would leave and never come back. But that'll never happen. She's a partner and gets much respect at Clark and Howard. They say she's hell in a courtroom and I believe it too, 'cause she gives me hell every day.

I hope my eleven o'clock meeting for the Barron account doesn't run over. An hour should be enough time to negotiate the final terms of the contract.

I look at the conference room clock again and I'm irritated that Mr. Barron wants to haggle over one small detail about the verbiage around license renewal. I do all I can to meet the needs of the Barron Group as well as Clark and Howard's terms and conditions. Finally, at twelve-fifteen, Mr. Barron agrees to sign the contract. I give the final drafts to the paralegal to type up and return to me by close of business today. I return to my desk, grab my purse, and head to the elevator.

I anxiously wait for the elevator to descend to the lobby level.

I rush out the front doors of 191 Peachtree and race across the street. I hope Bishop is still at the Westin. It's twelve-twenty-seven. I know he's probably gone, thinking that I'm a no-show. But I'll go check just to be sure.

The hostess greets me with a friendly smile and I ask for Bishop Thomas.

"Right this way."

The hostess leads me to a table alongside the large, wide window. Bishop stands to greet me.

"I thought you weren't gonna come. What happened?"

"Closing the Barron account took longer than I anticipated. I'm sorry. I didn't mean to keep you waiting."

"No harm, no foul. Are you hungry?"

"Starving," I answer as I feel my stomach rumble.

The waiter approaches us, gives the lunch specials, and takes our order. While we wait for our food, I initiate our earlier conversation again. I'm curious as hell to find out more about Bishop and his wife.

"So, Bishop Thomas, tell me, why are you cheating on your wife?" I go straight for the jugular to see what he has to say for himself. I know my reasons for cheating on Keith. I don't know one female who says she likes an undersized penis. Whoever says, *it's not the size of the boat, but the motion of the ocean* is a damn liar.

As Bishop clears his throat to speak, I lean further toward him.

"Well, Connie, you see, it's kinda like this. I told you that she's ten years older than me, right?"

"Yeah, go on."

"Well, she, uh, well, uh, she um—"

"She what?"

"She, um, doesn't have a sex drive anymore. I thought after she lost weight that she would feel sexier, be more active, but she doesn't. I tried to be understanding and patient and all those things. But I got a sexual appetite like King Kong. A brother got needs. You know what I mean?"

"Yeah, I sorta do."

"I don't regularly cheat on her. I mean, I've had a lady friend here and there over the years, but the sex doesn't last long because they can't handle me. My wife doesn't satisfy me. Hell, she doesn't do anything with me. I'm doing good if I get a peck in the morning and at night. But you and I, oh my God. You got the golden gate I want and need."

"Oh, really." I play coy even though I know he's telling the truth about our sex. I tame his black stallion every time I ride him and make him breathless every time he fucks me.

"Yeah, Connie, you know our chemistry is off the chain." He leans forward across the table and whispers even more softly, "And when I get all of me in you, that shit feels like warm butter. You give me chills every time."

I hang on to his every word, watching his LL Cool J lips move. I want to jump across the table right now and attack him. *Damn! He has such a wicked effect on me.*

"Yeah, I know," I reply with my female arrogance. "You haven't seen anything yet." I challenge him because I want to see all of his naked body on me, not just his pants around his ankles. After he fulfills this desire, then I'll cut him loose.

"No shit?" He's surprised at my arrogant statement.

"No shit," I solidify. He knows where I'm taking this conversation. Ain't no two ways about it.

"You do know this *is* a hotel."

"I know that. What I'm wondering is why are you still sitting here telling me about it?"

"Oh shit! Connie, you are my kind of woman. Sit tight." He places a twenty-dollar bill on the table to cover the cost of our drinks. I watch him whisper to the waiter, and then exit the restaurant. About five minutes later, the hostess hands me a note that reads, "Come to room 619." The card isn't signed but I know who it is. I give the waiter the twenty dollars and tell him to cancel the lunch order. He informs me that it's already been taken care of.

I go to room 619 and knock on the door. Bishop answers in his birthday suit and immediately starts ripping off my clothes. We go at each other like two wild, hungry animals, gnawing and clenching each other. He sits me on the edge of the bed facing his cock. He lifts his right leg and places his foot atop the mattress. He guides my mouth to his saluting dick and I take him into my mouth and deep-throat him.

"Suck that shit, Connie. You know how I like it."

I give him what he wants, strong long sucks and quick lollipop licks. I then consume his dangling scrotum.

"Yeah, that's what I'm talkin' about. Damn, girl, you're good."

I say nothing. Handling his large sex organs requires concentration. He grabs the back of my head and pulls me back and forth, on and off his dick. He moans with ecstasy and I feel his big rod grow larger in my mouth.

"Don't stop, Connie."

I keep sucking and jerking his penis. He palms my head with his right hand and presses my mouth all the way to the base of his thick shaft. Then suddenly he snatches my head off of his dick, takes hold of his dick, and shoots his cum on my face as he pumps his hand back and forward along the shaft. I tilt my head upward to show him how delightful it is. He releases my head and uses his right hand to rub his cum all over my face.

"Yeah, Miss Connie, you like that shit, don't you?"

"Yeah. It's my pearly shower." I lick my lips and his cummy fingers. He lowers his six-foot-two, Hershey-dipped, Adonis frame onto his knees.

"Open your legs."

I comply and he kneels so that he's eye level to my wet zone. He wraps his arms under my thighs, then jerks my body toward him. I watch him eat my cookie until I feel myself losing consciousness to the sensations he sends throughout my body. He makes my clit engorge with blood, then sucks it so hard, I cum again and again. He finger-fucks my pussy while giving fast lollipop licks atop my clit, sending creamy juices down my sugar walls again. Damn, he knows how to satisfy me. He lifts my legs higher into the air, places one finger in my ass and two in my pussy, leans over me, and suckles my 36DDs. I cum so hard I scream his name and damn near black out. Before I can recover, Bishop flips me over and fucks me doggy style. My diva sings her wet, juicy song and saturates our pubic hair again. Bishop digs his hands into my hips and thrusts me back and forward onto his gigantic rod. My body quivers with every stroke. He's so damn big! He grabs the back of my hair, pulling my head up. I yell, "Bishop, fuck me harder, baby." I point my ass higher into the air. Somehow we always know what the other means.

"You want the king dick?"

"Yes!"

He withdraws from my pussy, spreads my buttocks far apart, and slowly slips his rod into my asshole, one inch at a time. I moan with each down stroke. We work together until we get him all the way in. My body adjusts to his girth and I let him know that I'm ready.

"Fuck me, Bishop."

Then he pumps in and out, faster, then faster. He pounds my ass hard. I grab the sheets and place them in my mouth to keep from screaming out loud. Tears come to my eyes 'cause he hurts so good. After a few more strokes, Bishops grunts, "Damn, girl, your ass is so tight around my shit, you're gonna make me cum again." And with that he withdraws and busts his nuts across my ass. His hot fluid drips down my crack as I turn and kiss his six-pack abs, chest, and neck. I stand on the bed and wrap my legs around his waist. He holds me mid-air, carries me to the bathroom, and sits me on the countertop. I say nothing and continue to suck and bite at his neck and chest. I like munching on him. He quickly wipes down his dick; I'm glad 'cause I don't want brownie crumbs mixed in with my cookie. He crouches a little, finds the center of me, and then pounds my pussy again. He has cum twice already, so I know this time we're in for the long haul, nothing but rock-hard, thick, long dick.

We move from the bathroom and fall onto the floor leading into the bedroom. I mount him and ride the black stallion full throttle. I lean my breasts over his face and he squeezes and sucks them so good and hard that I cum again on his joystick. Damn, he knows how to get to me!

We return to the bed, me on my back and him hovering above me, both of us sweating like crazy. My hair is frizzy, makeup gone, deodorant worn out, and Adonis blanketing me. Nothing but the smell of wild sex fills the room. As we take a moment to breathe, Bishop gently removes straggly pieces of hair from my sweaty forehead, places a peck on my lips, and says, "You're a beautiful young lady."

"Thank you." I try to think of something else to say but I have no words. I feel him take his penis into his right hand and find the opening to my wet center.

"Are you ready for round three?" He smiles with a mischievous grin like he's so happy to have someone of his caliber.

"Of course," I reply, thinking strength and stamina, what these two healthy bodies can do together.

"We don't have much time left," I inform.

"I don't need much," he replies as he begins to stroke my inner meat with the tip of his big poker. And he's right. Our chemistry takes over and we're two wild animals again for a solid thirty minutes.

Exhausted from our midday escapade, we lay on the bed, naked and satisfied. I give five minutes of what could be considered cuddle time, then I head to the shower to keep from dozing off like Bishop. I don't want to be more than fifteen minutes late returning to work, even if boss lady is out of town. I know her secretary keeps tab. "Hawk Eyes," as we call her, will allow you fifteen extra minutes. It's like being fashionably late, but after that, your ass is grass. And although I have a good job, I don't have a senior position like Bishop where a person can bend the rules a little more. He can nap all he wants, but I'm gonna have my behind back at my desk smelling like sweet roses in no time.

As I exit my steam-filled, ten-minute shower, Bishop greets me at the bathroom door as I towel-dry. I purposely moon him as dry my calves.

"Woman, you better stop bending over like that before I have your ass back across the bed again."

"Oh really?" I brush my breasts against his well-defined Hershey chest and arms, making my way back into the main room. I sense him staring at me, so I peep in the mirror opposite the bed and catch him not only staring at me, but also seemingly having a personal conversation with himself.

"What did you say?" I face him to see what he does while sliding one lean leg into my skirt, then the other.

"Uh, nothing. I'm just thinking about what I have on my agenda when I get back to the office."

Liar. I know a look of contemplation when I see it. He's probably wondering what the hell has he gotten his married ass into. I understand how he feels, wanting to cut someone off for something you think is better but can't. There's no question in my mind that he cheats on a regular basis with other women, but I know that I rock his world the best. I can have his player ass whistling "Dixie" right about now, if I want. My coochie is dangerously addictive. Too bad he's only getting a taste 'cause when I walk out of the door, this hot and nasty affair is over.

"Bishop, I gotta go. I'll chat with you later," I yell from the living area. He pokes his head out from behind the white shower curtain and summons me.

"Connie, hold up. Come here."

I turn the corner to see him gesture me for a peck with his soft, scrumptious lips. I can't resist. I kiss them ever so sensually. My subconscious won't let me walk out the door like I want. *Grab that dangling cock one more time* rushes through my head. My thoughts shift between *walk away, Connie, and touch it again. One more time won't hurt. Walk away, Connie.* I can't resist my urge and give into my temptation to squeeze Bishop's genitals again.

I reach behind the curtain and get a handful of dick and balls. *Damn, he feels good in my hand, warm and wet.* I stroke his cock while I continue to kiss him. He opens the curtain all the way, exposing himself to me. I wrap one hand around his muscular ass and continue stroking his dick with the other. He unbuttons the top button of my blouse. Water from his fingertips drips onto the delicate garment. Do I care? Hell, no. I'll just make good use of the wall-mounted hairdryer.

"Get in." He entices me in a whisper that sends chills down my spine. *How can we possibly have this much attraction for each other?* Bishop extends his hand.

"Join me, Connie."

"Hawk Eyes" crosses my mind for a split-second. Fuck her! I slowly undress, giving Bishop a personal striptease show. He smiles as my taunting pleases him. His gun loads with the ammunition I need, and I'm more turned on, watching the barrel get thicker and longer. My breasts stand at attention and my nipples harden as I anticipate touching him in the shower.

I step in and watch the water bead down his face onto his chest. I instantly lick his chest and circle my tongue around and across his nipples, then slowly cover the territory of each muscle that composes his six-pack abs. As the moments pass, I'm quickly reminded that I stepped into the shower without anything on my hair. My blow-dried hair is saturated and begins to curl. There's no use in trying to save it now, and quite frankly, I don't care. It is what it is. I feel Bishop's hard pole against my belly as I kiss him around his neck. He sucks my neck hard. I pray he doesn't leave hickies—that's a no-no in my book. Keith would kill me, but this shit feels so good I can't stop him. He squeezes my 36DDs and presses them together making the water puddle in between them. He slurps the puddle dry, then releases the water onto my lips as his kisses them again. He grabs my breasts harder this time and proceeds to suck and bite the shit out of my nipples. He pulls on my nipples with his teeth and gets me more excited. My pussy wants his dick so badly I can hardly stand it. The element of the water always turns me on.

"Eat me, Bishop."

His lips and tongue travel over my breasts, down my abs, over my belly-button piercing and ventures through my forest. I watch him part my pussy with his thumbs and index fingers. He slides three fingers in and out, and sucks my creamy juices off them.

"You're always so wet, Connie. I love that shit."

I grab the back of his head and press him toward my snatch. He parts me again, then glides his tongue in and out, up and down, and all around. He takes my clit between his teeth and tugs at it gently. I moan with ecstasy. He licks my cunt hard and intentional with the sole purpose to make me cum in his mouth. Using his tongue and fingers, he makes me do just that. I cum all over his mouth.

"Awwww, Bishop, that feels good, baby."

"You like that, huh?"

"Yes, baby."

I'm hotter than ever. He stands and gets his footing on the wet shower floor, squats a little and raises one of my legs. Aaaahhhh, yes! I love how he navigates his big Johnson into the center of me. He pounds my pussy with such force that I scream with hurtful pleasure.

"Ouuuuch, Bishop!"

He grabs the metal towel rack and drives deeper, sending my pussy to the back of me.

"Ouuuuch, Bishop!"

"Your pussy is so good, Connie, I can't stop."

He drives deeper and my tears join the cascading water.

"Do you like how I fuck you, Connie?"

"Yessss!"

"You like my dick, don't you?"

"Yessss!"

"You want me to fuck you harder?"

"Yessssss!"

"Grab on."

I lock my arms around his neck. He swings open the shower curtain and lifts me around his waist. I watch him step over the tub like it doesn't exist at all. With our wet bodies never parting, he lays me on the bed and proceeds to hammer my pussy. He uses the spring of the mattress to help suspend himself above my sex zone. And right at the point when his dick is about to come out of me, he thrusts himself into me, time, after time, after time. I fear the bed is going to break.

"Cum with me, Connie. I'm gettin' ready to explode!"

"Me, too, Bishop."

"Ohhhhhh shit! Goddamnnnnn!" he grunts with that ugly face I like to see.

"Ohhhhhh Bishop! Damnnnnn, baby!"

I grab his Hershey ass and dig my fingers into his flesh. I gyrate my hips and without fail, we cum simultaneously.

"Whew! Oh my goodness, girl. You are somethin' else," he says breathlessly.

"You ain't too bad yourself," I reply, exhausted as well.

"We are two horny toads," Bishop jokes. We laugh at each other. I get a glimpse at the clock on the desk.

"Shit! Look at the time. I gotta go, Bishop. 'Hawk Eyes' is gonna have my ass." I run to the shower.

"Who?"

"My manager's secretary. I should've been back by one-thirty." I turn on the shower water and barely hear him say, "Don't worry about that. I'll cover for you."

I shower and dress in record time while Bishop takes another one of his quick naps. I wake him.

"How are you going to cover for me?"

"Don't worry about it. Trust me."

I don't have time to haggle over his meaning. I'll just face the music. He sits up and we give each other a peck.

"I'll call you later, Miss Winslow."

"That's fine."

As I head toward the door, I see Bishop reaching for the phone. I pretend to take one last look in the mirrored closet door, but really, I'm curious to know whom he's calling. He waves at me like a signal that everything is okay and to go ahead and leave. As I turn the door handle, I hear him say, "Hello, Ms. Matthew." I gasp. He's calling the secretary. *Who is this guy that he can do that? Nonetheless, if it gets my ass off the hook, who cares?* I leave the Westin Peachtree Hotel as one damn happy camper.

I open the front glass doors to the legal department with my head held high. "Hawk Eyes" sits at her desk like a bird on a perch.

"Ms. Winslow," she begins, "Mr. Thomas called and informed me that your meeting ran over causing you to return late. He was very apologetic as he knows we run a tight ship around here."

"I'm sorry, Ms. Matthew. I should have called you."

"No need. Bishop Thomas is a respectable man who stands in high regard here. I'm sure your meeting was productive."

"Thank you, Ms. Matthew."

Who the hell is this man to have pull like that? I return to my office and can't help but to sit and daydream about my escapade with Bishop. My pussy is throbbing like mad. Every time I think he has fucked me hard, he fucks me even harder the next time. His wife doesn't know what she's missing. That bitch must be crazy not to want him. It's a damn shame, too. Think about all these women out here trying to find a husband and her crazy ass has one, a well-endowed one at that, and she won't give him any. He's right. She's got some serious issues. The phone rings and interrupts my thoughts.

"Clark and Howard. Connie Winslow speaking."

"Hey, baby. Did everything go okay when you got back to the office?"

"Yes, Bishop. Thank you. How did you manage that?"

"Don't worry your pretty head over that."

"Don't tell me. You had an affair with Ms. Matthew," I joke lightheartedly.

"Hell no. Are you out of your mind?"

I laugh and he joins me. "Well, are you going to tell me or not how you managed this?" I ask again.

"Not this time. What matters is that you're set, right?"

"Right. I'll let you get away with it this time, Bishop Thomas. But sooner or later, you're gonna tell me."

"Okay, if you say so. I have a meeting at three so I have to go for now. I'll see you at the car at five, right?"

"Yeah. How else would I get home?"

"True. See you then."

"Ciao, Bishop."

The rest of my day creeps by probably because I want five o'clock to hurry up and arrive. I review purchase contracts, one after another.

Finally, at five p.m., I exit the building, enter the lower-level parking garage, and head toward Bishop's car. Behind me, I hear the scrawny man and Bishop.

"B, there's that pretty young thang again. Is she riding with us again?"

"Yes, George, Connie is riding with us again, so act like you have sense and manners."

"Okay, already. But she sure is a beautiful African Queen. Just look at those legs."

"George—"

"Okay, B, damn. I'll be on my best behavior."

I arrive at the car first, turn and watch them approach. Bishop gives me a warm and loving smile. Snaggle-toothed George can keep the jacked-up smile he offers. I roll my eyes at him to let him know I ain't having any of his shit on the way home. Bishop, being the charmer that he is, instantly smoothes the waters between the snaggle-toothed Oompa Loompa and me.

"Connie and George, how about we stop at the ice cream shop just outside the mall? I could go for some frozen yogurt."

"B, I don't know. Ice cream doesn't cost what it used to."

"Damn, are you that stingy with your money?"

"Hey, pretty thang, don't mouth off at me. Every penny counts."

"Well, who can turn down ice cream on a hot Georgia day? I'm game."

"George, it's my treat," Bishop offers.

"Oh, well, why didn't you say that? Ice cream sounds just fine."

No, he didn't. This cheap prick won't buy his ice cream. Ironically, he probably has a million dollars stashed somewhere, just saving his money while he spends other people's hard-earned dime.

We pull into the parking lot of the ice cream shop, and George acts like a little kid. He's the first one out of the car and rushes to be next in line. Bishop opens my car door and we walk together. He opens the entrance door for me and taps my ass when I pass him. He still wants to play games. I get my ice cream to go. We return to the car and drop George off at the Lenox Mall Marta station. We head home.

"Bishop, turn right here." I point in the direction opposite of where we should go.

"What's up? Where do you want to go?"

"I need to make a quick stop," I inform. "Now turn here."

"Are you taking me to where I think you're taking me?"

I smile in a naughty fashion and navigate him to a secluded area in Chastain Park. I come here sometimes just to think. It's serene and beautiful, full of Mother Nature. But I never stay long and don't get out of my car. There are weirdos in the world, and I'm not trying to be on the evening news. Nonetheless, I do like it here.

"Park right over there," I instruct.

"Word."

Bishop pulls into an empty space and parks the car.

"What's up, Connie? Why'd you want to come here?" He looks around and while he admires the scenery, I unbuckle his pants, whip out his flaccid dick and give him a lesson about the birds and the bees, and what they do with ice cream. Before he can say my name, I cover his dick with some of my double-scoop cookies-n-cream.

"Ohhhh shit! That's cold!" he bellows. I ignore him and go to work with my deep-throat action I know he loves. I enjoy watching him rise and fall, squirm and churn as I lick and eat away my evening snack. He's so excited but manages to reach behind my leaning ass and find his way under my skirt. His middle and index fingers penetrate my moist box and we pleasure each other once more. I'm so glad I don't have on my panties; easy access is best when you're with your ideal sex partner.

"Connie, I'm about to cum!"

"Give it to me, Bishop."

He rises and falls, squirms and churns, and grabs the steering wheel. Then just when his dick is about to explode, I cover the tip of his penis with more of my cold ice cream-filled mouth and swallow his cum with my cookies-n-cream. He falls back into his seat.

"Damn, Connie. You make me weak. Whew!"

"Just thought I'd give you something to think about tonight."

"Like everything else we did today wasn't enough? You gonna hurt a brother."

Strength and stamina, I love it. Bishop holds my hand as he drives me to my dropoff at the Sandy Springs Marta. He pulls up to the curb and a few other late commuters are returning to their cars.

"Connie, I'll meet you here seven-thirty a.m. sharp tomorrow, okay?"

"Okay. See you then."

We give a quick peck and go our separate ways. I feel like I've been horseback riding all damn day. My pussy is worn out and I'm glad. It's an excellent accomplishment for our last encounter.

I look up to see someone staring at me. No, it's not George, but Quincy Perkins, one of Keith's boyz.

"Whatz up, Connie?"

Oh shit, here we go. "Nothing. How are you, Quincy?"

"I'm fine. Looks like you doing fine, too."

Shit, he knows. I look in the direction of Bishop's car and can see the taillights at the traffic light before he turns the corner.

"It's not what you think, Q. I'm carpooling. That's all."

"Out here? Seems like you'd be at the North Springs station."

"Look, Quincy, this is the station that's most convenient for everyone. It's that simple." I hope his dumb ass believes me. What does he know about corporate America, anyway? What I don't need is for him to alarm Keith. So, I have to go along with this bullshit until he's satisfied with my answers.

"So, that brotha works at your job?"

"Yes, Q. He's the director of accounting and has been there for a number of years. What's your point?"

"My point? My point is, does Keith know you're carpooling with this brotha?"

Damn! Now he's got me. Do I lie or tell the truth? Lie, of course. I'll make this right with Keith when I get home.

"Yeah, he knows and is cool with it." I pray this suffices.

"Uh-huh, aight. I'll see you two at my BBQ on Saturday."

"Okay. Tell Daphne 'hi' for me." I hope I sound sincere.

"Yeah, aight."

I call Keith the moment Quincy is out of my sight. I know his ass is going to call him regardless of my explanations. I toss my laptop and purse in the SUV and dial Keith.

"Hello," he answers. His cool-sounding voice is music to my ears.

"Hey, sweetie. How are you?"

"Hey, Connie. Whatz up?"

"Nothing much. Just calling to say I'll be home soon."

"Yeah, aight. Well, look, I got Q on the other line right now. Let me call you right back."

"Okay. I'll chat with you soon."

Shit, shit, shit! I pound the steering wheel and drive like a bat out of hell to fix whatever damage Q causes.

Quincy is cool and all, but he and his girlfriend, Daphne Raquelle, are nosey as hell. Whenever I'm around them, they get on my nerves cause they always argue like two Chihuahua on steroids. She constantly yaps after him, and he barks at her. I don't know how they stand each other. They are too much alike. They are both control freaks and power hungry. They each have to be right all the damn time. Maybe that's the source of their problems. You don't have to be Oprah or Dr. Phil to figure that shit out. I can only imagine what sex must be like between them— *"No, you get on top." "No, damn it, you get on top." "Give me some head." "No. You eat my pussy."* So sad, but it makes me appreciate the serenity of my relationship with Keith. One thing is for sure, we get along great. No arguments here, except, well, you know, pencil dick, but of course, I can't tell him that. I just hope Q doesn't screw up things between Keith and me.

I arrive home and Keith greets me with a hug and kiss as usual. I watch his behavior and demeanor. He seems the same. Hopefully, Q passed on telling him anything. I walk into the kitchen and he informs me that there's a Boston Market chicken Caesar salad in the fridge for me. I take it out and sit with him at the kitchen table as he finishes his meatloaf with three sides.

"So, how was your day, Connie?"

"Good, how was yours?"

"I've had better. Negotiations didn't go well with an artist today. But, I have another potential I'm checking out tonight at the Pit. Do you want to come with me? He's supposed to be real good."

"Sure, sweetie. I'll go with you anywhere."

"Is that right?" The look he gives me makes me feel a little uncomfortable, so I excuse myself from the table to get a glass of white Zin and pull my act together. I return to my seat a bit more composed.

"What time do I need to be ready?"

"Eight. Show starts at nine. He's the first emcee."

"Okay. Eight, it is."

He excuses himself from the table and goes to watch TV. I finish my salad and then join Keith in the family room on our favorite sectional. I like resting with him at the end of my day. I snuggle under his arm with my legs curled to my side. He touches my thigh, and I react oddly, immediately rising to my feet, alarming him.

"What's wrong with you?" he asks, looking bewildered.

"I, uh, I, uh, need to go to the bathroom. I think my cycle just started."

"Oh, you act like something major is wrong."

Shit! How could I forget I'm not wearing any panties? I've gotta be more careful. I race upstairs, strip down to my natural birthday suit and proceed to the shower. Just as I'm about to step into the warm oasis, Keith turns the corner, reaches into the shower and turns off the water.

"Come here," he says, taking my hand and leading me to the bedroom. I quickly grab my towel.

"Sit down." He points to the California King bed and I sit my towel-wrapped body on the white goose-down comforter and say nothing. I wait to see where this is going.

"Connie, are we cool?"

"Yeah. Why?" I make an extremely puzzled expression to pretend he has asked a silly question.

"Everything is everything, right?"

"Right. Keith, what's up? Why are you questioning me?"

He says nothing for a moment and an awkward pause fills the air.

"I'm your man, right?"

Holy mother of Mary, where did that come from? Remain calm and answer the question, I think.

"Of course, sweetie. Don't be silly." His intense, concerned expression is anything but silly.

He looks right into my eyes and says, "Remember that shit."

Then he stands and walks away. I reach for him and purposely let my towel drop. If I'm lucky, I'll cloud his judgment with the sight of my cocoa, fine ass.

"Keith, what's gotten into you? You are my man." I press my naked body against his chest and wrap my arms around his waist.

"What's this I hear about you riding with some nigga from work? Don't I give you everything you need?"

"Yes."

"Yes, what? Yes, you're ridin' with someone or yes, I give you what you need?"

"Yes, you give me what I need. And yes, I carpooled today, but I only did it once to see what it's like and to see if it's beneficial. You know the traffic is horrible and the gas is expensive. We get to and from work twice as fast 'cause we use the HOV lanes. It wasn't bad."

"Who the fuck is 'we'?"

"The driver and another rider."

"Male or female?"

"Both male."

"Ahhh, hell no, Connie. You leave that carpooling shit alone. I don't want you riding with two mothafuckas I don't know. You've only been at the job six months. You don't know these people. Why would you do that?"

"Keith, the driver is a respectable, senior manager at the company, and the other man is a total geek. They're harmless."

"Half the crazy mothafuckas in the world are geeks. Next thing I'll know, you'll be on the six o'clock news missing persons report."

"Ahhh, sweetie, you're just concerned." I rub his back to soothe him. "Thanks for caring so much about me, but I promise you that I'm fine, really."

He looks at me with his intense brown eyes. "I just don't want anything to happen to you. You don't need these men to help you with anything; that's what I'm here for. We can afford the gas, the ride, everything."

"Okay, Keith. I don't want to argue. If you don't want me to carpool, then I won't. I'll send an email from my Blackberry and inform the driver I won't be there tomorrow.

"Word. Who's your man?"

"You are, sweetie."

"That's right. Remember that shit." He seals his boastful statement with a peck.

"I do remember, Keith, every day. You don't need to worry." I hug and kiss him lightly about his face and neck, reassuring him everything is fine.

"Aight. Let's get going before we miss seeing this new artist. I hear he's the shi-zite."

He grabs a handful of my ass, then quickly pats it as he walks away. I stand there thinking, *that damn Q; he needs to mind his own business, for real.*

❈❈❈

I fumble to turn off the annoying, chirping sound of my Friday six a.m. alarm, and linger beneath the Egyptian cotton sheets, snug as a bug. I'm exhausted from my exhilarating encounter with Bishop yesterday and hanging out with Keith at the Pit last night. We should have left the hip-hop club no later than midnight in order to get a decent night's sleep before having to go to work this morning. But Keith is always quick to remind me that the crowd doesn't get good until after eleven o'clock. Plus, he likes to see how the mass of patrons responds to an artist. It's one way he determines whether or not an artist has crowd appeal. Luckily, his potential client is a crowd-pleaser.

As I recollect about last night, I gotta admit, Phoenix, as people call him, brought the house down. Thursday nights will never be the same at the Pit when he's on the mike. His rap style sort of reminds me of Mos Def, who happens to be one of my favorite rap artists. Although Phoenix is not quite as polished as Mos, he certainly is an up-and-coming talent. Keith is still bouncing off the walls from Phoenix agreeing to work for him.

"IIIIT'S FRRRIDAY! Wake up, Connie, baby. Time to go to work." Keith pulls the cozy comforter and sheets off my naked body and exposes me to the cool air-conditioned room. My nipples quickly harden and Keith zeroes in on them like a suckling babe to its mother. He lies atop me with his sexy, naked muscular body and cups my 36DDs with both hands, sucks and gnaws at the tips of my breasts. I watch him take a mouthful of each breast, work his way to my pointed nipples, then tug just hard enough to make me moan with pleasure. The tension turns me on, and my breasts swell, as I desire for him to play with them more.

"I love your Betty Boops, baby. They're so full and perky, and soft to the touch."

"Yeah, I know you do."

As he places his face in my cleavage, I vigorously shake my breasts from side to side, smacking his cheeks with each backward-and-forward motion. He laughs and enjoys our playful moment. I'm glad to see that his mind is off our conversation last night about me sluggin'. Speaking of which, I need to meet Bishop at seven-thirty a.m.

"Sweetie…" I interrupt Keith's exploration that seems to be headed to my hot zone.

"Shhhhh. Lay back and relax. Let me give you what I know you like." He parts my long, slender, brown legs and rubs my clit with two of his fingers. This is going to be hard, but I gotta stop him.

"Keith, sweetie…"

"Shhhh."

He licks around my labia and I fight the urge to let him have me for breakfast. I push back on my elbows toward the headboard and force him to lose his position over my moist box.

"Keith, I can't this morning. I have to be at work early and don't have time to serve you my biscuit. I'm sorry."

As I leave the bed, a disappointing look consumes his face, even though he tells me that he understands. I feel strange, not because I'll miss out on his good, pussy-eatin' skills, but because today I need to tell Bishop no more carpooling and no more hot, crazy sex.

I stare at my reflection in the bathroom mirror, thinking I must be nuts to let go of Bishop's big, ten-inch, pussy-satisfying penis for Keith's small rod. How in the hell am I going to do this? Just thinking about Bishop and the fire we create is getting me excited. Shit, to tell the truth, I can't wait to see him. I'll wear something extra special today so that when I tell him my news, he'll crave me, but can't have me. I'm gonna drive his ass crazy with my control and power over our lustful affair. Yeah, I know, some would say this is teasing, but do I care? Hell no. If I gotta let him go, then I'm gonna do so in a fashion that will leave him desiring me. This way, if ever I have an itch, I know he'll be willing to scratch it.

Thirty minutes later, I kiss Keith good-bye and I'm ready to walk out of the house with just one thing on my mind—Bishop Thomas.

I arrive at Perimeter, waiting for the silver metallic 500 Mercedes to pull up. I know wearing these four-inch heel sandals with my mid-thigh, wrap-around dress is going to make him drool. I love how the material feels against my skin, especially since the only undergarment I have on is my bra for perfect cleavage. I have a thong in my purse for wearing after I complete my mission this morning.

At seven-thirty a.m., an immaculate 2005 Black Escalade slowly rolls up to the curb. The SUV is outfitted with a serious chrome grill, sparkling spinner rims, and dark-tinted windows, looking like it has been spit-shined from the rooter to the tooter. I commit the license plate, "THA BLKNT," to memory in case the person inside is up to no good. But I gotta admit, "The Black Night" does suit this armored vehicle. I stand on guard as the right passenger window lowers. I hear, "Mornin', precious," and am relieved to discover the driver of the Black Night is Bishop. I open the door and slide in, admiring the interior of the pimped-out ride. This is far more impressive than the Mercedes.

"Nice," I comment.

"You like?" he questions as his wet tongue tries to meet mine. I succeed in not slobbing him down like normal. I have to control this situation in order to end it, but I think this is going to be more difficult than I had planned.

"Yeah, this is cool."

"So, how are you today, Connie, my sizzling tamale? You look hot in that dress."

"How cute. I'm fine."

"Really? You look concerned about something this morning. And the conservative way you reciprocated my kiss is not exactly what I was expecting from you. Anything wrong?"

I'm trying to hide my thoughts, but I guess I'm not doing a

very good job. *There's nothing to do now except get this out of the way. The sooner, the better, right?*

"Well, Bishop, now that you mention it. There is something on my mind."

A huge pause occupies the space between us before he replies, "Sounds serious. What's up?"

I adjust the way I'm sitting to slightly turn and face him. *Damn! This is hard.* I look at my ideal sex partner—smart, career-minded, handsome, muscular, passionate—and think, *do I really want to give up his ten inches of rock-hard, thick, solid dick that consumes all of my deep cavity? Do I want to give up this Adonis who understands how I like my pearly showers?* Keith pops into my mind—a caramel-coated, take-no-shit, intelligent, successful entrepreneur who is handsome, athletically built, considerate, and loving. He does all he can to please me with the six inches he's blessed to have. But am I happy with him? He makes me laugh in ways no other does, appeases my senses; he always smells so damn good and is pleasing to watch. I feel at ease when we're together and he's easy to talk to and always listens to me, no matter what subject I choose to discuss. With Bishop, I never have much to say.

So, here I sit with a dilemma: *Do I give up Bishop for Keith's sake?*

"Connie, are you okay?" Bishop asks, interrupting my thoughts.

"Yeah, uh sure."

"Something's up. Let's go chat a moment," he suggests.

Bishop tries to make small talk as we drive to Lenox Mall where we pick up George. I moderately entertain the conversation but am mostly silent along the way. I see the signs for the Lenox Marta subway but instead of going straight to the Park & Ride to get George, he detours. He drives to a nearby parking garage and parks the Escalade on a secluded upper deck. He turns off the engine, killing a mellow groove by KEM that's soothing to my ears.

"Okay, Connie, let's talk. What's going on?"

Everything in me wants to just say, "I can't see you anymore," but nothing comes out of my mouth. I merely look into his beautiful hazel eyes and wish I could have him all to myself—no Keith, no wife.

"Connie, what's gotten into you?" His tone is changing, becoming stern. I realize I'm frustrating him and that's not my intention.

"Bishop, there's something I think you should know."

"What?"

"I uh, I think today is my last day carpooling. This isn't working out for me."

He looks at me blankly, then out the window and then back at me. I assume it's to gather his words.

"Connie, what happened? Did George say something to you 'cause I'll—"

"No, George hasn't done anything. It's just not working out for me."

"How so? Give me two good reasons why not."

Without exposing Keith's wishes, what else can I say? I lie. "Well, it's just that during the day, I feel trapped at work without transportation. Like yesterday, I could have gone to the post office to update my passport, but I couldn't 'cause I didn't have my car."

"All you had to do was mention it and I would've taken you."

"That's the point. I don't want to have to ask you or anybody else. I just want to get in my ride and go."

"I'm not buying this, Connie. It's gotta be something else. Is this about my wife? 'Cause—"

"No. It's not about your wife. It's about me and what I need."

Well, actually what Keith needs but I can't say that. "Are you feeling guilty about your wife? Is that why you ask?" I try to flip the script and turn the attention to him.

"No. Hell no. I want to be around you as much as possible and don't want you to pull back because of my wife. I explained where she and I stand to you, and I hope you believe me."

"Yeah, but what I don't get is, why do you stay?"

"Let's not dwell on that. What I care about right here, right now, is you. So tell me the truth. Why don't you want to carpool with me anymore?"

Umph, the truth, the truth is what I get from Keith even when it's brutal. I don't think Bishop is a truthful person, but he sure is hellasexy. *Do I care about his honesty? Not really, his sex is what I'm after.*

"Well, Bishop, the truth of the matter is, I'm not comfortable in this situation with you."

His perplexed expression indicates he's totally confused. So, I continue, "I don't think we should see each other anymore." I lean forward just a little to let my 36DDs put an exclamation mark on my statement.

"Stop playin,' Connie. You know we are equally yoked."

"Maybe I don't want an equal. Maybe I want an opposite."

"What the hell are you talking about?"

"Maybe I don't want a corporate eagle like myself. Maybe I just want an educated roughneck."

"Oh, I see where this is going. Some other nigga is tappin' that ass, or you want to start seeing somebody else, huh?"

"Bishop, time out. I don't need your permission for nothing and I don't have to tell you shit. We don't have any strings attached."

"Fuck that, Connie. What hoodlum nigga are you sleeping with?"

He catches me off guard with his jealousy but I'm quick to reply, "Hoodlum? Who said I'm sleeping with a hoodlum? Besides, just because a brother can be thuggy doesn't mean he's stupid or insensitive. I know brothers who have just as much as you, and some who have more, and their ass didn't have to go to West Point to get it."

"Those street mothafuckas can't touch me. And that's what you want, huh? A thug."

"I didn't say that."

Suddenly, somehow, we get into a heated discussion about our so-called relationship. I call it a "fuckship." For the first time, I witness Bishop's temper.

"Shit! The very time I find someone I want to be close with who is my equal sexual partner, you want to stop seeing me for a thug. Ain't that some shit."

"He's not a thug," I retort.

"That might be so, but can he make you feel like this?"

Bishop suddenly dips his tongue into my mouth and grabs my breasts. He then reclines my seat to the level with the rear ones that are already folded down. He runs his hands under my dress and discovers my bare ass and pussy. He breathes heavily in my ear, "Damn, you're so fine. I know you still want me because you wouldn't offer yourself to me like this if you didn't."

I say nothing and kiss him back with the same degree of passion his tongue demands from my mouth. He pulls apart the bow that keeps my wraparound dress together, exposing my mostly naked body. He reaches down and unsnaps my bra, then tosses it aside.

"Yeah, now that's what I'm talkin' about." He views my entire naked body, and then engulfs my breasts and I'm turned on even more.

"I know that nigga doesn't make you feel like I do. And I guarantee you that he doesn't have this."

He unzips his pants and exposes what I love best about him. I can stop now and end this, but I'm again under his wicked spell. I jerk his pants and boxers down and become more animalistic than ever, biting at his penis. I then rip open his freshly pressed, Sean John business shirt and lick his six-pack abs.

"Move your fine ass to the back," he orders as he slaps the side of my hips. I like being in the midst of his aggressive side. He makes a few adjustments to the seats and presto, we have good-sized flat surface.

As our heated, naked bodies touch, and I feel the exhilarating pulse of his heart against mine, and the warmth of his breath on my neck, sudden thoughts of consequences enter my mind. They are thoughts about Keith and the loyalty he expects from me.

"Bishop, do you have a condom?" I hope he says no and I can end this right here, right now, no more excuses. I can honor Keith's wishes.

"Uhhhh. Hold on a sec." He rises off of me and searches inside his center console.

"Got one right here."

Damn! He holds the super-sized Trojan pack in the air like a trophy that he's proud to have on hand and quickly returns to hovering my body. I try to bring Keith back to my forethoughts, but our chemistry takes off like a dragster racecar, engines roaring, wheels churning, full combustion, racing to get to the finish line. Bishops holds the Trojan pack between his teeth and tears it open with one hand while his other continues to find the center between my wet labia. I squirm with excitement, spreading my wetness upon his fingers as I gyrate my hips in a circular motion.

I want him, got to have him, and let him whip that thang on me one last time.

"Bishop," I moan.

"Yeah, baby?"

"Put your scrumptious dick in me."

I wrap my long, dark-brown legs around his waist and pull him toward me. He seals the remaining part of his long shaft with the condom just in time as I guide him straight into my opening. He works his big cock into me, one inch at a time, with slow, intended down strokes until his base reaches my labia. He stirs up my juices, getting our genitals soaking wet, and then he puts a hurtin' on my pussy. I know he's going to have rug burns on his elbows and knees, but he doesn't seem to care.

The Escalade rocks with the force of our humping bodies. Bishop continues to blow my back out. I return the favor by making him lie on his back while I ride his black stallion.

"Damn, Connie, your shit is good!"

"Yours, too!"

"Turn your ass around," he orders.

I ride his stallion backward. With one hand, he grabs a handful of my hair for his reins and spanks my ass with his other—the entire time, one slap after another.

"Ride my dick, Connie. Harder. Harder," he commands.

I pounce up and down on the long, thick pole until I concave and cum so hard that I see flickers of glitter about my sight. My cum drains down his latex shaft with each thrust I give. My orgasmic juices reach his pubic hair and balls.

"Damn, you're so wet. Don't stop, baby," he orders. I try not to but my body has just experienced the hardest orgasm ever. I continue to give enough of myself to keep him excited and satisfied.

After a few moments, he sounds off, "Oh shit! I'm cummming!" Just for kicks, I rise to the tip of his penis, spin around, face him, and then slam my pussy to his base. The spin sends him into a frenzy.

"OHHHH SHITTTT!"

His body seizes and I feel his penis pulsate and grow that extra thickness just prior to ejaculating. I watch his eyes roll upward inside his head, then close with each contraction as his body releases an abundance of cum. I'm glad he's wearing a condom 'cause this would be a serious mess. I look around the SUV and discover that the tinted windows are completely fogged. I can't see shit and that concerns me. We can't see if anyone is walking up on us. I let Bishop enjoy a few more seconds of my insides, then I suggest, "We should get going. We'll already late getting George."

"Forget about George. He can wait."

"Bishop, stop playin.' Come on, we gotta get to work."

I remove myself off of him and search for my clothes. He slowly gets up and does the same.

"Damn, it's hot in here." He climbs to the front, butterball butt-naked, and starts the engine to initiate the A/C.

"Shit!"

"Bishop, what's wrong?"

"I got a cramp in my leg."

I watch him grab his hamstring and press his head against the headrest.

"Open the door and stretch it," I suggest.

"In a sec. I can't move right now." His face displays the discomfort and tightness of his muscle spasm. I feel sorry that there's nothing I can really do. He grunts more. I quickly put on my undergarments, wrap my dress, exit the vehicle, and race to the driver's side. I open the door and he practically falls out. I try not to laugh, but here he stands naked outside of the SUV in broad daylight.

"Bishop, you gotta pull yourself together and get dressed."

"Woman, you don't understand. I can't until this shit goes away."

"Woman"? Who does he think he's talking to? I turn and leave his ass leaning alongside the Escalade and climb back into the truck. That did it for me, no more. I hear the sound of screeching wheels like a car is steadily coming up the ramp. I see Bishop fighting to get back in the Escalade. I feel sorry for his ass and gather his clothes and button his shirt while he puts on his pants. We see the yellow lights reflect off the concrete wall as the security car approaches further up the ramp. I do a final check in the visor mirror.

"How do I look?"

"Fine," Bishop replies.

The windows unfog just in the nick of time. The security car approaches us slowly. A well-fit Caucasian man sits behind the wheel. Bishop lowers his window and places both hands on the steering wheel so they are visible to the guard.

"Is there a problem here?" the guard asks, looking across Bishop's seat at me.

"No problem, sir," Bishop answers. The guard looks at me again like he needs reassurance. So, I give a slight wave, indicating everything is fine.

"Well, you can't loiter here," the security guard informs with a condescending tone.

"I understand," Bishop complies.

"You folks have a nice day."

"Yeah, whatever," Bishop mumbles. He then puts the Escalade

into gear and drives away. He reaches across the console and holds my hand. Before I get a word out of my mouth, he kisses the back of my hand and I say nothing. Sometimes you just have to let a moment be.

We arrive at George's pickup spot twenty-five minutes late. Bishop lowers his window and instructs George to get in. He looks miffed. I know he's going to talk about this all the way to work. He opens the rear passenger door and gets in admiring the SUV. Bishop watches him through the rearview mirror and tries to take George's mind off of the tardiness.

"You like my new ride?"

"Damn that. B, man, where the hell have you been?"

Bishop smiles and puts the car in "drive" and looks at me.

"Oh, I see, late on the lady's behalf. Good mornin,' Connie.

"Mornin,' George."

"Tell me something, Connie. Why do women always take too long getting ready in the morning?"

"George, before you get started, I was on time." George looks at Bishop with frowned brows and asks, "Well, B, if she was on time, why the hell you twenty-five minutes late getting my ass?"

"George, man, ease up. We'll be at work in no time."

"Yeah right," George snarls as he stares out of the window. He settles in but just like I suspect, he questions Bishop the entire way to work.

The day zooms by. Thank the Lord; it's five o'clock on a Friday. I can't wait to leave Clark and Howard—no more contracts to write and review, no more conference calls, no more negotiation meetings, and no more filling-in for boss lady, who I'm still reluctant to say will be back in the office on Monday. Nothing left to do now except take my final ride home with Bishop and George.

We all meet at the car in the garage at five-oh-five. This time on the way home, George entertains us about the latest gun laws in Congress. Being an attorney, I debate with him about some of his wacky points of view. The ride home is full of conversation, probably more than Bishop wants this time of day. But that's okay—after today he won't have to hear George and I go at each other anymore.

We arrive at the Lenox Marta subway station and George exits the SUV. I must admit I won't miss riding with him.

"Later, B. Later, little Miss Missy."

"Whatever," I announce out of my window. He squints his nose at me and I squint mine back at him.

"You two are a trip," Bishop proclaims as he drives away.

"At least I don't have to deal with his crazy ass anymore."

"What do you mean by that?"

"Bishop, we talked about this this morning. I don't want to go through this again."

"Don't worry, we won't. Do you mind if I make a stop on the way to your car?"

"That's fine."

Twenty minutes later, Bishop drives into the archway of the Ritz-Carlton in midtown.

"I'll be back," he announces with a kiss to my hand.

"Bishop, wait. What are you doing?"

"You'll see."

He leaves the car and walks through the entrance of the hotel. About fifteen minutes later, he returns.

"Everything is set."

"Everything like what?"

"You'll see."

He signals for the valet to park his SUV. He then walks around to my door and opens it in his gentlemanly fashion. I'm curious about what he's up to, but I also need to get home. Maybe a quick peek won't hurt.

We reach the twelfth floor and Bishop leads the way to suite 1220.

"Close your eyes," he requests and I oblige without hesitation. I'm more curious than ever. I suspect that the surprise is for me and I'm dying to know what it is. He opens the door and the sensual scent of roses fill my nostrils. I smell the aroma of vanilla-scented candles.

"Bishop, can I open my eyes?"

"Not yet. Walk this way." He guides me from the entrance and I notice my heels no longer click on marble flooring but are silenced by plush carpet.

"Now?"

"Yes. Open."

My mouth falls open at the beautiful sight of a rose petal-covered bed, with calla lilies in crystal vases on each nightstand accompanied by chilled champagne and two crystal glasses. I follow the rose-petal trail on the floor to the European spa bath in the next room.

"A jasmine bubble bath awaits you," Bishop whispers in my ear. "I know we got a little carried away this morning, and there was no place to really erase our encounter. So I thought I'd bring you here before letting you go home."

"Thank you, Bishop. This is so nice of you. But—"

"But nothing. No strings attached, just enjoy yourself. I'm gonna take a shower."

I undress by the side of the Jacuzzi tub and let my dress and undergarments fall onto the white marble floor. Bishop watches me through the mirror and I don't mind. After I slide into the bubbles, he walks back into the living area, turns on some jazz, and then returns to the bathroom, undresses, and steps into the shower.

"How does it feel?" he yells above the running water and rumbling Jacuzzi jets.

"Fine. Thank you. I needed this."

"No problem."

He finishes his shower way before I finish soaking. Finally, I rise out of the tub and dry off. The water drains and Bishop returns to the bathroom right at the moment I'm about to put on my thong and bra.

"I don't think you want to put those back on, do you? I bought you these." He hands me a pretty, silk, indigo panty-and-bra set.

"Thanks. How thoughtful of you."

"All day I thought about you not being able to freshen up the way you like. We both could've used a shower this morning."

We laugh and the moment is lighthearted. I'm so glad to have fresh undergarments.

"Just put on the bra and panties and come join me to relax a while."

"Okay."

I feel my heart racing. I know where this can lead and I really don't want it to. He's seducing me and I can't fall for it. *But how do I show my appreciation? What he's done is really nice.* I pace the bathroom floor trying to figure this out. *Hell, screw it, I didn't tell him to get this room.* I wrap my dress around my body and slide on my high-heel sandals. *Damn it, I'm in control and my ass is leaving.* I open the bathroom door but don't see him.

"Bishop?" I call out, peering around the corner.

"Yeah baby, I'm in here." His acknowledgement comes from the kitchenette. He turns the corner and walks toward me with his dick swinging in the wind the way I like to watch it. *Be strong, Connie*, I tell myself.

"Why are you dressed? I thought we'd hang out here for a while."

Be strong, Connie. Don't look down at his penis. If you do, you're gonna want it.

"I, uh, I, um, I really need to go."

"You're joking, right?" He intentionally steps toward me with his dick an inch away from my pelvis. He leans in for a kiss but I turn my head.

"No. I'm not joking. I have to go."

He wraps his arms around my waist and I feel weak in the knees.

"What are you going home to that's better than what you have right here, Connie?"

He kisses the side of my neck and I feel his loaded gun against my dress. I raise my arms not sure whether to embrace him or push him away. He kisses me harder and I begin to kiss him back. His dick grows longer and wider. I feel my hot zone throbbing, yearning for his long dong. I'm saturating my new indigo panties and my breasts are standing at attention. I tell myself, *I have to gain control. I can't do this anymore. Keith is my man even if he doesn't have a huge penis. If he ever finds out about this, my ass is as good as gone.*

"Bishop, I'm sorry, but I gotta go. I can't do this anymore." I try to push him away but he holds me tightly. I like the way he's fighting to keep me.

"Look me in my eyes and tell me that you don't want what we have together. Look at me, damn it!"

I slowly affix my distant stare upon his hazel eyes and for the first time, I feel something in me flutter. It's not supposed to, but it does.

"Bishop, look, this has been a wonderful week and I've had a lot of fun. But I can't see you anymore."

"Can't or won't?"

"Don't try to twist my words. I don't want to continue to see you anymore. Is that clear enough?" I lie. *Shit, this is hard.*

"Why, because of that unsatisfying thug you have? Connie, I can give you everything he can and more, if you let me. I know that I satisfy you sexually. Please, let's work this out."

He's begging and ironically, his pleading is touching places in me that should not be tapped. I say nothing and let him continue to spill his guts.

"Connie, if you can honestly tell me that you don't want me, I'll leave you alone and never look back."

Damn, I don't want it to be like that. I think about Keith and ending this affair with Bishop, right here, right now. I have Bishop where I want him. I can kiss his ass good-bye, walk out this door, and forget this ever happened. *Hmmm. What shall I do? Sorry, Keith, but a girl's gotta have what a girl needs.*

I interrupt Bishop and tongue him passionately. He lifts me and lays me gently onto the rose petals that adorn the California King-sized bed. Our encounter is different this time, slow and meaning-ful, drifting into a place I know it shouldn't be, a place of intimacy. I watch Bishop peel my clothes tenderly. I follow suit and enjoy this moment of truth. Could it be that we've revealed another layer of desire for each other, another need? No words are spoken; they would only get in the way. Our bodies entwine into several positions. Kama Sutra has nothing on us. For some strange reason, screaming, "Fuck me, Bishop," would be out of place in this setting.

For forty-five minutes, we're suspended in a matrix of romance, and oddly, I enjoy the transition. My sensual movements and direct eye contact speak every word I dare not say. The caressing grip of Bishop's masculine hands and soft kisses of his LL Cool J lips express a tenderness from far within. The wave of his body with mine, a slow, repeated, penetrating motion takes us to a heightened orgasm we experience simultaneously. Our bodies quake and we hold each other tight. Afterward, I rest my head upon his chest. The room is filled with the muted sound of Will Downing. I say nothing but lie thinking, *this moment can't be revisited or I'm going to be in a bigger dilemma.* Bishop interrupts my thoughts.

"Baby, I'm going to take a shower. Do you want to join me?"

"No, I'll, um, take one when you're done."

"Sure?"

"Yeah."

He kisses my forehead and leaves the room. *Shit, shit, shit! What the hell is going on? This isn't supposed to end like this. We're suppose to have wild, butt-naked sex, not, well you know, the alternative. Keep this in perspective,* I tell myself. *He's married and has never said anything about leaving his frigid wife. I wonder why? This is a dangerous, dead-end road and I need to get off of it as soon as possible.*

Bishop returns to the room about ten minutes later with a white towel around his waist. He sits on the edge of the bed and touches my thigh.

"Baby, are you all right?"

"Yes. Why wouldn't I be?"

"No reason."

"Tell me something, Bishop. What are your plans regarding your unfulfilling marriage?" Surprisingly, he gives me a straight answer the first time around.

"I plan to file for divorce shortly."

"You 'plan to,' oh really. I see." *Liar. He could at least be more original.*

"Seriously, Connie. My wife is a well-connected woman. I have to be careful with our situation or she will drag my ass through the mud in court. I've already set the wheels in motion. If everything goes as planned, I should be done with the process by Christmas next year. What a gift it's going to be to me." He smiles as he discusses his divorce.

"Yeah, if you say so. It doesn't matter, anyway. I was just wondering."

"Forget about that, Connie. I've got it under control. What I'm interested in is, how are you feeling?"

I know he probably wants to talk about what happened between us, but I'm not letting him have that upper hand.

"I feel fine."

Annoyed by my quick, nonchalant reply, he stands and walks to his clothes. I rise and enter the bathroom where I relax in the shower. Thirty minutes later, I'm dressed and ready to go to my car.

The ride to my car is unusually quiet but Bishop still holds my hand the entire way. He turns onto Perimeter and I see my SUV.

"Well, here you are, Connie."

"Thanks."

"Next week is George's turn to drive, but I'm going to drive on Monday 'cause his car is in the shop."

"Bishop"—I stop him from further explaining the carpool situation—"I'm not riding with you next week or the week after. This is it for me." He just doesn't want to accept the facts.

"Why? I thought we—"

"I know what you thought and trust me, you need to stop thinking it because it's not going to happen. I simply can't see you anymore, especially now." He leans in for a kiss and I ignore his attempt and try to exit. He grabs my wrist, firmer than usual.

"Connie, let's talk this through."

"You best let go of my wrist," I demand with a threatening, escalated voice. He obviously doesn't take me serious and tries to hug me.

"I said, let me go! I don't want this!" He tries to kiss me again. "Bishop, no!"

I hear Keith's voice in my head. Gradually, he reaches my subconscious and I feel him shaking me saying, "Connie, baby, wake up, wake up." But in my dream, the motion is me, frantically pushing Bishop away, not because he's attacking me. I'm fighting my own desire to remove myself from this hypnotic state of wanting his big dick. I continue to swing my arms and say, "Leave me alone! I can't do this!"

"Connie, WAKE UP!" I feel Keith shaking me vigorously, snapping me out of this exhilarating, highly implausible yet probable fantasy.

Slowly, my eyes open. I look around the room dazed and see Keith sitting beside me on the sofa with the most perplexed look upon his face. I say nothing because I'm not sure what all I revealed in my sleep. But he does and he's staring right at me.

"Baby, that must have been one bad-ass dream. I ain't never seen you do no shit like that before. What the hell were you dreamin' about?"

I gaze out of the window and see the black blanket across the sky and the diamonds that lay upon it.

"What time is it?" I look past Keith at the clock on the wall, trying to change the subject. But before I register the numbers, he answers, "Twelve-thirty."

"Wow, I've been asleep that long?"

"Yeah. You've been knocked out since you changed clothes when I was grillin.' Judging from how much wine is left in the bottle, you had a little too much. But squash that. What I still want to know is, what the hell were you dreaming about?"

I orient myself and sit up on the sectional sofa, pulling my knees to my chest, recalling my dream. I look at Keith and wonder what does he really know.

"Keith, sweetie, come here." I pull him into my 36DDs and whisper, "It was just some midnight madness, that's all. Nothing to worry about. Just a crazy-ass dream."

"Oh really. Well, who the fuck is Bishop?"

I laugh to buy time in order to try to figure out my answer. Calling out another man's name is not something Keith, or any man, would take kindly to. This is a delicate situation. I must be victorious or the night is going to get real ugly, real fast.

"What the hell is so funny, Connie? I don't see anything so damn humorous."

"Sweetie, don't get mad. I was just dreaming, okay?"

"No, this shit is not okay, Connie. Who the fuck is Bishop?"

"All right, I'll tell you but don't judge me for what I say."

Keith sits at attention like a Rottweiler ready to pounce.

"Bishop was…" Keith leans toward me, eyes fixed and ears alert.

"Bishop was a man at my job that I was having explosive sex with because he had a huge dick." I look at Keith in a matter-of-fact way to get him off balance. He leans back and looks confused.

"What the—"

"I told you it was crazy."

"Connie, you had a dream about another man and his dick?"

"Yeah. That's why I said don't judge me. I can't help what I dream about."

"So that's why you were moaning, 'Oh Bishop, yes.'"

"Yeah. I gotta admit that it was the bomb, too. And sweetie, it was weird. There were these people in my dream that I don't even know, like this nosey lady who kept popping up, and a nerd who carpooled with me."

"Ain't that some shit," Keith announces, looking off into the distance.

"What?" I ask.

"Well, either you're dreamin' about another man's dick because you've been involved with someone or you're not satisfied with me. Maybe you're dreamin' about it because you want something or someone different."

"Keith, I assure you that I don't want anyone else. And sweetie, you please me like no other."

"So, why is Bishop's dick on your mind?"

This is the one time I wish he would be less analytical and just accept my answer that it's only a dream. But no, he's pushing, and I know he's not going to stop until he's satisfied.

"Well, Keith, the truth of the matter is, well, you know how in dreams things can be jumbled up and incidences and people switched around? You know how sometimes dreams just don't make sense at all?"

"Yeah, go on."

I place my feet onto the floor and sit at the edge of the sofa with him to better position myself for his response. You know a man's ego is a sensitive thing, especially when it comes to his prize possession.

"Well, actually, I dreamed that you had a miniature penis, and it wasn't satisfying me. But your real dick was on this man named Bishop who sexed me the way you do."

Keith looks at me like I have lost my mind. He tries to reply but apparently can't find the words. I watch his mind work behind his curious eyes.

"So, what you're saying is, I wasn't me in my own body, yet I was me in another man?"

"Yeah, something like that. Look, Keith, the dream made no sense. I've dated guys with small penises and was satisfied because it takes more than the size of a dick to please me. Then I have you, who just happens to have the largest damn cock I've ever had, and I'm satisfied more than ever."

Naturally, his ego kicks in and suddenly the direction of our conversation changes.

"Yeah, I know you're glad you got a man with a big pipe who knows how to give it to you, aren't you?"

I try not to feed into his ego too much, so I merely smile.

"Tell the truth, Connie. You love how I pound your pussy with my giant." He leans toward me and makes me slowly fall onto my back. His left hand unties my summer dress and travels from my stomach to my breasts. He cups my perky mountain peaks with both hands, then gnaws at my nipples the way I like.

"Slide back," he orders. I find my footing and push myself backward until my entire espresso body is fully on the sofa directly under him. He removes his right hand from my breast and teases my clit with one finger while two others find their way into my cavity. I moan with excitement as my creamy juices seep onto his fingers. I want him and he knows it. I rapidly kiss and suck his neck and chest, craving for him to fuck me.

"Tell me, Connie, what did Bishop do to you in your dream that you and I have never done?"

His question catches me off guard and I look at him shocked. He looks at me sincerely and repeats the question in a soft, warm whisper as he nibbles at my ear. Hearing his baritone voice ask me about fulfilling a fantasy makes me hotter, but I'm somewhat embarrassed.

"Baby, don't be shy. It's just you and me. I want to please you. I know there's something in your dream you must want to do. Let me fulfill your desire."

I want to respond but the words are silenced by Keith's tongue in my mouth. He kisses me so deeply and presses his ten-inch dick against my pelvis so hard that I almost cum from sheer desire to have his big cock in me. He slurps my bottom lip as he removes his tongue. He gives my body quick lollipop licks down my neck, between my 36DDs, down my stomach, pass my pubic hair, and right into the creases of my labia. He spreads my legs further apart and goes to work, eating my pussy like never before. He sucks my entire wet box into his mouth, holds it there, then finds the opening to my center with his tongue. How the hell he does that shit, I don't know, but the sensation is out of this world. He releases my labia and only his tongue remains in the center of me. He uses his fingers and spreads my pussy further apart until my clit is fully exposed. He hones in and makes me squirm and scream with pleasure as he licks, sucks, and bites his way into my subconscious state. I feel myself rise and fall as my body spasms to a breathtaking orgasm unlike any other I've experienced with him. My dream is causing a profound impact on us both. Keith returns to my ear and whispers, "Baby, let me please you more. What do you want? Trust me. I'm your man."

I look into his loving eyes and confess, "I want to know what it's like to have you…"

"Go ahead, baby, tell me. I'm here for you."

"To have you cum on my face." I feel weird and immediately cover my face with my hands. *Why the hell am I embarrassed with him?* Keith tenderly peels them away and smiles at me.

"That's nothing to be ashamed of. I never knew you wanted

that. I just assumed you didn't, therefore, I always remove myself before that happens. I'm sorry. I never meant to leave you feeling unfulfilled."

"Keith, you don't have to apologize. How could you know? I never said anything."

A brief period of silence lingers in the air before he says, "Do you love me?"

"Keith, you know I do."

"You're my girl, right?" He kisses me just below my earlobe in a spot he knows is an instant turn-on.

"Yes, sweetie. I am."

"Who's your man?"

"You are, Keith."

"That's right. Remember that shit."

He straddles my face and lets his genitals hang over my lips. I suck his large cock into my warm, wet mouth and hear him release a sigh. I go to work with the action I enjoy giving him. I draw his entire dick into my mouth and down my throat until my lips touch the base of his rod. I release him slowly with the right amount of pressure, turning my mouth into an oral oasis. I work my way to the head, grab onto the shaft with my hand, and begin jerking his cock in and out of my mouth while concentrating on licking and slurping the head. And then without notice, I down him into my throat again back to the base of his penis.

"Shit! Connie, baby, you know how I like it."

I release his dick from my mouth, grab it with my hand, and smack my face with the hardness of the shaft. I moan as I release my inhibitions and attack his penis the way I want. I gobble and twirl his cock, spinning my tongue around the head and the shaft without releasing it from my mouth.

"Damn, baby, you've been holding out," I hear Keith say.

I hold him by his athletic, tight ass and pull him further into my mouth. I suck harder and go up and down on his loaded pistol. He gets it and begins to hump my mouth.

"Yeah, baby, take what you want, Connie."

I moan and suck his cock even harder, spinning it in and out of my mouth, jerking it with my hand, stimulating every inch from the tip to the base. I hear what I've often heard from him.

"Shit! Baby, I'm gonna cum, don't stop."

I continue to eat his meat like it's the best damn steak I've ever had. Suddenly, he removes my hand and takes over with his own. I feel his dick swell even larger as he takes his final slow, long strokes in my mouth. Then suddenly, he retracts from my mouth, points his shooter at me, lets out a loud grunt, and fires his hot load all over my face. I squint to keep his cum from getting in my eyes and try to watch him through the tiny space I leave between my lashes. I want to see his expression during this first experience. He continues to shoot the final remains of his orgasm and I get a glimpse of his closed eyes and concentrating face. He seems to be in another world. I wait until he opens them and then I let him see me rub his moisturizer into my skin and lick the remnants from my fingers.

"Thanks for my pearly shower. It was all that and a bag of chips," I tell him.

"I'll say. You make me weak in the knees. Pearly shower, huh?"

"Yeah, that's what I called it in my dream."

"I like that," he replies.

He lowers his body over me, takes his big-ass dick into his right hand and fondles my genitals until his giant is full length again. He's always good for multiple orgasms. That's another thing that I love about him.

"Well, baby, you know what I want." He flips my legs over his shoulders, points my pussy to the ceiling, hovers above me and places his thick, long dong in me, one inch at a time, in deep, in deeper, in all the way. Suddenly, I feel his dick consume the center of me and we fuck like rabbits all night long; strength and stamina, what these two healthy bodies can do.

I stretch and rise with the early-morning Saturday sun. The rays feel warm and fresh against my naked body as I walk into the bathroom to start my day. I turn on the shower and brush my teeth while the shower water warms to the perfect steamy temperature. After a few minutes, I step into the shower and begin to lather. Through the glass doors I watch Keith enter, stand over the toilet, and drain his lizard to start his day.

I yell, "Are you joining me this morning?"

He doesn't answer which is strange. Usually he's only quiet in the mornings during the week when he's thinking about his workday and all he wants to get done. On the weekend, he's more easygoing and talkative. He opens the shower door, steps inside, takes the washcloth out of my hands, and scrubs my back in a circular motion. I close my eyes and enjoy the tender side of him. Moments after washing my back and shoulders, he asks, "Connie, do you love me?" I'm glad my back is to his chest because my mouth unintentionally falls open. *Where the hell did that come from?* We don't walk around saying *I love you* often like some couples. He tells me once every blue moon, never twice in a row like last night and now. And I make it a practice never to tell a man *I love you* first and surely not often. They'll eat that mess alive and think they have you sprung. If Keith tells me *I love you*, then I'll tell him. But this time he's asking about it again like he has doubts. I'm sure my dream registered with him and now he's questioning his manhood. How many people would take kindly to their mate dreaming about some other person? Not many and certainly not Keith, even if he did fulfill my fantasy. I compose myself and face him.

"Keith, sweetie, of course I love you. You know that." I seal my words with a soft kiss under the warm waterfall. He presses his forehead against mine and continues, "Connie, do I satisfy you?"

I press my 36DDs against his chest and wrap my arms around his neck.

"Keith, you are the smartest, kindest, most loving and giving man I've ever known. Yes, baby, you satisfy me."

"Are you sure?" He sounds like he's troubled.

"Yes, sweetie, I'm more than sure. I told you that I enjoyed you fulfilling my fantasy."

"Yeah, but you had it with some other cat first."

"Keith, it was a dream. I was too embarrassed to tell you and it just played out that way."

He stands silent looking at me. I gotta get his mind off of this. I cup his testicles in my hand and stroke his long shaft. I kiss him passionately across his wet chest, up and down his neck. I suck his earlobes and whisper, "I love you, Keith Nelson." I break my rule because desperate measures call for desperate action. He can't doubt me. Nothing can disrupt the flow of me being his platinum princess. Finally, he shows a sign of belief and relief. I'm happy to see I've won his thoughts over again. We bathe each other under the waterfall and enjoy a sensual shower together. Afterward, we dress and head to his friend Q's barbecue on the east side of Buckhead to kick off our Saturday fun. Later we drive to the Pit and as usual, the crowd gets cranking after eleven o'clock.

✸✸✸

Monday morning arrives quicker than I want, but I'm glad to be here to witness it, another day, and another dollar. Keith rolls over and greets me with a warm good-morning kiss. I cuddle next to him and think about our adventurous weekend, mainly about my dream and how it strangely brought us closer.

"Baby, what's on your schedule today?" he asks while stroking my pubic hair.

"I don't know 'cause boss lady is back in town. I'm sure she's gonna want to catch up on what's been happening in her absence, in spite of the fact that we emailed her daily."

"Do you think you'll be free for lunch?"

"I should. Why?"

"Maybe we can go to the revolving restaurant at the Westin Peachtree across from where you work. You've always wanted to go there."

"Keith, you're kiddin,' right?"

"No. What you think, a brother can't afford it?"

"No, no, nothing like that. It's just that, well—"

"Well, what?"

"It was in my dream."

"Come on, Connie. Stop with the bullshit."

"No lie."

"Well, who did you go with?"

"Huh?"

"You heard me, who?"

"Bishop," I answer.

"Are you serious?"

"Yeah, why?"

"I think there's more to that dream than you're telling me." He rises from the bed, obviously annoyed and heads to the bathroom. I join him.

"No, there isn't. Don't trip. It's just ironic, that's all. Maybe I dreamed it because, like we both know, I've always wanted to go. The subconscious is a powerful thing."

"Yeah, tell me about it. Yours is in overdrive." I pay him no mind and dress for work.

An hour later, we're both ready to greet the workforce, me in my pantsuit and Keith in his Rocawear. I commute the usual hour-and-a-half drive during rush hour to Atlanta and think about the carpool experience in my dream. I laugh aloud, what a dream.

The parking garage is unusually full this morning so I drive down two more levels than usual. I park near the elevator entrance, exit my car, and proceed to the entrance when I notice a metallic silver Mercedes 500 in the far corner. Strange. What a coincidence. I reach the lobby and wait for an elevator car with the rest of the morning crowd. The bell dings and an elevator arrives. The doors open and everyone boards. I hear a familiar woman's voice screaming, "Hold the door, please. Hold the door." She enters with a laptop, briefcase, and folders in hand. The doors close and she looks around. "Thank you." She sees me to her left.

"Connie, hi. How's everything?"

"Fine, Ms. Collins. Everything went smoothly while you were out of town. How did the cases go?"

"Great. We got a lot done. We have a number of new contracts to handle, lots of good business."

"Wonderful. I look forward to it."

"Stop by my office later this afternoon. There are a couple of contracts I want you to handle."

"Okay." *Bitch*, I say to myself.

The day passes quickly with boss lady back. She has so many things she wants the staff to do and so little time to do them. I finally get a chance to meet with her like she requested this morning. Our conversation doesn't take long. She's a very organized, middle-aged woman who knows exactly what she wants, and communicates her expectations with precision. She instructs me to go to the accounting department downstairs on the fifteenth floor. She wants me to review a contract with Mr. William Johnson, the lead senior accountant and director of his division.

"I've already spoken with Mr. Johnson. He's very familiar with your work and is expecting you at three o' clock."

"Yes, Ms. Collins. I'll be there at three o' clock sharp."

"Very well."

She shuffles her papers with the usual signal to anyone standing before her that the conversation is over. I leave her office wondering how is my assignment going to work out with someone who knows more about me than I do about him. I'm already at a disadvantage. Usually, I'm familiar with my clients and have done my homework to understand who or what I'm dealing with. But this is straight off the cuff and my meeting with Mr. Johnson is only an hour away. Nonetheless, I'll go there like Ms. Collins asked.

At three p.m. sharp, I enter the glass doors of the accounting department on the fifteenth floor where the receptionist greets me.

"You must be Connie Winslow."

"Yes."

"Mr. Johnson is waiting for you."

She gives me instructions to his office. I stand there like a deer in headlights because her instructions are straight out of my dream—how eerie. I reach my destination and almost pass out— right there on the spot where the door opens and a tall, handsome, thirty-something, Hershey-dipped man stands before me.

"Hi, Connie. I'm William Johnson."

I damn near scream and gasp at the sight of him. He looks strikingly similar to the man in my dream. The only difference is Mr. Johnson is more pepper-gray and his eyes are dark brown. Instead of a shadow beard, he sports a refined mustache. I catch my breath just enough to say, "Yes, I see that on the nameplate, sir. Nice to meet you."

"Come in. Bernie tells me that you're an excellent contract attorney."

"Bernie, sir?"

"Yes. Bernadette, your manager, my wife."

"Wife, sir?"

"Oh that's right, you're new here. How could you know? She uses her maiden name at work. Bernadette Collins is my wife."

"Ms. Collins is your wife, sir?"

"Yes. We've been married for—"

"Don't tell me. Let me guess, thirteen years?"

"Yes. How did you know? Did she tell you?"

"No, I just took a wild guess." I walk to the huge window to collect myself. But when I touch the thick glass, I'm quickly jolted back to my dream when we were spread eagle fucking against the window like two wild animals.

"Connie, is everything okay?"

"Yes, sir."

"Please, call me Bill. Have a seat."

I sit across from this Adonis man trying not to make direct eye contact, but it's inevitable, as we must discuss the contract on the table in front of us.

"So, this is the much-talked-about Hoffner contract," I mention, trying to stay focused.

"Yes. Here, let me show you the sections in question."

We reach for the document at the same time and it happens—our hands accidentally touch and a bolt of familiar desire flashes throughout my body. Our eyes fixate on each other a few seconds beyond what's professionally acceptable. I wonder what he's contemplating. I know what I'm thinking: In my twisted state of mind, he knows how to rock my world.

₮℞

Janice N. Adams is an enthusiastic author who ignites life into fictional characters and story lines. Her arousing novels and novella take your mind away from the daily hustle-bustle as you laugh, cry, and cheer for her characters. She is a native of Richmond, Virginia who moved to Maryland in 1992 where she currently resides. She earned a bachelors of science degree in sociology from Virginia Polytechnic Institute and State University in 1988. Her professional career spans over twenty years in the areas of project management, information technology, and human resource management. She is an active member of her community providing support and contributions to local churches and charities. She is married and has two young sons. She enjoys photography, interior design, sports, music, and movies. In addition to her novella, "A Twisted State of Mind" featured in Another Time, Another Place, *she is on the horizon of publishing two completed novels,* A Heart's Journey to Quench a Thirsty Soul *and* Undeniable Passion: A Heart's Journey 2. *She is also working on her third novel,* Hale and Fury: Two Sisters, Two Worlds, One Destiny. *You can learn more about Janice and her upcoming novels at www.janicenadams.com or email her at Janice@janicenadams.com*

ANOTHER TIME, ANOTHER PLACE

ZANE

Dear Diary,

His dick was curved. Not a huge curve but curved just enough to work my pussy in all the right spots. When a man's dick is too straight, it can be painful. A sister needs a brother to be able to move with her groove. I remember my ex-boyfriend, Tony. His dick was like a wooden plank. It would not budge for anything and even when I tried to get on top and maneuver to get some serious action going, it was too much damn work. He would leave me sick, unsatisfied and feeling like I had gone through an OB/GYN examination with that duck lips tool.

Back to the one with the curved dick. I licked it last night, like it was the most delicious chocolate ice cream cone in the world. No, not a cone, a Popsicle with chocolate on the outside and vanilla cream on the inside. I wanted that cream, too. I wanted him to shoot it down my throat like a human geyser. I wanted him to cum so much that I could gargle with his sperm. I know all this sounds nasty but I am simply a woman who loves dick. Now the men that dicks are attached to are another question. There is Darrell. He's nice enough. We met at the grocery store the other day. He seems like a brother who is about something other than trying to see how many pairs of panties he can get into. We will have to wait and see what happens.

Anyway, back to last night. I was standing on a balcony, the wind blowing the curtains outward and teasing my hair as I overlooked the skyline. I could sense his presence as he walked—no, glided—up behind me. I could smell his cologne. Mmm, he smelled like heaven. He was wearing all white. A doubled-breasted suit with no shirt. His chest was chiseled, like the rest of him. His skin was moistened—his deep dark skin. His bald head was shaved smooth, like his face, and his thick lips encased perfectly straight white teeth.

"Did you miss me?" he whispered in my ear, after joining me on the balcony.

I could not answer. I only managed a whimper. My entire body, from the soles of my feet to the tips of my fingers to the baby-fine hair of my pussy was calling out his name. Strange as this is, I still do not know his name. I know every inch of his body, his voice; his dick, but not his name.

He comes to me every night now, no matter what city I am in, no matter what time zone. I cannot wait to get through the performances at work so I can rush to be with him. Our favorite fucking song is "Do Me Baby" by Prince, followed by "Fire and Desire" by Rick James and Teena Marie. Both of those songs make me so fucking hot. My pussy stays drenched from merely thinking about being with him. Once we are together, we ignite. I am surprised the bed has not caught fire from all the serious fucking we engage in.

He always gives me a serious dick down and I do mean dick down. I can hear the sound of his balls slapping up against me as I type this. Mmm, damn, I wish he was inside me right now. I wish that I was sitting on his dick, with my back to him, rocking back and forth as I sit here at my computer. A sister can get a lot of work done that way. When he fucks me, a feeling comes over me that I cannot quite express. I shiver, but I feel calm at the same time. No man has ever made me feel so desired, like he is so pleased by my efforts.

He eats my pussy until I detonate all over his tongue. It is such an amazing feeling. I only wish that I could fuck him twenty-four seven, but life intervenes. If I could, I would walk around with his dick in my ass; in my pussy; in my mouth. Ooh, yes, definitely in my mouth.

Damn, I am getting fired up just writing this. I hope he comes back tonight so we can "cum together" and fornicate under the consent of the king. I know he'll be here. I need to go bathe and get ready for him, so he can bury his dick into me balls deep and put me to sleep like a baby.

Kisses,

Kiss

ALECK

"Man, there are a ton of fine women over here," Mike said to me as we headed to the beach in the late afternoon. "We should have had our asses over here years ago."

"You are such a pussy hound." I swatted him on the back with my beach towel. "We're here to relax and take a break from a hectic work schedule. Not to get laid."

"Shit, you might not be here to get laid, but I am. If I don't get pussy every day, I feel sick. It's my medicine. It keeps me alive. I'm trying to see as much pink meat as I can before we head back next week."

"You are so damn nasty. Better watch out with these Jamaican women. You might try to fuck one that has a man slinging a machete. Then the only color you'll be seeing is red and I'll be carrying your body back in a bag. Imagine that, me having to explain that you got murdered in Jamaica because you were trolling for pussy in another man's marked territory."

Mike waved me off and started flexing his muscles. "Aleck, please. I know how to handle any motherfucking thing that comes my way. If a man can't fuck his woman good enough to keep her at home, that's his damn issue. Women don't cheat when they're satisfied."

"That's complete bullshit," I said. "Men can have the best woman in the world. Perfect in every way and some will still cheat."

"The key word was *satisfied*." Mike glared at me. "A real man is never satisfied. Not when there are more varieties to be sampled." He pointed in the direction of three women sitting on lounge chairs near the tip of the ocean. "Speaking of which... Damn, check them hookers out."

"What makes you think they're hookers?" Mike really disgusted me sometimes with the way he referred to women. I glanced at the women and all of them were drop-dead gorgeous. "They don't look Jamaican. They're probably vacationing here from the States; like us."

"That's even better. We can fuck them over here and then collect some more ass when we get back stateside. I have a shit load of frequent flyer miles. I hope they live in one of the cities where Delta flies. "

I chuckled. "I see that you've got it all figured out."

Mike rubbed his chin and gloated. "I always do, my man."

"What about Candace?"

"Who?" Mike asked sarcastically.

"Candace? Your wife?"

"Oh, her..." Mike sighed. "Look, Aleck. I realize you think that I'm wrong for cheating on Candace, but she knew what she was getting when she walked down the aisle. I'm a man and men are going to do what men do. Candace saw that writing all over the wall. Shit, I practically spelled it out for her. Like most women, she decided that my feelings were more important than her self-respect and I ain't mad at her. She wanted a husband, a bad crib, kids, all that. She has it and as long I'm paying all the bills, I can do whatever the hell I want."

I shook my head. "I don't believe in cheating. I believe in karma. When I do find Mrs. Right, I don't want my past catching up to me."

"Yeah, well, that's you. I am an All-American man and I will not live my life dedicated to one pussy—not even if it's made out of Kryptonite."

There was no use in continuing that discussion. Mike was not going to miraculously grow a conscience; not in Jamaica with half-naked women everywhere. If we were at a convention of convents, Mike would try to fuck a bunch of nuns who had sworn off sex. He was convinced he could talk any woman into spreading her legs.

Besides, he was right. Candace realized what she was getting into. Mike disrespected her time and time again while they were dating. Despite everyone warning her to move on, she was determined to get him down the aisle. Sure, on the surface he was a good man, a good provider. The ugly truth was hidden underneath the fancy six-bedroom home, the Jaguar and Mercedes, and the limitless spending sprees Candace got to enjoy.

Even though the sun was about to go down, the sand was still piping hot between my toes. "Damn, it's hot out here."

"We're in Jamaica, Fool," Mike said, continuing the topic I had decided to drop. "And don't even go there about cheating. You've cheated plenty of times. You forget; we go way back."

"Exactly—way back. I cheated on sisters in college but I have outgrown that since then. I believe in honesty and if I'm not feeling a woman enough to be with her and only her, then I tell her straight up and let her make an informed decision."

Mike laughed. "Maybe that's why you don't currently have a woman. Fuck that honesty nonsense. Women can't handle the truth."

I hated to admit it to myself, but Mike did have a somewhat valid point. Every time I tried to tell a woman that I was feeling her but not yet in love, she would get offended. All the women that I met tended to want to go from casual dating to shacking up or getting engaged in less than six months. At the age of 29, I had only had one close brush with marriage but Brenda decided that she wanted to get back with her high school sweetheart. That practically destroyed my faith in women, but I continued to date—in protect mode.

It had been hard for anyone to break down that barrier for nearly seven years. I had doubts that I would find a woman who could be my complete package. Then we walked up on those three women so Mike could make his move and the one in the red bikini instantly made me think twice.

KISS

My heart skipped a beat; then it fluttered. It was the man from my fantasies—all my sexual fantasies. The one with the curved dick. He was wearing black swim trunks and walking toward us with another man in a blue pair. They were both attractive, but the one in the black…I couldn't believe it was really him.

"Humph, do you see what I see?" Nancy whispered and then poked me and Calibri in the arms, in that order. She was sitting between us but she sat up slightly so she could get a better look. "Here comes some of that Jamaican Mandingo meat."

Calibri giggled. "They don't look Jamaican, but they do look damn scrumptious. I hope they're single."

Nancy said, "I don't care if they're single or married, as long as they're available to play with my kitty kat."

Calibri smacked her lips. "Nancy, we're here to relax. One last week of girl fun before the big day. We didn't come here to get fucked."

"Speak for your damn self," Nancy replied. "Ain't nothing wrong with fucking as long as it's good. It's been two weeks since I rode, sucked, or intook any dick and that ain't good. I'm used to getting some at least twice a week."

"No one wants to know your fucking schedule," Calibri said. "Two weeks is nothing. Some sisters go years because they refuse to have a lousy fuck…or a casual one."

"Well, crucify me then," Nancy said. "I'm living this life once and I'm going to do what the hell I want to do. We all have separate rooms. What goes on in mine is my business."

"True that," Calibri agreed. "Thank goodness for it, too. I wouldn't be able to stomach seeing you fuck or, heaven forbid, listen to you slobber all over some man's dick."

I did not say a word. I was still in a state of euphoria while they went back and forth with each other. For nearly a year, I had been experiencing these crazy fantasies and masturbating myself into a frenzy over a man in my dreams—the one now walking in the sand less than a hundred feet away.

As they got closer, Nancy started smoothing down her short hair and repositioning her tits in her white crocheted bikini top. "I want the one in the black. No, the one in the blue. Shit, I'm undecided."

Calibri said, "Calm yourself down. For all you know, they might not even want you."

Nancy got offended and glared at Calibri. "What man wouldn't want all this?"

Nancy had recently gotten a breast augmentation and had gone from 36Cs to 36DDDs and you could not tell her that she was not God's gift to man.

"Hello, ladies," the one in the blue trunks said as they grew nearer. "Enjoying yourselves out on this lovely beach?"

"Things are definitely looking better," Nancy said, jumping up and extending her hand. "Hey, I'm Nancy."

The guy took her hand and kissed her knuckles. "I'm Mike." He pointed to his friend, with whom I had made eye contact; we were staring each other down. "This is my buddy, Aleck."

Mike was about five feet nine inches, light-skinned with amber eyes and a great build. But he was not my type. Aleck was around six feet four inches, dark as midnight and bald and he had the darkest, most alluring eyes. *Damn, he was definitely the man from my dreams.*

Nancy pushed her breasts out at Mike. He seemed disinterested in them and pointed at Calibri and me. "Are these your friends?"

After sighing and making a show of it by putting her hands on her hips, Nancy said, "Yes, we're from Los Angeles. And you?"

"We're from the D.C. area," Mike said.

It did not escape any of us that she did not bother giving our names so Calibri chimed in. "I'm Calibri and that's Kiss."

"Kiss?!" the one named Aleck exclaimed, still staring at me. "As in K-I-S-S?"

"Yes," I replied, getting up off my lounger and brushing the sand off me. "My daddy said he fell in love with my mother during their first kiss, so it's kind of an inside joke."

Aleck looked my body up and down. I was doing the same damn thing to his. "Well, it's a nice joke. I've never met someone named Kiss before. It's definitely unique."

Calibri had stood up, without me even noticing it, until she rested her arm on my shoulder. "Kiss is a unique woman all around. Tell him what you do for a living," she urged.

Mike looked at me with interest then. "What do you do, Kiss?"

I knocked Calibri's arm off my shoulder. "I hate you." We both laughed. "I'm a clown and I'm proud of it."

"A clown?!" the two men exclaimed in unison.

"Yes, as in a circus clown," I stated, used to that reaction from people. "It's a family tradition."

"Both of her parents are with the circus," Nancy said, like it was a crime. "Her dad is the ringmaster and her mother is a trapeze artist."

"Wow, I didn't know that there were many black people in..." Mike started to say.

I interrupted him. "There are not that many, but it's what I do. Got a problem with it?"

Aleck crossed his arms and smiled. He was too fine. "I think it's cool."

"Baby, if you like it, I love it!" Mike yelled out. "As fine as you are, I bet you look sexy as all get out in a clown suit. I've never gotten it on with a clown before."

"No, you just act like one every time you open your mouth," Aleck remarked.

"Whatever, Man." Mike shot him a wicked look. "So, are you ladies busy this evening?"

"I'm available." Nancy moved closer to him to make sure he understood the ramifications of her statement.

He seemed turned off. "What about you, Calibri and Kiss?"

Calibri responded, "We don't have any major plans. We were going to dine by the water back at our hotel."

"Where you staying?" Aleck asked. "We're at the Ritz-Carlton."

"So are we," I said. "Great place."

"It's off the chain," Aleck added.

There was definitely chemistry between us. Little did he know that I had already fucked him in my imagination hundreds of times. My eyes dropped to his swim trunks, trying to figure out if his dick was curved.

ALECK

A clown named Kiss, I thought as I showered and prepared for an evening of promise. The only down side was that she was from Los Angeles and I resided in Washington, D.C.—a recent implant from Atlanta. *Since she's with a circus, that has to mean she travels constantly, which could be an up side or a down side depending on how I look at it. Hopefully the circus heads East and I can see her often. On the flip side, she might be so tied up with work that she'll have no time for me. Then again, she is in Jamaica on vacation.*

"Stop it!" I warned myself out loud. "You just met the woman!"

I finished rinsing the lather off me, got out the shower and began to get dressed. I chose a white linen casual suit, no shirt, to show off my pectoral muscles, and a pair of black sandals. Mike had recently convinced me to start getting pedicures. He said that men with smooth feet and shiny, clipped nails turned women on. Since my feet had seen better days, I decided to get one biweekly a couple of months before we headed to Jamaica.

Kiss was fine. She was about five feet six inches and thick. I loved a woman who fit comfortably into a size fourteen. She had a flat stomach, but the hips, thighs and chest were on point enough to sport that red bikini. She had mocha skin, smooth like a baby's, and dark brown eyes. Yes, I was definitely feeling her—to the point where it almost frightened me. It was like déjà vu. Like I had known her some place before. That was crazy. I had experienced my share of one-night stands in my younger years, but I never would have forgotten her.

Mike, that fool, would forget a woman in a heartbeat. I was so embarrassed one night while we were clubbing on the D.C. waterfront. He spotted a woman and walked to her, proclaiming, "You're going to have to help me out here. I remember the pussy but I don't remember the name."

I was so embarrassed, but surprisingly, instead of slapping the living daylights out of him, the woman laughed and seemingly found it flattering. For the next two minutes, Mike tossed out name after name until she finally revealed that she was Jackie. They flirted for a good thirty minutes before her friend, who obviously did not find the situation amusing at all, said she was tired and ready to go. Mike got the digits—again—and then ended up fucking her the next night and never called her again.

I don't believe in being disrespectful to women, being that I come from a single-parent home and I have five sisters. If any man ever spoke to my mother or one of my sisters that way, they would be eating teeth mixed with blood. That was part of the reason why I was sort of stressing the upcoming dinner with Kiss and her friends. I wanted her—badly—but I did not want to come off the wrong way. I realize that a lot of people vacation in the islands to get laid, but that was not my purpose at all. Mike and I had been working on a crazy schedule for months, trying to lock down a merger deal with a competing corporation. We were the crème de la crème of financial analysts but we also put in a lot of hours.

The only jacked-up thing about meeting someone on vacation is that if you want to pursue something other than sex, it's difficult. Even though I had not been in a bona-fide relationship for a long time, I was already hoping for something long-term with Kiss. Never one to believe in the proverbial "love at first sight," I now found myself contemplating if that was actually possible.

Men do think differently from women, so I was already assuming that in order to see her again after we left Jamaica for our respective home towns, I would have to lay some sex on her that she would never forget. Otherwise, why would she even pursue it? Women can claim otherwise all they want, but ultimately, sex is an integral part of a relationship to them and they want a man who can blow their back out. I was going to have to prove myself worthy or forget about it.

Women might worry about their bodies when it comes time to have sex but men have a lot of worries. Will our dick be big enough for the sister? Will we even be able to get the damn thing up? Will we be able to perform over and over again? Will we have enough stamina to wear her out? Will we serve up better dick service than every man who came before us?

I finished dressing and went down the hallway to knock on Mike's door. He and Candace had been married for going on five years and had two sons. He stopped wearing his wedding ring by year two, claiming it was too tight, but that was a lie. Candace did not seem to care, as long as she could lay claim to having a husband and a family. Many women feel that way but they are selling themselves short. Mike would nail anything he could and I was not surprised when a Jamaican maid, half-clothed, opened his hotel room door instead of him.

"He be ready in a minute," she said with her accent, walking into a disheveled room that reeked of sex. "He in da bathroom."

I could make out the smell of soap, mixed with pussy from the bed, and was glad that Mike had at least washed his ass. He came prancing out of the bathroom a moment later, dressed in black linen pants and a tan island shirt.

"Let's roll, Man." He looked at the maid. "Honey, can you change my sheets and tidy up the room before you leave?" He rubbed her on the head, like she was a puppy. "Thanks, Ma."

"Me see you later?" she asked.

"We'll see," he said hesitantly. "I know where to find you, Sugar."

She grinned from ear to ear, thinking that Mike was going to lay up with her again during our vacation. There was zero chance of that. Mike was not looking for love. He was searching for pussy and either Calibri or Nancy was next on his list. I had made it perfectly clear to him that Kiss was off limits and that he better not even gaze in her direction. That was another thing that I felt badly about—her unsuspecting friends. I had been alive long enough to know that women often held men responsible for the actions of their friends. Rarely did it work the other way. I had dated plenty of women whose "associates" had dogged over one of my boys but I never made the women feel bad about it. Let a man dog out a sister and all his friends are immediately just as guilty.

Part of me wanted to convince Mike to simply go to dinner and not try to sleep with one of Kiss's friends, but he would never go for that. His mind was made up; more than likely on trying to bed Calibri. Mike did not like aggressive women and Nancy looked like she was ready to fuck both of us on sight. Mike liked the challenge of obtaining the pussy. Even that maid had probably played hard to get at first, but he had eventually gotten the drawers and now she had been tossed into the pile of past notions.

"That pussy was a nice appetizer—Caribbean Jerk Punany," Mike bragged as we descended on the elevator to meet the ladies in the lobby. "Now I'm ready for the main course—Los Angeles Cream Pie. I wonder if I can get a two-for-one deal tonight. Too bad they're leaving tomorrow. If I had until we leave next week, I most definitely would fuck them both. Tonight's going to be a challenge, but I'm up for it."

I smirked. "I seriously doubt that. You might not get any play at all, so don't be surprised. Haven't you had enough sex for one night?"

"Hell no!" Mike exclaimed. "If there was only one chick as an option, then I might not want to bang her again, but I'm always down for new meat."

"That's all women are to you, huh? Meat?" I shook my head. "Did you talk to your *wife*?"

"Yes, I damn sure did," he replied, "and she loves me to death, my sons are fine, and you can drop the guilt trip act. I'm enjoying myself and you know how I am. You need to take a note from my book and enjoy life."

"I do enjoy my life, Mike. I simply don't feel like my dick has to regulate my every move."

It was his turn to smirk at me. "Yeah, right. I saw the way you were looking at Kiss earlier. You know you want to salute her with your wing-wang tonight. If you play your cards right, you might get lucky." As the elevator doors opened, he added, "Damn, I wish that I could make it with a clown. That's a new one. I wonder if she wears a red rubber nose and a wig to bed. That shit makes me hot just thinking about it."

"You are truly sick," I said, then laughed, halfway turned on by the thought myself.

KISS

When they walked into the beachside restaurant, I wondered how a man could grow even finer within the span of a few hours.

Aleck had on this white linen suit that brought out the beauty of his dark skin. He smiled as they approached us and my black thong got wet. Then again, I had been wet all day. I had returned to my room and masturbated for an hour, fantasizing about him...being inbetween my thighs. I imagined him fingering my pussy and then staring at me as he licked his fingertips one by one. I imagined him flipping me on my stomach and eating me out from the back as I buried my head in the sheets and held on to the bedposts. Mmm, yes, it was something. The great thing about this particular fantasy was that I now had a name to go with the face, the body and the curved dick.

"Hey, ladies," Mike said once they arrived at our table. "I don't know what smells better, the food or the three of you." He sat down next to Calibri and sniffed her neck. "What's that scent called? Paradise?"

Calibri blushed. "Oh, you have mad game."

"Hello, Kiss...Nancy...Calibri," Aleck said and each word sounded poetic.

"Hey, Sexy," Nancy stated seductively. I shot her an evil glare. She would not even want to go there.

We sat in that restaurant for a good three hours, eating, laughing and drinking. That get-to-know you period. Nancy and Calibri started vying for Mike's attention but it was obvious that he was down to fuck one of them, or both. It didn't matter to him as long as he got some pussy. Definitely not my type of man, but Nancy and Calibri thought he was hot.

"Would you like to take a walk on the beach?" Aleck asked me out of the blue.

"Absolutely." I quickly got up to follow him.

"Be good, or be good at it!" Nancy yelled out after us.

As we walked toward the shoreline, Aleck took my hand and nothing had ever felt so natural.

"Your friend is a trip," I said.

"Don't hold it against me." He laughed. "Mike can be a character, all right."

"Is he married?"

Aleck stopped dead in his tracks and let go of my hand. "What makes you ask that?"

"Women's intuition. It does exist, you know."

Aleck did not respond.

"It's cool," I said. "Nancy and Calibri really don't care; especially Nancy. They're only here to hang out and have fun. We're all grown."

He stared at me. "Aren't you going to ask me?"

"Ask you what?"

"If I'm married."

I shrugged. "Like I said, we're all grown."

I could tell that he was dying to ask me if I was married. There it was, on the tip of his tongue, but he swallowed it.

"Why'd you let go of my hand?" I asked. "I was enjoying that."

He took my hand back into his. "So, Los Angeles. Is it really as hot there as everyone claims?"

"You've never been to L.A.?"

"No, not yet. I've always planned to visit but haven't made it there yet." He smiled at me. "Maybe I'll have a reason to come now."

I cleared my throat uncomfortably. "Los Angeles has tricky weather. During the day, it can be hotter than hell and by nighttime, you might need a parka. It's beautiful, though."

"And obviously full of beautiful women to boot."

"Ooooh, Aleck, you have mad game."

We both laughed. "No, not me," he replied. "I simply recognize beauty when I see it; both inside and out."

In my entire life, I had been many things. Bold was never one of them. Yet, something overcame me at that very moment and it changed me.

"Aleck…"

"Yes?"

"There's something very sincere about you; something I want to experience…if only for one night."

"What do you mean, Kiss?"

We stopped in place while he awaited my answer. I took a deep breath, contemplating my next move.

"Do you believe in destiny?" I asked. "Like, do you believe that it's possible for two strangers to mesh so well together that it seems surreal? So much so that it seems like we've been in this place before?"

"I feel that way right now. I've felt it all day," he replied.

I wanted to feel him inside of me. Something about him made me feel so comfortable, so unique. I decided not to waste another moment of valuable time.

"Aleck?"

"Yes?"

"Would you like to fornicate under the consent of the king?"

ALECK

At first I thought that I was hearing things. Then she said it again. "Well, Aleck, would you like to fornicate under the consent of the king?"

The smile that spread across my face could have probably lit up the sky. "Kiss, it would be my pleasure but—"

"My pleasure, too." She placed her hand over my lips. "There are no buts...not tonight."

I kissed her fingertips. "I want you to understand something... first."

"What's that?"

"I'm not ordinarily the type of man to do something like this." She smirked and I could tell that she thought I was full of shit. "Seriously. Normally, I would never sleep with a woman on a vacation like this. I'm not the type to bed just anyone."

"That's nice to know." She pointed toward the hotel with her free hand, the one holding the straps of her sandals. "Your room or mine?"

I shook my head. "That doesn't matter, and you're missing the point."

"I understand what you're trying to express, Aleck, and I appreciate that." Kiss sighed. "This is not the norm for me, either. I certainly didn't come to Jamaica to get laid, but I want you. I want you bad...tonight."

She stood on her toes and I leaned down so she could kiss me. It was incredible when her tongue slipped into my mouth. I could feel the tip of her tongue exploring the inside of my cheeks and the roof of my mouth. Her breath was sweet, like candy. She grabbed one of my ass cheeks; I went tit for tat and cupped my hands around one of hers. It was round, juicy.

"Kiss, I really want tonight to be special," I told her as we broke the kiss after a good two minutes.

She started rubbing my dick through my pants. It was already throbbing and I felt like I could explode right there.

"Aleck, will you let me put it in my mouth? I want to taste you... your essence." I was speechless. "I want us to pretend like this is our last night...not in Jamaica, but on Earth. Will you take that special journey with me? Will you fuck me like there's no tomorrow?"

"Damn!" was all that I managed to get out before she glanced up the shore toward the restaurant, where people were still laughing and drinking.

Then she dropped to her knees, right there. She stared up into my eyes as she undid my belt buckle, then the zipper on my pants. She gently tugged at my dick until it was exposed. She laughed, which made me nervous. I was packing all of nine inches, admittingly having measured it. I wondered what was so funny.

"What?" I asked. "Something wrong, Kiss."

She giggled. "No, not at all. It's just that it's curved."

I used to feel uncomfortable about the curve in my dick, but figured out that most women enjoyed it. I was hoping she did not see it as a fault, not that there was anything I could do about it.

"Is the curve a problem?"

"Hell to the no." Kiss looked at me serious then. "It's all that I imagined it would be. That makes me so happy."

I was relieved. "What can I do to make you even happier?"

She did not hesitate. "Feed it to me. That's how you can make me happier."

Kiss opened her mouth wide and waited. She wanted me to bring it to her. I grabbed the base of it and slid the tip inside.

"You taste so sweet, Aleck," she whispered as she tickled the head with the tip of her tongue. "You have the nectar of royalty...of a king. Just like I always imagined."

I had no idea what she meant by that "just like I always imagined." Nor did I care. She licked the underside of my dick and squeezed my balls gently. Then she took me inside, deep, until her bottom lip was rubbing up against the top of them. She held me there, lost in that single moment, while she tightened her jaw muscles around me. It was so pleasurable that it was almost painful. I felt something incredible, something that could only be described as pure ecstasy. This woman craved my dick in a way that most men would kill for. My only thought was that I had to find a way to make it last...beyond that night...beyond Jamaica.

She held me tightly inside her mouth for several minutes, staring up at me in the moonlight. Then she let me go.

"The perfect fit," she said. "I want you to fuck me in all three holes tonight. Is that cool?"

I almost had to slap myself to believe this was really happening. I realized it was on and popping when she started gliding my dick in and out to imaginary music and humming on my dick like it was a fine musical instrument. She was enjoying herself and did not break her rhythm as these two men walked past us on the beach. I had not even seen them coming.

"Damn, Brah, you're lucky as shit!" one of them commented as they stood there for a minute, watching.

"Shit like this never happens to me," the other one said.

I grabbed the back of Kiss's head, trying to get her to ease up. "Kiss, maybe we should go up to the room," I whispered.

She was relentless, still humming, still staring up at me, like the other dudes did not even exist.

They finally moved on, discussing how they needed to find some women—and quick—to get laid.

I exploded before I even felt it coming. It was the biggest orgasm of my natural life. Kiss still did not let my dick go, not until she had extracted every drop of semen that my body had to give. She stared at me.

I tried to fake a laugh, but I was overwhelmed with the sensation of what she had done to me. "What next?" I asked jokingly, thinking that surely I needed at least a two-hour nap before I could do another damn thing.

Kiss finally released me and stood back up. She glanced at the water. The waves had started crashing up against the shore. Her chest was heaving; not from exhaustion, but from excitement. She pulled down the spaghetti straps of her black dress and stepped out of it, leaving her in nothing but a thong that tied on the sides. She undid the strings and pulled them between her legs to the front. She took them and lifted them to my lips. They were wet.

"Lick them," she whispered.

Normally licking a woman's drawers would be unappealing to me, but I was caught up. I took them from her, spread them out and licked, then sucked the crotch.

"How do I taste?"

"Like heaven."

"Then I taste like you," she said, grinning and then making a dash for the water.

I watched her splash around in the waves for a few seconds. Then she lifted her left breast to her mouth and flicked the tip of her tongue over her nipple. I did not think that I could get hard again so quickly but, sure enough, my dick sprung right back up to attention.

"Aleck, are you going to keep me waiting?"

I looked around, and while there were people still at the restaurant, and others walking further down the shore, I decided that I was not about to pass up an opportunity to see where she was trying to take things. I was in Jamaica and, outside of Mike, I did not know a soul anyway.

KISS

I asked Aleck if he was going to keep me waiting. He stood there looking around, probably worried that someone else would see us. Those two bastards had walked by but they were not going to deprive me from what I had yearned after for so long. I am sure they had seen their fair share of pornos, not to mention getting head themselves, so it was not a big deal to me. Granted, I had never imagined myself sucking dick in front of strangers, but I was a grown woman and life is what it is. You only live once.

I watched Aleck as he came to his senses. Maybe it had something to do with the fact that I was standing there, butt ass naked, slobbering all over my own nipple. He started taking off his white suit, which was already damp and his pants were already down around his ankles. He kicked his sandals off into the sand. I had noticed earlier that he took good care of his feet. That was a definite plus because I could not stand a man with jacked-up, rough feet, and nasty-ass toes. Even his feet turned me on and I could envision sucking his toes and licking his soles; something I would never have considered before that night.

Once he was nude, I could make out his "perfect" silhouette in the moonlight as he merged toward me in the water. In my lifetime, I had endured times when I was aroused by men, but never such as this. I had so much to look forward to, based on what had happened in all my fantasies about this man. I only hoped that I would not end up disappointed. So far, so good.

"Well, here I am," Aleck said when he was close enough for me to touch him.

Touch him, I did. I let go of my breasts and rubbed the fingertips of my hands over his expansive chest. I pinched both his nipples. "Are your nipples sensitive?"

"Yeah, I guess," he replied. "Most women aren't interested in my nipples," he said, looking down at his erect dick.

"Oh, you already know I'm feeling your dick." I reached down and gave it a quick yank. He winced in pain, then grinned. "But I want to play with your chest."

"You can play with whatever pleases you."

"Have you ever had a woman show you how she wants her nipples sucked by practicing on you?" I asked him, pinching and then pulling on his nipples harder.

"No, but if you intend to suck on them any way near the way you just sucked on my dick, I'm not sure I can handle it."

I giggled. Dirty talk always turned me on, and even though I was the instigator, he was a quick learner, or an old pro. Whichever, I did not care.

The water was lukewarm, but it would not have mattered. The steam emanating from our bodies would have kept us warm. I moved even closer to him and drew one of his nipples into my mouth. It was salty and hard. I held onto it and worked my tongue over it. Aleck moaned. For the next few minutes, I showed him what I wanted him to do to my breasts. How I wanted him to knead them with his powerful hands, then slurp and lick all over my nipples until they could cut diamonds. How I wanted him to devour my breasts like they were the best two things on earth. My breasts had always been my weakest link. When a man even brushed across them, my pussy got wet.

I looked up and he had his head thrown back, his eyes closed. His hard dick was poking into my belly button so I must have hit upon one of his weak links as well. While I craved to have him inside of me, we had all night. I wanted to make the most of every second.

"There," I whispered, letting go of the chest action once I felt him come all over my stomach, even under the water. "Did that feel good to you, Baby?"

"Yes...yes...hell, yes," he managed to get out. "You're doing all this sucking on me. When do I get to suck on something?"

"Right now." I pulled Aleck down by his shoulders onto the knees in the water and then held up one of my breasts so he could suckle on it. "That's right, Aleck. Suck it like it's the sweetest thing you've ever tasted. Suck it like you always do."

Oops. I did not mean to let that slip out. I waited to see if he would question my last comment. He did not; just kept sucking.

"Mmm, that's it, Papi." I caressed the back of his head with my fingertips. "Show me how much you want me."

"I do want you," he whispered. "I want every part of you."

"So you'll do it...you'll give it to me in all three holes."

He stopped for a minute and grinned at me. "One down, two to go." He started planting kisses all over me and I felt his fingers enter my pussy. "Damn, how can a pussy be so juicy under water?"

"Because you turn me on," I replied.

I lifted my leg and he helped me brace it up on his shoulder, both of us realizing what was next. He did something nothing short of incredible. Aleck took my other leg, threw it over his other shoulder in one quick movement and then stood up as he began to lick my pussy lips.

"Oh, shit!" I exclaimed, shivering a little in the cool night air. He moved his head from side to side, licking every spot and then he did it…he slid his smooth tongue inside of me and my thighs trembled. "Ooh, Papi! Yes! Do me just right. That's it, Baby! Um, it feels so damn good!"

I had never talked that much during sex but I had dreamed about it. Now I was letting all my inhibitions go.

I stared at the moon as my body went weak. The orgasm came like a lightning storm and sent a streak from my big toe to my eyelids. Aleck kept eating me and I wanted to beg him to stop but I could not even find a breath, rather less my voice.

Aleck gripped me tighter by the ass cheeks and carried me out of the water, then lay me down on the sand. He never broke his stride with his tongue action. Not for a second.

"Enough!" I screamed out, as another orgasm rippled through me. "I can't take anymore."

Aleck stopped and caressed my thighs, which were now shaking like a washing machine during the rinse cycle. "You like the way I eat this pussy, Baby?"

"I love it, but I really can't take anymore."

He grinned. "Maybe later, then." Suddenly he looked concerned. "Damn!"

"What?"

"I don't have a condom. I had hoped but… I really didn't think that we would…"

"It's okay," I said, rubbing my fingers across his chin. "I'm on birth control."

"You sure?" he asked.

I snickered. "Positive. I'm the one that swallows every morning." The connotation of that was cute. "I swallow pills every morning."

"Maybe soon you'll be swallowing something else every morning."

We both laughed.

"I want you to put that beautiful curved dick all up in me." I reached down and grabbed; his dick was rock hard. "I have an itch and I need it scratched."

"Where are you itching?"

"Inside my belly button." I rubbed up and down his thick shaft. "Will you fornicate under the consent of the king with me now?"

"Absolutely." Aleck started sucking on my breasts again, causing me to moan with intensity. I anticipated his entry, and like a surgeon, he delicately placed himself inside my sugar walls. "Aah, that's it," he said. "Let me show you what making love really feels like."

I rubbed the back of his head. "Is that what we're doing? Making love?"

"We're making history," he replied.

That was a new one on me; "making history."

Aleck put his arms underneath my knees and pushed my legs up over his shoulders.

"That's it. Go deeper," I said. "Rub it against my special spot."

"You like this dick," Aleck said, turning me on by talking dirty. "Tell me you like this dick."

"I love your dick. Give it all to me. Take all this pussy."

I started gyrating my hips, trying to work his dick like a vise by contracting my muscles on it.

Then…I screamed. Not a sexual scream but a painful one.

Aleck freaked and pulled out of me. "What is it? What's wrong?"

"Something cut me," I said, sitting up and reaching under my ass. "I hope it wasn't a jellyfish."

Aleck started reaching to and came out with a broken seashell about the size of a golf ball. The ragged part of it had torn into me. I could tell that I was slightly bleeding.

"You okay?" he asked.

"I'm fine." I put my arms around his neck and pulled him to me. "Can we continue what we were doing?"

"How about back in your room?" he suggested. "That way we won't have to worry about needing a first aid kit when we're through."

I giggled. "Good point; but this is so peaceful, so sexy, being out here...with you under the moonlight."

"I'll tell you a secret."

"What?"

"I look the same under regular light bulbs."

We both laughed and got up, searching for enough clothing to wear back to the hotel without arousing suspicion. We went back to my room and fucked in three more positions that night. First, I was on top. Then, we did it sideways. Finally, he fucked me doggy style and I could feel the tip of his dick all the way up in my stomach as his balls slapped into my ass from behind.

Later on, after I sucked his scrumptious dick yet again in the shower, he ate my pussy so tenderly, like it might break if he was too rough with me. The ceiling was mirrored and I watched the back of his head as he got lost in my goodies. He was serious about his business and after we fucked about three or four more times, he put me to sleep by eating my pussy all over again. I slept like a newborn baby.

THE AFTERMATH

ALECK

She was so beautiful, as she lay sleeping. What a workout! I had never fucked or been fucked so hard in my entire life. I was in love, pure and simple. I was ready to make a commitment. I was ready to move to be with her; whatever it would take to make her mine.

Kiss and her friends were leaving that day and I had to let her know how I felt. I could not let her get away.

We sat out on the balcony, overlooking the ocean, an hour later. We were nude, but had a blanket wrapped around us as we cuddled.

"Kiss, last night was wonderful." I kissed her hand, then her cheek. "I wish you didn't have to leave today. Can you stay a day or two longer? You can sleep in my room."

She giggled. "How thoughtful of you."

I winked. "Hey, I'm a gentleman."

Kiss suddenly looked upset.

"What's wrong?" I asked.

"There's something I have to tell you."

"What's that?"

Kiss blurted it out, like it was nothing. "I'm engaged."

I stood up, naked, dick swinging for the world to see. "What did you just say?"

She gazed up at me. "His name is Darrell. We're getting married in two months. I met him last year in the grocery store."

"What?" I asked again. "Tell me that you're joking, Kiss."

"No, I'm not. What's so crazy about this entire thing is that I dreamed about you before I even met him. Life is strange, but who are we to question things?" She stood up, but kept the blanket wrapped around her. "Calibri and Nancy decided that we should come here for a last girlfriends' getaway before I tie the knot. That's why I'm here."

"You mean so you could come over here and get fucked before you tied the knot."

She slapped me; it stung. "I didn't come here to get any dick, Aleck. I resent that. What happened between us wasn't that *basic*. It was something special. Something electric."

"Okay, so if it was that damn special and electric, then dump him to be with me. You said you dreamed about me before you met him. That technically makes me first. I'll move to California; whatever it takes. Just don't let this end like this…not like this."

I knew the words sounded ridiculous as they were leaving my mouth but I did not care. This was not fair, for me to meet the woman who possessed every quality that I could ever ask for and then have to give her up to another man.

"I cannot break up with my fiancé, Aleck. I feel something for you, I won't lie, but he and I have made plans."

"Plans are made to be broken."

"But promises are not," she said, cutting through my heart like a knife. "I made Darrell a promise and I have to keep it. Would you want someone to break their promise to you?"

"No, I suppose that I wouldn't," I readily admitted. "This is just hard for me, Kiss. Last night, I felt something. I felt it from the moment I saw you."

"You have no idea how long I've been feeling you," she responded. "This is insane. All those dreams I had, and here you are."

"It's not insane at all, if it's true."

"It is true. That's why I had to be with you. That's why I had to take the opportunity when it was placed in front of me."

I smirked. "So, was I better in the fantasies?"

"No, you were better in real life." She punched my arm lightly. "In my wildest dreams, I could never have imagined what happened last night. How you felt inside of me. How you tasted. How you tasted me."

My dick got hard all over again. "Down, boy, down," I told it, trying to swat the hardness away.

Kiss had other ideas. "No, let's not let that erection go to waste. Will you dick feed me one last time before I leave?"

Before I could reply, she was on her knees on the balcony, trying to swallow me whole. She let the blanket drop and I was mesmerized with the way her tight ass bounced up and down in the air as she devoured her last meal.

It hurt me to say good-bye later that day, but what else could I do? I had the seashell from the night before and gave it to Kiss when she was in the cab leaving for the airport. I stood there until the cab carrying her and her friends was out of sight. Something within me wanted to rush to the airport and beg her not to leave, but I had my foolish pride. Plus, I could not make her do something she did not want to do. No matter how special our one night together was, I was being egotistical to think that I could make Kiss forget about her fiancé. I would simply have to live with the circumstances and let the memory of her carry me through the rest of my life.

Mike and I still had several days there. I spent them sulking on a lounge chair on the beach while Mike chased tail. He had slept with Nancy that night; Calibri wasn't having it. Mike said Nancy was "aiight" but nowhere near as fly as she wanted men to think.

He claimed that she was scared of the dick and gagged while she was giving him head. I asked him if he ate her, and he said, "Hell, no! The only pussy I eat is the one lying in the bed at my house! Fuck all these other tricks!"

I had given Kiss my number but I knew that she would never use it. Other women tried to distract me in Jamaica. Mike even came to my room with one woman who was down for whatever, but I politely asked her to leave. I loved Kiss and prayed that one day our paths would cross again.

ALECK

"Kiss, it that you?"

I couldn't believe it. After all those years, to run into her inside an airport. It was so cliché.

She spun around to face me inside the American Airlines terminal.

"Oh, my God! Aleck?"

"One and the same."

I set my briefcase down and slung my garment bag over my shoulder as she approached me. I was preparing myself to throw at least one arm around her. She was still a stunner—remarkably so. She had on this black business suit that made her look incredibly sexy; even though I am sure she was going for the more conservative look.

Our hug was nice, but reserved. She smelled like shampoo mixed with floral body spray. Even with all of those scents masking it, I could still smell her pussy. It was calling out to me. Heaven help me, but that was one call that I yearned to answer.

"What are you—" we both started to ask in unison.

She threw her head back in laughter. I remembered that mouth, those lips, engulfing my dick and filling me with pleasure. "I'm on my way to a business meeting in New York. My flight was cancelled, engine trouble, so it looks like I'm stuck overnight. What about you?"

"I've been here for two days. My flight leaves in an hour."

"Oh…" Her voice reeked with disappointment. "That's too bad."

It took everything in me not to try to devour her right there in the airport. Every inch of my being wanted her. I had to do something to protect my emotions, so I asked sarcastically, "So, how's the hubby?"

"I guess he's fine." I eyed her strangely, with a raised brow. She shrugged, then added, "I wouldn't know how he's doing. He's my ex-hubby now. We still speak, but I don't get into his business."

I was stunned. "What?"

"We got divorced last year. It was amicable; nothing too nasty."

"Did he cheat on you?" I asked, thinking the man would have to be a damn fool if he did.

"No, at least not that I know of. We weren't compatible; had different goals. That sort of thing."

I motioned over to the seating area by Gate 31. After we sat down, I reflexively took her hand. "What type of business?"

"Huh?" Her mind seemed a million miles away; she was lost somewhere in my eyes.

"You said that you're on your way to New York for a business meeting. What kind of business?"

Kiss grinned. "Well, I gave up being a clown. I had to, after I realized that I was pregnant."

I could tell by the expression on her face that the look of anguish on mine was obvious.

"I have a little boy, Aleck. He's seven."

I forced a smile. "What's his name?"

"Aleck."

"Yes?"

Kiss laughed. "My son's name is Aleck, Aleck. I named him after you."

Her grip tightened on my hand.

My mind started running rampant. *Did she say that he's seven?*
"Kiss—"

That was when she glanced down, noticing my wedding ring.
"You're married?" she asked, yanking her hand away.

"Kiss, you walked out of my life...after one night. I needed
someone to...to fill the void."

She was visibly upset. "How long?"

"Just two years."

"Oh..." That one word hung in the air like a thick fog.

Meanwhile, I will still doing the math in my head. "Kiss, is
Aleck my—"

She shook her head adamantly. "No, he's not. What happened
between us meant a lot to me, Aleck. I enjoyed our time together
and he reminded me of you...a little. Or maybe I just wanted
him to remind me of you. I really wanted to be able to at least
say your name on a daily basis, even if it wasn't to you directly."

I sighed in relief, or disappointment. I was not quite sure which
emotion outweighed the other. There was no way that I would
want a child of mine in the world and not know him, or have him
know me. I decided that I was more disappointed than relieved.
God, I would have given anything to have a baby with Kiss. *Snap
out of this, Aleck*, I told myself.

"To answer your previous question," Kiss said, interrupting my
thoughts, "I work for a major property management company
with offices in twelve cities along both coasts. I have to go back
and forth to New York quite often."

"Sounds interesting. At least you get to travel."

"I used to travel with the circus year-round, Silly."

I laughed. "Good point."

"I only recently started to travel again. After I had my son, I wanted to be there for him; but I need to make a living now that I'm single...and this works."

"Your parents watch him when you travel?"

"They pitch in, but I have a great nanny. He's a wonderful kid!" Her face beamed with pride, making me feel even worse that he was not mine. After a long pause, Kiss asked, "So, what's her name? Any kids?"

For a second, I had no clue who she was talking about; then I remembered. Janice. Janice and I met during a jazz festival in Richmond, Virginia, in 1992. We dated for a little over a year before deciding to settle down. She was a schoolteacher and I admired that. Kids had become serious behavior problems, particularly in public schools, but Janice was one of the few teachers who was totally committed to making a difference. She was from a large family in North Carolina but had relocated to the D.C. area to get her degree from Howard University. She was quiet, a home-body, and all she wanted to do was make me happy when she was not teaching. She volunteered for a lot of programs and I could not ask for a more loving individual in my life. Yet, sitting there with Kiss, all I could think about was being inside of her. I should have left...before it was too late. I should have told her that I needed to head to my gate so that I would not miss my flight. I should have done something else...something other than what I did.

KISS

"Did you forget her name?" I chided, after Aleck did not answer.

"What?" he said, coming back to reality.

"Your wife. Her name?"

"Her name is Janice. She's a schoolteacher, from North Carolina."

"What grade does she teach?"

"She teaches middle-school math. Grades sixth through eighth."

"Any kids?" I held in my breath, hoping he would say no.

"No kids yet. We've both been pretty caught up with work."

"You still a financial analyst?"

"Yes. I'm not like you. I'll probably be doing the same thing when I'm ninety."

Hopefully you'll be inside me when you're ninety, I thought. Aleck looked like time had stood still. He was the same man that I had fallen for in 1987—perfect. He had on a golf shirt and khaki slacks and I could see the outline of his dick. The curved dick that I had missed for many years, along with the man attached to it.

"Do you love her?" I asked blatantly. "More than me?"

Aleck could not find the words.

"You do love me, don't you?" I leaned over and drew his bottom lip into my mouth, suckling on it. "I fell in love with you that night in Jamaica, too, Aleck."

His eyes watered as we stared at each other. "Then why didn't you say something, Kiss? Things could have been so different. So damn different."

"It wasn't our time." I touched his wedding band; it glared in the setting sun through the picture windows of the airport. "I guess now isn't our time, either."

I stood up before I broke out in tears. "You'd better get to your gate. I called for a car and it's probably waiting outside to take me to a hotel."

Aleck grabbed my hand and pulled me to him. He buried his nose in my belly button, whispering, "Let me go with you."

"We can't, Aleck. It wouldn't be right."

He stared up at me. "Nothing has ever felt so right."

"Then get your things," I blurted out before either one of us started thinking with an ounce of clarity.

We were out of the airport, inside the black Lincoln sedan, and all over each other in less than ten minutes. I climbed on top of him, not giving a damn what the driver could see, and gave him all the tongue he could handle. He hiked my skirt up around my hips and worked his fingers inside my black lace panties, fingering my sweltering pussy.

"I want you so bad," I said, coming up for air. "But..." I climbed off of him.

"Kiss, what are you doing?"

"The question is...what are we doing...here...together."

Aleck grinned. "I guess we're about to fornicate under the consent of the king."

I could not help but laugh. "You remember that, huh?"

His grin turned sensual. "I remember every second that we spent together. Every touch. Every lick. Every orgasm."

I blushed. "So, I laid it on you good, right?"

He chuckled. "It was alright."

I frowned, then swatted him away from me. "Fine, then." I glanced up front at the driver, who was pretending to keep his eyes on the road. "Um, Driver, I think we need to turn around. Aleck wants to go back to the air—"

"Shut the hell up!" Aleck grabbed my hand gently, lifted it to his mouth and kissed it. "We're fine," he said to the driver. "How much longer to the hotel?"

"About ten minutes," came the driver's reply.

Aleck glanced at me, holding my hand tighter. "We can do a lot of things in ten minutes."

"But what about him?" I asked, pointing up front.

"You weren't worried about him less than five minutes ago."

"That's because I got carried away."

"Then get carried away again."

Aleck unbuttoned my suit jacket and maneuvered one of my

breasts out of my bra so he could devour it. I do not think my nipples have ever been as hard as that day. He sucked on my breast like I yearned to suck on his dick. There was something purely magical about this man and I could not wait to get him into a hotel room.

In fact, I did not wait. By the time we pulled up in front of the Hilton, Aleck was balls deep inside of me and the driver had no clue what to do…so he watched. I could make out his eyes in the rearview mirror, full of lust and wonderment. He was an older man, one who had surely seen his share of action in the backseat of his sedan. But we were not simply fucking…we were trying to fuck each other to death.

"You feel do damn good," Aleck whispered in my ear. "I love being inside of you."

I grabbed his head and licked the top of it. "Right the hell where you belong."

"Oh, shit!"

Aleck made a mess inside of me, and all over the backseat. I came right behind him. I held onto him like he was my lifeline until we both got our breathing back under control.

Once we were in a room, it was like we had not just fucked in the car. Our erotic dance began anew.

Aleck threw me back on the bed, yanked my pumps off and starting working to get my skirt off.

"I have something for you," I whispered. "Something I want to give you."

Aleck eyed me seductively, taking my foot in his hand and kissing my ankle, then licking my insole. "I'll bet you do have something good for me. Something plump, wet, and juicy."

"Oh, I've got that for you, too, Papi." I took the same foot and rubbed it across his chest, down the middle of his stomach and massaged his dick through his pants. "That's not what I mean, though. It's in my suitcase."

He raised a brow. "But you didn't know you were going to see me."

"It's something that I carry with me all the time." I could tell his curiosity was piqued. "Hold up a second."

I lowered my foot and got up from the bed. Aleck slapped me on the ass as I headed for my suitcase. My skirt was falling off so I let it hit the floor as I walked, revealing a white thong.

"Baby still has back," Aleck said jokingly.

I rummaged through my belongings until I found what I was looking for and returned to the bed. "Hold out your hand," I said. He did as instructed and I placed the seashell that he had given me in Jamaica into his hand. "Remember it?"

He grinned from ear to ear. "You still have this?"

"It has been my lucky charm. It's the only physical memory that I have of the night we spent together."

Aleck grabbed my waist and pulled me to him, burying his head in my chest and holding me tightly. "I have missed you so much, Kiss. I missed us."

I lifted his head by the chin and stared into his eyes. "Then let's not waste tonight."

"You ready to fornicate under the consent of the king some more?"

We both laughed, but there was nothing funny about our situation. We were addicted to each other and when the morning came, we would have to say good-bye. I decided not to worry about it; to let it all go and make the most of the time we had together.

"Speaking of baby still having back," I said. "You didn't finish your job in Jamaica, Aleck."

He seemed bemused. "What?"

"You said that you were going to fuck me in all three holes that night." I grinned. "Remember the whole 'one down, two to go' thing. Well, we handled my mouth and we handled my pussy but I still haven't had the pleasure of having you inside my ass." I finished taking off all my clothing. "It's so strange. I have no problems getting naked in front of you."

"Why would you?" he asked.

I shrugged. "Even when I was married to Darrell, I didn't feel completely comfortable baring myself like this. With you, it's never an issue."

"What do you think that means?"

"That what I feel is real."

Aleck pulled me onto the bed. "Lie on your stomach. I'm always a man of my word."

Once I was on my stomach, Aleck got undressed and lay beside me. He reached between my legs from behind and started fingering my pussy, which was really more like a fountain at the point. I squirmed and moaned. There was something about his touch that drove me wild.

He used my own juices to lubricate my ass for a few minutes, playing with my hole with first one, then two fingers. When he thought that I was ready, he climbed on top of me and took his time entering a little of his dick at a time until he filled me up.

"I don't want to hurt you, Baby," Aleck whispered in my ear.

"No, it feels good, Papi. Real good." I grabbed onto the sheets and got lost in a rapture as my first orgasm achieved through anal sex pulsated through me. "I've been dreaming about this."

"Then let me put you to sleep the right way."

Aleck started working my ass then, giving it to me good. I

screamed out in pleasure and then he came. The sensation of his sperm in my ass made me lose it. I lay there shivering as he placed tender kisses on my back. He fell asleep with his flaccid dick inside my ass. We both slept like babies and parted sometime during the night. I ended up clinging to his chest...hoping.

THE AFTERMATH

ALECK

I woke up the next morning, before the sun had risen, with Kiss snoring lightly in my arms. The fear, the guilt, it all hit me at once. What had I done? Part of me instantly regretted it; that was the side with morals. The other part of me wanted to wake Kiss up and go two or three more rounds. Wanted to take Kiss back to Jamaica and never come back. Wanted to love her for the remainder of my natural life.

I gently pushed Kiss onto the bed pillows, which she grabbed to replace her hold on me. It was hard to get out of the bed, but I managed. My entire body was sore from the sex. Kiss was no joke when it came to pleasing me, and pleasing herself. After twice having my mind blown in the span of one night, I wondered if I could even hang with Kiss if we were together all the time.

When I peed in the toilet, it hurt—a good kind of hurt. Now I knew what women meant when they said that their pussies were sore from being fucked hard. I ran cold water over my face and looked into the mirror. My reflection was that of a man full of confusion; one who wanted to have two women for different reasons.

"Couldn't sleep?" Kiss asked me as I tried to sneak back into the bed.

"I had to use the bathroom."

"Oh…" That one word spoke volumes. I could tell that she was also worried about what we had done.

"Kiss, I want you to know that I do not regret what happened."

"Nor do I." She flipped over to face me and gazed lovingly into my eyes. "But I understand…that you have to go home to your wife."

"I don't know what to do," I admitted. "I cannot believe we ran into each other like this. It's like time has stood still. Like we are continuing where we left off in Jamaica."

"Yeah, I know what you mean." She ran her fingertips across my chest. "But time didn't stand still, Aleck. I got married, had a child, got divorced. You got married, and you're happy. Right?"

I had to struggle for a response. Finally I said, "I'm content. I made the best decision based upon the circumstances. You broke my heart back then, when, out of the blue, you told me that you were engaged…after that night we spent together."

"I was dead wrong for that and karma is a bitch."

"What do you want me to do, Kiss?"

"Oh no, please don't put the ball in my court. I don't want it." She kissed me tenderly and we got lost in each other once again for a moment. She stopped it as quickly as she had started it. "You have to go home. I will not be responsible for breaking up another woman's home. I would not want someone to do that to me."

"But what about us?" I asked.

"This is what it's supposed to be," she replied. "If it was meant to be more, things would have been different. We would have run into each other and both been free to love, but maybe we're not supposed to be that. Maybe we're supposed to cross paths every now and again."

"For what reason?"

"So that we can remember what it feels like…to have such passion in our lives."

"I do love you, Kiss."

"And I love you; but sometimes, love is not enough."

"And sometimes, love is everything."

With that, I took her back into my arms and made love to her until checkout time. It was painful to say good-bye at the airport that day. I was weak as I watched her walk away down a gateway to get on a plane. By the time I settled into first class on my flight, I craved to be with her. But that was not to be. Kiss refused to even trade phone numbers with me. I was willing but she said that it only meant trouble. I prayed that I would be able to forget her, or at least function without her.

KISS

Calibri picked me up at LAX when I got back to Los Angeles. She was looking fly in a hot red pant suit that complemented her flawless skin. As I climbed into her Infiniti SUV, she couldn't wait to ask me questions.

"So what happened between you and Aleck in Dallas?" she inquired before she had pulled out into the next lane. "Did the two of you fuck?"

"Damn, Calibri. It's nice to see you, too," I said sarcastically. "I shouldn't have told you that I ran into him."

"Well, you told me, so you can't take the shit back." She paused as I tried to adjust my seatbelt. I must have been taking too long to answer. "Kiss, what went down? Don't do this to me. I need to know."

I rolled my eyes at her. "Why do you need to know if Aleck and I had sex?"

"Because this is a monumental moment in your life, Sis. It's been nearly a decade since you've seen him. I'll never forget the expression on your face in Jamaica after the two of you got busy. It was one of the happiest moments of your life."

"That was a long time ago."

She pulled on I-405 and headed toward Santa Monica. The sun was setting; she put down her visor so she could see. The traffic was crazy, as usual. We both knew what topic was being avoided so I decided to come out with it.

"No, I did not tell him that A.J. was his son."

Calibri gawked, stared at me and almost slammed into the back of a delivery van. She hit the brakes just in time but we swerved to the left and almost ended up in the other lane.

"Why didn't you tell that man the truth? You should have contacted him in the first place when you found out that you were pregnant."

"Really? Should I have called him before or after I was walking down the aisle with Darrell?" I sucked my teeth and laid my head back on the headrest so I could clamp my eyes shut. "This damn sun is relentless."

"You admitted fooling around to Darrell," Calibri said. "He forgave you and agreed to raise another man's child. Why couldn't you—"

"Hmph, and we see how that situation turned out," I whispered.

"You and Darrell didn't split because of A.J."

"Thanks for reminding me why my marriage failed," I said sarcastically. "For the record, I was there."

The fact was that my marriage had not ended because of A.J. It had ended because I was still in love with my son's father, Aleck. Over the years, I had tried to get him out of my head, tried to appreciate the love that Darrell offered. It was not to be. Aleck was inside my head, inside my heart, inside my soul.

I had lied to my friends, though. Not really lied. I told them that Darrell and I had different life goals and, in a sense, that was true. His goal was to love me and my goal was to love someone else.

Calibri fell silent for the remainder of the ride back to my house. I had a lovely little bungalow in Santa Monica, not that far from the Third Street Promenade and within walking distance of the boardwalk. Like everyone else, I would have loved to live directly on the water, but wasn't in that income range yet. So A.J. and I would get up on the weekends and run with our two Shar Peis, Max and Ruby, named after A.J.'s favorite cartoon characters.

A.J. and Nancy were waiting for us on the front stoop, along with my nanny, Rosalita. A.J. ran into my arms, reminding me what my main purpose in life truly was.

"Mommy, I missed you!" he said, before throwing his arms around my neck and placing a kiss on my cheek. He had the same dark skin as his father, along with his eyes, lips and just about everything else. It looked like Aleck had spit him out, which is why I lied about not having any photos of A.J. when we were together in Dallas.

"I missed you, too, Baby. How was school this week?" I asked him as we walked toward the front door.

"It was *so* boring. It's always boring."

Everyone laughed because that was A.J.'s newest favorite word. He would find a word he liked and wear it into the ground. Sometimes, he would not even understand what the word actually meant, but he had the "boring" concept down. A.J. was a bright child and school was not a challenge for him, at all. In second grade, he was reading on a sixth-grade level and doing math on a fifth-grade level. His principal had discussed skipping him, but I had done that as a child, and I wanted A.J. to have the childhood social experience.

"How was your trip?" Nancy asked as we reached her and Rosalita.

"Interesting," I said, knowing good and well that Calibri had opened her big mouth already. When I asked Calibri to pick me up from the airport, I mentioned running into Aleck but gave no details. "It was a productive trip."

Nancy smirked and then winked at Calibri, who was helping to bring in my luggage. "I'll bet it was productive."

They both giggled; made me sick.

"Hello, Rosalita. Everything okay?" I asked my nanny.

"Everything's great, Miss Kiss. Dinner's ready." She looked at her watch. She should have been off work an hour earlier. "Would you like me to stay and get A.J. ready for bed after dinner?"

"No thanks." I patted her on the shoulder. "As always, thanks for staying around the clock so I could go out of town on business."

"Anytime." Rosalita rubbed A.J.'s head. "I love A.J. It's nothing but a pure pleasure to take care of him."

A.J. beamed with pride. He was a good kid.

After we had eaten dinner and A.J. was bathed and in bed, I went back out into my living room to hear Nancy and Calibri whispering on the sofa. They stopped when I entered.

"Let me guess. The two of you were out here speculating about my pussy's activity." I sat down across from them in a recliner and hit the button to elevate my feet. "Okay, get it over with. Ask your twenty questions so I can get ready to watch *Martin*."

Calibri laughed and tucked her feet underneath her ass. "Girl, that Martin Lawrence is hilarious!"

"I love the show. When he does that snot-nose kid character, Roscoe, I can hardly contain myself," I replied.

Nancy folded her arms in front of her and smacked her lips. "Fuck television! What happened between you and Aleck?"

I shrugged. "Like I said, ask your twenty questions and I'll answer…the ones I feel like answering."

"Fine," Nancy said. "Calibri told me that you didn't tell him about A.J. Why not?"

"Because Aleck's married now." I could hear—and see—them both suck in air. "Breathe, dammit! It's been years; I had no expectations of him being single. Hell, I had no idea that I would ever see the man again."

"What do you think it means?" Calibri asked.

"What do I think what means?"

"That you ran into him."

I smirked. "I haven't a clue. It happened; it's as simple as that."

Nancy seriously copped an attitude, like I had done something to her. "Married or not, the man has a right to know that he has a son. Do he and his wife have any kids?"

"No, but I would assume they're working on it."

"You have a beautiful, intelligent little boy," Nancy continued. "You're not being fair. Not to Aleck, not to yourself, but especially not to A.J."

"What have you told A.J. about his dad?" Calibri asked.

I sighed. "This is not what I need tonight. Forget the twenty questions thing. I'm not up for it, after all."

Nancy stood up and started pacing the floor in anger. "Who gives a shit what you're up for? I cannot believe you. We've been friends forever, and I would never expect such a thing from you. It was one thing when you and Aleck lost touch and you decided to let it go. Even though I didn't agree with it, I let it slide. A one-night stand is a one-night stand."

"Exactly," I said vehemently. "Seeing Aleck in Dallas didn't change that, either. In fact, with him being married, I couldn't possibly throw a monkey wrench like that in his total existence."

"Don't you see that this is fate?" Nancy was determined to make her point. "You're the one who's always preaching about how there's always a reason. You said there was a reason why you and Aleck met and slept together in Jamaica; so that you could have A.J. You got married, cool, but that shit didn't work out. Now God has given you another chance to—"

"To break up Aleck's happy home?"

That shut her ass up...for all of three seconds.

"Did you sleep with him in Dallas, Kiss?"

The question hung in the air like a cloud of smoke.

Calibri tried to break the ice by snickering. "You all calm down. Nancy, you shouldn't ask her that. I'll admit that I asked her in the car, but that was before I realized Aleck was married. I'm sure Kiss wouldn't sleep with a married man. She's not that woman."

I started flipping through television channels with the remote, looking for *Martin*.

"You're not that woman. Right, Kiss?" Calibri asked.

I found the correct channel and even though I was tempted to turn the volume all the way up, I hit the mute button instead.

"Not that it is any of your business, but I will tell you...only because the two of you have been there for me and A.J. from the beginning." I paused. "Yes, Aleck and I succumbed to a moment of weakness and engaged in intimacy in Dallas."

I realized that I was making it sound more like a romance novel than straight, cold fucking.

"The next morning we both came to our senses and realized that we can never have a true relationship. He went his way and I went mine. I have no regrets about it, so I hope that you ladies will drop the subject. I don't wish to discuss it further."

They were quiet for a good two minutes while I turned the volume back up and the opening scene came on. Holding true to form, Nancy had to get in the last word.

"Kiss, okay, I am going to make one comment and then I swear that I will leave this alone."

I glared at her. "What comment?"

She sighed. "You can sit here and try to pretend like what happened was no big deal. You can be nonchalant about it until the end of time, but you love that man and I don't think that's ever going to change."

"Thanks for the revelation," I stated sarcastically. I got up from the recliner. "I'm going to grab a wine cooler. Anyone else want one?"

As I headed toward the kitchen, they both said, "No thanks."

I got my wine cooler and reached into the drawer to get a bottle opener. I struggled to get the cap off and finally gave up, after I could not get my hand-eye coordination together. It probably had something to do with the tears that were streaming down both my cheeks, blurring my vision.

KISS

A.J. was starting college and I could not be more excited. He had gotten a full athletic scholarship to Morehouse College for football. All the years of driving him back and forth to practice has paid off financially and we sure could use the assistance. It has not been easy for me over the years. Going back and forth to New York from California had proven to be too much for me. While I did not mind the travel before I had A.J., he was the reason that I had given up performing in the circus. Yet, there I was still away from home constantly. I started guilt-tripping and feeling like an unfit parent, even though he had a nanny. I wanted to be the one there for him.

I gave up my property management job shortly after I ran into Aleck in Dallas and started selling life insurance. It was quite a career jump and it was not for me. People do not like discussing life insurance because that means discussing death. The only job more difficult than a life insurance agent is selling cemetery plots. People really aren't trying to deal with that concept—being lowered into the ground. There is no way to make "final resting place" sound appealing.

After three years of selling life insurance, I was bored to death—no pun intended. I got into the whole cellular phone boom and sold a bunch of those bad boys until the fad became the norm and people were no longer looking for new service, just upgrading to the newer gadgets. Plus, I was still bored. Calibri opened a restaurant and wanted me to partner with her but that did not interest me. Nancy wanted me to go into this "virtual assistant" business with her. I was proud of my friends being entrepreneurs, but those were their dreams, not mine.

I searched to "find myself" and keep food on the table and clothes on our backs. Then I decided to do something drastic and moved to Atlanta in 2001, shortly after the terrorist attacks. If life was going to be that unpredictable, I was definitely going to begin treating every single day as a gift—something that I should have been doing all along.

There was something about Atlanta that had always appealed to me. The Dirty South, the way African Americans were doing so well there, the cleanliness of the downtown area. A.J. had mixed feelings about moving because he had only ever lived in California. Let's face it; most people in the East are trying to get to Cali. I was trying to get the hell out of there.

It was a huge undertaking, leaving my friends and family like that. My parents were retired and chilling at their beach home. They offered to let us come stay with them, assuming that my move was totally financial instead of because of my needing a change. Of course, they wanted their grandchild near them. He was their only one and that made him the most precious thing on Earth to them. They would be able to visit often, I assured them. I also promised to send A.J. back west to see them several times a year, during his school breaks and the summer.

Things worked out well those first years in Atlanta. I decided to get over all my fear factors. I went skydiving; I rode a motorcycle; and I got me a monster truck with tires that came up to my shoulders. I had a sticker in my rear window that read "Not only boys have big toys" and people were shocked when they realized a woman was driving it.

A.J.'s friends at Benjamin E. Mays High School thought I was the coolest mother around and I agreed. I did not try to smother him and while it was hard not to be too overprotective once he started dating, going to parties and driving, I managed to find that perfect equilibrium. He was the captain of the football team at Mays and the girls adored him. He looked so much like Aleck that it was scary. I was always reminded of the man that I wanted to love up close but had to cherish from afar.

I had dated several men over the years, but nothing serious. I had sex with them to meet my basic needs but steered away from developing any real feelings. The men in Atlanta thought they were special and in high demand because women put them on a pedestal. As I grew older, I realized that a lot of women my age were willing to accept a bunch of nonsense from men just so they could lay claim to one; even if they were sharing him. None of that was for me, so I fucked a man from time to time and then sent his ass home or got up and returned to mine. I liked it that way, too. No one to demand food on the table when he got home from work. No one to try to be the head of the household. No one to shove his dick into me when I was least expecting it, or wanting it.

On the day that A.J. was moving into the dorm, everything changed for me. A.J. had told me that his new roommate had a similar nickname, M.J. Even though I had never acknowledged that A.J. was really a junior of a man he had never met—I told him that was his great-great-grandfather's first name—I figured that M.J. was definitely a junior. What I was not prepared for was that his name was Michael, Jr. and that his father was the same Mike from Jamaica, Aleck's best friend.

Mike was in the room when we showed up, helping to unpack his son's belongings. It turned out that M.J. was the second youngest of Mike's four sons. He had had two already when we met in Jamaica and his wife became pregnant shortly after he returned home. Mike took one look at A.J. and knew the truth. There was no point in trying to deny it when he followed me to my truck, asking questions faster than I could register them all.

I agreed to meet Mike for drinks later that night, begging him not to cause a scene or tell A.J. anything about his father. We met in the Omni Hotel lobby and had a lengthy conversation, where he lambasted me for not being honest with Aleck. Aleck had told him about running into me in Dallas, and about the sex that had ensued. Mike also informed me that our indiscretion had ended Aleck's marriage a few years later, when he came clean to his wife, Janice, about the affair. I was in shock and I was speechless.

I apologized to Mike but he said, "Kiss, I'm not the one you need to be apologizing to."

"You're right," I said hesitantly. "Do you have a number where I can reach him?"

"I can do one better than that," Mike said. "Aleck's upstairs, in Room 932."

My mouth fell open. "He's here…in Atlanta?"

"Yes, he rode down here with M.J. and me to help me drive back. He didn't come to the dorm earlier today because he had a stomachache." Mike slid a pass key across the table to me. "I'm in a different room but he gave me one of his keys, so I could check on him later."

Mike stood up. "I'm going to take M.J. and A.J. to the movies." I gasped. "Don't worry. I promise that I will not say a word to your son. This is not my mess." He paused. "Kiss, as you know, I am anything but perfect. Far the fuck from it. There's one thing that can never be denied, though. I love my kids; they're everything to me. Aleck has always talked about having a son. Here it is that he has one, in college, and he doesn't even know that he exists."

I fought back tears. "I was wrong. I see that now."

He caressed my shoulder. "Then make things right."

I watched Mike walk off and then stared at the pass key while I finished off my rum and Coke. I sat there another thirty minutes or so, trying to find the guts to go upstairs. He was going to hate me, I was convinced. Why wouldn't he hate me?

I called Nancy and asked her to get Calibri on three-way. I needed a serious pep talk. Nancy got onto the entire "I told you so" trip and I wanted to reach through the phone and strangle her ass. Calibri was more sympathetic and told Nancy that we cannot focus on the past but deal with the present. Calibri even offered to get on the first thing smoking from California so she could be there by the morning. There was nothing she could do so I told her thanks, but no thanks.

After I got off the phone with them, I went into the ladies' room and sat on the toilet for another ten or fifteen minutes, with the lid down and my pants up, trying to practice what I was going to say to Aleck.

"Hey, Aleck. Long time, no see. By the way, we have a son in college."

"Aleck, I have to tell you something. My son is your son. I lied. So what else is new?"

"Aleck, sorry to hear about your divorce. Want to go meet your son?"

No, none of that shit was going to fly. I sucked in my chest and got up off the toilet, flushed it to pretend like I was using it, and then put on a show of washing my hands. I played with my hair because it had become ruffled, put on some fresh lipstick and powdered my face. Then I went out to find the bank of elevators.

As the elevator ascended to the ninth floor, I could feel my heart leaping in my chest. There were butterflies in my stomach. I was sweating. Room 932 was in the middle of the hallway. I rapped lightly at first, then remembered the pass key and pondered on using it. I hesitated when he did not answer but then slid it into the lock. The green light came on and I pushed. The room was dark and the air was dry. Aleck had the heat up high, even though it was August in the South.

I could make out his form on the bed, his beautiful form. He was snoring loudly and it made me smile. I remembered his snoring, even though I had only heard it twice. He was a heavy sleeper. I was not sure whether to climb into bed with him or cut on the light. I wanted him badly. The thought of him lying there in that bed made my pussy wet. It was calling out his name: *Aleck*.

As much as I wanted to get butt naked and attack him, I had to be sensible so I walked over to the bed and cut on the light on the nightstand. Aleck stirred. I sat down beside him and rubbed his back.

"Aleck?"

"Kiss," he replied in his sleep. He knew my voice.

"Aleck, we need to talk."

One of his eyes popped open, then the other. "Am I dreaming?"

"No, you're not. Mike gave me your room key. We ran into each other today."

Aleck wiped the drool from the side of his mouth and sat up, adjusting his eyes to the light. There was a discomfort as we both tried to decide whether to hug, kiss, or do nothing at all. Instead, he ran his fingers through my hair.

"What are you doing here in Atlanta?" he asked.

"Long story." I laughed. "Long-ass story."

"Mike's son is going to Morehouse. I rode down here with him to—"

"I know," I said, cutting him off. "That's where we first ran into each other. M.J. and A.J. are roommates. What are the odds of that?"

"A.J." I could tell that it hit him. "Your son's name is Aleck, right?"

"Yes."

"But he's not a junior. Why do you call him A.J.?"

I stared at him. "You've always been smarter than the average bear."

"Maybe you need to explain this to me, Kiss. What I'm thinking could not possibly be." He sat up even further. "You told me that he wasn't mine."

"I lied to you, Aleck. He is your son." For a moment, Aleck stared me down and I could see the pain in his eyes. "I realize now that I was wrong, but I was trying to do the right thing."

"Do the right thing?!" He got loud then. "How could not telling me that I have a son be doing the right thing?"

"It's okay if you hate me, Aleck. I have hated myself on and off throughout the years. It was never an ideal situation. Raising a child alone, him never knowing his father, me lying because it was a one-night stand."

"But what about when you saw me in Dallas?"

"You were married. Like I said then, I could not be responsible for breaking up another woman's home."

"Does he know that I'm his father?" Aleck asked.

"No, he hasn't a clue and I'm not quite sure how I'm going to tell him."

"Who does he think his father is?"

"I told him that you died in an automobile accident before he was born."

"Damn, Kiss!"

Aleck got up from the bed and started putting on his clothes. He had on boxers and a wife beater but was quickly getting into some jeans, a T-shirt and a pair of sneakers.

"We have to go tell him, right this second."

"Mike took the two of them to the movies. I'm not sure what time it started but they've got to still be there."

Aleck stood in the middle of the floor. "Does he look like me?"

"He looks like you spit his ass out. I was merely the vessel."

Aleck grinned. "What's he like?"

"Smart. Athletic. He has a full scholarship…for football."

"What do you think he's going to say?"

"He's going to be mad, that much I know for sure," I said, then immediately broke out in tears. "He's going to hate me…just like you do."

I buried my head into a pillow. I felt Aleck sit down on the bed and then he caressed the small of my back. "I do not hate you, Kiss. I love you. I've always loved you."

"But can you forgive me?" I asked, even though my voice was muffled.

"I have to forgive you. Love is forgiving." He continued to console me and his fingertips sent electricity up my spine. "I'm divorced. I told Janice about my feelings for you and she ended the marriage."

"You shouldn't have told her," I said, sitting up and looking at him. "It was a good marriage."

"It was a matter of convenience, not love. I went back to her, after Dallas, and tried to resume a normal relationship. But she was just a substitute for you, Kiss. Every woman that I have been with since 1987 has been a substitute for you."

"God, I can't believe that it's been almost twenty years."

"Twenty years of time wasted." He leaned in and placed a soft kiss on my lips. "I don't want to waste any more of it."

Aleck and I made love for the rest of the night and made a promise that we would fornicate under the consent of the king for the rest of our lives. The next day I was a nervous wreck as we set out to tell A.J. the truth. Kids are interesting people. They take things better than we ever could. A.J. was confused and inquisitive at first, but never angry. He was happy to have a father in his life and neither of them could get over how much they resembled each other.

Aleck moved to Atlanta to be with us and we were married that New Year's Eve. To this day, we make the most of every day and never look back. Every night, when Aleck settles down to sleep inside of me, because I love to feel his dick pulsating against my walls while I am in a deep slumber, I thank God for him…for us.

Let this serve as a lesson for those of you who have loved someone and had to let them go. Things never happen on our time… they happen on His time. If things do not work out the first time, or even the second time, there can always be another time and another place.

A.J.

I was stunned. No…stunned did not describe it. It had to be some type of mistake, or a weird coincidence.

"What's wrong, Honey?" my girlfriend Jasmine asked, taking my hand.

"Do you see this?" I asked, pointing with my other hand. She stared at the painting and I could feel her start to shiver. "Can you believe it?"

"It can't be," Jasmine whispered. "Impossible."

"Yes, it's impossible, but yet, there they are…in vivid color."

Jasmine and I had been dating for a year. My parents insisted that they wanted me to take a historical vacation and decided to pay for the two of us to travel to Ethiopia. My dad had paid to have a genealogy test done—one of those mail order things where he swabbed the inside of his mouth and sent it off for the results. It came back that his genes traced back to Ethiopia, which was news to him. He was so excited that he suggested that we go see the culture there.

We are inside an art museum looking at a display about Menelek II, the King of Kings of Abyssinia, who lived from 1844-1913. He was considered one of the great leaders of world history because he was able to unite several kingdoms that had fiercely opposed each other. He was baptized as Sahle Maryam, but later was given title of emperor. All of that was well and good but could not explain what Jasmine and I were looking at. It was a portrait of Menelek II and his wife, Taytu Betul, a noblewoman of imperial blood. While they were dressed in traditional garb with head wraps, there was no denying it. Even with the beard, I was staring into the eyes of my father...and my mother was standing beside him. There was a scroll in her hand and I squinted to make out a few of the words. It said: "Under the consent of the king."

৪০৫৪

Zane is the New York Times *bestselling author of more than ten titles, the editor of numerous anthologies, and the publisher of Strebor Books, an imprint of ATRIA Books/Simon and Schuster. She is also the executive producer of several television and film projects, including* Zane's Sex Chronicles, *an original Cinemax program loosely based on her life. You can visit her online at: www.eroticanoir.com, join her mailing list by sending a blank email to eroticanoir-subscribe@topica.com or visit her MySpace page at www.myspace.com/zaneland.*